Deviant Resurrection

Deviant Ascension

Book 1

Cover Typography by Karen Dimmick / ArcaneCovers.com

Sally M. Jenkins

smwitchjenkins@gmail.com (please email for mailing address)

www.smwitch.com

Ebook ISBN 979-8-9892703-0-9
Hardcover ISBN 979-8-9892703-1-6

Acknowledgements

Developmental editing services provided by K.B. Spangler (https://kbspangler.com) and Breyonna Jordan (https://editingyourworlds.com)

Copy editing services provided by Emily Loveall (https://emilyannloveall.com/editing)

A special thank you to my alpha readers, my sister the Sand Witch, my sister The Grey Witch, and my dad, the best grumpy badger ever.

Also thank you to all my beta readers and critique partners, your help was invaluable!

CONTENTS

A PLACE BEYOND TIME AND SPACE

No *there* existed for them to be in. Moments vanished into nothingness as soon as they formed, unconnected to any mortal, demonic, or divine experience, and yet these moments were both shaped by and an influence on all of space-time.

They, the five entities, did not appear into the infinite void. There was no light to reflect off them, and no words could vibrate through the vacuous darkness between moments.

Yet they could see and hear each other perfectly.

There were five thrones for them to occupy, arranged in a circle, evenly spaced, vibrating subtly, as if unstable in structure and dimension.

As they entered this emptiness, this non-space, a false time began.

Gemma, Earth Goddess of the Mortal Realm and Queen of Faerie, formed the foundation of their out-of-phase existence. She was a vast presence within a delicate form, terrible and beautiful and somehow both human and decidedly *other*. She coiled in her green and gold throne, Eldritch and draconic. Life-fire shimmered through her in veins of primordial blood.

"Who has a grievance not covered by the Treaty?" she said, her voice unhurried and perhaps slightly resigned.

Micheal, representative Archangel of the Divine, flared violently and stood. In this place no mortal would ever see, he did not suppress his glory. He was pure white flame, power and hunger and authority. His throne was impossible, both indestructible stone and ephemeral light, a pale reflection of Micheal's Divine glory.

"Ah *yes*, to the surprise of no one," said Zee, the Psychopomp Monarch, Head Librarian of the Earth Archive, wreathed in starlight and mystery. Their throne was a twisting labyrinth of a thousand different writing systems carved into stone and parchment and paper, yielding and fragile, but also eternal. "What *will* it be this time, Micheal dear?" Gemma narrowed her eyes at Zee in warning. Zee leaned back, an unapologetic smile on their elven face, and winked.

Lucifer, Former Guardian of the Seal, The Divine Opposition, The Underworld Anchor, scowled. His throne was obsidian lit with chromatic firelight, the easiest for mortal eyes to comprehend. "Let's just get this over with." His eyes were fierce and dark, his posture strong and self-assured. His tone dripped with skeptical disrespect.

Micheal ignored them both. "We—" Micheal always spoke with the *royal* we, "—want to reopen the discussion on vampires."

Lillian, Queen of Magic and Demons, soft white and glittering black, leaned forward. She shone with silver mirror-light, the moon to Micheal's ostentatious sun. Her throne was darkness woven into a filigree of wishes and dreams, the thread from which souls might be born. "That matter is settled."

Vampires were under her exclusive administration, demons that could not settle in the Underworld or within the carefully regulated witch familiar system. Unlike Lucifer and Zee, Lillian was very good at playing celestial politics with Gemma and Micheal, and she *knew*

Micheal could not actually be worried about vampires. He had another goal.

Micheal burned steadily. "Things have changed. Your Pit is overrun with unrepentant, uncooperative souls, and you refuse to destroy—"

Lillian hissed, "That has *nothing* to do with my vamp—"

Lucifer stood, his cloak flashing with fire. "It is *not* overrun—"

A minor tremor shivered between Time and Space, and silence fell.

Gemma's eyes flashed, bright with surging life-fire. "Do *not* speak over one another. Micheal has the floor. He may speak *uninterrupted.*" She glared at Lucifer and Lillian.

Zee groaned delicately into the stiff silence. "Oh, come *on*—"

Thunder cracked and a forked rift flashed through the circle, causing everyone to jump.

"Enough!" Gemma's voice thundered so loudly their pocket of reality splintered with hairline fissures. Whispers and chittering seeped in from outside before the fractures resealed.

No one spoke— all eyes were, only slightly begrudgingly, fixed on Gemma.

She nodded, satisfied. "Micheal, state your grievance, but do so *without* commenting on the internal affairs of the Underworld."

Micheal's expression morphed into something a bit less haughty and more angry. Still, he maintained his stately composure. "We have *concerns* about the number of vampires among the various disparate mortal populations. With the limited number of Paladins we're allowed, we are unable to keep Divine territory free of your *vermin*. We suspect there is a surplus within witch territories and they are moving into Divine territories in search of prey. Further, we have noticed that mortals killed by vampires have a higher chance of remaining unrepentant and resistant to divine influence. We find this unacceptable."

Gemma tapped a claw on the arm of her throne. "Unacceptable?" she said, slowly. "There have been no Treaty infractions, and yet you find the situation *unacceptable*?" One scaly eyebrow arched almost imperceptibly, and a trail of sparkling smoke trickled between her teeth.

Micheal's flame dimmed slightly, but he remained resolved. "We do."

Earth-quaking thunder rumbled, covering any reactions from members of the Underworld Triad. "Is this causing any instability within your Divine gestalt?"

Micheal winced. "Gemma, please don't use gestalt, we prefer Divine Unity or Divine Collective to—"

There was a reality-shattering crack somewhere in the distance. Something chittered from very far away. "Answer the question!"

Micheal's fire dimmed further, exposing the beatific humanoid guise beneath. "No. We remain stable."

"Alright then," Gemma said, leaning back on her throne. "Your concern about the abundance of vampires entering Divine territory has been noted. However, you already have the means to counter that problem—your existing exorcists should be more than up to the challenge. As for the second point, do you have any evidence that these souls would have joined Divinity if they hadn't been consumed by a vampire?"

Micheal burned stiffly. "We do not. We could not. Alternative fates are inaccessible."

Gemma nodded. "That is a valid point. I assume, Zee, that there has been no progress on replacing the lost Oracles?"

Zee flicked their scarf with an elegant hand. "No. All Oracle souls are still in hiding or destroyed." Their posture was casual, overly relaxed. Anger simmered behind their otherwise aloof expression.

"Which is *Divinity's* fault," Lucifer said, his tone clipped. His anger was proud within the set of his jaw and the fire in his eyes. He glanced at Gemma, who allowed the interjection.

Micheal scowled. "That was before the Treaty. We hardly think we should be punished for that now. The matter has been settled."

Lillian snorted delicately and muttered, "Much like the vampire issue," but her words were drowned out by Lucifer's incredulous, "*Settled*? You caused an apocalypse the mortal realm has only *just* recovered from!"

"I don't know about *recovered*," Zee said, affecting neutral thoughtfulness while examining their ink-stained fingertips. "Stabilized, maybe."

"The Earth's magic is very much still in flux," Lillian added with more convincing sincerity, her voice a light and mysterious stratospheric breeze. "There are a number of shards and Mantles still unaccounted for, which could cause future instability in unexpected ways, especially if they are embedded in a mortal soul."

Micheal's glower was somehow angelic. "We were only trying to restore harmony during a time of Chaos. You all have committed plenty of atrocities of your own." He glared at Zee, who placed a hand on their chest and blinked innocently.

"We have very different definitions of *atrocity*," Lucifer growled, his eyes flashing with golden fire.

Gemma sighed irritably and said, "Regardless of who is at fault, the point stands that Divinity has no means to conduct any proper investigation into the vampire situation. An allowance must be made."

"Gemma," Lillian said, laying a hand on Lucifer's arm before he could explode, "what allowances are you proposing?"

"Divinity must be allowed to investigate whether or not the souls vampires hunt are beyond rehabilitation."

Lucifer raised his chin, his eyes sparking with promise of white flames. "Investigate how? And, more importantly, even if there is some causality, are you suggesting we interfere in the mortal justice systems?"

Lillian added, before Lucifer could flare up into a rage, "Vampires were meant to be a compromise to give vigilante souls a manageable outlet."

"A compromise Divinity *already* agreed to," Zee said—pointedly.

Gemma made a dismissively placating gesture. "I am only suggesting Divinity be allowed to gather information."

"We want to create a new Paladin Relic specifically for this purpose," Micheal said. "We have the Mantle already set aside."

Crackling green energy surged up from the Triad half of the circle as Lucifer, Lillian, and Zee all tensed.

"*You*," Lucifer said, carefully venomous, "want us to let you bind another *living* soul to your will? We allowed you to keep the Relic-enslaved souls you already bound, to reincarnate at your discretion, but you have been *explicitly forbidden* from creating new ones!"

"None of the Paladins we have are suited to this kind of delicate investigation. We need something new."

Lucifer's eyes flashed with chromatic fire, but Zee put a hand on his arm, and he stilled.

"The process will be unchanged from the Breaking?" Zee asked, silkily. "The soul will retain the potential to recapture its autonomy?"

Micheal scowled. "We would prefer—"

Zee laughed, delighted. "Ohh, this will be *interesting*. Micheal, dear, are you *sure* you want to do this? It might *ascend*."

"Ascension is not *meant* for mortals," Micheal roared, flaring into a fierce white sun. "Their fragile souls will break under the weight of eternity, and We will reclaim them, and every one of the other so-called *Ascended* souls, including yours. The Divine is *inevitable*, Unity *will* prevail, and We will consume every hell-spawned—"

Lucifer launched himself at Micheal, howling with rage. Micheal drew his flaming sword, and Lillian and Zee leapt to their feet, summoning glittering silver magic and twisting arcane symbols that clashed against Micheal's Divine fire, protecting Lucifer from harm.

Lightning started to flicker at the edge of the false space, the battle threatening to escape the carefully crafted circle. Small, chaotic hands tipped with black claws began to scratch at the thinning walls.

Gemma glared at her fellow deities, profoundly disappointed. She could feel the fae building into a frenzy in the back of her mind. If she didn't act soon, the conflict would spread into space-time.

The conversation was clearly over.

"Meeting adjourned." The quiet words sundered the temporary space, sending the gods back to their respective realms. The chittering laughter abruptly cut off.

GREATER PROVIDENCE RI, SEPTEMBER 6TH, 47 YAR

That's Years After Rapture, in case you were wondering

The man pushed June against the car, his erection straining against his too-tight jeans. June gasped for air as he broke their kiss and moved towards her neck, sucking hard enough to leave a mark.

"Wait, wait, please, stop!" she gasped, pushing weakly at his chest.

With a frustrated grunt, he let her push him back and hold him away. He met her eyes, his gaze hot with desire.

"Stop? But you said—"

"I know, I know. I'm sorry, I just—" June shivered, hugged herself, and tried to make herself small inside the cage of his arms. "I changed my mind. I'm sorry. *Please.*"

He shoved away and adjusted himself. "Whatever."

June watched as he walked back towards the bar. His shoulders were tense and the flush on his neck was visible to her even in the dim light of the small parking lot. He ran his hand through his hair and swore softly under his breath. He was halfway back to the entrance before June recovered from her surprise. She pulled the straps of her top back into place and tugged her skirt back down.

Well, fuck. She'd really thought this one would bite.

She smiled ruefully and *flickered*—between one blink and the next she was in front of the man, and her eyes flashed.

The frustration melted from his face and his expression went blank. His shoulders lost their tension as he became quiet and compliant.

"You will forget me," she said, and she felt the command take hold in his unprotected mind. Unable to help herself, she gave him a small peck on the cheek. Then, after a moment of consideration, she drew a suddenly sharp and claw-like fingernail across her own wrist and pressed it to his mouth.

He groaned in ecstasy as she smeared her blood on his lips. He tried to latch on.

She pushed him away gently. "No no, that's enough. You'll be free from harm for a good week with that, and I don't have any more to spare. Go on, have a good evening."

With another *flicker* she was behind him again in the half-empty parking lot. Her hold on him broke as soon as she lost eye contact. He shook himself, now confused instead of angry, and walked back into the bar.

June ached with hunger. This was the third guy in a row who took no for an answer. She hadn't eaten in nearly three weeks, and she was worried about what would happen if she didn't find someone.

"Maybe I should try a God-fearing city. Fucking witches, and me, are doing too good a job here," she grumbled to herself, not actually serious. There was no way she was moving, and especially not to God-fearing country. Plentiful prey wouldn't help her if she ended up obliterated by an exorcist.

She took a moment to regain control of herself, ruthlessly pushing her hunger back. She was fraying around the edges, but she needed to keep it together until she could find some prey.

There had to be *someone.* The city was huge.

Giving up on this bar, she walked down the block to visit Penny, feeling less than hopeful. It was nearly midnight, and the pickings were becoming slim.

The smell of pot nearly overwhelmed her when she pushed into the noisy space, and June dampened her senses just enough to be comfortable. Her well-worn boots stuck to the mildly sticky floor. She scanned the room as she walked, looking to see if she caught anyone's attention. June was dressed for the hunt—too little clothing for the relatively cool fall evening, and too much makeup for someone who was alone. Her hair was long, dark, and curly, and she'd given herself a side shave to expose her neck. The face she wore was not anyone in particular, crafted to look strikingly sexy without being particularly memorable. It was her favorite hunting face for this part of town.

More than one pair of eyes followed her as she prowled over to the bar, which was a promising sign. There weren't any fae or fae-bloods here that she could smell, which was even better. Fae could be unpredictable, and it was better not to hunt when they were watching—they might try to join in.

June draped herself on the counter, put an artful pout on her face, and looked disinterestedly at the dance floor. A husky voice from behind her said, "Hey, June."

"Hey. Any problems tonight?" June asked without turning around, unable to keep the hope from her voice. June had never told Penny she was a vampire, or what her prey was, but Penny seemed to know anyway. Penny was a witch, and her bar was registered Neutral Territory, so she was probably an important witch. Maybe that was how she knew. Her familiar told her or something.

However she'd come to suspect what June was, she clearly approved, because Penny always pointed her in the direction of deserving prey if any was nearby.

June felt a thrill of anticipation when Penny nodded towards the other end of the bar. A group of very drunk frat boys were being tugged onto the dance floor by their dates. All but one, who instead had his date pinned against the wall.

The girl, who looked like she'd gotten in with a fake ID, tried to push him away, but the guy grabbed her by the wrist and held her in place. June saw the brief flash of fear in the girl's face before she tossed her drink at him and fled. He sputtered, swore at her, and tried to follow, but she made it to the restroom and slammed the door in his face.

June smiled.

The frat boy cussed at the door, pounding on it angrily for a few seconds before turning back towards the bar. It took a moment, but he eventually noticed June watching him. She winked and turned away, tilting her head slightly to expose her neck.

When he reached the bar, he immediately crowded into her space. His smile was predatory. He probably thought it was charming.

"You look lonely," he said, his voice artificially low, and June had to resist rolling her eyes. She scanned him from beneath her unnaturally thick lashes, trying to decide if he was hot enough to get away with shitty pick-up lines. Probably. He had the overly muscular and athletic build of a football player, and his face would likely be appealing if he stopped sneering.

"Yeah, a little. My boyfriend dumped me," June said, trying to subtly ease away from him.

He was, delightfully, uninterested in her cue, and he followed her. "Yeah? Shit, what'd you do? Had to be bad for him to dump something as hot as you."

Dear fucking god, was he negging her? June crafted a blush into her cheeks and dropped her gaze but didn't say anything.

He took the bait, pressing in even closer. She forced herself to surrender, mimicking the pliancy of a caught mouse. "Let me buy you a drink," he said, "and you can drown your sorrows with me."

She looked up and met his eyes, her face sculpted into a perfect mask of vulnerability. "Okay. Sure."

He ordered for her without asking what she wanted and didn't leave a tip for Penny when he paid.

June almost dropped her fangs then and there. She pretended to take a sip, and then submitted to his flirting for another few minutes, during which time he downed both his drink and the rest of hers.

Fuck, this prey was *perfect*. June asked him if he wanted to walk her home, and his leer was so obnoxious she had to hide her face so he wouldn't see her expression.

They made it two blocks before he grabbed her and dragged her into an alley.

She let him get in one sloppy kiss before shoving at him. "Hey, no. I don't want to fuck in public."

His eyes were glazed, and he used his considerable bulk to trap her against the wall. There was a composting dumpster next to them, and it reeked.

"I do," he said, and he grasped the back of her head and kissed her again, forcefully.

She struggled more desperately now, trying to twist away from him. "Please, stop. No!" she said loudly, but not *too* loudly. She was really hungry, and the last thing she needed was a good Samaritan coming to her rescue.

He used one hand to cover her mouth and reached under her skirt with the other. She tried to kick him away and scream, but he seized her by the throat and pushed her onto her toes, cutting off her air and pinning her with one massive hand while the other pulled at her underwear.

Welp, that settled it. She'd given him more than enough chances.

June gave in to her hunger.

Claws burst from her fingers and sank into the asshole's shoulders. With inhuman strength, she kicked off the wall and they slammed into the brick on the other side of the alley. Too quickly for him to react, she tore into his neck with a mouth full of suddenly sharp teeth, gulping greedily while he choked on a scream. He heaved, trying to buck her off, but he could do nothing with her iron grip on him, her claws sunk into his flesh, holding him down. He lashed out desperately and managed to get in one solid punch that probably broke his hand.

Slowly, he began to weaken.

The blood that rushed down her throat was sharp with alcohol, and her eyes burned a dull red as her body broke it down before she could feel its effects. June felt the fierceness of her hunger wane with the rapidly slowing heartbeat of her victim.

When she'd drunk him dry, she felt his soul rip free and fall away. Her hunger quieted fully as her Geas, the bond placed on her demonic soul when she was reborn as a vampire, settled, satisfied. She let his body slump to the ground and took a moment to enjoy the warm pleasure of a fresh kill.

Finally, June shivered happily and flesh-crafted herself back to looking fully human. Now that she was well fed, it only took seconds.

With a contented sigh, June wiped her mouth and crouched down to check his pockets. She'd done a pretty clean job with the kill, and other than the stink coming from his pants there was very little mess. There were two cell phones, which she crushed in her hands before putting the pieces back in his pocket. She found his wallet and pulled out a surprisingly large wad of cash and two driver's licenses. One was for 'Todd Patterson, age 23' and another was for 'Sean DeNardis, age 20'. The school ID said Sean DeNardis, and so did the credit cards. His real license also had a 'pure human' registration seal, and he wasn't an organ donor, of course. She pocketed the cash and tossed the rest of the wallet in the recycle bin. Then she lifted the body carefully over her shoulder and *flickered*.

She flashed from spot to spot, moving too quickly for any human eyes to register her presence, not that there were many people on the street at this hour to see her. Even in a witch metropolis like Greater Providence, humans still kept mostly daylight hours. Those who didn't were either gamers who didn't leave their homes or musicians who wouldn't be heading home till closer to dawn. Even so, she didn't stop until she reached the river.

The bricks and industrial fishing net she'd stashed there were exactly where she'd left them, tucked under a bridge. She ripped off the corpse's head and used her boot to smash it into mush, grinding it into the mud and rocks below the tide line. She picked the teeth up and tossed them one by one out into the river. Then she used the netting to secure the bricks to the body.

She swam the weighted body out a few hundred feet before letting it sink to the bottom. The thick hemp fibers were sturdy enough to be used many times before they started to biodegrade. Fish and fae would chew through the body long before the netting deteriorated.

She climbed up the far side of the river and, dripping wet but utterly content, headed for home.

ATRIUM

WHEN ISN'T IMPORTANT HERE (USUALLY)

The soul landed on the polished stone with a soft *whump*. It took some time for the soul to pull itself together. Returning to a more familiar shape felt like struggling awake with too little sleep, but the soul—*he*—was determined. As soon as he had arms and legs, he pushed to his knees and trembled, desperately holding himself together.

He was surprised to find that he didn't hurt. It had been years since he'd had a clear head without feeling some kind of pain, either from withdrawal, or hunger, or...something else.

Eventually, his shivering stopped, and he felt more stable. He did not need to breathe, but he took in a breath anyway and rocked back onto his heels, tipped his head back, and opened his eyes.

He was in an atrium. Delicate arches towered above him, the only thing between him and more stars than he had ever seen in his life. The walls of whatever structure he was in were so black they seemed to absorb light, making it feel like he was floating in space. Despite that, he could somehow make out decorative carvings on the impossible walls, almost like symbols hovering in the darkness.

His eyes roamed, confused and fascinated, until they stopped short on a strangely modern-looking reception desk, sleek steel and glass that should have been at odds with the rest of the space and yet wasn't. Behind the desk was one of the most fabulous people he had ever seen.

The lean figure had on a black silk button-down shirt and matching silk pants. Their long legs stretched out to a pair of shiny black boots resting on the desk. A glorious coat, obviously tailored to be left open like a cloak, pooled behind them in a river of shifting, prismatic darkness and a scarf twinkling with starlight wrapped around a graceful neck. Flowing hair was secured into a tail at the nape with a kind of clip like one that the soul had a hard time focusing on, as if its relationship with reality was tenuous. A beautiful and androgynous face with an expression of languid boredom turned from inspecting purple-polished fingernails to meet the soul's startled gaze.

Their eyes were endless black pools, no whites, and the soul seized with fear.

"Oh!" they exclaimed, and a bright smile blossomed across the lovely face. The boots dropped to the floor and the person sat up. "You've *finished*! Already! Goodness gracious!"

The soul was too stunned to react.

The figure waved an elegant hand, and a holographic screen interface appeared off to their left. They pursed black-painted lips and studied what must have been an information file.

"Hmm, your record is...huh. Too clean. What could have...oh. Hmm. And that...ah." Their face turned sympathetic, and they glanced at the soul before turning back to the file. Fingers tapped for a second on the table, and then the person stood and walked over to crouch in front of the soul.

"Aiden," they said kindly.

Aiden's memories rushed back to him all at once, and his face crumpled.

He was dead.

He remembered a very distant feeling of panic, of being colder than he ever had before, lying in bed that last time. The customer that night had been an asshole and hadn't respected any of his boundaries. He should have expected it would happen when he took on someone without any referrals, but he'd been short on cash that month after visiting an anarchist-friendly healer, and he'd decided to take the gamble rather than dip into his savings.

He'd tried to leave, cancel the date, but the man hadn't let him go, had laughed in his face when Aiden threatened to call the cops. *We both know they don't help your kind in this part of the world, bunny.*

After, Aiden was less careful than he should have been when he measured out his dose for the night.

And now he was dead.

He hugged himself to try to hold in the sobs, but when the beautiful person wrapped their arms around him, they burst free. He wasn't sure what he felt on his face as he cried—maybe hot tears or maybe just the memory of them.

Eventually, he calmed down and the person drew their arms back. Aiden scrubbed his face, surprised to find it damp with...something. When he licked his lips he tasted sparkles, and nothing.

"So, um. Where am I?" Aiden asked, very afraid of the answer.

The beautiful person studied Aiden and then helped him to his feet.

"You know. But it's not what you think."

"This is Hell, right?" Aiden asked, and he yelped when the floor shook slightly beneath him. The beautiful person glared at the floor and the shaking stopped. "I mean," Aiden went on in a rush, "it seems kinda nice right now, beautiful and peaceful, but this is just the entrance. The bad part is still coming, isn't it? You don't, um, you look..."

They tipped their head back and laughed. "I don't look like an angel? I should hope not. White is *so* boring, and they're really no fun, I promise you."

Aiden flushed, embarrassed and still very scared. "What's going to happen to me?"

"That depends." The beautiful person studied Aiden again, and then cocked their head to the side. "What do you think will happen to you?"

"I..." Aiden didn't know how to answer. His parents had told him he was going to Hell, a terrible place of pain and suffering, worse than he could ever imagine. The pastor at church had said the same thing, and Father Luke at during 'therapy' before he—

No. He wasn't thinking about that. It was over, long over.

After Aiden ran away, even though he'd tried to be a good person, he never believed he was. He'd run away from everyone who'd ever loved him. Most of his gaming friends told him that his parents were wrong, that they and the Church had fucked him up and it wasn't his fault. But they lived in places where witches ran for office and won, so he wasn't sure they were any better off than he was, as far as damnation was concerned.

The lady who handled his client referrals had told him that there was nothing wrong with doing what he wanted with his life, and that he was a sweet boy and shouldn't take shit from anyone. But she was an anarchist, and the Church claimed that was hardly any better than being a witch.

Aiden shivered, curling in on himself. It wasn't like he thought the Church was right either, not when he knew how hypocritical it could be, but it didn't lessen his guilt, or his certainty that he was broken and unworthy. Besides, plenty of people, not just his parents and Father Luke and the other priests and nuns, told him he was exactly that.

Broken, unworthy, damned.

And now he was in Hell.

The beautiful person gave his shoulder a quick squeeze and stood. They walked back to the plush chair behind the desk. Aiden followed for a few steps but then stopped, uncertain.

"I'll explain some of your options in just a moment, but first I have a few questions to ask so I can complete your file here."

Options? So, what, he got to choose how he wanted to be punished? Aiden felt a little thrill, and then very sick, because how could he *like* that idea? This wasn't a game. This was *Hell.*

Right?

He swallowed and meekly walked over to stand in front of the desk. "Um, what should I call you? What pronouns do you prefer?" he asked, as deferentially as possible.

The person glanced at Aiden, slightly surprised, and then they smiled. "Use whatever pronouns you like. You can call me Zee." Zee winked.

Aiden blushed again, and, ashamed of his blush, mumbled something and looked down. Zee chuckled and turned back to the screen.

"Alright then, is there anything holding you to the mortal plane? A lover, a soul debt, an oath of vengeance?"

Aiden thought about it. He had a few exes, but they hadn't been *lovers.* He'd tried to love them, in all the ways that he knew how, but what he gave hadn't been what they wanted. Part of him would always care for them, but they'd all told him to go, and he had. He didn't blame them for it. They'd had good reasons—they couldn't deal with his addiction, he was too messed up, and Aiden had understood. He *was* pathetic.

He'd deserved to be alone.

Aiden shook his head. "No, nothing like that."

"Mmm, alright. Were you ever visited by any divine entities, or had any encounters with demons?"

"I don't think so?"

"Oh, you'd know if you had. Okay, last question, do you feel as though you have any unfinished business?"

"I..." Aiden wanted to say yes, but he knew it would be a lie. He felt a deep sense of loss, but nothing was *unfinished.* If anything, he felt like he'd never really gotten a chance to *start.* Except that would also be unfinished, right? So it wasn't that either. He'd just—his life had been... "No. There's nothing."

"That's it then," Zee said, and waved a hand through the screen, which vanished. They looked at Aiden with a soft expression. "So, you're not *exactly* wrong about where you are, but mostly. It's the opposite of Divinity, sure, but we try to avoid the 'H' word down here. *Some* people are overly concerned with labels." Zee glared at the floor for some reason. "We prefer to call it the Underworld, but that's also not entirely accurate. In the most basic sense, it's a gathering of souls uninterested in joining Divinity."

Aiden nodded mechanically, unsure how to feel. He vaguely remembered telling *something* to leave him alone, but it was like a dream mostly forgotten.

Had he damned *himself*?

Well, yes. How else?

Zee studied him with that same compassionate expression before continuing, "Your biggest problem right now is the amount of guilt you're carrying. I'm pretty sure it's the root of all this anxiety that's—" Zee pressed a finger to their mouth and looked briefly embarrassed. "Sorry, not the time. Regardless of what you decide to do, I'm going to recommend you see one of our therapists so we can help you with that. Is that alright with you?"

Aiden shivered again, feeling sick without any thrill this time. "Is this, like, punishment therapy?"

Zee stood up, as if they'd been slapped, and Aiden flinched.

"No! Oh, no." Zee reached towards Aiden, then paused. When Aiden didn't flinch again, Zee took his hand. "No, this would be real, proper therapy. The kind where you just talk to someone who can give you advice with no judgment. Okay?"

Aiden hesitated. "Like in witch territory?"

"Yes."

Something in his chest unclenched, and Aiden found himself nodding. "Alright."

Zee carefully let go of Aiden's hand and smiled warmly. "Great." A different screen appeared, this one with strange, scrolling decorations on the side, and Zee tapped their fingers on the desk. "I've set up an appointment for the day after tomorrow, Nexus time. Nexus is used as the temporal standard down here. It has Day-Night cycles close to Earth's, so it should be an easy transition for you. Be careful if you go anywhere else, though— time can get wonky around here. I'll assign you a room in Nexus as well, but you don't have to stay there if you find someplace you like better."

Zee waved the screen away. "Now, with a record like yours, there are *quite* a few options available to you. I think it might be best if we take you—"

Zee was interrupted by a loud crack. Aiden whirled around, eyes wide, to see a black mass writhing over a huge crack in the stone floor.

"What the *fuck*, Lucy?" Zee yelled, vaulting over the desk and putting themself between the thing and Aiden. "I don't care how angry the soul is, you can't let them—*shit!*"

The black mass surged outward in every direction, stretched thin and oily. Zee made a frustrated noise and their hand glowed silver-iridescent. Arcane symbols appeared in the air, forming a shield, but the darkness was moving too quickly. It flowed around Zee in a wave and kept going, rushing straight towards Aiden.

Aiden turned and bolted. In a flash, he was scrambling over the desk. He didn't need to look to feel the darkness coiling around him. Distantly, he heard Zee shouting after him, genuine panic in their voice.

Aiden didn't stop, didn't even think.

The darkness caught him anyway.

</<*That fucking bitch killed me*!>/> the thing roared, and Aiden felt its rage try to consume him, swallow him whole.

Aiden curled in on himself, a tight, impenetrable ball. He let the rage flow around him, through him, but he didn't let it touch him.

The darkness paused.

</<*What the fuck is this? Where am I? What* are *you?*>/>

Aiden stayed small and quiet. The darkness reached for him again, condensing around him. Again, it passed through and around Aiden, but could not touch him.

Confusion and fear colored the twisting mass of anger. The darkness changed, and Aiden could see that under all the rage it, whatever it was, *hurt.*

Aiden made a small sound and reached out. Nothing should hurt so much. Maybe if he—

There was a flash of brilliant color and the darkness *screamed.* Aiden flinched back and returned to his tight ball.

"That's *enough*!"

The voice cut through the darkness like fire. With another scream, the darkness split and boiled away.

Aiden, still tightly curled, was lifted into strong arms. A feeling of safety washed through him, and, without any real understanding of why, he relaxed. With a small pop, Aiden uncoiled back into something like a body, arms wrapped around shins, head pressed into his knees.

Whoever the arms were attached to made a low grunt of surprise.

"Give him to me, let me see if—oh. Oh! Look at him!" Zee's voice was full of a strange mix of worry and wonder.

The strong arms set him into something cool and soft, but also bright, like silk made of starlight. Zee? Then who picked him up? Aiden lifted his head enough to open his eyes. He found himself looking into Zee's face, their delicate brows knit with concern. "Sorry," Aiden said, reflexively.

Zee shushed him, and gently petted Aiden's head. "Nothing to be sorry for, sweet. That was—" They broke off, those fathomless eyes searching Aiden's. "Are you alright?" They still sounded a little awed.

Aiden squirmed, uncomfortable with the attention. After a moment Zee opened their arms and Aiden slid downward to land on his feet. "Um, yeah." Aiden blinked at Zee—they were hovering in the air cross-legged. Zee seemed to notice Aiden's confusion, and they unfolded until they were standing on the floor again.

Embarrassed, Aiden looked down. "I'm fine. Really."

Zee hummed inscrutably and opened their mouth, but a howl of rage cut them off.

Aiden whirled and saw the darkness behind him, still boiling with rage. After a terrible moment of horror, he sagged with relief— it was contained somehow. The poor, hateful darkness screamed incoherently, splattering itself against an invisible barrier marked out by a glowing chalk circle.

Next to the circle stood an *incredibly* attractive man, a warrior with a presence so fierce and protective Aiden had to stop himself from doing something embarrassing.

Were demons all hot? That... didn't seem right. Certainly that terrible darkness wasn't hot. Were there some nice demons and some mean demons?

What was going *on*?

The warrior was frowning at the raging darkness. He wore black tactical armor and, incongruously, a kind of cloak that hung off one shoulder, the fabric impossibly dark and dancing with chromatic flames. His eyes shone with the same starlight as Zee's scarf, and he radiated a powerful aura.

It was the same warm, protective aura that had lifted him out of the darkness, so Aiden figured this must be the owner of the arms that carried him over to Zee.

The warrior noticed Aiden staring and turned to give Aiden a nod and a scorching smile.

Aiden made an overwhelmed noise in his throat as heat bloomed in his cheeks. The warrior winked, and Aiden shivered.

Not with fear.

"Good work, bunny," the warrior said. His voice was deep and strong. "Let me know if you want a job."

Aiden was stunned. Did he know? But no, he couldn't possibly—

"Lucy!" Zee said and stamped their foot. "That is *not* funny. We got *very* lucky no one was hurt. What the *hell* happened?"

Lucy's face turned thunderous, and Aiden was suddenly slammed with unexpected desire. He gasped and fell back a step, his knees going weak.

Zee groaned. "Ung, turn down the sexy, Lucy, I'm sorry for using the 'H' word. Look, you're scaring our little hero."

The warrior—Lucy?—looked at Aiden sheepishly. The unexpected lust faded back to something that felt like it might be normal, and Aiden rubbed his face, trying to smooth away his blush.

Lucy turned his attention back to the darkness. It was rapidly coalescing into the shape of a man. Lucy's frown returned.

"I'm not a hero," Aiden said, his voice a little hoarse.

Zee patted his shoulder before walking over to join Lucy. "Sure you are. If you hadn't distracted that asshole long enough for us to trap him, who knows how many souls he would have ripped through?"

"What?" Aiden whispered, horrified. "I didn't—"

The darkness screamed loud enough to shake the floor, and Aiden shrank away.

Zee glared at the darkness. "Stop being such a drama queen, you're fine." Zee considered the figure and frowned. "Odd, that."

The darkness twisted and a ragged, half-formed mouth said, </<*What the fuck did you do to me?*>/>

Zee ignored the question and turned to Lucy. "Are you going to apologize to Aiden or what?"

Lucy glared at Zee, then sagged and nodded. To Aiden's horror, the imposing warrior dropped to a knee in front of Aiden, clapped at fist to his chest, and bowed his head.

"My sincerest apologies for my failure to keep you safe."

Aiden shook his head and took a step back. "N—no, it's, I'm fine. Don't, um." He pressed his hands to his stomach to hide their shaking.

Lucy stood up in a single fluid motion and gave Zee a pointed look. "See? He didn't want it."

Zee sniffed. "You still needed to give it. Now *what happened*?"

Lucy looked at Aiden, then back at Zee with a raised eyebrow.

"Ah, right. One moment darling," Zee said to Aiden, and they and Lucy stepped away.

Aiden made a small sound and wondered if it were possible to dissolve back into oblivion.

Inside the circle, the darkness had taken on a form that was almost human looking. It pressed a ragged hand against the invisible barrier and Aiden *felt* it look at him with its twisting, angry face.

</<*Come here, little rabbit.*>/>

Aiden shivered and glanced over at Zee and Lucy, who were obviously having an intense conversation. Aiden heard Lucy say something about someone named *Sam*, and Zee's irritation dropped away. They clapped their hands, delighted.

</<*I said come* here *you disgusting little fa—*>/>

"Okay! That's enough of *that*," Zee said, appearing quite suddenly between Aiden and the monster. They drew a symbol in the air, right at the edge of the circle.

The nasty soul's voice cut out, and Aiden felt tension he hadn't even known he was holding leave him. He sagged in relief.

"Are you alright, bunny?" Zee asked again, coming over to lightly rest a hand on his shoulder.

Aiden shrugged. "It's, um, nothing I haven't heard before." Then he frowned. "Why does everyone always call me that?"

Zee's eyes went wide, horrified.

"No! Not that!" Aiden flushed. "I mean bunny. Rabbit." Aiden's hands fluttered helplessly. "People always call me that. I don't mind, but, do I, um, look like a rabbit?""

Zee blinked once before their head tilted back and they roared with laughter. They collapsed onto Aiden's shoulders, weak-kneed with mirth.

Aiden wasn't sure what was so funny, but he felt warmer, more stable, as if the laughter was filled with sunlight and air. He smiled tentatively and awkwardly patted Zee's back.

A flash of reddish-purple light blossomed over where Lucy was standing. Aiden twisted around to look and saw Lucy pull an angry cat through a glowing doorway that immediately vanished afterward.

The cat hissed and Lucy dropped it to the floor. With another flash of light, the cat turned into a stunningly beautiful naked man. Another beautiful man, and this one was *naked*.

Aiden was really starting to wonder what the catch was. Why were there so many beautiful men in Hell?

This was all so *confusing*.

"What the fuck, Lucifer, you couldn't just call me? I can make my own door, you know."

Aiden felt the room tilt slightly.

Lucy was short for *Lucifer*.

Lucifer, who'd saved him from the angry darkness?

Aiden gave up. It was that or burst into tears.

Zee, clearly unaware of the reason behind Aiden's sudden tension, finally pulled themself together. They stood back up and wiped their eyes, which were wet with a sparkly fluid that was distinctly *not* normal tears.

"Sam! Bunny, this is Sam." They gestured grandly at the man who, Aiden realized with a start, had *cat ears* growing out of his silky hair. "Sam, darling, will you take Aiden here on a tour of Nexus, and anywhere else that seems appropriate? I won't be able to finish his orientation until after we deal with this mess." They waved vaguely in the direction of the thing inside the circle. "Aiden's got a room in the Nexus Hotel, and he's *incredibly* stable, but he has essentially no knowledge of the afterlife or experience with magic, so try not to shock him too much."

Sam turned a startled gaze towards Aiden, and Aiden felt his cheeks heat. Sam's fluffy cat ears twitched adorably, and Aiden couldn't stop from staring.

He wanted to touch them. They looked soft.

"*Re*ally?" Sam said, and smiled, tiny little cat fangs dimpling his lower lip. "Sounds like a good afternoon. Come on, bunny, let's go."

Again with the rabbit thing! What was he missing?

Sam turned around, a piece of glowing chalk suddenly in his hand, and started drawing the outline of a door. Unfortunately, as soon as Sam's back was to him Aiden's eyes landed on Sam's tail and extremely nice ass. His *naked* ass. Aiden was half hypnotized by the way the tail twitched back and forth. He closed his eyes and shook himself before fixing his gaze determinedly on the back of Sam's neck.

Sam had really nice shoulders, too.

Ah! Stop it, Aiden! Don't be a creep! Be confused and scared like a sane *person*.

What the hell was wrong with him?

Aiden pressed his palms to his eyes and focused on taking breaths he didn't actually need.

Sam finished his drawing and the door flashed with a riot of color before settling into a softly glowing film shifting like a sunset underwater.

Sam turned back to Aiden, flashed a fanged grin, and stepped through.

Aiden hesitated and looked back at Zee, who made a shooing motion. "Go, go! I'm terribly sorry I can't finish your orientation myself, it's the *least* I should do, but I'm sure we'll see each other again soon. And don't worry about all the, ah, H-E-L-L stuff. You're in for a bunch of very pleasant surprises." Zee winked.

For some reason Aiden couldn't bring himself to believe Zee would lie to him, and since the alternative was staying here with the monster inside the circle, Aiden gave Zee a small nod, turned, and followed Sam through the doorway.

GREATER PROVIDENCE RI, SEPTEMBER 8TH 47 YAR

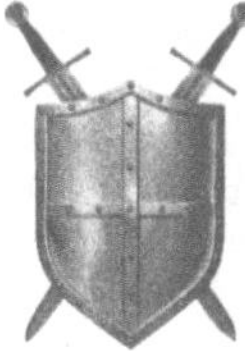

Emily drank half of her second cup of coffee in one gulp, desperately trying to feel human again. She rubbed at aching eyes, pressing the heels of her hand against them to relieve the pressure. At around two in the morning, she'd been called in on a domestic dispute. The Crisis Security Responder had requested an investigator once she'd secured the scene, suspecting an assault.

Her mind's eye filled with the stony expression on the woman's face. She'd insisted, no matter how Emily prodded, that she didn't want to press charges against her spouse, that she'd only fallen down the stairs after *sleepwalking*, of all things.

It wasn't impossible. The woman was heavily invested in Dreamscape VR and sleepwalking was a symptom of overuse—but Emily knew in her gut the woman had been lying. The responder had told Emily that the injuries were more consistent with being hit, and the smooth way the woman's spouse had answered Emily's questions had set her teeth on edge.

Emily's partner had wanted to charge her spouse anyway, evidence be damned, but George DeNardis could be an idiot about stuff like that. He was, technically, more experienced than Emily—he'd been with the Greater Providence main investigator office much longer than Emily—and he should have known better. Maybe he'd watched too many pre-Rapture cop shows as a kid, because he often didn't understand that abusing the law to play hero usually only made things worse.

After one more sip of coffee, Emily finished adding her notes to the incident report, submitted it, and then put a reminder into her personal note app to order another burner phone to replace the one she'd given to the woman.

She might have expected better of a witch city like Greater Providence, and perhaps it was something that the resources to help in these situations did exist, but it was still depressing just how many burner phones she'd given out over her career. Even though the woman had refused to allow Emily to file any charges, the flicker of relief in her expression, and the careful way she'd tucked the burner phone away in her jacket, had Emily hopeful the woman would, eventually, call the pre-programmed number and get help.

She left the part about the burner phone out of her report. It wasn't relevant to her job, and what she did with her own money was her own business.

She did make sure to flag the household for a wellness check in a few weeks.

Just to be sure.

Emily filed the report into the proper archive and leaned back in her chair. The plants she had on top of her desk glowed cheerfully under their little grow lamps, bringing a spot of brightness to her gloomy little corner. One of them, a small purple orchid her sister had given her, was growing a new flower stalk.

Emily jumped when her phone went off with DeNardis's ring tone. Emily frowned at it before she picked up.

"This is Scott. Everything okay?"

"Emily, I need a favor. I'm with the captain right now, can you come in here?"

Emily's frown deepened, but she made affirmative sounds and stood up. She dropped her mug off in the kitchen on her way and hoped no one would get mad at her for leaving it in the dispenser during her impromptu meeting.

She had a feeling she was going to need more coffee.

After she closed the door behind her, the captain said without preamble, "You're cleared to take this case if you want."

When he didn't say anything else, Emily turned to look at DeNardis.

He didn't look awful, precisely, but there was tension in his jaw and the lines around his eyes were deeper than normal. His posture was always stiff, but today there was a brittle rigidity that reminded Emily of a mast holding a sail against a strong wind.

"Sean is missing."

Emily took in a sharp breath. "What, really? How long has he been gone?" Sean was George's son. Emily had never met him, but George sometimes talked about him. Emily wasn't entirely sure how to react. She tried to keep things as professional as possible between them, and DeNardis wasn't a touchy-feely sort of partner.

"Since Saturday night. He didn't come home after going out with some friends. I got a call from his roommate this morning. I did some checking, and I was able to verify his phone went dead right around then."

Emily blinked once and glanced at the captain's impassive face quickly before refocusing on DeNardis. Pulling records for personal business wasn't *illegal*, but it was ethically frowned upon. Emily knew that DeNardis was friends with the captain, but she hadn't realized they were close enough that he felt comfortable openly admitting to skirting the edge like that.

"I'll take on your other cases while you look into this. Go ahead and pull in any magic consultants you need— anything the department won't cover, I will." DeNardis looked briefly at the captain, then back to Emily. "You're the only one I trust on this. Please."

Just that. *Please.* His voice was even, without any pleading or vulnerability, but Emily felt like she'd been slapped. She looked at the captain, who gave her a nod.

"Like I said, you're cleared to take this. I spoke with Public Safety, and they agree that your relationship with DeNardis is enough to justify claiming jurisdiction as long as he's not on the case himself. If you're not comfortable, it'll end up going to the Bristol inspector office. They'll do good work."

The captain left the *but* unsaid. It filled the room regardless. The Bristol sub-office *did* do good work, but they didn't have the same resources as the main Greater Providence office. It was ostensibly all one department, but everyone knew the main office always got the cases with higher political significance.

Or the ones where someone could pull personal strings.

Ethically, she should probably still say no, but Emily didn't think she could turn George down. Her caseload wasn't light, exactly, but there was nothing that she felt needed her personal attention.

And it was his *son*.

"Alright," she said. George's posture relaxed slightly, but significantly. "Can you send me whatever you know about his schedule, friends, all that?"

DeNardis nodded and tapped on his tablet. "Already done. Thanks, Scott. I owe you one."

Emily nodded and left. She stopped by the kitchen to grab her fresh cup of coffee before burrowing back into her corner.

Technically, Emily had been with the main office long enough to request a desk upgrade, or even an office, but she liked her spot. It wasn't glamorous, but it was constructed with all the feng shui mindfulness that defined a high-profile witch city building.

More importantly, no one bothered her unless they really needed something.

When she opened the file DeNardis sent her, she had to take a moment to remind herself that she'd already said yes, and changing her mind now would be unacceptable. In addition to the phone records, the report had extensive profiles on all of Sean's friends—their names and contact information, hobbies, their parents' names and hobbies, even some of their frequent hangouts. The file on Sean's girlfriend was even worse, including a full financial background check. The file also contained a list of every class Sean had taken at Roger Williams University and contact information for every professor, not just the ones teaching classes he was currently enrolled in.

There was no way DeNardis had gathered all that since the call he got that morning. Emily suspected DeNardis had gotten the call and gone straight to the captain first thing. He had to have this file *before* Sean went missing.

The poor kid.

Emily took a sip of coffee. It was still hot— the dispenser kept it at optimal serving temperature until the cup was removed— and the flavor was rich and deep. Emily didn't know much about how coffee beans were grown, but she did know that one of the dispatchers knew a divine coffee farmer and the brew from their beans was *heavenly*.

Divine territory definitely had its problems, but Divinity sure knew how to keep a body fueled.

Most of the people she needed to talk to were at the Roger Williams campus, so rather than try and get them all to come to the station or try for phone calls she decided to go there in person. She sent a message to her car to meet her in the waiting area outside the office, grabbed her yellow investigator's coat, tablet, badge, and taser, and left.

On her way over, she called one of GPI's regular magical consultants, a witch named William Davis. Emily liked Will—he was far less invested in all the spooky, stars and smoke and candlewax *witch aesthetics* than most, and she trusted him to be open with her as much as Coven law allowed. Witches, as a rule, were cagey as well as eccentric, but there was something unusually grounded about Will. He was always honest about what he could and couldn't do or say without trying to bullshit her.

Will's receptionist answered, and Emily gave her badge number and asked to be put through. The line went quiet for about a minute, and then Will answered.

"This is Will."

"Hi, Will, this is Detective Emily Scott from GPI. I have a missing person's case that I'd like to bring you in on?"

"Emily! Been a while. When do you need me? The earliest I can make it down there is probably six, I'm tied up here till around five, and it will take me about an hour to ride down."

It would probably take her most of the day to interview all of Sean's friends, and she would hopefully have a lead by then.

"I can portal over sooner if it's an emergency, but I can't do it for free, not if it's official for GPI, so it will cost you," Will added, trying to be helpful.

"Nah, six is fine. Send me a text when you get close so I can tell you where to meet me. You still have my direct number, right?"

"Yeah. I'll flag it so you won't need to go through the receptionist next time. See you later. Oh! Don't forget to grab a personal item for me to use or this will take all night."

"Yup, I'll do my best, see you."

When Emily arrived at the campus, she told her bright blue and white investigator cruiser to find a place to park—the interview process would take a while, and Emily didn't want the car killing its battery trying to idle nearby.

With a sigh, Emily adjusted her bag over her shoulder and took off across the bright green lawn. The buildings were all Post-Rapture, but you wouldn't be able to tell from their design. Someone had clearly wanted the campus to feel like an old-world Oxford style *Learning Institution*, with sweeping arches, hempcrete spelled to look like granite, and cobbled paths laid out in elegant spirals and curves.

Witches loved their *Dark Academia* aesthetics.

Classes had been in session a full three weeks—the university started session in August—but the campus still had the fresh feeling of a new semester. Students not in class were still relatively bright-eyed, and the abundance of witch-assisted flowers filled the air with energizing perfume.

Emily, in her yellow investigator coat, stood out like a beacon. Eyes followed her all the way to the main administrative building. The wooden doors swooshed open as she approached, and a wary young man looked up from the glass-and-oak construction that served as a main desk.

Emily let the kid enter her badge number into the system and then he handed Emily an authorized visitor pass that would allow her access to most of the campus. Emily did her best to put the kid at ease, and eventually he warmed enough to give Emily access to his computer so she could double check the list of professors and student contacts DeNardis had provided.

DeNardis's list was unsettlingly thorough.

Sean was studying law, and it seemed he had a particular interest in *copyright* law, of all things, which meant a lot of crossover with puffed up neo-philosophy and political science. As a rule, most of his professors, at least those he'd been working with for more than just this semester, spoke very highly of his character and performance, expressing their surprise that he hadn't shown up for class and speaking platitudes about his safety. Only one professor had anything to say about him that wasn't overly flattering, and it was an ethics professor who said that he might be anti-witch, but he hid it well.

After the professors, Emily started the much more time-consuming process of tracking down his friends. The first few she found were able to identify some of his friends who'd been out with him at a bar the night he disappeared.

Sean had disabled his GPS function, but the cell company was still able to narrow his location down to about a quarter-mile radius. The bar was in the same general area where Sean's phone had gone dead.

She grew even more concerned when she asked Sean and Olivia's mutual friends about the relationship. Olivia Weaver had been dating Sean for six months, and her friends didn't seem to think it would last much longer. None of them said anything specific about why they thought that, but Emily got the distinct impression they *hoped* it wouldn't last much longer.

One of Sean's friends, a boy named Richard, told Emily that Sean left the bar with a dark haired 'bombshell,' a word Emily was entirely sure didn't deserve a revival, especially since it wasn't helping her identify the woman in the slightest. She'd have to hope the woman's face showed up on a security camera. The kid hadn't seemed concerned about what Sean's girlfriend might think of him leaving with another girl and had laughed outright when Emily asked if he thought Olivia knew, or if he thought Olivia might break up with Sean over it.

The whole conversation left a bad taste in Emily's mouth.

His girlfriend, Olivia, had gone home early, alone, the night Sean disappeared.

Why?

Emily caught Olivia between classes and offered to buy her a coffee. She was pretty, small, and a little bit baby-faced, but her expression was wary. She asked to see Emily's badge and actually ran her investigator license number through a quick search on her phone before agreeing to come.

"You're not working for Sean's dad, right?" Olivia asked as they walked towards one of the campus cafes.

Emily considered how to answer and decided to be honest. "No, but I was assigned the case because Detective DeNardis is my partner."

Olivia thought about that. "They let you investigate your partner's missing kid?"

Emily nodded. "Yup. Public Safety apparently liked my odds better than the local office."

Olivia chewed on her lip. "Sean's dad is a stalker." She hesitated a moment, then said, "Sean doesn't like him very much."

Emily nodded but didn't say anything.

Olivia didn't let the silence stretch. "Sean said his dad leaves all kinds of bugs all over his apartment, and that he's probably bugging me too. I've never found anything, but Sean always checks before we go anywhere. He—" Olivia stopped, glanced at Emily, and looked away. "He hasn't called me since Saturday. I thought about reporting it, but I..."

Emily watched Olivia's body language carefully. She had a slight tic in her left ring finger, and she was studiously avoiding eye contact. There was a very slight bruise on her right wrist.

Emily forced herself to stay calm and not get angry. It was her job to *find* Sean, not build a case against him.

Except, fuck, maybe she should be doing both.

"Is he alright?" Olivia asked instead of finishing her previous thought.

Emily kept her expression neutral. "That's what I'm trying to find out. So you haven't heard from him at all since Saturday night?"

Olivia shook her head.

They paused their conversation long enough to give their orders to the barista. Emily paid for Olivia and asked her if she wanted to sit down.

Olivia glanced at her phone nervously. "Is it okay if we walk? I have class in fifteen minutes, and I want to get there early. Sean says I need to keep my grades up, or—" she cut off, and blushed. "He's right. I need to keep my grades up."

Emily sucked her coffee in through a clenched jaw and let out a slow breath. “Sure, we can walk. Lead the way.” Emily stayed quiet until that tic in Olivia’s left hand started up again and then asked, “What time did you leave the bar? Did Sean walk you home?”

Olivia shook her head. “I was, um, not feeling well, so I left early. I didn’t want to ruin Sean’s night, so I left by myself.”

She rubbed her wrist absently, and Emily took another sip of coffee to cover her reaction. “Did you see him talking with anyone else? Who else was with you?”

Olivia gave an accurate list of the friends that were with them but made no mention of the dark-haired woman. She did admit to sneaking out the back, but said it was because the smell in the bar made her feel sick.

When Olivia went into her class, Emily stood there for a long moment, compartmentalizing her anger.

Her first job was to find Sean.

Afterwards, assuming the kid was alright, she’d have a conversation with DeNardis and his son about *several* things. If they wouldn’t talk to her, they’d talk to the Social Work office.

Emily went to Sean’s dorm room next to get a personal item for Will to use. From what she understood, objects he was emotionally attached to, or were the focus of strong emotions, had the best chance of giving Will something to follow. She didn’t see anything that spoke of sentimental value— his room was fairly spartan. She ended up taking a backpack and a game controller, hoping that something would be significant enough for Will to latch on to.

She went into the bathroom to find something with his DNA on it in case Will had to resort to following a DNA sample. It took more magic to trace with DNA than emotional resonance, according to Will, but it also had more consistent results. All she could find was his toothbrush, and she rubbed it through some of the scum on the sink, hoping to pick up some stray hairs just in case the toothbrush wasn't enough on its own. Fortunately, each bedroom in the apartment had its own bathroom, so she was fairly certain it was only Sean's DNA she was picking up. She dropped the now very disgusting toothbrush in an evidence bag.

The kid could get himself a new toothbrush when he turned up. *If* he turned up.

That taken care of, Emily checked the time. She decided it was probably late enough that someone would be at the bar by the time she got there. She sent a quick message to Will asking him to meet her there and put the address for Thoughts and Prayers into her car's GPS.

As she crawled through streets flooded with rush hour pedestrians and buses, she pulled up as much information on the bar as she could find. She did a quick search of the Rhode Island incident database and scrolled through the list of reports it was mentioned in.

There was the normal smattering of incident reports for a popular bar in a college town, but Emily was surprised to see that there were also over a dozen other missing persons cases that mentioned the bar over the last two years.

"Why the fuck didn't this get flagged?" Emily grumbled, compiling a list of them all.

It didn't look good. Every single one of them was an adult male, and human, not witch or fae-blooded. They didn't seem to have much in common, but Emily had a bad feeling. None of them had ever been found or heard from again.

Shit.

Emily called DeNardis.

"Emily, do you have an update on my son?"

Emily braced herself to give her partner some bad news. "Did you know that there is a bar in Bristol that has been mentioned in *fourteen* missing persons cases in the last two years? And none of them, not one, was resolved?"

There was silence on the line for several minutes. "No. My son was there before he disappeared?"

"Yes," Emily said, as neutrally as she could manage.

Another moment of tense silence. "Thanks for the update, Scott. I'll let the captain know so they get someone to look into why that wasn't flagged by the system. Let me know when you find anything else." He hung up without waiting for a reply.

Emily took a deep breath, and then pulled up a picture of Sean on her tablet. He was a good-looking kid, hopefully memorable.

Hopefully alive.

NEXUS

Aiden stepped through the doorway and into the strangest city he'd ever seen.

On the surface, the city was normal, with paved roads running between buildings, sidewalks and street lamps, store fronts advertising things, but that was where the similarities ended. The buildings didn't make any sense. There were massive skyscrapers right next to tiny three-story Victorian houses, and there didn't seem to be any divide between where businesses and homes were located. There were a few spooky-looking places, and a number of buildings that he couldn't even begin to guess what they were for. Walls and billboards, some floating above the street like banners, held advertisements for every vice Aiden had ever heard of, and some that he hadn't.

What was a treegasm experience? The banner had a stylized tree in full bloom on it and promised *accurate tree memories, sped up to animal time scales*. It couldn't mean that *literally*, right?

The air smelled like chaos, but in a good way, with food, spices, strange perfumes, and other, sharper scents he couldn't identify. Almost as jarring as the pleasant cacophony was the complete lack of any of the normal unpleasant city smells. There was no exhaust, ozone, or garbage. Nothing foul at all. The air was thick with *something*, but it was crisp and energized and utterly enchanting.

Aiden looked up. There was no sun, only an orb of multicolored fire that was quite clearly being pulled by a chariot and four flaming horses. The horses ran, hooves flashing, but the chariot crawled, hardly moving at all. Though the chariot was near the zenith of the sky, the light given off by the ball of fire was much dimmer than normal daylight, leaving everything feeling like it was on the edge of dusk or just after dawn.

The sky itself didn't seem to want to decide on a color, shifting like the prismatic darkness of Zee's coat. Despite the relative dimness of the sky, the colors of everything around him were improbably vibrant, and in more shades than he'd ever seen before.

And the people! There was clothing in every style, from every culture and time Aiden had ever heard of and many he hadn't, combined in every way imaginable. There was also a shocking amount of people wearing nothing at all. Many of them had animal parts—ears, horns, tails, hooves, claws, and wings—with no regard for what belonged together. There were people with too many arms, or too many eyes, sometimes in strange places like the tips of their fingers or on the end of long tentacles.

As he watched, there didn't seem to be any care for what was allowed on the street versus the sidewalk. People and cars and bikes and carriages were going in every direction, fast and slow and practically teleporting, but somehow nothing crashed and everything fit. The carriages were being drawn by all sorts of creatures, from horses to monsters, to...a unicorn?

Aiden stared after where the unicorn had disappeared around the corner, blinking rapidly.

It was all so much. It should have been overwhelming, but he *loved* it. It was better than anything he could have imagined.

But he was *damned*. It didn't make any sense.

He found himself suddenly sitting, the pavement sun-warm beneath him, but not uncomfortably so. The people and creatures flowed around him, so beautiful and exciting that he could have cried. He was suddenly very, very afraid, certain that *this*, seeing this city and its people, hoping that he might get to *live* here only to have it all ripped away was going to be his torment.

"Sam, are, um. Am I... I thought he—I mean, I expected—"

"You expected eternal torment, fire and brimstone and pools of acid and horned demons running around stabbing people with pitchforks?" He laughed. "We need to invest in better PR. I know Zee said you had no knowledge of the underworld, but still, people can *talk* to demons. They can just ask for the truth! Instead, they repeat tired old stories that never made any sense to begin with."

Aiden looked away and mumbled, "People get killed for talking to demons where I grew up."

Sam winced and crouched down to ruffle Aiden's hair. It felt *odd*. Like there was something there that was...

"Sorry," Sam said, and Aiden shrugged awkwardly. He hadn't been fishing for an apology, not on purpose. "You lived in Divine territory? Didn't have much access to trustworthy information, yeah?"

Aiden nodded, and Sam looked even more sympathetic. "Times change, but people don't. There will always be people who won't let themselves know the truth even after we beat them over the head with it." Sam paused and grew thoughtful. "But there are those willing to see the truth, eventually, once they shake themselves free of whatever bullshit lies they were raised on. They're the ones who will win this war, if it can be won."

Aiden swallowed and nodded again, but reflexively this time, not really understanding what Sam was saying. He was having too hard a time believing what he was seeing.

He blushed when he realized that was *exactly* what Sam was talking about.

Sam groaned. "Stop blushing like that, bunny boy, or we're not going to make it very far." Aiden blushed harder and looked at his knees. Sam laughed. "Don't worry so much about it. It's okay to take whatever time you need before you let yourself believe it's real. Honestly, you're handling it all *way* better than I did. It took me ages to get over myself."

Aiden looked up at Sam, focusing hard on his bright green cat eyes so he wouldn't stare at his ears, or his stomach or his...other parts. "I am? How did you handle it?"

Sam sighed and sat down next to Aiden on the curb. Aiden felt Sam's tail curl around his waist, and he relaxed a bit more.

"My arrival was a little different from yours. They teach you about the Rapture up there, right?"

Aiden nodded, but felt compelled to add, "Yeah, but they also teach about He—, I mean, this place, being filled with fire and brimstone, so maybe assume I don't know anything."

Sam laughed again, and it filled Aiden with warmth. He really liked Sam's laugh.

"Fair enough! Okay, story time." Sam stood up and drew a box in the air with his finger. One of the holographic screens popped into existence. Sam pushed it down so it was hovering at Aiden's eye level, and then he sat back down next to Aiden.

Tiny stick figures appeared and waved cheerfully at Aiden. A few of the people on the street glanced at Sam and Aiden as they walked by, but mostly they just kept walking. To escape his self-conscious embarrassment, Aiden focused intently on the screen. A title appeared above the stick figures that read:

'Sam Tells History. Probably Badly.'

"So, life began on earth," Sam said, looking at Aiden and not the screen. The stick figures exploded and resolved into what appeared to be several single-celled amoeba wiggling on the screen. Aiden poked the screen, and as his hand passed through it, the cells dodged out the way and tiny angry faces appeared on them. Aiden pulled his hand back and wrapped his arms around his knees.

"Every time something died, it left behind a little echo, a soul. As the souls built up, they started collecting and merging, forming like...a soul planet. Or maybe a soul-star? It was this big dense soul thing that radiated, um, soul energy, what we call magic these days. The denser it gets, the more it burns and radiates, just like light from a star." The cells on the screen started passionately dying, leaving behind tiny, dramatic ghost cells. The cell-ghosts clustered together on the screen, and then they smooshed themselves together, looking very confused as they tried to make themselves into a planet. Then they seemed to disagree on how to make a star, and there was a bit of chaos before they finally formed a single glowing orb.

"So this big soul-star slowly became self-aware. As it did, life got more and more complicated. Don't ask me about causality, life-chickens or sentience-eggs or whatever, no one knows because it was before things like, *knew* stuff." The orb on the screen tried to demonstrate what Sam was saying as weird little jellyfish and clams appeared around it, dramatically dying, and then smushing into the orb. The orb grew a little face so it could glare at Sam, who was still looking at Aiden and couldn't see it. Other animals started crowding onto the screen, acting out more and more ridiculous death scenes.

Aiden laughed, and Sam frowned and looked back at the screen. The face disappeared, and Sam shrugged, seeing nothing wrong, and looked back at Aiden. The face reappeared and winked at Aiden.

"Okay, so, as the big soul-star got bigger, it realized it could be bossy. At the same time, some of the animals realized they could use magic. Sometimes they did things with the magic that, like, broke the planet and caused an extinction event, and the soul-star, which started calling itself Divinity, got a *huge* influx of souls all at once, and then it couldn't be bossy, or something, until it sorted them all out."

The orb grew itself a little crown as a few of the animals started flinging lightning and firebolts at each other. The fire and lightning filled the screen, and then all the animals started silently screaming as they boiled alive. The souls all rushed the Divinity orb at once, and the crown fell off.

It fell slowly, as if sinking through thick liquid, and as it sank other animals and plants appeared. Just as another crown appeared on the orb, the old crown fell *on* the new animals and smooshed them all, and the new crown vanished for a moment before reforming. Strange land animals appeared on the screen, and the Divinity orb started poking them. The animals all got big frowns on their faces and started throwing exploding question marks all over the screen. The Divinity orb was overwhelmed again, the crown breaking into pieces, and then dinosaurs appeared. One of them summoned a volcano, and then there was an asteroid, and then it became too confusing to follow.

"So, eventually the animals and Divinity all got tired of this cycle, and they both tried to fix it. Divinity got even more bossy, and it was throwing off ridiculous amounts of magic because it was so huge. The animals gathered it all up to do something with it and then, I don't know, the Seal happened." The figures on the screen started trying to act it out, and then they threw up their arms in defeat and a massive circular symbol appeared on the screen. It was outrageously intricate, and Aiden's head hurt when he tried to focus too hard on it.

"With the seal in place, souls had nowhere to go. Oh! Shit! I forgot to talk about the Library, and reincarnation. Go back!" Sam looked at the screen. The stick figures appeared again, arms crossed, looking mutinous. The seal hovered dimly in the background.

Sam made a frustrated sound. "Fine. Never mind. Just know souls can choose to reincarnate, and there's also the Library, and it might be full of aliens, but I guess we need to move on."

"Wait, aliens? What?" Aiden was very confused, and he looked at the screen for help. The stick figures were shaking their heads sadly.

"We're getting off track! Without a place to go, souls just *froze*. No thinking, no feeling, no doing. We call it oblivion, lots of us were in a state of oblivion for hundreds or thousands of years before waking up during the Breaking. Some of the early Seal-age souls apparently knew enough to force their reincarnation anyway, but doing so destroyed their memories and they ended up caught in an endless reincarnation loop. Other, later-born souls were angry or sad enough that they were able to haunt the mortal plane, half in and half out of oblivion, but that was really rough on them and most went loony and fell apart. I think maybe the fae started eating them, or maybe the fae used them to make new fae? No one knows, it doesn't matter."

The figures on the screen abandoned all pretense of following along with Sam, making silly faces instead. One of them tried to start a game of pick-up basketball with the others, and they formed themselves into rough teams.

"Anyway, there was a standoff. After thousands of years of pressure from all the souls that had nowhere to go, Divinity managed to do some shady fascist shit to erode the Seal. Eventually, the Seal broke, what you probably know as the Breaking, and we, the souls of those who died during the time of the Seal, all started waking up."

Sam waved his hand through the screen and it shuddered, the edges frayed. The figures started screaming and running around, and random fires appeared. "Magic, both Divine and other, flooded the world. Human infrastructure crumbled and creatures, both human and not, were slaughtered by the hundreds of millions, flooding more and more souls into the chaos. Divinity went positively batty, drunk on a flood of souls larger than any before on a titanic scale. It created monsters that shouted nonsense like 'BE NOT AFRAID' while chomping down on deviant souls who wanted nothing to do with Unity."

The figures on the screen started rioting. Whether they were acting out Sam's words or were just mad at Sam, Aiden couldn't tell.

"Pretty quickly, a bunch of humans and independent souls organized a resistance. Lucifer, the Guardian of the Seal—or well, formerly—teamed up with Lillian, a pre-Seal soul that managed to get sole control of the entire Mantle of Magic pretty much right away, and Zee, who runs the Library. They collected all the deviant souls and here we are."

The screen vanished, and Sam put his clawed hands on his naked hips.

"The end!"

NEXUS

I KNOW WE NEVER LEFT. HUSH.

Aiden nodded and clapped politely. Most of this was somewhat familiar, though with a heavy dose of silly and all the church propaganda and anarchist conspiracy theories scrubbed away. Divinity was, according to its own lore, the Unity of Souls. He'd grown up being taught that evil Demons had locked everyone away from Unity until finally righteousness prevailed and Lucifer, the keeper of the Seal, lost and fell and Divinity was free. Divinity taught that the Rapture was a war fought to keep the demons from locking Divinity away again, but anarchists always said it was Divinity who was the aggressor.

Aiden tentatively raised his hand, not sure what else to do. "What about the Rapture?"

Sam snapped his fingers. "Right! The earth manifested a soul—her name is Gemma and she's super scary. She got help from the fae, or maybe she was originally fae, I don't know, and they froze everything for a few days, ending the Breaking. During that time, the Triad—that's Lucifer, Lillian and Zee, they're kind of a team—and Divinity negotiated the Treaty. Divinity gets to try to seduce humanity to its side, but it can't use magic to dominate any unwilling souls, living or dead, while it does. In exchange, us Demons—their word, not ours, but we're stuck with it now—can assist humanity in its quest for Ascension, but mostly just within witch territory."

Aiden blinked. "I'm...still a little confused," he said carefully. He absently brushed a hand over a strange mossy plant growing between the cracks in the pavement. It almost looked like it was *fixing* the pavement, which made no sense. "What's Ascension?"

Sam shrugged. "No idea! Future knowledge is restricted. Whatever it is, Divinity can't gobble up Ascended souls. There's a couple Ascended souls kicking around besides the Triad, but I think they're still alive? Sort of? It's confusing."

Aiden nodded slowly. "I, um. Can tell."

Sam smiled sheepishly. "Best I can do. Sorry. The Triad tells it better, but they never have time." Sam climbed to his feet and stretched, completely unselfconscious about his nudity. His tail coiled into a little question mark.

Aiden quickly looked down at the moss, which had sprouted an array of tiny glowing flowers under his fingers.

"So, back to your question—how did I handle waking up? Well, my last memory was dying in a trench during the Great War. The first one, before the Breaking, back when we killed each other with guns and gas and most of us died of flesh-rot and the flu. Shell-shocked doesn't even begin to cover it. Nexus had already been somewhat established by the time I pulled myself together—trauma can make it take longer sometimes. My best guess is it took me maybe fifteen years to regain awareness after the Breaking. Even together as a self I was still a mess for like, twenty years."

Aiden tensed. "So, wait, how long have I been dead?"

"You? Hmm, what's the last date you remember?"

"September 7, 47. Ah, 47 YAR"

Sam's mouth fell open. "Wait, really? Fuck, that was only yesterday!" He reached out a clawed hand and tentatively poked Aiden's shoulder, as if checking to make sure it was solid. Aiden felt his chest growing tighter. "Shit, kid, that's kind of unbelievable. Didn't Zee say anything?"

Aiden looked down and fidgeted, thinking about the terrifying confrontation with the angry darkness and the weird way Zee and Lucifer acted afterwards. "They were a bit busy."

Sam studied Aiden for a few seconds, then shrugged with exaggerated nonchalance and offered Aiden his hand. "I guess they must have been. Come on, let's get moving, we have a lot of ground to cover." He smiled encouragingly. "I'll try to answer as many questions as I can for you as we go."

Aiden felt a little unstable, but he took Sam's hand anyway and let himself be pulled to his feet. They started walking down the street. Despite the number of people, there always seemed to be plenty of space, and after a moment Aiden decided the sidewalk had to be actually changing size to avoid congestion.

"Alright, so basically, navigating the underworld is more about knowing where you are going instead of how you get there. There are places, but they are more the *idea* of a somewhere rather than a physical space. In order to get around, you picture where you want to go and then step onto a pathway." Sam demonstrated by turning a corner, which brought them to an even larger street. Aiden hesitated when he realized there weren't any sidewalks on this road, but Sam still had his hand, and he gave a gentle tug that Aiden didn't want to resist. "They're like trains of thought—the more people who know about and use a pathway, the easier it is to find and follow."

Sam pointed to the street they were walking on. "This is one of the largest and most stable pathways in the underworld. Think of it as Nexus' Main Street. So many people have used it that it's become a *place*."

Sam tugged Aiden between two slowly rolling carts, one of which seemed to be selling singing flowers, the other full of strange, glittering vials. "Nexus is all like that—you can get to almost anywhere from here, as long as it's a place you are able to go—not every soul can go everywhere. There are no maps of Nexus because it isn't bound by physical rules—the city doesn't *want* to be mapped, and it gets irritated if you try."

"Irritated?" Aiden asked nervously.

Sam glanced back at Aiden and smiled. "Nothing nefarious, but it will deliberately move buildings into your way, or fill a street with glowing fog or swarms of distracting butterflies, stuff like that."

Aiden eyed the pavement suspiciously. "What about those doors you keep opening?"

Sam stepped out of the way of a pumpkin carriage full of white doves and his expression turned sly. "Ah well, those are a special demon privilege. You can only open doors to places you've already been, but it allows you to short circuit pathways. You've been like, two places so far, so I wouldn't worry about it yet, and you'd need to register as a demon with the Library anyway. But, there are other little shortcuts you can take, if you don't want to rely on the main roadways. Here, let me show you one."

Sam took Aiden's hand and pulled him over to what looked like an old-fashioned phone booth, the kind cities used to have before the

Breaking. He opened the doors and pushed Aiden in before following. It wasn't bigger on the inside, not really, but there was exactly the right amount of space for the two of them to comfortably maneuver. Sam picked up an ancient looking phone and entered in a number using some kind of strange, spinning dial that clicked after each number he entered.

He let it ring once, then hung up, and when they stepped back out to the street they were in a totally new part of the city.

Aiden's chest got tight. "Wait, do I need to memorize numbers to get around this way? How many different numbers are there? Are there phone books, or would that be too much like a map?" Aiden started to shake a little and his hands twitched. He had no notebook or phone or anything to help him keep track of *anything*. What was he going to do?

"Whoa, hey, easy there," Sam said gently. He took Aiden by the shoulders and led him over to a bench. It was covered in pretty green and gold vines. They smelled faintly of vanilla, and Aiden drew in the scent as Sam guided him to a seat. "It's okay, you don't have to memorize stuff if you don't want to. It's just a shortcut, you don't need them. They're only for fun, okay?"

Aiden nodded, but he felt terrible for his stupid breakdown. He *wanted* to learn all about Nexus, and the idea of small secret paths, or coded doors that lead across town *should* have been exciting.

"I'm sorry. I'm glad you showed me the phone booth thing," he said, miserably.

Sam threw one arm over Aiden's shoulder and gave it a quick squeeze. "Bunny boy, you have all of eternity to learn secret tricks. You'll probably even make your own—I learned about the phone booth from the lady who built them. I've been here and sane enough to enjoy it for like, maybe fifteen years and I've only scratched the surface. There's no rush, and you don't have to do anything you don't want to."

Aiden just nodded again. He couldn't bring himself to explain to Sam that he *did* want to, *so much*, and that terrified him. Part of him still half believed this was all going to be ripped away from him any second.

Which was *stupid*. He knew it was.

Aiden resisted the urge to curl into a ball and cry and settled instead for closing his eyes and taking another deep, slow breath. The scent of vanilla was even stronger now, cut through with something else, something that reminded him of fresh air and soft grass. Aiden opened his eyes and saw that small white flowers had opened up all along the vines. He reached over and brushed one lightly with his fingertips.

"Do they always do that?" Aiden asked, softly. "The plants, I mean. Do they always bloom when you touch them?"

Sam nudged him gently with his shoulder. "Only when they like you."

Aiden smiled and nudged Sam back. "Let's keep moving. I want to see the other shortcuts, but maybe after I've had some more time to get settled?"

Assuming this wasn't all a trick.

Sam smiled encouragingly. "Sure, kid. We'll stick to the main roads for today."

Even sticking to only the wide, crowded streets, there were still tricks to learn. Sam showed him there were ways to move faster over long visible distances by stepping up to a streetlight and swinging around it. When you got all the way around the pole, you were a mile down the road on another streetlight. It was really simple, you just had to pick the streetlight you wanted to jump to and off you went.

Aiden *loved* that trick. They spent what seemed like hours chasing each other up and down the streets.

As they moved through the city, Aiden started to get a rough idea of its layout. Every so often a building, or an alleyway, or, oddly, a playground inside of a little park with purple grass and rainbow colored trees, would *call out* to him. He somehow knew he could go back there if he wanted to, and he had a weird certainty that he *would* go back.

The more places he found that called to him, the better sense of the city he got. As Sam chatted to Aiden about all the different places he knew, it became very clear *no one* really knew the place, no one *could*, since places appeared and disappeared without warning or apparent cause.

The size of it, the chaos of it, should have been overwhelming, but Aiden felt better knowing that it was too big to completely understand.

After a while, Aiden noticed that the sun-chariot had moved most of the way across the sky. He wasn't nearly as tired as he thought he should have been, and he wondered why he wasn't feeling more foot sore—he wasn't exactly used to being on his feet all day.

He was about to ask Sam why when Sam pulled them to a stop in front of a strangely colorful cafe.

"Hey kid, I'm hungry. Wanna stop for a bite?" Sam asked, pulling Aiden towards the building.

"I'm not a kid, you know," Aiden said, letting himself get dragged along. He wasn't annoyed by being called a kid, but he felt like he needed to say something to hide how much he liked the way Sam was leading him around.

"*Sure* you aren't. You died at what, 17?"

"I'm 26. Or, I guess I was?"

"Oh man, really?" Sam said, pushing him through the door. "That means I'm younger than you, sort of." A wave of marshmallow and chocolate-scented air hit Aiden in the face, and he was momentarily dazzled by the massive displays of brightly colored cookies and intricately decorated cakes. The place was all steel and shiny bubblegum pink-and-blue ceramic, like a picture from a mid-twentieth century magazine.

Sam continued, "We count our ages in two ways here, because the amount of time your soul is in a living body affects how much, like, soul density you have. I died at 20, so you've got six mortal years on me. But you're still a kid, because I've been around here for decades and you've been here for like twelve hours." They joined a line full of people waiting to order. Apparently Hell, despite being not at all hellish, still had lines. It made Aiden feel better, like maybe it wasn't a trick.

"Oh," Aiden said. "So I'm like a day-old baby?" He wrinkled his nose.

"No," Sam said, frowning. "I'm sorry, I'm not explaining things very well. I usually kind of, you know, *do* stuff." He batted lazily at his own tail. "If Zee wasn't *Zee*, I probably would question their judgment in picking me to be your tour guide. But Zee *is* Zee, so I won't question it, not unless..." He suddenly looked uncertain. "Would you like me to ask Zee to take over? They're probably done with whatever they were doing. Or I could find someone else who's better at explaining if you want."

"No! No, it's okay, I like—" Aiden cut off and clasped his hands together to stop them from fluttering. "I get it. I'm both older and younger than you, right?"

Sam smiled. "Yeah! But you're not like, *way* older than me. The important thing to remember is that it makes sense for me to call you kid. Got it, kid?"

Aiden scowled at him. Sam laughed and bumped his hip against Aiden affectionately, and his scowl twitched into a smile. He really liked Sam's laugh. It made his green eyes sparkle.

He was glad that their mortal age difference wasn't...gross. Aiden had slept with plenty of guys who were way older than him, but...

It didn't matter. Sam was his tour guide and not his date.

Aiden turned his attention to the menu posted above the counter. Even though most of the options were very strange and made no sense to him—what was Egyptian Scarab-aide?—it was all definitely in English. It occurred to Aiden that it was odd.

"Does everyone here speak English?" Aiden was sure that couldn't be true, but so far he'd understood everything around him.

"What! Oh, no, of course not. Souls don't speak any mortal language. We're not speaking English right now."

"We aren't? But..." Aiden looked back at the writing on the menus and blinked. Sam was *right*. The markings on the signs weren't English, they weren't anything like English, but they were also perfectly understandable.

Aiden spent a few moments with his mind blown as he went through everything he had heard and said since waking up in the Atrium with Zee. He had been speaking whatever language this was the *whole time*. Why the hell hadn't he noticed before? Was there something here affecting his thinking? Was he...

Aiden felt himself growing cold and tense, so he pushed the thoughts away. It was *fine*. He'd just been a little overwhelmed, is all. If he didn't think about it, he wouldn't get upset, and then he wouldn't panic. *Again*.

Sam's tail wrapped around Aiden's waist, and Aiden looked down, surprised and pleased, and then back at Sam, who smiled and gestured at the menu board. "Some humans call it the Language of the Birds, or Demonic, or Angelic if you're talking to an asshole, but it's just the language of souls," he explained. "If you ever end up back on the mortal plane you'll find that all mortals, human or otherwise, can understand it, but only witches with a bonded familiar, oh, and fucking exorcists, can actually hear it and speak it without the assistance of some kind of spell or tool."

He sighed dramatically, tail twitching. It ticked where it touched Aiden's skin. "We *used* to be able to talk to whoever we wanted, but now it's in the *rules*, so we can't. Anyway, whatcha having? Want me to pick for you?"

Aiden nodded since he was still too busy thinking about words to summon the fortitude to make a decision. Sam leaned over the counter to fiddle with something behind one of the displays, and the barista slapped his hand away and scolded him cheerfully. They chatted about a bunch of people Aiden didn't know for a minute before Sam ordered two unicorn milkshakes. He entered a code into a small screen that popped up.

"Message me a receipt, Kel. I'm gunna bill *Executive*." He sounded very pleased with himself.

"What, for a milkshake? How come?" The barista had horns like a gazelle, and was dressed in what looked like some kind of predator fur. Her posture screamed danger, but it was covered with a veneer of warm, beautiful softness that Aiden found irrationally off-putting. She looked behind Sam to Aiden and her eyes lit up. "Oooh, where'd you catch this sweet pet?" She gave Aiden a slow smile, but continued speaking to Sam. "He's *cute*, are you *sharing*?" Her smile was full of fangs.

Aiden froze, and then tried to hide behind Sam. Sam curled his tail tighter around Aiden's waist, but didn't turn away from the barista. His tone remained friendly, and he laughed. "He's not my pet, Kelsy, he's *new*. Zee asked me to give him the tour, so it's paws off until he's decided what he wants to do."

Kelsy pouted, and Aiden blushed, but he wished desperately that he hadn't. He wasn't... he didn't...

Kelsy's expression went sharp, and she laughed in delight, "Oh *honey bunny*, once you're settled you better come right back here, alright? I'll give you something on the house." Kelsy winked at him and then turned to make their shakes.

Aiden covered his face with his hands and didn't remove them until the heat from his blush was gone. By the time he did, Sam had pulled him over to a table. Aiden accepted the bright rainbow milkshake Sam held out to him. It was cold in his hands through the antique style glass, solid and real. Did that make sense? Sam offered him a chair, and he sat down.

Aiden's shake had a thick straw, but Sam's didn't.

"Do you want me to..." Aiden drifted off as Sam dragged his glass over and started lapping at the milk shake like a cat.

Because he *was* a cat. Partly.

Aiden watched in fascination until Sam looked up.

"What, you don't like it?" he asked, licking his lips. Aiden stared at Sam's tongue, realized what he was doing, and hastily looked away and sipped from his own drink.

The flavor that burst onto his tongue was like laughter and sparkling sunlight. He made an indecent sound and he sucked greedily for a few seconds before he forced himself to slow down so he could savor it. He eventually looked back at Sam, who was smiling at him.

"Awesome, right? I thought you'd like that." He looked smug.

"I thought milk was bad for cats?" Aiden asked, ducking his head to cover his blush.

Sam laughed, "Bunny, where do you think you are? We can do whatever we want here, without feeling bad about it, as long as it doesn't hurt someone else. Unless they want to be hurt, but that's its own whole thing. Basically the only thing off the table down here is forcing someone to do something they don't want to do, understand?"

Aiden nodded, and took another euphoric sip from his shake.

"Besides, I don't think unicorn milk has any lactose in it anyway," Sam said.

Aiden choked and snorted rainbow milk out his nose, sending Sam into another fit of laughter. When Aiden stopped spluttering, mostly, he asked, eyeing his shake. "This is what?"

"A unicorn milkshake. As in, made with *unicorn* milk. Obviously."

"Someone *milked* a unicorn?" Aiden tried to picture it. "It was a girl unicorn, right? Not, like..." He blushed, and Sam fell out of his chair.

Aiden smiled slyly and kept drinking.

When they had both finished, Aiden looked around for a rag or napkin to wipe the table. Sam noticed and gently pushed Aiden to the side.

"Watch this."

Sam flipped the table with such force it smashed into pieces against the wall. Aiden yelped and jumped back, but then watched in amazement as the broken bits vanished and a new table, perfectly clean and undamaged, materialized.

"That's handy," Aiden said, a little shocked, "Do people not like to clean in He—here?"

"Nah, some people like to clean, but they don't *have* to. At its core, everything here is just an idea, even though it feels solid to us, because souls and all the stuff they feel are made of ideas." He waved his hand around as if that might make it all make sense. "You see?"

Aiden thought maybe he did. Carefully, he said, "So you and I and everyone, *we're* ideas too. Our own idea of ourselves, made tangible by our desire to continue to *be*. The ideas we share between us are as real as we are, which is why everything feels real, until it's not."

Sam beamed. "Yeah! That's a much smarter way of saying it!" He took Aiden's hand and pulled him towards the exit. "Come on, it's late, so I'll show you where you can sleep. I'll pick you up in the morning and we can visit a few other places tomorrow."

They walked down the street in companionable silence. Aiden tried to grapple with everything he'd experienced, but he had a hard time focusing on anything other than Sam's hand holding his. The sun-chariot had set below the horizon but the city wasn't dark. It glowed with the same riot of nonsense colors it had in the daylight, except in the darkness it was more like everything was illuminated by a black light.

The people on the street seemed different too, nocturnal creatures rather than daylight ones. Some of them waved at Sam, and one of them, a gorgeous man who also had cat eyes, though his were yellow and his hair was long and gold, just straight up asked if Sam wanted to go have sex.

Sam laughed and waved him off. "Nope! And a no for bunny here too. He's too new. Shoo." The lovely man shrugged and gave Aiden a knowing wink before walking on. Sam's tail wrapped around Aiden's waist again, briefly scanning Aiden's face to make sure he was okay, before pulling him along.

He *was* okay. Somehow, even though he was dead and damned, he was...happy?

Aiden felt an ache form in his chest, part fear and part hope. He didn't want to spoil the happiness he was feeling, so he focused on the dark, empty sky to keep from thinking about it. A moon that rippled with the colors of a bloody sunset was rising, only just beginning to peak above the horizon.

"Why aren't there any stars?" he found himself asking. "There were stars in the Atrium."

"Ah, well. That." Sam was quiet for a moment. "You noticed the bars on the ceiling of the Atrium?" Aiden nodded, thinking of the arches. Only in hindsight did he realize that's what they had been.

His good mood evaporated.

Sam squeezed his hand. "That place is essentially the gate house. Lovely as it is here, it's still...well, a fortress."

Aiden grew very cold. "I see."

Sam turned to face Aiden and wrapped his tail tighter around Aiden's waist. In spite of himself, Aiden felt a little warmer. "It's not a *prison*," Sam said gently, "It's a *fortress*, to keep us safe."

"But we can't leave." Aiden was trying to decide if he minded that.

"We can, actually. Not right away, and there are certain conditions that need to be met, again for safety. I mean, I guess in theory you can give up your free will at any time and leave to join Divinity, but if you wanted to do that you wouldn't have landed here at all. I don't recommend it either way, since you get eaten and lose your individuality forever. But there are other ways to leave, including reincarnation."

Never, he thought, inexplicably. Aiden was almost overwhelmed by the instinctively visceral rejection of the idea of reincarnation. He physically shuddered with the force of it.

Sam noticed and, misinterpreting his reaction, gave Aiden's shoulder a small squeeze. "I'll tell you more about the ways to leave later. For now, just know that, whatever you were told when you were alive, you *always* have a choice. A *free* choice. The Triad cares a lot about making sure no one is coerced. It's kind of their whole deal."

Aiden nodded, but he was still uncertain. He wanted to believe it. Wanted to *so* badly.

And yet.

Sam took his hand again and they walked together until they came to what looked like an old-fashioned hotel. It was scary looking, but in a way Aiden found comforting. Aiden hesitated at the door, letting himself feel a fear that made *sense* for a relieved moment. Sam looked at him, worried, until he saw the expression on Aiden's face, and then he pushed open the door and tugged gently on his hand. Aiden swallowed, shivering but still smiling, and let Sam pull him through.

The lobby was furnished like a spooky but grand World Wars-era hotel, with plush furniture, a massive chandelier hanging from a vaulted ceiling, and an ornately carved wooden desk. There was a fountain that splashed red liquid, but it was much too thin to be blood. It looked more like punch, or maybe wine. The air smelled oaky and fruity and a bit musty, but with a sharp coolness that made the air feel oddly fresh, like the space was often exposed to an ancient garden.

A snake person stood behind the desk. They had a massive hood like a cobra, but their face was human, gaunt and genderless, except for the eyes, which were obviously snake eyes. They had on a pinstripe uniform, and a cap teetered on the top of their head.

"Welcome! Do you have a resssservation?" the snake person hissed cheerfully.

"There should be one under Aiden?" Sam said, gently tugging Aiden forward.

The snake person summoned up a holographic screen, which was stylized in a way to not clash with the old and pleasantly decrepit atmosphere. "Ah, yessss, room ssseven thirteen. Right thisss way, pleasssse."

The snake person slithered out from behind the desk and led them down a hallway to an elevator. There was an operator standing next to it who appeared to be some kind of rock person. Their skin was mottled grey and copper, and their features were sharp and angular, maybe masculine. Their eyes were brassy, but they looked real enough. The mouth was human looking, but not particularly expressive. They were dressed in a pinstripe uniform.

"Hugo, I'd like you to take thesssse two to room ssseven thirteen? Take the direct route pleasse, there was a ssspecial request from the top to keep thingsss ssssimple for thissssss one, at leassst for now."

The rock person, Hugo, nodded and pulled open the elevator doors. Hugo bowed Sam and Aiden through and then stepped in behind them. The elevator car felt ominous, which Aiden thought was fitting, though incongruous with his experiences of damnation so far.

Aiden wondered briefly if this was when they stopped messing with him and the torment began.

Hugo opened a panel in the wall and flipped a switch. The lighting in the elevator became softer, warm instead of menacing. Almost immediately the sense of doom vanished, and Aiden was confused again. A holographic screen popped up and Hugo tapped in the room number.

Aiden twisted his fingers together as the elevator began to ascend. He wanted to ask questions, but he was also afraid to say anything to the rock person in case he offended them.

Sam seemed to sense his unease, because he turned to Hugo and asked, "Hey, Hugo, it's been a while. How're you doing?"

Hugo shrugged casually, and there was a rumbly rocky sound that gave the impression of contentment.

"Great! This here is Aiden, and it's his first day in Nexus. Will you do me a favor and keep him safe for me while he stays here?"

There was another rock sound, which this time felt like an affirmative.

"Good fellow!" Sam winked at Aiden, and he felt his cheeks heat. "Just so you know, this place can be...weird. More so than the rest of Nexus, believe it or not. It's sort of its own separate zone. There's a whole series of places like it throughout the underworld, usually at least one in each of the main realms. They're all a little different. This one is probably the safest, but I'd still hold off on playing around for now. You've got plenty of time, and you'll be able to stay here as long as you like."

Aiden nodded, wondering how Zee, how *anyone*, could have known that a space like this, spooky and old-fashioned but also warm and welcoming, would make him feel safe. It reminded him of the scary-silly movies he liked best as a kid, with friendly ghosts and affable detectives. It also felt a little like the better hotels he would meet clients in, old but sturdy pre-Rapture buildings, worn on the outside, plush and well kept on the inside, run by friendly anarchists who backed him up if a client was cruel or tried to rob him.

No one had ever guessed someone as easily frightened as him liked spooky places. No one had ever tried to know him well enough to care.

The elevator stopped, and Hugo opened the doors directly in front of room 713. As they stepped out, a screen materialized on the door, and after an awkward moment Sam guided Aiden's hand up to press on the screen. It flashed green, and the door swung open. The room beyond was dark, but there were hints of plush furniture in the same style as the rest of the hotel.

Sam stepped back and bowed dramatically, gesturing Aiden towards his room. "Here we are! Do you have any other questions before I go?"

Go.

Aiden swallowed. He didn't have any questions that couldn't wait till tomorrow, but he wasn't ready to be alone. He wanted to ask Sam to stay, but who was he to ask for that? Sam would say no. *Of course* he would say no. Sam was only there because Lucifer and Zee, who were the gods of this place, told him to be.

But the thought of Sam leaving made him feel sick. He stood there stupidly, gaze flickering between Sam and the empty room.

Before Aiden could pull himself together, Sam's face softened. He nodded at the room questioningly, asking silently if he should go in.

Hope, blind and idiotic, followed by a massive wave of guilt twisted in Aiden's chest. He nodded anyway, and closed his eyes against tears of shame, trying to hide his relief. He followed Sam into the room and closed the door.

They stood there in the dark for several minutes, Aiden facing the closed door, too afraid to turn around. Maybe he should have left the door open. Was he horrible for trapping Sam in here? Should he open the door again? Or would that be worse?

Sam didn't make a sound, but Aiden could *feel* him there, behind him, waiting patiently. Aiden finally worked up the courage to turn and meet Sam's eyes. He was instantly caught in the deep, vivid green. They shined faintly in the dim light.

Slowly, carefully, Sam blinked and smiled. Aiden felt the tightness in his chest ease very slightly.

"So, um, this is damnation?" Aiden asked awkwardly. He pressed on, unable to look away from Sam. "It is, because when people talk about joining Divinity and the Will of the Divine, they're talking about that big soul star, and I told it *no*, so now I'm here. I did this, damned myself."

Sam tilted his head to the side, considering, then he nodded once, his expression becoming more neutral.

Aiden took a deep breath, which he didn't need to do, because he was *dead*.

The air smelled cool and earthy, a bit flowery. The carpet was soft under his feet. The dim light was soft, soothing. Familiar. Safe.

He let the breath out slowly. It helped, breathing, which was...strange. But also good.

Like this place.

He wanted to ask Sam if demons dated. Wanted to ask if Sam liked him. Wanted...

He found himself asking a different question, one he'd been avoiding all day. "Why is everyone so nice? Why are y—" *Nope, don't say that*. "Why is *everything* so beautiful?"

Sam's next smile was soft, but also brilliant. "You think it's beautiful here?"

"I...of course I do." Confusion sliced through some of Aiden's irrational fear. Sam started *purring*, which was even more confusing. "How could I not?"

"Bunny," Sam said, stepping closer to Aiden, "not every soul likes it here. *Most* souls, when they arrive, are overwhelmed. It's too much color, too much chaos, too much *freedom*, and it burns them. They shut down. Sometimes they fall apart completely, their souls shattered into fragments never to be reforged." Sam stopped scant inches away from Aiden and raised his hand up to hover a breath away from Aiden's cheek . "Only a small percentage of souls ever fully pull themselves together enough to stabilize the way you have. Even then, there are plenty of people who walk through Nexus for the first time and feel as if they actually are in some kind of hell." Sam's smile became a little enigmatic. "Not you, though. I wonder why that is? Do you know?"

Aiden...he might...but he...*couldn't.*

He wasn't special. He was a *mistake.* A mess who'd failed at living. He wasn't... He didn't deserve this. He'd told heaven *no,* over and over, and he deserved...not this.

Right?

He shook his head and backed up until his back hit the door. He didn't *want* to back away, but he...

He started to shake.

Sam dropped his hand, but the purring intensified. Aiden followed the motion of Sam's dropped hand, and something on his face must have communicated a fraction of his disappointment to Sam. Sam reached out again, slowly, leaving Aiden plenty of room to move.

"Is this okay?" he asked softly.

Helplessly, desperately, Aiden nodded.

Sam gently cupped Aiden's cheek with a clawed hand. "Can you tell me what you're afraid of?"

"Everything. Nothing. I don't know what to do. What I'm supposed to do. What I *am.*"

Aiden shook harder, ready for Sam to call him stupid and leave.

Sam gave another slow blink. "You could try getting some sleep. You've had a big day, and souls need to rest."

Aiden winced, but managed to keep from pulling away. He didn't *want* to pull away. "I don't know how to sleep," he whispered. "I need...I don't have..." Aiden couldn't finish.

Sam rubbed the palm of his hand against Aiden's cheekbone, and Aiden leaned into it and closed his eyes. "Aw bunny, tell you what, you crawl into bed and I'll stay till you fall asleep. I have some work to do tonight, but I'll come back first thing in the morning, okay?"

Aiden nodded, so relieved he felt his eyes finally burn with tears. He turned away and stumbled into the bedroom.

The bed was huge and canopied, with thick, dark curtains pulled back and held with lavender cords. The bedding was very dark brown with a slightly iridescent sheen, like black gold. He stuffed himself under the fluffy down comforter and buried his face in the pillows.

As soon as he settled, he felt a soft weight start kneading his shoulder. He twisted onto his back and looked. A black cat blinked at him with Sam's bright green eyes.

Aiden smiled, daring to hope, to pretend, and Sam settled himself on Aiden's chest and started purring again.

They lay like that for a while until, to Aiden's amazement, he started to feel drowsy, something he hadn't felt without drugs since he was a little kid. Half asleep, he absently scratched Sam's head and mumbled "What if I get lost? How will I find you?"

"Call me," Sam's voice said, quietly, and a word, a <[name]>, landed in Aiden's mind. He felt it settle deep inside him, and his sleepy self somehow knew it would always be there for him if he needed it.

After that, Aiden drifted off into sleep, feeling safer than he had in his entire mortal life.

GREATER PROVIDENCE RI, SEPTEMBER 8TH 47 YAR

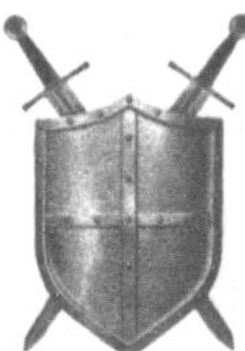

Emily arrived at Thoughts and Prayers and put in the code that let the car park itself in an emergency vehicle zone. The bar wasn't open yet, but the area was a designated pedestrian neighborhood and the closest parking was six blocks away. Emily didn't want her car that far away right before rush hour hit its peak.

The bar was in an artistically repaired pre-Rapture building, with a mix of old-fashioned red brick and magically reinforced hempcrete. The sigils on the door declared it Neutral Territory, though it obviously didn't have a gateway to Faerie within city limits. Still, just the possibility of fae and fae-bloods probably added to its appeal among the college crowd, not to mention the possibility of lawlessness.

Emily quickly checked her notes on the owner, a witch known as Penny, full name Penelope Reed. She had an agreement with the Covens to cooperate with local law enforcement, which meant Emily could ask her questions, but that was it. Emily wouldn't be able to hold the witch accountable for any illegal activity she discovered, and any evidence she wanted to submit would need to be approved by a member of the Providence Coven before going to the city courts.

It was a pain, but nothing Emily wasn't used to dealing with. There were several dozen single-building Neutral Territories inside Providence, and all of them were on good terms with the local government.

Just as she was stepping up to the door, she got a message from Will. She sent him the address, and he gave a twenty minute ETA. The door was locked, but Emily peered through the door and saw a woman working behind the counter. She knocked and showed her badge when the woman looked up.

The woman came over and unlocked the door. She was in her early thirties by the look of her, with a glorious mane of pink and orange coils, warm skin dusted with freckles, and an abundance of witch-forged bracelets on her long muscular arms. Her eyes were a very dark green. Emily recognized her from the photo in her notes as the bar's owner, Penelope Reed.

"Hi, I'm Detective Scott. I'm looking into a disappearance and I was wondering if I could ask you a few questions?"

Penelope nodded and opened the door wider to let Emily in.

Even at this hour, and completely empty, the bar still smelled like pot. She double checked the bar's information and saw that it did indeed have a license for indoor cannabis use. She wasn't here to bust them for code violations, but you never knew when you would need a little leverage.

Emily held up the picture of Sean. "Have you seen this man? He would have been here Saturday night, if you were working then."

Penelope studied the image for a few seconds, and then slowly nodded. "Yeah, he was here. I scanned his ID when he ordered, I'll pull it up for you." She went over to the bar and started tapping on the screen. After a second, she spun it around to show Emily the picture.

It was definitely a picture of Sean, but the name said Todd Patterson, and the age was listed as twenty-three. Emily tapped the screen and zoomed in. It was an astoundingly good quality fake. She snapped a picture of the screen, making a quick note to follow up on where the fake might have come from, and nodded. "Yup, that's him. Can you tell me who he was with?"

"Hmm, I think he was here with a bunch of friends? I can probably pull up some of their IDs as well." More tapping, and she pulled up three other IDs. One was Olivia, and the other two were the friends Emily had spoken to earlier. Emily dutifully snapped pictures of each one, noting that all but one of them was also fake.

"Do you know if he left the bar with his friends or alone?"

Penelope thought for a moment, and then shook her head, "I'm not sure. I know he and his friends left before last call, but I don't know if they left together or not."

"Do you have any security footage? I don't have a warrant, but I can go get one," Emily said, careful to keep her tone friendly. Some systems wouldn't even let people access camera footage without either the owner present or a warrant, and maybe both.

Penelope shrugged apologetically. "A warrant won't help you. The system is closed loop, and footage is automatically purged after twenty-four hours unless an alarm is triggered. It's standard for registered

Neutral Territory to not hold on to anything other than purchase and ID information."

Damn. She should have remembered about that. This was a dead end. Probably at least part of the reason why the system never flagged the bar. Goddamn witches and their goddamn special treatment.

She checked the time and saw that there was only a few minutes before Will would show up. Emily decided to take a gamble.

"There seem to have been a lot of missing persons cases in this area recently. Have you seen anything suspicious?"

Penelope blinked at her in surprise, and Emily watched her face carefully, trying to decide if the reaction was genuine. Witches were usually masterful at hiding their thoughts. There were truth spells, but the witches were the only ones who could cast them, and all they did was identify when someone spoke intentionally false words.

Emily couldn't detect any deception when Penelope shook her head and answered, "No, I haven't. Should I be worried? What should I look out for?"

Emily sighed. "We're not really sure. I may come back with some more questions about it, is that okay?"

Penelope nodded again. "Yeah, alright. I need to go open up now, but there probably won't be anyone in right away if you need to look around more."

She went to unlock the door. When she did, Will was standing there with his hand raised, about to knock.

"Oh, uh, hi Penny! I'm looking for Detective Scott? She asked me to meet her here." Will was wearing a pair of sturdy jeans and an old-fashioned leather jacket, his dark grey shirt the only piece of fastfab clothing. He was fairly tall, built like a runner, and had long locks pulled back into a knot at the nape of his neck and glasses that he wore low on his nose.

Emily had her suspicions about how much he even needed the glasses—witches always used magic to correct physical impairments—but she'd never figured out a way to ask without being rude. She wasn't sure if they were a fashion choice or if they had a magical purpose.

Penelope gave Will an inscrutable look and opened the door wider so Will could see Emily standing behind her.

"Hi Emily! Sam also says hi." Will gestured at the large black cat poking its head out of a canvas messenger bag.

"You shouldn't carry him around like that. You're spoiling him," Penelope said, but without any real censure.

Will rolled his eyes. "You know how he is. He said he was sleepy because he *'spent all day using every ounce of will he had not to pounce on the baby bunny'*, his words, and he wouldn't come unless I carried him." As if to illustrate this, Sam yawned and disappeared into the bag where he presumably curled up to go back to sleep.

Penelope snorted and turned back to Emily. "Is there anything else I can help you with, detective? I need to finish opening up."

"No, I'm all set for now. I'll be in touch later. Is this a good place to reach you?" They both knew Emily could pull up Penelope's personal phone number if she wanted, but some people felt more comfortable pretending.

"However you contact me is fine. The only day I'm not here this week is Wednesday. Good luck."

Emily stepped out and let the door close behind her. She saw Will's motorcycle parked next to her own car, and she gestured Will over so she could open her trunk where she had the stuff she'd taken from Sean's dorm.

"So, you know Penelope?" she asked casually.

Will knew what she was doing, but he smiled anyway. "Yeah, everyone does. Thoughts and Prayers is one of the more important Neutral Territories in the city."

Ah, Emily should have guessed. She held up her tablet with the picture of Sean. "Sean DeNardis disappeared after leaving this bar late Saturday night." Will's eyes went wide when he heard the name, but he didn't say anything. "His phone went dead right around the same time, somewhere nearby, and no one has heard from him since." Emily indicated the backpack and controller. "This was the closest thing I could find to personal items in his dorm room. His father might have something, but I'd prefer not to have to ask DeNardis for anything else if we can avoid it. I expect he's having a hard enough time staying out of the investigation as it is."

"I'll bet," Will said, picking up the controller first. He focused on it, and his eyes filled with white smoke. After a moment, he grimaced and put it down, moving on to the rest of the contents of the bag, his eyes still whited out. As he touched each item he started looking more and more concerned.

Emily got another sinking feeling as she watched him.

"I don't suppose it's all stuff he hasn't imprinted on?" Emily asked, and she knew she didn't sound hopeful.

"No. The controller especially has quite a lot of personal energy invested in it. It just isn't leading anywhere. In theory, he could be out of range, but..." Will drifted off, obviously uncomfortable.

"How far is your range, typically?"

Will rubbed the back of his neck and sounded sad when he said, "Pretty far. He would have to be on the other side of the Mississippi."

Fuck. Emily didn't think that was likely.

"He might be behind some kind of magical barrier, or in Faerie," Will suggested with a small wince. Neither of those possibilities were much better.

Emily sighed. "Do you mind hanging out for a bit? I want to see if any of these stores have any footage. Maybe we can pick up a trail the old-fashioned way. I grabbed his toothbrush as well, so let's try a straight up tissue trace."

Will nodded and started pulling stuff from the saddlebags on his bike. "If you want, I can get started on the trace while you talk to people. The longer I can charge the spell, the larger the range it will have."

Emily grunted an affirmative and gave him the skuzzy toothbrush.

It took her another hour to sort out a warrant to get the footage she needed. With Will's failure to pick up a trail using emotional resonance, she had enough probable cause to suspect a possible homicide or magical kidnapping. She ran the footage from as many stores as she could through a facial recognition scan and lucked out—a camera two blocks from the bar picked him up at about a quarter to one in the morning.

Emily felt a chill settle into her bones as she watched Sean drag a dark haired woman down an alley. The camera angle didn't show the inside of the alley, but neither of them ever appeared to leave it. She checked with the owners of the buildings that had doors to the alley, and none of them reported any break-ins or disturbances.

She sent all the footage back to forensics with a note to put together a more complete timeline and see if they could identify the woman who was with Sean. Based on what she saw, she wasn't hopeful. The camera had only found Sean's face when he'd looked around to check if anyone was on the street before he grabbed the woman's arm to pull her down the alley, out of sight.

Emily was *not* looking forward to giving an update to DeNardis. She thought about calling it in so they could secure the alley, but felt like she ought to find out what kind of scene she was calling in first.

She found Will setting up his circle in the emergency parking zone between her car and his bike. It looked complicated, with dozens of tiny sigils all around it. Inside the circle was the toothbrush and a small crystal carefully placed and surrounded by more sigils.

"Will, can you take a break from that? I, uh, found something." He nodded and ducked his head into the bar. Penelope came out to watch the circle while Emily showed Will the footage. When it finished, he looked grim.

"I take it you want me to check out the alley?" he asked. Emily nodded. "Alright, give me a second to finish this, and then we can use your car to keep people from walking through it." He turned to Penny. "Are you able to keep eyes on it while I'm gone?"

Penny nodded, and Will bent down and added a few more sigils before closing the circle. Emily moved her car, and then the two of them walked back to the alley.

As soon they entered, Sam poked his head out of the bag. He meowed, and Will looked sad.

"Sam smells death. Faint, but less than two days old. Human."

"Can he tell how many?" Emily asked. Sam and Will exchanged a glance.

"He can't tell. Not many, probably not more than one. Do you want me to read the scene first, or do you want to call it in?"

Will's psychometry, in addition to letting him track objects, was able to pick up the echoes of strong emotions, allowing him to witness the events that caused them. Death usually came with strong emotions.

Emily sighed. "I need to call it in first."

It wasn't a pleasant call.

The captain listened in silence while she outlined what they had found. They told her, in a perfectly neutral voice, that they would contact Bristol precinct and work it so Emily remained in charge of the case.

"Emily, I'm going to let George come out to observe. Can you keep everything under control?"

Emily gritted her teeth. Letting DeNardis come to the scene was a bad idea, but not because she couldn't handle it. "Yes, if you're sure he needs to be here."

The captain sighed. "If I don't let him see it for himself, he'll break himself trying to poke holes in everything."

"Yeah, I guess you're right about that." Emily hung up.

Will went back to finish his DNA trace casting while Emily stayed in the alley to wait. Forensics arrived fairly quickly, and they set up lights to keep back the growing darkness while they searched for anything that might tell them what happened. Fortunately, or unfortunately for the forensic techs, garbage day was Tuesday, so anything that had been tossed Saturday would still be there.

They found Sean's wallet, but nothing else.

Emily, in spite of DeNardis's earlier insistence he was only there to observe, went over to him and asked, "Do you want Will to read it here, or back at the lab?"

Will, with the wallet as a focus, would be able to describe exactly what happened at the scene without needing to be in the alley. The reading would be much clearer in the alley, but he could do it in a private recording booth at the lab. The case wasn't classified, so standard procedure would dictate doing it at the scene, but if they did it here, out in public, whatever they found would become tomorrow's gossip.

DeNardis gave her a scathing look. "Do your damn job, Detective."

With another sigh, she called Will over. She explained what they wanted, for the record, mostly, since Will already knew what he needed to do, and handed him the wallet. She took out her own phone to record anything that Will said, even though the forensic team had already set up their own, better, recording equipment.

Will knelt down in the middle of the ally and took a small knife out of his pocket. It was obviously dull, and it looked more like a fancy antique letter opener than an actual knife. He used it to draw a tight circle around himself. The circle flared with light when he finished, then settled into a steady glow. Sam, who was still tucked into the messenger bag, stuck his head out, and Will swung the bag around so it was right against his chest.

He took the wallet in his left hand and the knife in his right. After a second, his eyes started to glow with the same light as the circle.

He spoke carefully, with a practiced attention to detail. It was incredibly uncomfortable to listen to the scene he described, but especially while standing next to Sean's father. Emily's gaze flickered to DeNardis when Will said *vampire*, but DeNardis's face might as well have been carved out of stone.

When it was over, Will slumped forward, gasping. Emily knew from experience that Will did not want to be helped, and that until he broke the circle it was dangerous to try. Instead, she grabbed a bottle of water and an evidence bag. As soon as Will broke the circle and got to his feet she held the water out to him. He accepted it gratefully and dropped the wallet into the evidence bag.

DeNardis left without saying a word. Emily waited while the forensic techs finished up. It didn't take them long. She told them to look into the fake ID as quickly as they could, and she was met with somber nods. It was after midnight when the van finally pulled away.

Will was waiting outside the mouth of the alley, sitting on an iron bench. Emily pulled out her tablet and searched for a nearby hotel. “I’m getting you a room. Go get some sleep. Finding the body can wait till morning—it could be anywhere.”

Will shook his head and stood. “No, I’m almost done with the trace. I’d rather not have to start over. If it’s alright with you, I’ll cast the spell tonight. I appreciate the room, though—no way should I be riding this late after casting two major spells.”

They walked back to Emily’s car. Will waved at a little green snake that slithered its way back into the bar. Emily figured it was Penelope’s familiar, keeping an eye on the spell while Penelope worked the bar. Emily used her tablet to command the car out of the way while Will used his knife to break the circle.

As soon as he did, the crystal started glowing brightly. He pulled out from his saddle bags a map and a delicate silver cage that hung from a short chain. He spread the map out on the pavement and dropped the crystal into the cage which had a small needle-like point at the bottom of it. Without drawing another circle, he knelt down in front of the map and his eyes began to glow again. He swung the crystal slowly, in gradually wider and wider circles until it suddenly jerked down and impaled itself on the map, right in the middle of the Providence River. An ‘x’ burned itself onto the map and then the crystal went dark.

Shit.

Once again, Will slumped forward, gasping. Sam mewed softly and nudged Will’s face. Will was shaking, and the cat turned to Emily with what she thought might be a beseeching look, though it was hard to decipher the expression of a cat. Taking that as a sign she wouldn’t cause a magic explosion by touching him, Emily helped Will to his feet and into her car.

Continuing to pray for an explosion-free night, Emily crouched to gather up the map and crystal. She handed the crystal to Will then stared in dismay at the map. The body was in the fucking *river*. Retrieving what the river fae hadn't eaten was going to be a goddamn nightmare, if there was even anything left to retrieve.

Will looked terrible, so she tried for some levity. "Really, Will, an 'x'? It's a body, not a pirate treasure." She stowed the map in her glove compartment and then made sure he'd buckled his seatbelt.

Will smiled tiredly. "What makes you think that's something I control? Maybe it was Sam's choice."

"Uh huh, *sure* it was. I know he's a demon or whatever, but he's still a cat. He'd probably make it look like a mouse or a laser pointer." She looked over at Will's bike. "If you want, I can drive your bike to the garage at the hotel for you."

Will nodded gratefully and handed her the key fob before tipping his head back against the seat and closing his eyes.

Emily used her tablet to direct the car to the hotel and followed along behind on his bike. After dropping Will's bike off at the hotel garage and making sure he made it safely to his room, Emily headed for home. Even though she was exhausted, she couldn't sleep as the car drove itself through the mostly empty and silent streets. Her mind kept spinning as she finally let herself emotionally process what had happened.

Sean, her partner's son, had tried to rape someone. A someone who turned out to be a vampire that killed him.

Emily had quite a lot of feelings on the matter, and most of them left her gutted. A vampire hunting in the metropolis was potentially a big problem. Vampires were rare, and no one really knew what their deal was. They were demons, and they fed on humans, but little else was known. Each one seemed to have a different kind of person they hunted. Some didn't seem to need to kill.

Obviously this one did.

Emily had a really bad feeling about the other missing persons cases and what they might all have in common with each other. She wondered how many bones they would find when they went to retrieve what was left of Sean.

Hunting vampires was way outside her job parameters, but she would still need to investigate further. She'd have to prove, beyond a shadow of a doubt, that not only was the vampire a serial killer, but that it was still in the area. That was going to be difficult, if not impossible. If she managed it, the city would then need to facilitate negotiations with the Providence Coven and the local Church of Unity representatives, probably the embassy over in Fall River, to get a permit for an exorcist to come into the metropolis and hunt it.

If she couldn't find sufficient proof, the Providence Coven would not allow an exorcist into the city, and if the killings stopped or remained under the radar, the city council wouldn't be able to do anything about it. Shit had to be pretty dire for them to allow a witch-killer into their home.

Emily was acutely aware that there might be nothing she could do to bring justice to the vampire's victims.

Victims who might all be rapists.

Fuck.

Emily felt her jaw creaking, her hands squeezing into tight fists, and she forced herself to take a deep breath.

She had a duty to discover the truth and do her best to help stop the vampire from murdering people, no matter what other *circum-*

stances there were, but part of her was afraid that once she had all the facts she wouldn't...

Fuck.

Vigilante assassination, if that's what this was, wasn't *right*. Illegal, obviously, but also *wrong*. She believed in rehabilitation. *Witches* believed in rehabilitation. Witch cities didn't have prisons or death penalties for a *reason*.

But.

But she would be a liar if she didn't admit that part of her thought it might be a kind of divine justice. That the world might be better off with these people dead.

That her *partner's son* might have deserved to die.

Emily closed her eyes and swallowed.

That part of her left the rest of her feeling sick, but *fuck*. It was there.

Please, she found herself praying, with all her heart, to whatever might be listening, *please help me do the right thing. Help me know what is right.*

She pulled up in front of her house and climbed the stairs to her apartment, her soul aching and her body exhausted. Out of the corner of her eye, something gold and bright flashed. Emily whirled, hand on her taser, but there was nothing.

Then—

~This one~

"Who's there!"

Her voice echoed in the empty stairwell. Nothing answered.

Emily pinched her nose and leaned against the door, listening hard. Still nothing. She entered her apartment, rubbing her temples, hoping all she needed was rest.

It took her several minutes before she noticed the odd quality of the light in her living room.

It took her even longer, once she found the source of the strange glow, to realize it was an *angel.*

Impossible.

He was beautiful, of course he was beautiful, shining and Divine, but the beauty was an attack. As she struggled to understand what she was seeing, her knees gave out and tears filled her eyes.

There were wings, wings that hurt to look at, and she couldn't quite tell how many there were. His face was perfect, awe inspiring, and her chest ached so fiercely she was afraid she was having a heart attack.

He was more human than the Divine creatures she'd seen in old videos from the Breaking. Those angels had been made of fire that seared the soul, or massive monsters with hundreds of eyes that saw every sin you'd ever committed, or twisting vortexes of judgment and fury.

This creature was peaceful by comparison. Seductive. Well-contained within a humanoid form.

But he was not a video. He was raw, searing. Magnificent and terrible.

Emily found that her hand had reached for the taser again, and she hastily let it drop.

Tasers didn't work on angels. Probably.

Still, she refused to be cowed any more than she already was. Knowing it was stupid, she lifted her chin and met his eyes.

A horrible burning sensation rolled through her body. Her breath abandoned her, forced out by bright agony. Her whole body seized as if she were being electrocuted.

The angel smiled proudly and blinked, releasing her. <<Hello Emily. Your prayers have been heard.>>

The burning subsided, leaving Emily gasping. “What?”

She was *way* too tired to deal with this.

The angel’s expression softened into something more serene. He repeated, <<Your prayers have been heard. We are here to offer you the guidance you seek, and to offer you a gift.>>

She felt light-headed, nerves still alight with the aftershock of whatever the angel had done to her, but she climbed to her feet anyway. “Uh, okay. I uh, may I sit down?” She staggered towards the couch without waiting for an answer, barely making it there before her knees gave out again.

The angel, fortunately, didn’t seem to mind. He waited patiently for her to collect herself.

Emily couldn’t quite wrap her head around his presence. Angels weren’t supposed to be in witch cities. There were rules. They couldn’t use their powers here except for healing, and they could only appear if they were specifically called on with...with prayer.

But, no. No, that was ridiculous. She’d prayed before, at church when she was a child, at home with her parents before holiday meals, and alone after particularly upsetting cases. She’d never felt anything more than a little comforting warmth, or enough peace that she was able to fall asleep.

Fuck, she wasn’t even a member of the Church of Unity! She only prayed out of habit, because her parents had!

“Why me? Why now?” she found herself asking, stupidly. She looked towards the angel without focusing on any one part of him for too long, hoping that would keep herself from being burned again.

He didn't seem upset, exactly, by her questions, but the expression on his face as his head cocked to the side made her spine tingle. <<Child, are you questioning the Will of the Divine?>>

She literally was. "No," she said automatically, which was *lying* to the Divine so she quickly amended, "I mean, I'm sorry? Sorry. I'll stop."

The Angel's smile turned radiant. <<Exactly right. You are well chosen.>> The angel pulled out a hotly glowing necklace from inside his robes. The brightness dimmed suddenly to reveal a large pendant about three inches across hung from a golden chain. He placed the seal in his palm and held it up. It began to shine again, so brightly Emily had to close her eyes. It kept getting brighter anyway, and she tried to cover her eyes with her hands, futilely trying to stop the light as it grew brighter, and brighter, and *brighter*.

It *burned*, searing into her mind and body, blocking out all other sensation, all breath, all thought. She seized, clenching against the agony, desperately trying not to scream, but having no way to tell if she was succeeding.

After an eternity of pain, it stopped, leaving her reeling.

She felt something settle around her neck.

The light faded completely, and she dared to look.

There, resting against her bare chest, was the pendant. Her shirt had burned away underneath it.

Numbly, she picked it up. It was warm to the touch, suspiciously comforting. After the agony, it was almost euphoric.

She had no fucking idea what it was.

<<When you are ready, declare your acceptance of the Will of the Divine, aloud. You will be filled with Our light, and your doubt will burn away. Ever after, you will know, without doubt or trepidation,

what is right, and you will possess the strength to do whatever you must to see Justice done.>>

And then he was gone. There was no flash or sound to mark his passing. He was simply there one moment and gone the next.

Emily sat on her couch, holding the pendant in her palm, stunned.

The pendant was intricately carved and made of a material that made no sense. It felt like metal and stone at the same time, cool to the touch and very solid, but it was also somehow weightless, impossibly insubstantial. The twisting design was incomprehensible, but it reminded her of some kind of religious seal, like the ones they put on official Church documents.

When she took it off, her head started to throb violently. Stubbornly, she went to put it on the table.

The moment her fingers lost contact, pain cracked her skull in two.

She hastily picked it back up, and the pain vanished. She stared at the mind-twisting seal resting in her palm, and then back at the empty space the angel had been in moments before.

"What the *fuck*."

GREATER PROVIDENCE RI, SEPTEMBER 9TH 47 YAR

June stood at the foot of a hospital bed, reading the chart of her last patient for the night. The girl was barely fourteen, and she was sound asleep. June skimmed over the chart, uninterested in its contents—her memory was flawless, she already knew everything it said.

She made a discrete cut on her thumb and, faster than any camera could pick up, she *flickered* over to the girl and swiped blood over the girl's lips. She was back at the foot of the bed before the chart had even begun to fall from where she'd left it hanging in the air.

In her sleep, the girl licked her lips and sighed before rolling over.

It was the girl's second dose of vampiric blood. With any luck her doctor would be able to send her home tomorrow. It generally took two or three days for the tiny amounts of blood she gave to the kids to do its work. Unlike divine healing, which relied on the chemo to kill the cancer before it was effective, her blood, once properly calibrated, attacked the cancer itself, and it was most effective against the hard-to-treat blood cancers that this hospital specialized in.

In the three years since she had been a vampire, she'd given small amounts of blood to just over sixty children. A third of those she'd done all at once in a Boston hospital, sloppily. She'd been back on earth for maybe three weeks, and she'd snuck in and given blood to the entire cancer ward. Not just a few drops, either—the adults had all gotten back ten years of their lives, and the kids were probably *still* healing a little faster than normal.

At the time, June hadn't really understood the sensation that would cause. The story had exploded all over human media, and within days someone had linked the deaths of her prey and the healed patients to the presence of a vampire. A fierce debate between the city council and the Boston Coven had ended in, to June's horror, the decision to allow Divine Paladins, exorcists that specialized in vampire hunting, into the city. June fled before they found her, but the city remained on high alert, even now, years later.

You would think that the people in witch cities might be more reasonable, but no. A scary vampire among them, who could be anyone, look like anyone, was, apparently, *too much*. In a city of hundreds of thousands, one little vampire was *too many*.

Humans were all the same, deep down. Ruled by base, mortal fear even when they had perfectly rational immortal souls.

Oh, there'd been some people in favor of leaving June alone. Who'd recognized that she was actually incredibly useful, necessary even in her main capacity, and wonderful in her extra potent healing abilities.

Just not enough.

Then there had been the people, people living in *witch cities*, who were supposed to be *better*, that wanted to capture her and put her in a box, using her blood to heal until she went mad and fell apart, instead of killing her.

That was what the Treaty dictated had to happen to vampires who didn't, or couldn't, kill to satisfy their Geas. They fell apart. Slowly. While *starving*.

It was not a pleasant way to return to the Underworld. Of the handful of demons unfortunate enough to experience it, barely half had been coherent enough to keep themselves together after.

Not that there were many pleasant ways for a vampire to return to the Underworld. Maybe if the Geas became impossible to fulfill, Lillian would find a way to break it that wouldn't cause massive amounts of soul-trauma. Even then, the process would probably suck.

Having never tried it, she didn't actually know.

So, June had to be more circumspect if she wanted to heal people and keep below the radar. She *really* didn't want to move again, and she couldn't quite explain why. It had something to do with the Geas. June had been able to move down to Greater Providence, somehow, but the idea of moving again was viscerally unappealing. She'd do it if she had to, but...

Well, she was doing her best to not have to. She'd stolen herself an identity that would allow her to work in the hospital, giving her access to exactly the kinds of patients who needed her the most.

It hadn't been easy. No matter what anyone said, women sexual predators were just not as common. Finding one who was also a medical professional had been even harder. She could have used a male identity, but—well. It wasn't something she could bring herself to do.

So, rather than choose between her morals and her needs, she'd gone looking in God-fearing territory.

She'd had to go all the way to rural freaking Georgia to find one.

It had been a massive risk going that deep into Church lands. People were more spread out there, living in cult-ruled suburban towns and Church-fortified compounds rather than the more diverse, comfortably warded-and-planned witch cities. There were a few God-fearing cities, but they were more local religious mecca than centers of commerce and education. Most cities in that region of the states were Neutral Territory, like Atlanta, but they tended to be positively *crawling* with exorcists.

Even with the spread out population, the prey down there had been uncomfortably plentiful. People in God-fearing territory didn't have universal access to mental health care services beyond whatever the local neo-Christian religious cult thought was appropriate. Some of the really bad areas reminded June uncomfortably of Puritans. Being among them had dragged up a lot of bad memories.

The extra prey hadn't been enough to make the trip any less grueling. She'd run the entire way, flickering to the point of exhaustion as she passed through the fae wilds, hiding in abandoned basements during the day. When she was in populated areas, she'd been constantly looking over her shoulder, expecting to be blasted by an exorcist at any moment. She couldn't rest the entire time.

Worse, she'd had a constant, almost painful ache in her chest that told her to *go home*.

But she'd found what she needed—a female nurse who was also prey. She'd killed the woman, stolen her face, and done a bit of hypnotizing to make sure no one questioned her sudden immigration into witch-territory. Now, she was a legitimate employee of the hospital, and she could heal people without getting run out of town.

June checked on a few more patients, but none of them really needed her blood—they were just recovering from particularly intensive healing regimes. She left the hospital when her shift ended, exchanging meaningless pleasantries with the other nurses and staff who were also leaving, or just arriving.

June decided to take the long way home, a walk that would take her through some of the prettier of the witch-gardens that dotted the pedestrian pathways of the city. The Providence Coven was big on native plants, or, at least the plants that had been native to the region before the Rapture, before the industrial revolution, even, which June liked. There was something soothing about seeing the familiar types of foliage and flowers that she'd grown up with, even if they were weirdly organized and overly-cultivated.

She didn't work at the hospital every night, only four nights a week, and she never hunted on nights she had a shift, even when she had time before sunrise, like she did now. If prey fell into her lap, she wasn't going to say no, but she could go at least a week before she would need to hunt again. June wanted to appreciate the break.

She paused when the path wound around to the river and the cultivated city forest opened to the river. After gazing at the view for a moment, she dropped into the ornate park bench with a peaceful sigh. The night was quiet, and a breeze from the southeast carried the scent of the ocean to her. Inky black water gurgled softly where it splashed against the warded canal, glittering softly whenever a wave caught the light from one of the softly illuminating lamps dotting the pathways.

She watched the barely-there sliver of moon rise over the river and wished for her guitar. There was no audience to play for here, now, but that would have been good, allowing the moment to be even more evanescent.

Tomorrow, maybe. She was off work tomorrow, and June had a busking license registered to one of her other faces. She could come back here—no, wait, there was a great little place on the other side of the river where she could play. There she'd be able to see this same moon sink back below the horizon, and she could play for the stars as the streets thinned of people and the night grew dark and still and calm.

June pulled her phone out of her pocket and checked the weather. The International Coven of Weather Witches, the ICWW for short, completely controlled the weather within witch cities. Rain was scheduled, meant for washing the streets and watering rooftop gardens. They couldn't defy the changing of the seasons, but each season was idyllic.

Early September was a particularly glorious time of year, the air smelling sweet with late blooming flowers and harvest. The city didn't grow all its own food, obviously—even a Divine farmer couldn't manage that—but a handful of agriculturally inclined witches maintained enough small farms to keep the local markets full of produce. Everything else was portaled in.

June didn't eat, of course, but she enjoyed the way food smelled, like peace and community prosperity.

June heard footsteps off in the distance and reluctantly rolled to her feet. There weren't many people who got up before the sun rose—magic made it so work was more option than requirement, at least within witch territory. Some humans dedicated themselves to careers, but they did it for prestige and self-satisfaction rather than out of necessity. Most people were happy to work a few hours a day at some relatively comfortable utility job, like healthcare, food preparation and distribution, or sanitation, and then spend the rest of their time investigating scientific curiosities, playing games or music, or any of the seemingly endless kinds of entertainment modern humans had at their disposal.

June wasn't in the mood for socializing, especially not with the kind of go-getter who woke up early to go jogging, so she *flickered* up into the boughs of a particularly sturdy oak tree to wait for the early bird to pass her by.

For June, who'd grown up living in a shack in the woods, eking out barely enough food to survive at the edges of untamed wilderness, modern life was paradise. She didn't want to reincarnate, though. She was very much over being human and all the...pitfalls. She'd rather enjoy it like this, existing between the cracks of society, between life and death, defying gods and mortals alike.

Besides, she did important work. Her Geas might be compulsory, but that didn't mean she didn't believe in it. It was necessary. Vampires existed to do what the humans could not, to cleanse the scum from the earth without becoming scum themselves.

Well. Perhaps some humans thought she was scum. Or, you know, a majority, technically, what with the whole *illegal to exist* thing.

But s*he* didn't think so. She killed rapists and used the power she gained from their deaths to heal people. She was like an immune system for the community.

She could do so much more for them if they didn't fear her.

It wasn't fair. They didn't have any problems ignoring the human predators who hunted in their communities, but even a *hint* of demonic magic about a person and suddenly there was a whole new set of rules. Rights and mitigating circumstances and everything else was thrown out the window in favor of good, old-fashioned monster hunting.

Below, the footsteps June had expected to pass along beneath her had instead stopped. With careful, supernatural stealth, June crept along a branch until she could see.

A human, she couldn't be sure of the gender expression, was setting up a small circle in the clearing near the bench by the water. Five pillar candles, white or possible pale yellow or pink, were set in each cardinal direction. The figure was pouring a line of fine white sand between them, guided by a grey fox with the demonically enhanced ability to make perfect, flawless arches.

A witch, then, come to make use of the cleansing sunrise.

June relaxed slightly. Witches weren't as dangerous as normal humans, functionally vetted by the process of becoming a witch. She was fairly certain they always knew what she was on sight—certainly their familiars did. But as long as they didn't see her doing anything illegal, they didn't act. Sometimes, like Penny, they even pointed her in the right direction.

Like her, they were bound by the Treaty to walk a fine line with the non-magical humans. So long as June didn't reveal herself, she was left alone, but the moment the humans caught wind they wouldn't, *couldn't*, hesitate to help the humans hunt her down.

Best they would do was use bureaucracy to give a girl time to escape.

When the little fox looked up and directly at June, she sighed and *flickered* her way up the path until she was out of sight. Once she was sure no one was around, she dropped back into a walk and turned onto a main street to head for her condo.

The sky was starting to lighten, and June's skin crawled with phantom itching. Enough brooding for one night. Dawn approached, and she had some composing she wanted to get done before sunset.

She had a date with the moon.

The itching intensified, becoming chills. Chills? June looked up at the still-starry sky. No way there was enough light for that strong of a reaction. She picked up her pace, not quite running through the still-dark streets, empty except for a few early morning joggers.

Something was *wrong*.

ATRIUM

CLEARED OF ALL MORTAL SOULS FOR AN EMERGENCY MEETING

Lillian, Queen of Magic and Demons, took a deep breath, trying to keep her frustration from eroding her sense and concern. "Explain it to me again."

Lucifer was still sprawled on the ground, his head in Zee's lap. Though Zee was starting to look more like their normal flippant self, they were stroking Lucifer's hair with a hand that trembled slightly.

Zee tried again, marginally calmer than before. "Lucifer and I were having an important conversation about which one of our dicks was bigger," Zee said. Their gaze was fixed on the rapidly shrinking wound in Lucifer's gut, but their smirk was almost normal. "It was *very* involved."

Lillian nodded serenely, resolutely holding on to her patience. "Right, like you do every night."

Zee nodded back without shifting his gaze from the wound. "Exactly."

Now that the bleeding had stopped, Lucifer shifted, trying to sit up, but collapsed back with a groan. Zee made a high whimpering sound, their hands fluttering helplessly over the smoking black hole.

Lucifer grabbed on to Zee's hands and used them to pull himself into a proper sitting position. Zee promptly wrapped themself around Lucifer, supporting him.

Lucifer picked up where Zee left off. "We'd been *discussing* this for some time when I blacked out. Not *passed out*, I didn't lose form or anything. This was—" Lucifer stopped, coughed, and gently caught Zee's hand to stop it from fluttering again. They waited a moment in silence while the wound continued to shrink. When the wound was nearly gone and his tactical armor was knitting itself back together, Lucifer took another, deeper breath, and went on. "For a moment all of my perceptions were focused on *pain*. I haven't felt anything like it since the Breaking."

Zee's eyes filled with tears again, and their arms tightened around Lucifer's shoulders. "Lillian, it was awful! He screamed and grabbed his stomach and he started *bleeding*! Bleeding! I didn't know that was a thing!" When Lucifer tried to turn around, Zee tightened their arms more.

Lillian knelt, pulling them both into a gauzy embrace. "Yes, dear, we know. It's not supposed to be a thing. So, do you know what caused the breach?"

Lucifer pretended he didn't need the hug as much as Zee did. "We think so, there was—" Zee's breathing hitched with a sob, and Lucifer wriggled free and opened his now-intact armor, displaying smooth, luminous skin marked with a very faint scar. "Hey, Zee, look, it's fine, I'm all better, see?"

Zee sniffed and pulled Lucifer back to their chest. "There's a *scar*. What does that even mean?"

Lucifer refastened his armor. "Probably nothing. It will fade like the others did."

Zee looked unconvinced and exchanged a worried glance with Lillian over Lucifer's shoulder.

Lillian's expression shifted back to neutral, and she pulled back and sat on her heels. "So, Lucy—" She gestured at his stomach. "—I take it the breach was in the Pit?"

Lucifer nodded and closed his eyes. "Yes." His eyes moved back and forth under his eyelids, searching. "Something tore through my shields from within the Pit and launched itself out into the Chaos. I... Fuck, it shouldn't have been possible. The shields around the Pit take a beating, there's a lot of soul density down there, but they weren't *weak*. They aren't weak. I—" Lucifer went pale and his eyes popped open. He put a hand on his gut. "Oh. Shit. That can't be good."

Zee and Lillian both froze. Carefully, Zee asked, "What can't be good?"

"The, ah. Pressure," Lucifer said. "From the high soul density in the Pit. It's gone."

Zee carefully removed one hand from around Lucifer and summoned a screen. In a few seconds, the Pit census was displayed.

"Impossible," Zee breathed. "That's...oh no." They summoned another screen, with a different list of names.

Lillian frowned. "Can you explain what you're seeing, darling?"

Zee's gaze never left the screens, their hands moving constantly. "It, there was a soul. The soul from earlier, Lucy, you remember, the one that attacked the bunny? It ate, fuck. Thousands. *Tens* of thousands!"

Lucifer pulled away, and this time Zee let him, too distracted to protest. "What do you mean? That mess of soul? It's only been, what, six relative hours? You mean something ate it? Even the Pit isn't that—"

"No," Zee said, a hint of panic in their voice. "It wasn't *eaten*, it *ate*. Look!" Zee gestured at a highlighted list of names.

Lucifer shook his head. "That doesn't make any sense. How? What the fuck happened?"

Zee continued to flip through data, muttering, "The vampire?" and "No, the other souls were random," and, "What about the—shit. *Shit.*" They stopped and looked at Lucifer. "Did you make sure nothing else fell into the Pit when you dumped the problem soul in?"

Lucifer winced. "I, uh, no. I guess not. I just grabbed everything that was inside your circle, I didn't want to fracture the soul by accident. Why? Did something else get in?" Lucifer frowned, "Not another soul, right? I didn't think it managed to touch anyone but the bunny."

Zee shook their head. "No, it didn't, but..." They shook their head again. "I don't *know*. There's <[redacted]> and <[unknown]> all over the goddamn record."

Lillian moved closer to Zee's screens. "I don't understand. Was there Chaos contamination? No, this was before the breach, right?" She tapped the screen. "Maybe we should check with this soul, the one that had contact."

Zee swore again. "Shit, Lil, he's still deep in his orientation. He only died *yesterday*, he shouldn't even be talking! We need to wait till he's ready to consent to an interview." Zee made a loud, dramatic sound and kicked off the ground to hover a full six feet above the floor. One by one they opened a new set of screens.

Lillian, still looking at the screen labeled <[Aiden]>, gently flicked Zee's scarf over her shoulder and out of her face. "An Oracle could decode this in seconds."

Lucifer, standing now, adjusted the fall of his cloak and scowled. "The rabbit-boy was Oracle coded? Zee, you should have told me!"

Zee shook their head. "I don't know what it means yet." He frowned, considering. "Maybe if we got him into the Library? It's too soon, but..."

"You saw how stable he was," Lucifer said. "He can handle it."

Zee nodded reluctantly.

Lillian moved to another screen. "Uh, Zee? This is a mistake, right?" She highlighted something.

"No," Zee said, immediately. "The record has no mistakes. What—oh."

Lucifer followed their gazes and swore. "No. How? That's not possible. It made it through the Chaos?"

Silence.

NEXUS

Aiden woke alone in an unfamiliar room. He wasn't surprised, he often woke up in unfamiliar rooms, but never before had he felt quite so safe, or warm. The lack of any ache from bruising or drug withdrawal was also a pleasant surprise, and very new to him.

The sense of warmth and safety fled as he remembered where he was. What he was.

Dead. He was *dead*.

And so far it had been...great.

Which was *terrible*.

Why was there no pain? He was damned, sort of, technically, but there was no pain, and he couldn't shake the fear that pain was coming. *Should* be coming.

If it wasn't coming, if everything here was as wonderful as it seemed, then why had he tried so hard to live?

Aiden tried to calm himself down, taking slow, deep breaths. They still didn't really do anything except remind him he wasn't alive—breaths you didn't need felt very different—but the ritual grounded him.

He felt great.

Aiden buried his face into the soft, perfectly cool pillow and groaned.

Stupid amazing pillow. Why did it need to feel so *real*?

Aiden reminded himself that there were people who didn't believe in eternal torment. Millions of people. Witches, mostly, of course, but still. He'd seen their propaganda once he'd had enough money to buy a phone with access to the uncensored internet. Witches believed that demons were just souls, no better or worse than any other person, and the idea of eternal damnation was a lie meant to keep people scared and stupid.

Aiden, raised deep within Divine territory, had certainly grown up scared and stupid, hadn't he?

The anarchists didn't believe in damnation either. They didn't believe in anything specific at all, really. Aiden had never taken them seriously, though—anarchists made good clients, but they were all crazy from constantly battling their way through fae wilds with nothing but guns and unstable magic. Their information was somehow even more biased than that of the Church, full of wildly contradicting conspiracy theories about aliens and mind control.

Hadn't Sam mentioned aliens? Maybe they weren't as crazy as he'd thought.

Aiden curled into a tight ball under the smooth covers. Without the need for food or air, he could have stayed there forever, an unmoving, perfectly safe lump.

What if aliens had harvested his soul, and he was being fattened up on happiness before they ate him? Was that more or less ridiculous than the idea that souls got to do whatever they wanted in an awesome rainbow city full of extremely conscientious, and sexy, demons?

Aiden didn't know what to believe. He was dead, and he was damned, but he didn't know what that *meant.*

As his thoughts spun, the warm glowing ember of the <[name]> deep inside him felt like an anchor. Sam's <[name]>. There was a weight to it, a surety that was so undeniably real there was no room to doubt that, whatever was going on, that <[name]> would be there, inside his soul, forever.

Maybe yesterday *hadn't* been a trick. Maybe this place really was all about healing and safety and magic.

He clung to that hope desperately as he finally crawled out from under the covers and began to inspect his room.

It was actually two rooms. One was a sitting area that included a writing table, a small sofa, and two overstuffed chairs. The other was a bedroom that held the stately four poster bed he had woken up in, as well as a wardrobe and an old-fashioned dressing screen. One wall had huge windows with heavy wooden shutters.

In the brighter morning light, Aiden could see the rooms were decorated in a spooky 1930s style, with grey wallpaper covered in stylized black rabbits, green velvet upholstered furniture, and an inordinate amount of wall sconces and paintings.

He looked at the paintings. Each of them depicted a jackalope in various poses. Each one also appeared to be in a different environment—a colorful meadow, a spooky forest path, a cavern filled with glowing mushrooms, even at a tea party with several other animals and cryptids.

Aiden turned away to look for a bathroom to brush his teeth, and then he remembered he was dead and his teeth didn't need brushing. He didn't even have breath, really, just the empty habit.

As he remembered the hot, yucky feeling of morning breath in his mouth, he suddenly *felt* it.

Confused, he touched his hands to his lips. As the memory faded away, so did the bad taste in his mouth. Carefully, deliberately, he remembered the feeling of brushing his teeth.

His mouth filled with bright, minty freshness.

That was...odd.

He continued his inspection of the room, and discovered that there wasn't a bathroom at all, only a massive stone tub and a mirror hidden behind the dressing screen that probably wasn't really meant for getting clean— there were too many faucets and what he assumed were water jets. Aiden didn't go near it, flinching away from the possibility of seeing his reflection.

He mentally jumped to the next morning task, getting dressed.

Wait.

He looked down at himself and blinked at his naked body.

He hadn't gotten undressed last night.

He'd woken up in the Atrium and hadn't thought about himself. His body. At all. He was naked, and he had been since he woke up in Atrium.

He blushed furiously as he remembered all the places he'd gone. Why hadn't he *noticed*? Was being dead messing with his thinking? Well, probably, if he could simply imagine himself into brushing his teeth.

He covered his face and replayed the previous day in his head. As he did, he marveled at the way his memories seemed...more vivid. Each memory he recalled flooded him with sensations, smells, feelings, textures, like he was *there* again. It took a conscious effort to focus back on where he was to shake himself out of it.

Thankfully, once he was free, there didn't seem to be any lingering effects.

Being dead was definitely messing with his thinking.

Maybe that was another one of those things about being in Hell that bothered other people. He wasn't bothered by it, but he probably should be. It might be really bad if he thought about a terrible memory, like his nightmares but worse.

Aiden felt a few of those memories start to surface, and he shoved them firmly away.

They went, easily, and Aiden felt relief wash through him. He had control over the memory experiences.

It was fine.

Cautiously, he thought about drinking a really good hot chocolate. The warm, sweet richness of sipping a hot drink first thing in the morning, the smell of the chocolate filling his senses, warming him from the inside out. He shivered with pleasure as the sensations of the memory washed through him.

After, Aiden felt much better, and not just from the lingering aftertaste of chocolate. The weird memory stuff worked on good memories as well as stressful ones.

He smiled to himself. It wasn't just *fine*, this odd way he could relive his memories. It was *wonderful.*

He was pulled away from his thoughts and memories when a knock sounded at the door. A voice that sounded like Sam's asked if he was awake yet.

Frantically, Aiden pulled open the wardrobe, hoping for something to wear. He felt a dizzy wave of relief when he found a robe. He threw it on and went to open the door for Sam, who was still calling for him, whining and *scratching* at the door.

Sam practically knocked him over when he opened it, and he immediately jumped onto the couch and sat down with his feet curled under himself. He was still very naked, and Aiden tried to not be distracted by it.

"Really, a bathrobe? You can wear anything you can possibly imagine and you choose a fluffy pink bathrobe? Why am I not surprised?"

Aiden blushed and snuggled deeper into the robe. He *liked* the robe. It was velvety soft and comfy. Then he frowned. "What do you mean? Anything I can imagine? This is what was in the closet."

Sam started to roll his eyes, then stopped, blinked, and looked at Aiden a little guiltily. "Right. Sorry. You wouldn't know how it works." He shook his head. "How can you be so put together and still so oblivious?" The words might have been mean, but Sam said them with enough admiration in his tone that Aiden was sure they weren't meant that way.

Sam got up and took Aiden's hand to pull him from the room. "So, I thought our first stop today should be the Library. It's actually a diff—"

Aiden dug in his heels. He might like the robe, but he didn't want to wander around Hell in it. "Um, wait. I want to wear something else. Where do I get other clothing?"

Sam turned to look at him, and Aiden found himself caught in his green, green gaze again. Sam smiled slowly, toothily, tiny cat fangs and perfect white teeth. "You could go naked again. I liked that." His voice was almost a purr.

Aiden's face grew so hot he was worried it would start glowing. Sam's expression turned briefly predatory, and heat bloomed in

Aiden's stomach. He made a small helpless sound, and felt himself start to go boneless.

Then Sam blinked and shook himself, breaking the spell. He spun and trotted quickly over to the wardrobe muttering, "*Nope*, nope, not yet, be good, Sam." He looked back to Aiden and this time his grin was sheepish. "You're definitely right. We should both wear clothes today."

Aiden felt a shock of disappointment, and he thumped his foot on the floor in frustration. Then he flushed with embarrassment. Sam blinked at him and then roared with laughter.

"Bunny, I swear if I weren't already dead, you would be the absolute death of me. Come on, I'll show you how the wardrobe works." Sam grabbed the handle. "It's really easy. You just grab the handle and then *expect* the clothes you want to be there when you open the door. Open the door, and voila! Clothes. Don't forget shoes if you want them, though honestly I don't know why you would."

Sam opened the door with a flourish. Hanging in the closet was what looked like a costume tuxedo made of a delicate, silky material. Sam pulled it out and Aiden saw that, other than the jacket, it was all one piece. It had Velcro seams in discrete places, like it was meant for a particularly speedy stripper. The lapels of the jacket were fluffy black fur, and there was a ribbon collar with a tiny bell instead of a bow tie.

"How is that supposed to be *less* distracting?" Aiden wondered out loud, and then blushed *again*. He hid his face in his hands and pressed at his hot cheeks in an effort to *push* the blush away. It did not work, obviously, and after a moment he gave up.

Sam just laughed and gestured at the wardrobe. "Your turn."

Aiden walked up hesitantly and grabbed the handle.

"But, where do they come from?" he asked, nervously. He wasn't procrastinating. It was a legitimate question.

"It's magic. Yours, to be specific. The wardrobe is a kind of focus." Sam narrowed his eyes at Aiden. "You're not stalling, are you? Open the door."

"Nope! Not stalling!" Aiden said, too quickly. He closed his eyes, focused as hard as he could on what he wanted, and opened the door.

Aiden felt a slight wave of dizziness, and then an absolutely *massive* pile of baggy jeans, rainbow t-shirts, and iridescent sneakers spilled out onto the floor.

Sam collapsed on the floor in a fit of laughter. Aiden hastily grabbed a set of clothing and started changing into them. He was so flustered that he ended up irrationally aroused, hopelessly tangled in the shirt he was pulling on. He wasn't even sure how it had happened—it was a t-shirt!.

Sam, still laughing, took pity on him and tugged things into place before booping him on the nose.

Aiden scowled and stuck out his tongue.

Sam's smile turned momentarily feral before he seemed to catch himself. He looked Aiden up and down once and blushed before spinning on his heel to head for the door.

"You look great, bunny."

Aiden drifted happily after Sam, tugging absently on the hem of his shirt.

Hugo was waiting for them just outside the room in the same place he'd been last night. Aiden realized that, unlike a regular hotel, there was no hallway and he couldn't see any other rooms—the elevator opened up onto a private landing.

"No stairways or fire escapes?" Aiden asked, slightly concerned. There were buildings like that in some of the anarch camps and Aiden had always tried his best not to stay in them long.

Hugo and Sam looked at him like he was crazy, and Aiden blinked at them, not quite sure what he'd said. Hugo made another one of those rocky sounds that Aiden interpreted as 'Is he for real?'

Sam rubbed at his cat ear. "We don't really have accidental fires. Even if the entire building was burning for some reason, unless you wanted your room to burn too, it wouldn't. The laws of physics are just recommendations here," he said, trying to explain. "It's not like the mortal world. Everything here fundamentally works on dream logic, except that things are still mostly fixed, because everyone has to agree on the dream. Not that everyone knows what your room looks like!" Sam rubbed the back of his neck and looked frustrated.

Aiden thought about it. "So, it all ties back to that cognitive realm, I-think-therefore-I-am reality system. There are no staircases because I, what, didn't want any?"

Sam nodded, then tilted his head to the side and shrugged. "Yes and no. The Hotel has its own sense of self, and it shapes itself according to the needs of its guests and residents. It probably picked up on your need for a single, controlled access point. Hugo and the elevator are currently the only way to get in. If there was an emergency, you, or the Hotel if you couldn't manage it yourself, could open a door that goes directly to somewhere safer or wherever else you needed to go. Inside your room, you have total control on who can access it."

Aiden felt an unexpected sense of gratitude towards the Hotel. He *did* feel safer knowing no one could get to him uninvited. Hugo, as if sensing that, made a warm rumbling that was not at all like purring but somehow gave the same impression.

Feeling bold, Aiden decided to ask Hugo a direct question. "Hugo, are you part of the Hotel?" Aiden wasn't entirely sure why he felt that was the case, but as soon as he asked he was so sure he was right he felt silly for having asked.

Hugo made a rocky sound that was clearly laughter. Aiden was starting to get annoyed by the way everyone kept doing that, but he supposed it was better than being yelled at or called stupid. At least this way he was making other people's day better.

Sam patted his shoulder. "Don't worry, I'm betting things will make a lot more sense once we've stopped at the Library. I'll make a door directly there as soon as we get outside—only guests can make doors inside the Hotel."

When they got to the lobby, the same snake person from before was still manning the desk. "Good morning! I trust your sssstay sssso far has been pleassssant? Would you like any houssssekeeping while you are away?"

"Um," Aiden said, thinking of the massive pile of clothing he had no idea what to do with. "No? Not today?"

"Not today? Doesss that mean you've decided to continue ssstaying with us?"

Aiden looked at Sam, who nodded towards the snake person. "It's your call, bunny."

Aiden bit his lip. "What does it cost?"

The snake person blinked. "Cosssst? Sssweet, there isss no cossst. The Hotel *needs* guesssstss."

Aiden looked between Sam and the snake person, unsure.

"Did you not explain thingsss to him?" the snake person asked Sam.

Sam rubbed at one of his ears. "That's what now is for!" He turned to Aiden. "Places in the Underworld want people in them as much as people want to be in places. You can stay at the Hotel as long as you want, it definitely likes you, but if you want to apply somewhere else all you have to do is ask."

Aiden thought maybe that sounded too good to be true, but he also couldn't make himself believe Sam was lying. "Um, I like it here, then. If that's really okay."

"Oh yess! ssSince you're ssstaying, you sshould call me ssSeptimusss. I am currently acting asss one of the Hotel'sss interpretersss, ssso pleassse don't hesssitate to assk me for anything you need."

Aiden had no idea what that meant, but he nodded anyway. "Okay, thank you, Septimus."

"You're very welcome!"

Stepping out into Nexus was not quite as overwhelming as it had been the first time, but it still stunned him for a moment. The colors, the incomprehensible number of people who somehow all fit without being crowded—it was mesmerizing. As he looked, he started to get *impressions* from some of the people. It was a little like what he'd felt with the places that resonated with him, but not quite the same.

Some of the people with *resonance* turned to look at him, and Aiden quickly hid behind Sam.

Sam laughed and reached around Aiden's not-so-subtly-hidden form to draw a door in some kind of chalk on the wall of the Hotel. When he finished, he said, <<*Library*>> in a way that Aiden felt ripple through him like a wave on the surface of a pond.

The door flashed gold, and Sam pulled him through.

AKASHIC LIBRARY

When his vision cleared of gold, Aiden froze, a wave of disorientation almost sending him to his knees.

Walls soared high above him, arching into an impossibly grand vaulted ceiling. The space was so large it defied comprehension, lacking any kind of buttress or support beyond the walls themselves. Despite that, there were staircases arching through the open air leading to levels of floors that somehow didn't impede his view of the walls and ceiling. On every surface, every wall and panel and bit of floor, there were images that looked like incredibly detailed frescos, and each one *moved*.

Aiden looked at the wall next to the doorway he had just passed through. Up that close, it was clear the images were actually made of *words*, words in so many languages it should have seemed like gibberish, but somehow didn't.

The images were slowly playing out stories, thousands of them. Aiden thought he recognized a few of them, the essences of myths or stories that everyone seemed to know. Some of the images, though, were incomprehensible, as if they were being told by and for someone that wasn't human.

Aiden shook himself free from the hypnotic images and looked back towards the impossible center. Every floor seemed to be filled with shelves, or...servers? Aiden felt another wave of disorientation at the juxtaposition of ancient looking bookshelves that were also, somehow, an impossibly huge server farm. Stairways seemed to twist and move until he focused on them and they would suddenly snap into sharp, stagnant detail.

The more he looked, the less it seemed to make sense, as if everything existed in a way that the normal three dimensions he was used to simply couldn't contain.

Aiden swayed on his feet, his head spinning and spinning. Someone, probably Sam, caught him before he fell.

"Whoa kid, stop trying to project your preconceived notions onto the Library. It doesn't like it, and it will give you a headache unlike anything you've ever felt before," Sam said, his voice far away and worried.

Aiden tried to close his eyes, to block everything out so he could re-orient himself, but it didn't work. Somehow he could still see everything around him, even with his eyes closed.

Helplessly, he continued to spiral out of control, everything making less and less sense. Pain bloomed in his mind, a pressure that threatened his very sense of *self*. He started to shiver with the force of it, as if the vastness of the library was trying to tear him apart.

He struggled against the pain, the madness, for an endless, foolish moment before he finally surrendered with a gasp.

Instantly the pain was gone as if it had never been. The space around him settled. It was still a massive, very library-like space, and the walls still had their moving stories on them, but nothing felt *wrong* about it.

He briefly tried to see something he recognized, to reconcile the space with anything he'd experienced before, but stopped when he felt the beginnings of disorientation flutter in his head again.

Clearly it was best if he just accepted the Library for what it was without trying to label it.

Aiden came back to himself. He was on his knees, though he did not remember hitting the floor. Sam was wrapped around Aiden, as if holding him together, and he was purring.

<<Is *this* your idea of an orientation, Samuel? You didn't warn him at all.>>

Aiden started and looked up at the voice. A massive owl was sitting on one of the bookshelves, looking down at them. The owl was *huge*, almost as big as Sam and Aiden combined. Aiden blinked. He thought he could see that strange black iridescence that Zee's coat had been made of swirling around the owl like a cloak. Aiden blinked again, and the owl was gone.

Instead, a human-shaped figure stood before them, shrouded in a black-iridescent robe and cowl.

Sam quickly disentangled himself from Aiden and jumped to his feet. "He's fine! He's a lot tougher than he looks, and warning him wouldn't have done anything other than make him stressed for no reason."

Aiden huffed and started to push himself up off the floor. Sam might have been right about how he would have reacted, but he should have let Aiden decide that for himself. He ignored Sam's offered hand with another little huff.

Sam's posture instantly drooped, and he turned his full attention back to Aiden. His eyes, brilliant and beautiful as glowing emeralds, got unnaturally huge in his head, and he looked tragically miserable. "You're fine, right?"

Aiden pressed his lips together, but nodded.

Sam blinked once, very slowly, and ducked his head. "I knew you would be." He rubbed his shoulder against Aiden in a very cat-like non-apology.

Aiden huffed again, but a smile tugged at his lips. "Warn me anyway next time, okay? If I can handle this, I can handle a little stress."

Sam bumped him again, insistently, head still bowed. "Of course. I—" he cut off and looked momentarily conflicted. "You're really amazing."

A flutter of warmth overrode the last of his irritation. Aiden thought he could probably press Sam to confess whatever was bothering him, but the idea made him feel like a bully, so he decided to let it go. He *was* okay, after all, and Sam's confidence in him was, in a way, one of the best compliments he'd ever received.

He bumped Sam back and turned to face the cloaked figure. Even though Aiden couldn't see the figure's shape or face, Aiden felt their attention shift to him. Aiden hesitated. What pronouns should he use for this person? Should he ask, or just assume they/them, like with Zee?

<<Female pronouns are fine for me, today,>> she said, answering Aiden's unasked question. Her voice sounded the same as when she was an owl. It wasn't particularly human.

"Um. Hi," Aiden said, not sure if he should extend his hand. "I'm Aiden? I'm new?"

She just stared at him. It lasted for a long, tense moment and Aiden felt her shrouded gaze scouring his soul, seeing farther into its depths than he had ever let himself look. He froze, not even letting himself blink—he understood that he was being judged.

For some reason he couldn't quite grasp, he really wanted to impress her. It was inexplicably vital to him, and he had a strange certainty that she was deciding whether or not he would be given something he very much wanted.

Before he had a chance to get really nervous or wonder *why* he felt that way, the owl lady nodded once, and the sense of judgment lifted.

<<Application Accepted. Follow me, and we will activate your demonic membership.>> She turned and swept down the aisle. Aiden hesitated only a second before hurrying after her, and Sam followed close behind.

"What, really?" Sam asked, stunned. The Owl glared at him, and Sam grinned. He turned to Aiden and whispered, "That's amazing! Good job, bunny. Getting accepted by a Librarian is the hardest part."

Aiden wasn't sure what to make of that, so he just nodded and kept after the Librarian. As he passed through the...archives...Aiden got impressions of topics or, even weirder, brief flutters of memories that were not his own.

Quite suddenly they arrived at what looked like an open reading area in the middle of the library. In the center was a large desk that gave the impression of being both imposing and welcoming without having any particularly describable features. It was a paragon of desk-ness.

The Librarian walked behind the Desk and waved her hand. One of the holographic screens popped up.

<<Open up a screen,>> she said to Aiden, and he blinked at her in confusion. She made a weird, vaguely unsettling clicking sound that Aiden had to assume was out of frustration. <<I have no tolerance for denial,>> she said sharply. <<You know how to do it, stop acting like you're still human and let yourself *be*.>>

Aiden blinked again, and then did as he was told, not letting himself think too hard about it. He *reached* and <[accessed]>. A screen popped up in front of him. It was blank except for a single blinking cursor.

<<Good. Now, in order to get full access you will need to choose a <[name]>. You won't be able to change it without special dispensation from the Triad, but you likely won't need to—despite your weird hangups you are remarkably put together, better than most people who've been around here for years.>>

Aiden felt panic clench in his chest. Choose a <[name]>? What did that even mean? The way she'd said it, it sounded important, too important for him to decide hims—

The Librarian made more clicking sounds, louder this time, and Aiden jumped. He knew his eyes were too wide, and the Librarian turned her full attention on him for a long second before the sound changed to something oddly soothing.

Aiden swallowed, and let out a long, slow breath. The Librarian turned back to her screen and grumbled something under her breath about <<weird ones>> and <<more work>> while she typed on the desk with clawed fingers.

Aiden focused on taking slow, even breaths. Why did it keep him calm even though he didn't have a heart that could race or lungs he needed to fill? Was it the rhythm of the movement, or something more, his belief that it *should* work? If the latter, could he just *will* himself calm instead?

Aiden wasn't quite ready to try, and he kept breathing.

Sam, noticing his distress, wrapped his tail around Aiden's waist and started purring again. It helped, and Aiden gave him a small, tense smile.

Why was he so nervous? Of choosing the wrong <[name]>? Why? Who would he disappoint? The Librarian? The Librarian was intimidating, but he had no reason to care *this much* about what she thought. Sam? He liked Sam, maybe a lot, but he barely knew him. Even Aiden couldn't have let himself get that attached so quickly, right?

Right.

Himself. He must be afraid of disappointing *himself*. There wasn't anyone else *to* disappoint. It was a horribly sad thought, but it was also a relief. The worst had happened. He was dead, and damned, exactly as his parents thought he would be. It was over.

And it was *really* nice down here. Maybe. Hopefully.

So long as you didn't make the eldritch Library mad about your preconceived notions about how a building was supposed—

Nope. Not going there.

He'd been terrible at living, but maybe he could be good at...being damned? It was why he'd become a whore. He'd been very good at it. Maybe he could be good at being damned too?

He did want this, whatever it was. He felt as if he *had* to do this, and it *wasn't* because of Sam or because he wanted to belong. He just...he just knew he was meant to do this. This was the right choice for him.

Even if he had no idea what he was doing.

But that had never stopped him before. He'd do it. He'd ask the Librarian for help, and he'd choose a <[name]>.

Aiden was about to say as much when the Librarian's attention returned to him. <<I will help. As soon as you're ready, I will open a <[directlink]> for you. It will be a little raw for you without a proper shard, but you should be able to handle it. Identify the <[words]> that resonate with you. Any of those words can be used as part of your <[name]>.>>

Aiden clenched and unclenched his hands, and stopped breathing. Could she read his mind? Had she heard *all* of his thoughts? Irrational guilt washed through him. "I'm sor—"

<<Hush,>> she said gently. <<It's alright. I could have been more patient with you, you certainly deserved it. Just do your best, and that will be enough.>>

Aiden let out a small breath and nodded. "Okay. Is there, um..." He hesitated, wanting to ask if there was anything more he should know. He liked Sam, he did, but it was pretty obvious Sam was a do-first-and-explain-after kind of person.

The Librarian's attention shifted to Sam, and Aiden could feel the judgment in her glare even though it wasn't directed at him. Aiden felt guilty all over again—he was pretty sure it was *his* thoughts that made her look at Sam with that piercing gaze.

Sam hunched his shoulders and pressed against Aiden's shoulder but otherwise pretended he was unaffected. Aiden wasn't fooled, though, and the absurdity of *Sam* hiding behind *him* broke through his nerves. He laughed, a little hysterically.

Aiden would have sworn the Librarian rolled her eyes. How she kept managing to communicate facial expression with her face completely obscured was something Aiden didn't dare try to guess at. <<Alright then, *I'll* explain. Once you have a <[name]>, you will have full access to the Records. That means you will be able to summon up the answer to any question you can ask, as long as it was experienced or answered by a soul, living or otherwise. The trick is learning to ask the right questions. No one will be allowed to help you ask better questions, and if you end up consulting for mortals, you will be required to ask their questions exactly, with absolutely no advice on how to better phrase it. That is part of the Treaty, unfortunately. If you need help, demons will often ask each *other* questions instead. It's a fairly simple loophole to exploit and it will allow you to refine your questions without getting the Library involved. Sam uses that method almost exclusively.>>

"Hey!" Sam said, and Aiden laughed again, this time without the hint of hysteria.

The Librarian ignored Sam. <<You will not have access to predictive knowledge, that is not your calling, nor will you have access to any knowledge not generated by Earth life.>>

Aliens again!

The Librarian gave Aiden a stern look, and he did his best to school his thoughts. Her tone became more serious and she leaned forward. <<The most important thing to remember is that your <[name]> is something you should keep private. Any soul you give it to will be able to call you anytime, and you'll be compelled to answer it at your soonest convenience. If you do choose to give it to someone, know that living mortals will forget it when they die, and mortal souls will lose it if they reincarnate or join divinity. Demons, though, will not forget a <[name]> once given unless they are torn apart. Most importantly, if you or anyone you have trusted your <[name]> to gives it to Divinity, you're fucked.>>

Aiden swallowed audibly. He was able to keep himself from looking at Sam, barely. He felt the <[name]> Sam had given to him, warm and comforting and, now, *terrifying*.

Sam had trusted him that much? *Why?*

"What happens if Divinity gets it?" Aiden asked, unable to keep the tremor from his voice. He wasn't afraid for himself.

<<If you're lucky, someone will eat you before Divinity manages to summon you. Most likely, though, you'll be torn apart by angels and absorbed into Divinity after being cycled through bacteria for a few decades. That is about as close to true death as a soul will

ever experience. If the <[name]> was acquired illegally, like ripping it from a soul's mind without their consent, the Triad will intervene on your behalf and you will get the opportunity to try to change your <[name]>. Changing your <[name]>, though, will take time, because you must change enough that a new <[name]> will fit you in a way your old one does not.>>

The Librarian looked at Aiden critically. <<You are strange, so things may be—>> the Librarian seemed to glitch, and she cut off. She fluffed her shroud as if it was made of feathers. <<Apologies, I overstep. Regardless, you will need to be careful who you give your <[name]> too, understand?>>

Aiden took a moment to think about that. Hesitantly, he asked, "Will getting my own <[name]> make me stronger? Better able to keep secrets?"

The Librarian made another strange noise. <<You do not have access to future knowledge. I *cannot* say what may or may not happen to you.>> An odd kindness entered her voice. <<Your application would not have been accepted if you were not right for it, but you can still withdraw your application if you wish. You can resubmit later.>>

"No!" Aiden was shocked at his own vehemence. He wanted to do this. There were things, things he couldn't remember, but that he still *knew*. He wanted to be able to...

Aiden couldn't hold on to the thought.

"Can you tell me if getting my <[name]> could make me stronger? Or weaker?"

The Librarian thought about that for a long time. <<Yes, it could make you stronger. I am not sure about weaker.>> Sam looked at the Librarian incredulously, but she went on. <<However, based on the information I have now, I don't believe you would become weaker.>>

Sam's incredulous look shifted to Aiden. Aiden shrugged self-consciously.

<<Do you have any more questions, or are you ready?>>

He tried to look confident and nodded. "I'm ready."

<<Alright. Type the words that resonate with you into your screen as they come to you.>> The Librarian looked at Sam and he sighed dramatically before moving far enough away from Aiden that he wouldn't be able to see Aiden's screen. "I wouldn't have looked, sheesh."

As soon as Sam was out of sight of his screen, Aiden felt the Librarian open a <[directlink]>. Words that were more than just words started rushing through his head, a massive flood of them. He was almost overwhelmed by it, but he knew how to function while feeling like things were out of his control—he'd had years of practice.

Besides, he'd *asked* for this, and that always made all the difference.

Aiden endured, and focused on his instructions, for feelings of resonance.

The <[words]> came. Too many resonated with him, way more than he could possibly type into the screen. He tried to focus on the ones that resonated the most strongly, but even then there were still too many. Desperately, he typed them into the screen in front of him as fast as he could. He didn't have a keyboard, but that didn't seem to matter. His fingers flew, and the words appeared on the screen.

He didn't know how long it took. It could have been hours, or seconds, or only a single instant. The rawness of the link began to burn him, and he felt himself beginning to fray.

The <[directlink]> broke.

Aiden knew his <[name]>.

It seemed kinda long for a name, but knew he wouldn't have any trouble remembering it. The <[name]> was now part of him. He could no more forget his <[name]> than he could forget his hand. Wait. Could he forget his hand? He held up his hand and looked at it. It seemed real enough, but...

Aiden shook himself. The fraying at his edges smoothed back out.

The Librarian was staring at him. Aiden looked between the screen, which now had a stylized search bar in the center of it, and the Librarian. The longer Aiden felt her piercing attention on him, the harder it was to keep himself from trembling.

"Stop staring at him like that," Sam said, putting himself between Aiden and the Librarian, "Can't you see it's scaring him?"

The Librarian's attention left him and shifted to Sam. Sam took it in stride this time, staring back evenly.

"I'm sorry. Did I do something wrong?" Aiden asked, trying not to cry. He'd done his best, but—

<<No. You did nothing wrong.>> The Librarian's shape became unstable until, with a *pop*, she exploded back into the giant owl. <<I need to do some research. Aiden, you now have full access to the Records and are a registered Demon of the Underworld. Please keep your profile up-to-date with any changes in residence and any hobbies or employment you choose to do. Also, *always* log any visitations to the mortal plane. Your profile will update automatically unless you disable the feature. I do not recommend disabling it.>>

With that, she launched herself into the air and flew off. The uber-Desk vanished.

Aiden looked at Sam, who shrugged. Aiden glanced at the screen, still open, but he decided that asking the Library what had upset the Librarian was probably *not* a good idea. He tentatively waved his hand through the screen, hoping to dismiss it. It winked away.

"Uh, I guess we're done here," Sam said, sounding just as confused and overwhelmed as Aiden felt. "Come on, I'll show you the regular way to get here without crafting a door. Theoretically, you might want to come back here for 'deeper research' or whatever and the doors are impressive as heck." Sam took Aiden's hand and led him back through the maze of shelf-servers to the main doorway.

Aiden let himself get dragged along, unable to take his mind off of the <[name]> buried deep within him. Not his own, that one was easy to accept. He knew how to take care of himself, mostly, and if he failed to keep his own <[name]> safe, no one would be hurt but himself.

But the <[name]> *not* his own was different. The <[name]> belonging to the beautiful cat boy pulling him along and chattering happily about nothing in particular.

The <[name]>, and the implicit trust that came with it, he *had* to find a way to be worthy of.

GREATER PROVIDENCE RI, SEPTEMBER 9TH 47 YAR

June's first thought was that the *wrongness* was an exorcist, or worse, an *angel*, but as panic tightened her chest she reminded herself it couldn't be that. Angels could only approach someone who prayed for them, and doing so in witch territory, in *public*, was grounds for seizure of the angel's shard. Exorcists were not allowed in witch cities at all without very publicly announced permits, the wards wouldn't let them through, and June would have known if one had been issued.

June calmed down enough to recognize that the magic was definitely not divine. The one time she'd been near an exorcist she'd felt a *burning*, like what old movies thought vampires felt in the sunlight. This wrongness did not feel like that.

No, this sense of foreboding wasn't Divine, but it wasn't quite demonic either. It felt *wrong*, like it was unstable, or...

Angry.

June wrestled with the pros and cons of ducking into an alley and *flickering* away. Humans had cameras everywhere, and if someone caught her going into an alley and not coming out she might lose the use of this face. She wasn't likely to find another one as good as this one.

She decided a persistent but inexplicable bad feeling wasn't worth the risk to her favorite human identity. She picked up her pace, but kept it within reasonable human movement speeds. It didn't help, and the sense of something *wrong* only continued to grow. She tried to lose it by taking a circuitous route, but gave up as she ran out of time.

She got home with only about twenty minutes to spare before dawn. The sky was bright, the stars almost completely gone. The alpenglow made her skin itch, and she quickly ducked inside and clattered down the stairs. When the door to her basement condo was firmly shut behind her, she scanned the open floor plan for any sign of intruders.

There were none. The dark, windowless apartment was empty.

The foreboding feeling continued to grow, relentlessly.

June had no fucking clue what it was, or what to do about it. Frantically, she ran around her apartment, looking for weapons. She didn't have much—no knives or pots or sports equipment. She looked at her guitars, some of which hung proudly on the wall, expensive collector pieces, and some in their cases stacked neatly in a corner, ready to be played. She decided that they weren't good weapons even if she were willing to smash them—which she was *not.*

Instead, she started fleshcrafting herself into a weapon. She stripped off her clothes—they would only get in the way—and put her back to a wall she knew had been carved out of the bedrock and closed her eyes, focusing.

She might have felt silly doing it, safe in her own home, if the sense of danger didn't *keep growing*. She bulked up her muscles until her skin split with small, white tears, not deep enough to bleed, but enough to push the edge of uncomfortable. The bones in her fingers lengthened, spitting open the pads and dragging nail keratin along with to form thick, razor sharp claws. She extended her fangs as well, and modified her jaw to be something almost wolf-like, optimized for shredding flesh without catching bone.

After a moment's consideration, she pushed a set of wings out of her back. They weren't enough to allow her to truly fly, but if she *flickered* up into the air they'd allow her to glide down at speeds unlikely to cause damage. She left them small and dense and grew another set of claws at each wingtip. That done, she toughened up her skin, leaving it thick and leathery, reinforced with more keratin.

She was considering whether or not she wanted to invest in any spikes when it arrived.

The *thing* flowed through the door like it wasn't there and splattered itself all over the landing. June felt a scream rise in her less-than-human throat as the thing started roiling and bubbling. Thick ropelike tentacles lifted an oily black mouth full of misshapen teeth. Eyes that wouldn't quite pair up locked onto June, and the mouth smiled gruesomely.

</<*Found you, bitch,*>/> it rasped wetly.

"What the fuck *are* you?" she hissed back, her flesh crafted vocal chords not quite up to anything else. She scanned the thing, not at all sure how to attack it. It refused to *be*, oozing over the carpet like oil. It appeared to be only half manifested in the physical plane, held here by some force June couldn't identify.

Without answering, the thing launched itself at her, teeth first. June *flickered* out of the way and picked up her couch. She flung it at the thing, but the couch passed through the creature like smoke to crash against the back wall and crumple to the floor in a misshapen heap.

The creature spun on itself, writhing in utter defiance of gravity or reason, and launched at her again. June *flickered* to the side and tried to swipe at it, but though her claw met resistance, it *gave*, like cold oil. When she tried to pull her hand free, thick darkness came with her, and she felt the thing *seeping into her flesh*.

June screamed, *flickering* around the room to try to get free. She crashed into a music stand, scattering sheets of smart-paper to the floor. Everywhere she went, the thing followed, towed along by the hold it had on her arm.

It started to climb farther up, sending sticky black tendrils along her forearm towards her elbow, the flesh bubbling and blackening as it went. It fucking *hurt*, and June grabbed her forearm at the elbow and twisted—ripping her arm off in an attempt to keep the thing from fucking *eating* her.

The next time she *flickered*, she left the arm behind out of desperation. The thing stayed with it. She watched in absolute horror as her arm fell apart, dissolving into the black mass in seconds.

June didn't even spare the time to open her door, simply *flickering* through to the other side and up the stairs towards the brightening dawn. There was no fucking way she was staying in there with whatever that thing was, sunlight or no sunlight.

The creature tried to follow her, roaring incoherent obscenities as it flowed up the stairs after her. June saw the door to her upstairs neighbor's apartment start to open, and she shoved one of her claws into the hinges, jamming the door shut. She hoped she hadn't just doomed the poor older couple, but the thing seemed pretty focused on her, and them coming out into the hall would not help.

The thing shrieked as it tried to pass through a pool of sunlight, curling away and around the bright spot to continue after June, relentless.

June wrenched open the front door. More sunlight spilled in, and the creature screamed again and fell back into the darkness. It actually *burned* in the sunlight, or maybe it evaporated, leaving behind nothing but wisps of smoke, as if it was unable to hold itself together. As June watched, the thing melted back through the door to her apartment.

She *felt* as it started seeping through the ground towards her, slower than when it moved through the air, but not nearly enough.

Unfortunately for June, the sunlight also destabilized her own flesh. Even in the relative shade of the building, her skin was beginning to look grey. If she didn't find someplace dark soon she would start to decompose in earnest.

But where could she go? The horrible abomination didn't care about doors or walls. Whatever dark place she managed to find, it would follow.

Angry darkness roiled beneath her feet, and June scampered back and out onto the street, not wanting to let the thing touch the soles of her feet.

A human scream sounded, and June whirled to see some terrified human holding a dog on a leash. The dog was small and definitely not a familiar, yipping and growling at her like *she* was the threat.

The woman screamed again, and June remembered that she was currently fleshcrafted into a fairly grotesque monster.

Shit shit shit.

Corruption reached for her again, and June *flickered* around to the back of the building.

Sunlight was the only safety, and sunlight was death.

She needed help.

With no other options, June began to *flicker* towards the only place she could think of that might have protection against whatever the thing was—Thoughts and Prayers.

By the time June got there, her entire body was soft with rot. It had taken her ten minutes to *flicker* her way across the metropolis, the sun rapidly putrefying her as she went. The flesh on her wings had fallen off about two blocks back, the bones beginning to bleach white. She couldn't feel them at all, which meant she'd need to snap them off if they didn't crumble into dust first. Probably the same with her fingerbones, which started bleaching as soon as she reached for the door.

Her hand shattered as she pulled, the door locked and unyielding, and she collapsed on the ground. She'd lost the horrible thing when she crossed the river into East Providence, but that didn't really matter anymore.

She was going to die. Again. Three years of freedom, of vengeance, was all she'd managed. *Fuck.*

At least rotting in the sun didn't hurt as badly as whatever that thing had been doing to her. And it had *nothing* on burning alive, which was how she'd died the first time, roasted like a fucking pig by her own family after she'd run away to live in Sokanon's village.

June barely noticed when the door opened.

"Holy shit! *June*? What the fuck happened?" June felt herself being dragged through the door. The relatively dim light slowed the rotting enough that June was able to focus long enough to forcibly slough off a good amount of dead weight.

Ha. *Dead* weight.

She started laughing. The sound was slightly grotesque, wet and juicy and not at all human, and for some reason that made her laugh even harder.

"This is *not* funny, June," Penny scolded.

"Buuufffhhsdh," June gurgled, trying to explain why it was funny. Penny didn't seem to get it, because she just kept swearing and hauling June down into the basement.

In the pitch darkness, June felt some of the mania leave her. Penny propped her against some crates, and it was cold. June realized Penny had dragged her into the walk-in freezer. Penny was so smart. It was too bad she liked dudes.

June's breath was rasping in her half decayed lungs, and there was very little of her that wasn't at least partially damaged. She probably stank. She gave up trying to fix the damage and just clung desperately to her ruined corpse of a body instead.

Penny choked, trying not to gag. "Fuck, June, I can't even breathe. Can you hold on for a few hours? I don't know where I'm going to find a fresh body on such short notice, but I'll do what I can. Tell me you can keep it together until I get back?"

June tried to speak and had even less success than before, so she just nodded. She would hold on.

Penny left, and June settled into the grim task of holding herself to the mortal plane by sheer force of will.

GREATER PROVIDENCE RI, SEPTEMBER 9TH 47 YAR

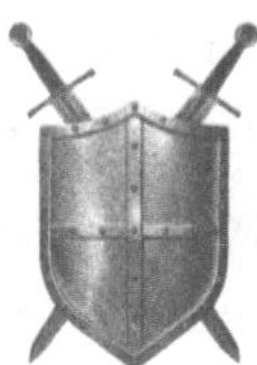

Emily woke, rolled out of bed, and was halfway dressed before she had a chance to wonder why.

The seal pulsed, frantic, and Emily felt something that reminded her of dissonant static rush by the street below her.

Evil.

Get it.

Without stopping, *unable* to stop, she pulled the rest of her clothes on, clipped on her belt, taser, and badge, and ran out the door.

It was late enough that the sun was well over the horizon and the streets were filling up with people. Most of them seemed oblivious, enjoying the magnificent fall sunshine, but a few were reacting as if to a bad smell, moving out of the way of an invisible pathway that blazed in Emily's mind like a beacon.

That way. It went *that way.*

Emily followed the sickly sweet smell of decay up the street, running as fast as she could. Faster, even, as she felt something warm and glorious flow into her from the pendant bouncing against her chest. There was no burn in her lungs, no ache in her calves as she sprinted fast as an Olympian down the street.

Too slow. She was still *too slow.*

She heard the screams first. Then she saw the people running.

Emily pushed her way through the crowd, wishing she'd thought to grab her bright yellow coat. At least she had her badge, which she started waving around like a talisman, hoping it would get her through.

She finally burst through the crowd to where a team of responders were setting up a perimeter.

Before Emily could find the officer in charge, she spotted a woman covered in blood exiting the subway. She hopped the gate and stopped, standing at the threshold between shadow and sunlight, unnaturally still.

I must kill it.

"What! No!" Emily said, out loud. The seal resting against her breast bone started buzzing at her painfully, urgently.

No, Emily thought at it with every ounce of will she possessed. *Shut up and let me figure out what to do.*

"Ma'am? I'm going to have to ask you back away."

Emily jumped and turned to the speaker, a responder with a roll of caution tape. She pulled out her badge. "I'm Detective Emily Scott with the Greater Providence Inspector office. Who do I need to check in with so I can witness the scene?"

They pointed to another responder a few feet away who was having a conversation with someone in an EMS uniform.

Emily walked over, passing by a few local inspector deputies who were trying to get statements from some of the people. Emily caught a few words, like *carnage* and *so much blood*, but she resolutely kept moving towards the officer in charge, clinging to procedure, desperately ignoring the way the seal kept urging her to *hunt it kill it*.

Emily had just finished signing into the scene when there was a gasp from one of the EMTs. Emily looked back towards the blood-soaked woman and sucked in a breath.

It was Sean's girlfriend Olivia. She still stood mostly in shadow, but now her arm was extended into the sunlight. The skin on her arm was mottled with blisters that slowly grew and burst, leaking black, oily-looking fluid that looked nothing like human blood.

No one approached—none of the responders here were witches, and there was clearly some kind of magic involved. Emily quickly relayed Olivia's identity to the EMS in charge as they took out a phone to call for magical backup.

Kill it.

No.

Emily, hands compulsively clenching and unclenching, did her job and watched without interfering. As the minutes passed, it became clear that, slowly, the skin was starting to heal faster than it burned. Eventually, the bubbling stopped, and the skin faded to an angry red, and then back to smooth, unblemished skin.

KILL IT.

No!

Olivia moved for the first time, the hand slowly rotating and flexing, like a robot diagnosing its motor control. Magical healers were still a few minutes out, but a terrifyingly brave EMT approached Olivia, speaking softly. Olivia ignored the EMT, pushing its arm farther into the sunlight. The newer fleshed bubbled once, and then settled.

A horrible mad grin split the girl's face, twisted and gruesome underneath the blood. She looked over at the crowd and spotted Emily and said, </<*What the fuck? No.* No!>/> The voice was *wrong*, as if it wasn't quite meant to reverberate in this reality, thick and guttural and monstrous.

It's not human kill it KILL IT.

Emily thought, as loudly as she could, *Shut* up, *you stupid thing. We do not shoot first and ask questions later. We are the questioner!*

There was a painful, static flash from the seal, and the thing wearing Olivia's body growled and ran down the stairs to the subway.

Emily was moving before she had a conscious thought. She heard people shouting for her to stop, she *tried* to stop, but her body kept moving half-against her will, the urgency overwhelming.

She had to slow when her foot slipped in the thick coating of blood on the base of the stairs. *What am I doing?*

Hunt it Kill IT.

Olivia stood at the bottom of the stairs, eyes blank, a sick smile twisting her lips. She opened her mouth and screamed. A thick cloud of black smoke poured out and pooled around Olivia before surging towards Emily.

A flash of blinding light surged outward from the seal, and Emily screamed with pain and determination as power blazed through and around her.

The darkness shrieked and recoiled, twisting into a snakelike ribbon before disappearing down the dark tunnel.

Olivia collapsed to the floor and started heaving up what looked like thick, chunky blood. Emily took a few steps in the direction the evil cloud had fled before shaking herself free from whatever compulsion the seal had forced on her and turning back towards the stairs to call for the EMTs.

By the time they'd loaded the now unconscious Olivia onto a gurney and sent her along to the hospital, the urgency to hunt had faded into something dull and easy to ignore. Now, the seal only radiated a soft, comforting warmth.

Emily determined there were at least fifty bodies in the gruesome mess of flesh and gore. She turned the scene over to the forensic techs and handed over her shoes when she got back to the street. They gave her a replacement pair and told her they would need a couple of hours before they'd have a detailed report.

"We also recommend hiring a magical consultant to assist. Your call, of course, Detective, but if you do decide to call one in, please let us know right away."

Emily nodded and promised she would before pulling out her phone. She sent a message to Will, asking if he was available, and then sent messages along to a few other witch consultants she didn't like nearly as much. The situation was too huge for her to rely only on poor Will, but no matter what, she wanted to see if he could track the evil cloud for her.

Emily moved into the sunlight and stopped to stand there for a long moment, letting it warm her. She needed to go back to her apartment and get her tablet and coat and rinse the blood off.

The clothing she'd dump into the incinerator.

Emily's amulet buzzed a warning.

"Detective Scott?"

Emily turned towards the speaker, tense. "Yes?"

A tired looking responder gestured towards an older man clutching a cat. He was studying the ground with a troubled expression. "I was told I need to check with you before I give this man permission to set up some wards. He says this place 'smells very wrong' and he and his familiar think it would be in everyone's best interest if they set up as many magical protections as they can manage."

The seal pulsed another warning, and Emily fought to keep the frown off her face.

The thing that gave it to her had claimed to be an angel, and it probably was, but that didn't mean it was benevolent. Hell, the damn thing might have been right about whatever had been possessing Olivia, but its solution had been to *murder Olivia.*

Emily decided she couldn't trust the seal or her own feelings just then, so she focused on logic instead.

"What's his name?"

Emily used her phone to do a quick background check on the witch, and, finding nothing suspicious, gave the go ahead for him to set up his wards. The moment he started working magic the damn seal started buzzing angrily, and Emily called the captain to find someone to take over the scene for her so she could go home, change, and get back in time to meet up with Will.

The captain, much to Emily's irritation, wanted her to stop by the office before she returned to the scene.

"Sir, I really think—"

"Emily, this is non-negotiable. You need to be cleared by the psychology department before you can be assigned a case like this, especially after what you've already witnessed. You'll also need to check in with counseling daily."

Emily gritted her teeth. "Sir, I understand, but—"

"*Emily,*" the captain said, and Emily snapped her mouth shut. "DeNardis was sent home on psychological leave this morning, which means we're short staffed. I *need* you on this case, which means I need you to come in and do things *properly*. Got it?"

Emily took a few slow breaths before she answered. Damn witches and their damn therapy. She was *fine*.

A little cold, a little scared, and maybe a lot sick to her stomach, but that was goddamn *normal*.

"I assume I can do these check-ins virtually after the initial evaluation?"

The captain sighed heavily. "Most likely, but you know how it is, if someone decides they need to see you in person, you'll have to go unless there's an emergency preventing you. I'm assigning you a small team of deputies to use on this case however you need. None of them are amazing, but they'll do their jobs while they're on duty."

"Thanks," Emily said, and she thought she managed to keep the bitterness out of her voice. "I'll be there as soon as I can. I assume I have time to wash the blood off?"

"Divinity, yes. Just be quick."

"Yes, sir."

Emily messaged Will to have him meet her at the office instead, and took off for home.

ATRIUM, SEPTEMBER 9TH, 47 YAR

YEAH, YOU KNOW IT'S BAD WHEN THEY START KEEPING TRACK OF TIME IN ATRIUM

Lucifer paced back and forth in front of Zee's desk. "We know its location now. It's in witch territory, which at least means Divinity can't declare war over it, *yet.* And it can, what, *possess* people?"

Zee tapped their screen, which had an alarmingly short list of names. "Or infect them, maybe. The record is a little vague, but, shit, look." Zee pulled up an image, and Lucifer stopped pacing and stared.

"That's very bad." He rested his hand on his sword. "Did the bunny make it to the Library? He's the only lead we've got."

Zee hesitated. "He's there now, but...well, see for yourself. His record is still more <[redacted]> than memory. A *lot* more." Zee hesitated, then said, "We need to be careful. Some of these tags... We could really hurt him if he gets it into his head this mess is somehow his fault."

Lucifer moved behind Zee's shoulder and his eyes narrowed. "You knew there was a connection earlier, didn't you?" Zee didn't acknowledge Lucifer. "*Zee!* We don't need to tell him why, but we *need* to talk to him. Look." Lucifer pointed at the screen. "He's registered as a Demon already. That's weird, right?"

Zee frowned, typing. "He's not even been here a whole *day*, how the hell did he register?" Lucifer growled half-heartedly, and Zee only frowned in response. "Sorry Lucy. Look, we can't talk to him until after his first therapy session. He needs *time*, I— Shit, this is such a mess."

Lucifer shook his head. "We need a goddamn Oracle. Can we contact any of the ones in hiding?"

Zee shook their head. "*We* can't, no," he paused, then their expression shifted. "But maybe we don't need to. Let me just..." They started typing. "There. I've positioned the Library next to Styx. That should do it."

"That should do what?" Lucifer asked, frowning at the screen.

Zee's expression became very sly. "Load the dice."

Light flashed, white and pure, and a shadow cast by nothing pooled on the floor. When the shadow was thick as water, reality twitched, and Lillian stood where the shadow had been. "I found another demon who's had contact—an active vampire—so she's not on your list, Zee. She was unable to fight the thing and is currently in critical condition. Her maker is patching her up."

Zee swore and summoned a new screen. "Critical condition? Did the corruption do something to her?"

Lillian shook her head, "No, but not for lack of trying, I guess. Zee, the thing was trying to *eat* her. While she was *still inside flesh.*"

Zee looked over, eyes wide. "That's...shit, Lil. That's very bad."

"What do you mean *unable* to fight? Hunting her *how*? Was the vampire targeted specifically?" Lucifer asked. His cloak flashed irritably in reflection of his mood as he resumed his pacing.

Lillian bit her lip, frustrated. "I don't know. Everything is second hand. The vampire's witch said the vampire showed up nearly dead. She ran into the sun to escape it."

Zee swore again and pushed back from the desk. They drifted into a hover above the floor and rolled back to stare up at the stars. "There's too much we don't know. If this thing is able to get at fleshbound souls... We aren't going to be able to handle this on our own. We need to tell the others."

There was a pause.

Together, they said, "*Shit.*"

STYX

Aiden eyed the boat suspiciously.

It reminded him of a small Viking ship, or maybe one of those boats they used to use in Venice back before it drowned. Which is to say, it looked like it might tip over, and Aiden was *not* interested in finding out what the magic water would do to him.

"Well *that's* new. Huh. These doors usually open into Nexus." Sam poked at the boat, then shrugged and, in a probable betrayal of all things cat, jumped into the boat and draped himself languidly over a cushioned bench.

The boat had been waiting for Sam and Aiden as they'd walked out of the Library. The grand stairs had simply *ended* at the river, disappearing below the dark surface.

Sam said, "Come *on*. I don't have all day. Will, my witch, could call me at any time, and I wanna see your face when we get to the scary tunnel."

Aiden blinked for a second.

Scary tunnel?

He narrowed his eyes at Sam. "What makes you think I want to go through a scary tunnel?"

Aiden did want to see the scary tunnel, because Aiden often made bad choices of exactly that type, but Sam had no way of knowing that.

Right?

Sam gazed up at Aiden through heavy lidded eyes, looking highly certain of Aiden's imminent compliance.

How the hell did they always know? *So many* guys would see him shivering and obviously terrified but they would still *know*. The good ones asked for verbal confrontation or just waited with an open expression, like Sam was, but they always *knew*.

Was it something on his face?

Without a word of explanation or hesitation, Sam stretched out a hand towards the hooded figure sitting at the back of the boat. The figure removed a bony hand from the long pole he was grasping and accepted the two gold coins that materialized and fell from Sam's hand.

"This is Char," Sam said, as if in explanation.

Aiden felt his chest go tight. Where had the money come from? Did he need money? He wanted to ask, but his tongue felt paralyzed—how could he ask a question before obeying Sam and getting into the boat, especially now that he'd *paid*?

The air this close to the river smelled distinctly of ozone, and the water did not move like water should. It was glassy smooth, even when Sam had jumped into the boat, but it also gave the impression of moving quickly just beneath the surface. Aiden decided that there was definitely something horrible under the surface of the water. Probably many somethings.

Sam studied Aiden for a long moment, concern pinching his brow. Aiden bit his lip and fiddled with his shirt hem, looking between Sam, the water, the boat, and the stairs.

"What *kind* of scary tunnel?" Aiden asked.

Sam's concern dropped away and he grinned evilly. Aiden shivered with that odd, familiar mix of fear and reassurance. "Are you saying you *don't* want to see a scary tunnel? If that's true, I suppose we could just go back to the Library. Maybe one of the Librarians will open a door for you."

Aiden's hesitation vanished and he jumped into the boat. The boat dipped and wobbled, and the water splashed alarmingly. He immediately pressed himself flat to the bottom, nearly crawling under the bench, eyes squeezed shut. The boat bobbed for a moment longer, then settled.

With an even, steady glide, Aiden felt the boat push off from the dock.

Aiden shivered for several seconds, until he felt Sam's hand reach down and stroke his hair. Unconsciously, Alien leaned into the touch, and soon enough curiosity won out over fear. He lifted his head. Sam was watching him, his face bright with amused compassion, and he blinked slowly at Aiden when their eyes met.

Aiden flushed and looked away, out towards the rapidly changing shore line.

The Library was nowhere to be seen, lost in misty darkness. For timeless minutes, or perhaps hours, Aiden watched the featureless shore slide by.

The first change was the high, haunting sound of some kind of bird. The darkness did not lift, exactly, but it became transparent, no longer impenetrable. Aiden's breath caught when he finally understood what he was seeing.

A line of distinctly Egyptian-looking tombs clustered along the edges of the river. In each of the tombs, a faintly glowing soul, indistinct but unmistakable, sat in meditative prayer.

The place was peaceful, restful, but also suffused with a sense of deep sorrow. The air smelled faintly of incense, and other than the sounds of the occasional bird or a suspicious splash, there was perfect silence. Some of the souls saw him and nodded in greeting, while others stared blankly, lost and oblivious.

"They are pilgrims," Char said. His voice, solemn and gentle, sounded like paper brushing over sand. "Many souls arrive in the Underworld broken. Each is set on a journey to repair the damage, to find themselves, or forgive themselves. These souls have finished their journey, but not...successfully. They come here to be judged, to see if there is still hope. Depending on how they are judged, some will be given another chance at redemption or reincarnation, and some will allow themselves to be torn apart."

Char paused his rowing as they passed a soul whose indistinct eyes wept red light. "Some of those who seek judgment hope for vindication, for permission to give up their own self loathing. For them, the risk of oblivion is worth the possibility of a second chance."

Aiden nodded, deep sympathy making his eyes sting. He felt for these people, for this place, but he didn't feel any...any *belonging*.

Aiden's problem wasn't that he didn't like himself. God, how much easier it would have been if that had been his problem? No, his problem was that, no matter how much the people around him told him he *should* hate himself, he didn't.

Except...no. He shouldn't think of that as a problem. They'd been wrong about Hell, and they'd been wrong about that. No one *deserved* to hate themselves, even if they needed to change to be better.

Guilt still churned in his stomach, irrational guilt about his own failure to be like these souls who believed, perhaps correctly, that a simple judgment from a stranger could help them.

It wouldn't work for him. He'd known too many judges.

Aiden looked at Sam and was surprised to see his own sorrow and guilt mirrored on Sam's face. He was looking at the tombs as if searching for someone he knew was not there.

Carefully, Aiden moved from the floor of the boat to sit next to Sam.

Without taking his gaze off the shore, Sam shifted to let Aiden join him. "It was a long time ago, bunny. Nothing to fret about," he murmured absently, but he did not stop looking at the shore.

Aiden was acutely aware of Sam's presence next to him. There wasn't any body heat, but there was an *energy*, soft and solid at the same time. Aiden felt warmer for its proximity.

Aiden leaned into Sam and looked back to the shore.

The tombs varied in style as they moved along the river bank. While the place never lost its Egyptian aesthetic, many of the little temples looked like they were from other cultures, perhaps matching the beliefs of those inside them.

He caught the eyes of one soul, startled by the recognition on their face.

"Stop, please," Aiden said, almost absently.

Silently, Char moved the boat towards the little temple. Sam stayed unnaturally quiet, watching Aiden with steady curiosity.

The boat bumped softly against the bank, and Aiden clambered out, never looking away from the soul.

The soul had gone very, very still. Nothing could have made it more clear that the entity was dead—such stillness was impossible in a living creature. It was indistinct, like a statue whose features had worn away. The temple it knelt in was very old, plain, rough stone lit by a single unmelting wax candle.

"Nakia?" the soul whispered.

The name shivered through Aiden, familiar and correct, but he did not *remember* it.

"Nakia," the soul said, more certain. Bright tears filled the soul's eyes. "Oh, *Nakia*, I'm so, so sorry."

Aiden swallowed, and panicked slightly. "I—" he hesitated, then said, "please, don't apologize to me."

The tears ran down the soul's face in thick, sparkling lines. "But, who else can I apologize *to*? You were the one I wronged. You were the one who deserved better. I am *sorry*."

Aiden wanted to say *I don't remember you*, but instead, he found himself saying, "An apology isn't a coin you use to purchase forgiveness."

The soul flinched as if struck, and Aiden reached out to take the soul's hand. "Hey, no. Look, I forgive you. I forgave you a long time ago. I forgave you before my body was even cold."

As he said the words, he *knew* they were true, even though he couldn't remember why they were true. He continued, "But, forgiveness is for the one wronged, not for the one who did the wrong. What you need isn't *my* forgiveness. You, you need to forgive yourself, yeah? Which you can do, because you know what you did was wrong and have taken steps to stop it from happening again, right?"

The soul's mouth opened, then closed. "No. Not yet. I thought..."

Aiden knelt in front of the soul. “Hey, you’re here, right? In a completely different place? A world nothing like the one we knew each other in?”

Slowly, the soul nodded.

Aiden smiled gently. “Then that might be enough. The places we choose to go shape us as much as the people we choose to be with. Right?”

Again, the soul nodded. “Right.” Then the soul smiled. “Oh, Nakia, how I missed you. I never deserved you then, and now? You’ve grown so strong, so beautiful. Thank you for visiting me. Perhaps, one day, I will be the sort of person who deserves to spend time with you.”

The soul closed their eyes, and the candle flared up. It caught at the soul and they went up in flames in a flash, like they were made of dried paper soaked in oil.

Without thinking, Aiden threw himself on the soul, twisting and rolling, trying to smother the flames. He felt them licking at his own soul-body, but he bore down and ignored the heat.

The flames didn’t go out, but they did change. Instead of hungry red fire, they shifted into something else, shining with every color imaginable, like fractured sunlight. The fire spread to surround both of them, but it no longer tried to burn.

They rolled to a stop against the wall of the temple, still wreathed in flames, and Aiden blinked up at the soul, dazed and weightless. For a moment, the light revealed the soul’s face, achingly familiar, and something squeezed in his chest.

The soul smiled, and vanished.

There was a strange sensation of vacuum, of something draining away, and then nothing. The fire went out, and there was silence.

Aiden scrambled to his feet and out of the temple, which vanished the moment he left. He looked around wildly, and he could feel that his eyes were too wide.

"Where did they go?" he asked, trying not to panic.

"Reincarnated," Char said, their soft voice loud in the strange quiet. "Peacefully, and whole, near as I can tell. I don't know what you did in there, but whatever it was, it restored the soul enough to survive the transition intact."

Sam was looking at him with a strange, almost wondering expression, except he was trying to hide it behind cat-like inscrutability. "We couldn't see inside the temple, bunny, but whatever you did saved that soul," he said solemnly.

Aiden made his way back to the boat. "But I didn't do—" He couldn't finish. He wanted to, wanted to say *I didn't do anything*, but the words would not form on his tongue, in his throat.

He frowned. Why couldn't he say it?

Sam snorted and stretched luxuriously. "You're cute, bunny. Come on, off we go. This isn't our final stop, clearly."

Confused, Aiden carefully climbed back in, eyeing the strange water with even more suspicion than before.

The temples vanished into the darkness and the river grew narrower. Aiden felt the brush of a feather against the back of his neck, heard a murmured whisper of what sounded like approval, and the scent of incense intensified.

A bridge appeared ahead of them, covered in souls. On one side, Aiden could almost see the twists of fear and hope rising from the waiting souls like smoke. The walls of the bridge were too tall for Aiden to see what happened at the apex of the bridge, but the few souls that came out the other side were bright with elation, moving with purpose. They even seemed more distinct, cohesive, the shapes of the intact person far more clear than any of the souls on the other side.

As the boat drew closer, the bridge towered over them, titanic and majestic, but also oddly difficult to describe. It somehow gave the impression of both stone and steel, and even intricately carved wood, without actually being any of those things.

Sam physically shook himself and his sorrowed reverie fell away. He grinned at Aiden. "Scary tunnel time!"

They passed under the bridge.

Aiden felt reality around him slide and fracture into fluttering chaos. It reminded Aiden, with uncomfortable familiarity, of the beginning of a very intense psychedelic trip.

Images that made no sense flooded his mind—flowers that bloomed inside of flaming rainbows, monsters that ripped their faces off to reveal Halloween candy made of vegetables, old records of forgotten music that rolled themselves into cigars, and so, so much more that he had no way to even begin to understand.

The chaos overwhelmed every one of his senses. He smelled things that should have triggered memories but instead made him laugh, or cry, or scream. Sensations danced over his skin, light, teasing touches mixed impossibly with bruising, possessive hands. He felt things filling his mouth, his throat, everywhere, and he held himself carefully, yielding and soft, without resistance or gagging, and his hysteria became euphoric because he knew he had done well, pleased...someone.

There was a subtle shift in the chaos, like the twist-crack of a joint being popped. A flash of identifiable memory crashed over him, and he re-lived agony he felt in the days after the text from his father telling him his mother's attempted suicide was his fault and that he wasn't to contact them ever again.

But then he felt that memory fracture, shattering under the weight of years of perspective. Suddenly, for the first time ever he truly *believed* that it couldn't possibly have been his fault, that he'd been a child, that his parents had wronged him.

The onslaught ended.

Aiden wiped wetness away from his face, and he stared at the glittering dampness on his fingertips. The tears, if that's what they were, dried and left behind a faint dusting of iridescence. Something had settled inside him, and much like the beautiful rainbows left behind on his skin, his soul felt cleaner, more stable. He blew lightly on his hands, letting the shining motes vanish into the misty river.

He looked up, wanting to ask Sam what, exactly, the 'scary tunnel' *was*, but Sam wasn't there anymore.

Aiden's chest squeezed, but before he could truly panic he saw Char gesturing at the bow. Aiden spun, barely concerned with the way the boat swayed, and saw him.

Sam was stuffed into the little cubby under the seat at the bow of the boat. He'd gotten almost entirely into the cramped space except for his tail, which had poofed up like a bottle brush.

Aiden blinked, and then burst into hysterical laughter. Sam extracted himself and turned to give Aiden a perfectly scathing look before slinking over to sit next to Aiden again. He took his tail in hand and smoothed the fur down, but it poofed halfway up again no matter how many times he tried.

Aiden laughed even harder, unable to stop himself, overwhelmed by relief and the aftershock of the tunnel. Sam sniffed and looked away.

Aiden eventually calmed down enough to speak, and he bumped gently into Sam's shoulder. "So, now that we're through the scary tunnel, where is the chocolate?" Aiden asked, grinning. Sam looked absolutely baffled, and Aiden gestured vaguely. "Like, a Wonka bar?"

Sam continued to frown, clearly not following.

"Come on!" Aiden said, "You must have—oh. Oh, no!"

Of *course* he didn't understand. If Sam had really died in 1917 or whatever, he wouldn't have ever heard of Willy Wonka. Not even the book! The thought was so absurd he started laughing all over again.

Sam waited with a very disgruntled expression for Aiden to pull himself back together.

Aiden was just about done when Char asked, in his whisper-soft voice, "Is this some kind of American Halloween thing? Scary tunnels and chocolate? This is not the first time an American has asked for candy after passing under the Bridge."

Aiden lost it again.

When he finally stopped laughing, any lingering darkness from the tunnel had been banished. He wiped more tears from his face and wondered aloud, "Can we watch movies down here?"

Sam thought about it, and then shrugged, "Maybe? I've never tried. I've looked up plenty of movie references though, since every soul born in the last two hundred years is *obsessed* with them."

Aiden was shocked stupid for a solid thirty seconds. Somehow, it hadn't quite processed that Sam wouldn't have seen *any* movies. At all.

"*Ohmigod*," he said, "we *have* to find out if we can watch movies. I *need* to show you movies. Like, *so many* movies."

Then Aiden realized what he'd done by asking Sam to watch movies with him. He froze.

Sam smiled, slow and predatory. "Movies, huh? I think maybe I'd like you to show me *movies*."

Aiden felt the oddest sensation. Like his entire body was suddenly full of tiny bubbles. He nodded and said, *stupidly*, "Okay, it's a date then," and every tiny bubble in his body started popping at once. Sam smiled, and held Aiden with his eyes for a period of time Aiden did not care to measure. Eventually he started to tremble slightly.

Sam's tail curled around his waist and he started purring. Slowly, Aiden let himself lean back against Sam. That strange energy he'd sensed before intensified, filling Aiden with warmth and safety and hope.

He closed his eyes and the trembling stopped.

"So...why'd you think I would like the scary tunnel?" Aiden asked without opening his eyes.

Somehow Sam kept purring, even as he spoke. "Honestly? A hunch. Firstly, the Styx was just *there*, which I figured meant it was for you. When you ride the Styx you almost always need to pass under the bridge, so I just..." He shrugged. "I didn't think too hard about it. I've been through the tunnel dozens of times now, and while it doesn't get easier, I look forward to it now, you know? The Bridge shows you the truth of your fears, and... I dunno. Clarifies them? I just thought you might be up for it." Sam scratched lightly at Aiden's scalp, and Aiden shivered happily. "I, ah, didn't explain again. I'm sorry."

Aiden smiled, eyes still closed. "S'okay. I didn't ask. I could have."

The purring increased. "So, you liked it?"

Aiden thought about it. "It was horrible, but I feel really great now. So yeah, a lot."

Sam laughed.

Aiden thought wistfully about asking if Sam liked kinky things too, if he might like to try some things some time, and suddenly remembered about the coins. "Sam, do I need money?" Aiden felt himself tense, and he mourned the loss of peacefulness fiercely.

Sam must have felt his tension, because he wrapped an arm around Aiden. Aiden appreciated the gesture, even though it didn't help much.

"We don't have money, not like the kind you're used to, so no. But you don't really need it. Like, remember at the Hotel? A lot of stuff is like that, an agreement between you and someone else for mutual benefit."

Aiden nodded, feeling a tiny bit of the tension leave him, except... "What do you mean there is no money? I've seen you pay for things."

Sam bumped Aiden's shoulder gently. "Watching me that closely, huh? The money system here isn't a currency, it's a debt system. You start out with none, and you can gather wealth by doing favors, or you lose it if you accept favors. The Library keeps track, so don't worry about that."

Sam rolled his hand and nudged Aiden. "Look here, this coin? This was made special. It's not really money, it's more of a token. I had to go to a particular demon to get these." Sam nodded towards Char. "Our ferryman here only accepts these tokens in particular. Some of his Mantle-brothers accept other tokens. Manning the ferry is Char's job—he accepted it when he signed the contract for the Mantle."

Aiden swallowed. "Oh."

Sam wrapped an arm around Aiden's shoulders and squeezed lightly before letting go again. "You don't need to get a job, bunny. No one will make you. But most of us demons look for one eventually. It feels good to have that kind of purpose, you know?"

Aiden nodded. He'd always taken jobs because he needed the money, but no one had forced him into sex work in particular. That, he'd done because he liked it.

It was another one of those things he'd been told he should hate himself for, but didn't.

Would Sam still be his friend if he knew?

Sam continued, unaware of Aiden's growing fear. "Me, I'm a familiar. I have a contract with a witch on the mortal plane. It's one of the jobs you can take that allows you to visit the mortal plane, and you need special approval from the Triad to do it."

Aiden closed his eyes and tried not to borrow trouble, instead focusing on Sam's voice as he continued explaining.

"Lots of people only pursue hobbies, though. You don't even need productive hobbies— there aren't really penalties for going into debt, except that if you accept too many favors from someone in particular they can demand restitution. That goes to a judge, and a contract is worked out. So that's the biggest thing to watch out for." Sam's tail flicked back and forth. "The most important thing to remember is never make a deal with a demon without reading the fine print—you don't want to promise more than you can afford to give."

Aiden felt his melancholy crystallizing into a familiar, isolating sorrow. He opened his eyes and looked up at Sam. "So, trust no one?" Aiden could do that, he *knew* that, but...

Well. He'd started to hope. He shouldn't have. It was almost a relief, to know—

Sam straightened, startling Aiden out of his thoughts. He turned Aiden enough that he could cup Aiden's cheek with his hand, very careful not to let his claws scratch. He held Aiden there, gazes locked, searching.

Finally, "You can feel the truth here, yeah?"

Aiden nodded, hypnotized.

Sam brushed a thumb over Aiden's cheek bone. "Demons, souls in general, are exactly what they seem. The outside is the inside. What you see is what you get. You *need* to trust your instincts, bunny, they're going to be based on truth. If you feel like you shouldn't trust someone, you can and should feel free to run the fuck away, or punch them, whatever, but if you feel like you *can* trust someone, it's safe to." Sam did another one of his slow blinks.

If someone had pulled a line on him like that when he was alive, he would have run the other way without a second thought. Here, though, now, Aiden knew, in a way that should have been impossible, that Sam was being genuine. It was almost certainly what Sam meant about *feeling the truth.*

Aiden's hope flared back to life. "Okay."

All of a sudden he felt a *powerful* sense of resonance. His head snapped up and he found himself standing, staring at the shoreline. The boat rocked slightly with the motion, but Aiden was so captivated by the *feeling* that he barely noticed.

"I see we have arrived at our destination," Char said, and he began to steer the boat to the shore.

The shore was bright with a very different kind of sunlight than Nexus's. It seemed to come from nowhere in particular, or possibly everywhere. Every drop of dew or lap of water on the marshy shore shone with rainbows. The air was filled with dragonflies and butterflies and other, stranger things that still looked enough like butterflies and dragonflies that the distinction was unimportant.

The shore gave way immediately to a riot of flowers that absolutely should not have been growing together, some familiar like daisies and poppies and some strange and ridiculous, like African violets, or cactus flowers with no cactus, or cherry blossoms that drifted down from sky without a tree in sight.

"Holy shit, Char, is that *Elysium*? It's *real*?" said Sam, standing up next to Aiden.

"Some who are of it have called it that, but honestly, you mortal souls call all kinds of things Elysium, including Nexus. I imagine Aiden here would have called Nexus Elysium if he could have remembered to. There are other places like it as well, though most are not quite so...sparkly," Char said dryly, with only the slightest hint of sufferance.

Aiden heard the words they were saying, but he didn't really understand them. He hummed with that sense of recognition, and he was filled with a desperate need to run and roll in the tall grass and...frolic?

He blushed at his own childishness.

Sam groaned helplessly. "Look, now he's *blushing* again. And his bouncing is rocking the boat and it's making me feel sick. 'Nauseous' and 'turned on' are not a pleasant mix of sensations, let me tell you."

Aiden forced himself to stop bouncing, but he only started trembling instead. He grabbed Sam's hand in his excitement and was too distracted to feel self-conscious about it.

When the boat reached the shore, Aiden could smell the flowers, and it made him feel dizzy. He wanted to leap onto the shore immediately, but he impulsively hopped over to Char and gave him a hug first. Char accepted it with an unreasonable amount of dignity, and then Aiden tried to drag Sam with him into the Meadow.

Sam resisted.

Aiden looked back at him, uncomprehending. Sam looked stricken.

"I can't follow you here, bunny. It doesn't want me."

Aiden was suddenly clutching Sam's hand, feeling torn in two. His eyes felt huge in his head, and they burned.

He *had* to go.

He *couldn't* go, not without Sam, but he knew that was wrong, he *could* and he *had* to, but he was so afraid to go alone, not because he was afraid of the idea of being alone, but because...because...

He ached with a thought he couldn't quite convince himself he deserved to understand.

Sam smiled encouragingly at him, but his expression was so sad. Aiden desperately wanted to do something to banish the sorrow from them.

"Bunny, I need to go to work anyway," Sam said, clearly trying to soothe Aiden. "I'm getting a summons. I'll send a message to Esther for you, she's your therapist. She'll come get you when it's time if you don't find a path back to Nexus on your own. Once you're done, she can take you back to Nexus. Or here, if you want, if you don't want to go back to Nexus, if you decide you'd rather st—"

Aiden kissed him.

At first, he just pressed his lips to Sam's to stop him from talking, from saying words Aiden didn't want Sam to need to say, but Aiden immediately wanted more. When Sam wrapped a hand around Aiden's neck, claws resting lightly against his skin, Aiden drew Sam's tongue into his mouth, sucking gently.

Sam moaned softly with pleasure and Aiden *melted*. Sam's tongue was strong and silky and tasted amazing, spicy and herbal and warm. Aiden drank in the flavor, wanting more, more, *more*.

Suddenly too weak to stand, Aiden found himself pulled into Sam's chest, supported and safe.

He didn't need to breathe. He could kiss *forever* and he didn't even need to breathe.

He didn't want to end the kiss, but the pull of the Meadow was getting stronger. He broke away, gasping reflexively, and clung to Sam with all his might. He buried his face in Sam's neck and inhaled Sam's scent—herbs and something light and fresh that he did not have the words for. It momentarily overpowered the meadowy smell of flowers that *pulled* at him.

Only momentarily, though. He had to go.

He whispered, *promising*, "I'll see you later. Maybe tonight? Come find me in Nexus." Aiden looked up at Sam's face and said, shocked by his own forwardness, "We have a date."

He turned away, half giving in to the pull of the Meadow and half running from his own bold words. In one single motion he flung himself from the boat and onto the shore.

GREATER PROVIDENCE RI, SEPTEMBER 9TH 47 YAR

Emily watched the footage from the subway again.

The Subway, an entirely post-Rapture construction part of the wave of high-tech urban infrastructure that defined all witch-run cities, had no camera blind spots. The *thing* still appeared out of nowhere.

Emily paused and clicked the video forward frame by frame.

There. The oily black mass seeped into the subway from somewhere in the ceiling. Emily cross-referenced a map she had opened on another screen and confirmed it was from the same direction she'd approached from. She did some more cross checking, and determined the thing might have been using the electrical utility conduits to move around underground.

Not that solid surfaces seemed to stop it. Maybe it was a speed thing? It seemed to move very quickly when it fled down the tunnel.

Emily let the video play for a few more seconds. Olivia stood in the passenger waiting area looking at her phone, mixed into the rest of the mid-morning crowd. She suddenly shivered, as if realizing the thing was there, and she looked up and saw it.

The indistinct, pulsing darkness, scared Olivia *badly.* She jerked back, dropping her phone and slamming into the person standing behind her. Emily paused the video again and watched, once again frame by frame, as the thing seemed to grab hold of her and pull her in. The girl writhed, screaming, desperate to get away. Around her, other people were starting to panic and rush for the exits.

They weren't fast enough. Once the thing had pulled the poor girl inside itself fully, which took only seconds, it formed itself around her shape. The darkness then seemed to sink into her body. When it was gone, the only sign something had happened to the girl was her sudden, mad grin when she looked up at the fleeing people around her.

Again, frame by frame, Emily rewatched the footage, looking for something, *anything*, to indicate what the thing might be, but there was nothing.

What happened next was worse than Emily had imagined. Even seeing the aftermath hadn't prepared her. She forced herself to keep watching, looking for details. *There.* She paused and went back a few frames. Olivia's hand was about to plunge into some poor victim's stomach and the darkness was visibly coating her hand. She snapped a capture of the frame and kept looking, finding every instance the darkness showed itself.

In less than two minutes Olivia, or, rather, whatever was controlling her, had shredded and *eaten* chunks out of everyone who hadn't made it up the stairs. The thing possessing Olivia stood, back and chest heaving with exertion, gnawing on a hunk of bloody flesh. The expression on its face was contemplative as it eyed the stairs for a few seconds.

With no one left to stop it, the thing walked up the stairs.

Emily knew what happened next, but she still went through the smattering of different videos gathered from store fronts and bystanders with phones. Then she watched the rest of the footage until the end, when light exploded out of Olivia's chest and the evil fled into the darkness.

So far no one had asked her about the flash of light. It was obviously Divine, but maybe no one who'd seen the video was opposed to accepting a little Divine help, even if it was frowned upon inside the city. Whatever that thing was, it was evil, and they might need Divine help to stop it. If the witches could tolerate divine healers, surely they could tolerate whatever this seal thing was?

Either way, she didn't have time to dwell on it.

She checked her messages again and was relieved to see that Will was waiting for her down in the lobby. He'd still been at the hotel she'd booked him last night, but hadn't checked his phone until he woke up about half an hour ago.

Emily finished compiling the screen shots she'd organized into one file, copied them into the case database, and went to get Will.

When Emily got to the lobby, she felt her seal pulse at her. She looked around, and the seal let her know the problem was Will and his cat.

Stupid thing. No matter what it thought, she knew Will was an ally.

Her trust in the seal eroded a little bit more.

Will appeared to be speaking to someone on speakerphone, which was somewhat out of character for the normally reserved witch. It was loud, too, though the deputy working the desk didn't seem to mind, which was also more weird.

Emily paused. Will didn't even have his phone out. What was going on?

<<—and I want to tug on them *so badly* but he doesn't even realize he *has* them yet,>> said a voice coming from somewhere inside Will's bag, <<It's *torture*. But he looks at you with these, these *eyes*, and they practically beg you to fuck him. Like, consensually, *obviously*. I want to—>>

"Spare me the gory details, Sam," Will said, very quietly. "So you have a date with him tonight, great. Detective Scott is here, so I need to focus on something besides your new beau, okay?"

Sam? As in, the cat?

It was confirmed when the cat poked its head out of the bag and looked around. <<Oh, we're working for curls and curves again? Tell her I need to be done by, like, four. Aiden's got his first therapy session, and I want to be there when he's done. He wants to show me some movie. Do you—>>

"Is your cat talking?" Emily asked, incredulous. Both Will and the cat turned to look at her.

<<"You can hear him/me?">> they asked together. Sam continued alone, <<Since when! She couldn't hear me literally *yesterday*!>>

"Yesterday, you didn't talk out loud like this!" Emily hissed at them. Except, maybe he wasn't talking out loud today, either. The cat's mouth certainly wasn't moving. She looked around, and noticed a few people giving *her* worried glances. Clearly, they did not hear a cat talking.

"I need more coffee," Emily said, loudly, and the glances stopped. Lack of coffee on a day like this would excuse quite a lot in the eyes of the GPI staff.

<<But seriously, how? Are you a witch now? You don't smell like a...>> The cat's nose twitched. <<Ohhhhhhh. Ugh. *Really?*>> Sam's ears pressed back against his head. <<Gross. Leave Will and me alone, okay? We're your friends, no need to attack us.>>

Will was looking between the two of them, baffled. Emily had no explanation except...

The seal. It was still vibrating slightly against her skin, and it felt almost itchy. Emily *did not* want to talk about her late-night visitor with a witch, even one she considered a friend, so instead she said, "I'm not going to attack my favorite consultant. Look, we'll have to figure out this whole talking-cat thing later. We have something of an emergency. Speaking of which—"

<<Ha! Witch. Okay, I believe you. For now.>>

"—*Will*, can you follow me?"

Emily led Will and Sam back to her little corner desk. Sam, apparently unconcerned by Emily's new ability to hear him, went right on talking about his not-yet boyfriend. He gave overly effusive descriptions of his beauty and personality, chattered about taking him to some library, and gushed about how he was already a fully registered demon even after only being 'put together' for a single day. Will, apparently used to Sam's prattling, ignored him.

Despite the seriousness of the situation in the subway, Emily found herself unable to do the same. "Wait. This 'new soul'. You were touring him around *Hell*. And today you took him to the library to sign up as a demon? So he's a demon now? This guy's soul just *became* a demon because you took him to a *library*?" Emily wasn't sure how she felt about that.

Sam, apparently, hadn't thought about it like that. <<I...oh no. You don't think I tricked him into becoming a demon, do you?>>

Emily *hadn't* thought that, before.

Sam yowled mournfully, and Emily was pretty sure *that* was actually audible. <<Oh Fuck. Oh *Fuck*. I didn't tell him! I never explained what it meant! I just thought because the Triad told me to take him there everything was good, but I didn't make sure he knew what he was signing up for! Divine *fucking* shit, what have I done?>> He sounded like he was crying.

Sam yowled again, as if in pain, and Will and Emily looked at each other, unsure what to do. Will gestured desperately at the bag at his side, and mouthed, *say something*, as if this was somehow her fault.

Since it might be, slightly, Emily awkwardly said, "Um, Sam, you, ah, didn't mean to trick him, right? So, when you see him tonight, you need to tell him, okay? Tell him, and apologize and, um, let him decide if he wants to forgive you?"

While Emily was pretty sure her advice was good, it was not the right thing to say to get Sam to calm down. He yowled again. <<What if he doesn't forgive me! He *shouldn't*!>>

Fortunately, Will took over from there. He picked Sam out of the bag and held him, scratching behind his head. "I'm sure he'll forgive you, Sam, if he's as sweet as you say. When you see him tonight, make sure you tell him, and apologize. It's not like you forced him, right? The Library wouldn't have signed him up if he was unwilling."

Sam stopped yowling and said, calmer, <<Yeah. Right. But—>>

"We need to do some work now, okay? We'll make sure to send you off by four."

<<Okay,>> Sam agreed, miserably.

Sam was mercifully quiet after that, and Emily refocused back on the case. She showed Will, and Sam—since he was still in Will's arms—the excerpts from the footage that contained the thing. She'd edited out as much of the horror as she could, but there was no hiding what had happened.

Will swallowed, and looked very worried. "I've never heard of something like that. Sam? What is it?"

Sam was staring off into space, whiskers twitching. After a second, he shook his head. <<I...shit. There's nothing in the Records that matches.>> Will's eyes went wide, and Sam continued, sounding seriously worried, <<Whatever that thing is, it's new. We should...we should go to the scene. Maybe I can pick up a scent you can use to scry its location.>>

Emily nodded. Even though taking Will and Sam to the scene was what she'd wanted to do, she still felt bad about it. Will, still focused on the screen, looked just as miserably resigned as she felt.

They took Emily's car and left Will's bike in the GPI garage after Will loaded his spell kit into Emily's trunk. She used her lights to cut through the mild traffic. It was easier this time of day, with fewer people on the street, and only a few unmanned delivery trucks and municipal buses.

Emily called ahead, and the deputy in charge of the scene gladly handed her back the reins, especially after she said she had Will with her. The massacre had them all spooked.

She felt a rather unpleasant tingle as they passed through the wards. It was not something she had ever experienced, or even really noticed before. She rubbed absently at her chest, and Sam gave her a knowing cat blink.

When they got out of the car, the first thing that hit them was the smell. Emily hadn't remembered it being that bad, but apparently a few hours made a massive difference. Even outside the subway it smelled like a slaughterhouse. Sam hissed, and Will pulled out a cloth facemask and traced a glowing symbol on it with his dull knife before putting it on.

One of the forensic techs handed Emily a mask, and wordlessly she handed it over to Will when he held up his knife, offering to spell it for her. He drew the same symbol, and when she put the mask on the smell was gone. It tingled unpleasantly where it touched her skin, but the seal could fuck right off if it thought she was going to take the mask off.

They both got a set of scrubs to put over their clothing, as well as gloves and wraps for their shoes. Will took Sam out of the messenger bag, which he left with one of the staff, and held him inside the scrubs.

The scene that greeted them at the bottom of the stairs was still rough. Emily realized she'd probably been in shock before, because it hit her hard. Some of the body parts had been removed, but medical technicians still had a long way to go.

Sam stuck his head out from Will's shirt and hissed again. <<Shit,>> he said, <<It smells vaguely demonic, but...*wrong*. Like it's...fuck, like it's *corrupted*. Will, I think we need to report this right away.>>

"I agree. Emily, I need to take this to the Covens. What's the procedure?"

"We need to go back to the station. We can start filing the release forms on the way, and I'll give you a conference room where you can run a liaison operation, if that's alright. First, though, I'd like you to try to scry for the thing. It's still out there. "

Will nodded. "Yeah. You sure you don't want one of the more politically savvy witches to act as liaison for this?"

Emily looked at him flatly. "I'm sure. I trust *you*."

Will smiled and rubbed the back of his neck, embarrassed. "Thanks."

Will spoke to one of the techs, and after some minor paperwork and remarkably little fuss they handed over the materials he needed.

"Let's set the spell up outside the wards. I don't want to interfere with them, and, well, I definitely don't want whatever this corruption is messing with my magic."

Emily nodded and they squelched their way back up to the street. They stripped out of the scrubs, sanitized, and walked back to where Emily's car was parked.

"Is here good?"

Will nodded and got to work.

Once the circle was set, they started filling out forms while it charged. When they'd filled out everything they could and were waiting for replies from the various bureaucracies, Will went back to the circle.

Nothing was different from the last time Will used a tracking spell. The seal was buzzing angrily, increasing steadily in intensity as the spell charged. Emily could only assume it was the same prejudice that had it buzzing about Sam.

She might have been mistaken.

This time, when Will broke the circle, there was a violent flash of green light. The crystal turned black and exploded.

Sam hissed, and the shards deflected away from Will. Emily's seal pulsed once, hard, and the shards deflected away from her as well. Her car wasn't quite as lucky, but fortunately the shards were too small to leave anything other than insignificant scratches. The self-healing paint would take care of them in time.

"Shit," Will said, shaking his head. "I don't even know what that means." He looked over at Emily. "I need to talk to some colleagues about this. Meet you back at the office? I'm pretty sure one of those forms covered the kinds of questions I need to ask, but I'll call if not."

Emily nodded, still staring at the black shards. "Sure. Do you want help cleaning this up?"

Will considered the destroyed circle. "Can I just throw up a ward around it and leave it? I'd like to have someone else take a look, see if they can make sense of it."

"Yeah, sure, I'll have one of techs yellow-tape the area, too." Emily's seal pulsed again, insistently, and she looked towards the east. "You can borrow the car if you want to get back to the station. I'll have it catch back up after. There's something else I'd like to follow up on."

Will smiled and adjusted his glasses on his nose before pulling out some chalk. "Okay, great. Thank you!"

Sam licked his paw, not looking at Emily. <<Try not to kill anyone we know while we're gone, yeah?>>

Will gave Sam a funny look, but Emily thought she understood. "I won't."

Sam nodded. <<Good. Let's get this ward up so I can go, I wanna report this as soon as possible, and I still want to go on my date. You can't stop living just because you're battling an unknown dangerous monster, right?>>

"Sure, Sam," Will said amicably and knelt to start his ward.

Emily took a few minutes to make sure the area would be properly defended, double checked to verify Will had been officially appointed by the GPI and the Covens as the official magical liaison for the duration of the investigation, and stopped ignoring her seal.

It's that way.

Emily started walking, following who-the-fuck-knew-what trail.

GREATER PROVIDENCE RI, SEPTEMBER 9TH 47 YAR

Penny handed June another bag of blood. The corpse Penny had found was relatively fresh and, most importantly, not embalmed. Where she'd gotten it, June had no idea.

They'd considered just transferring June over to the new body, because apparently that was something Penny knew how to do, but June had recoiled at the idea of losing all the flesh memory she'd stored up in her current one. Plus, neither of them knew what effect a full transfer might have on June's Geas, something Penny also knew a surprising amount about.

"So," June said, burning through the last of the blood she'd just drunk in order to properly absorb a new arm, leaving her ravenous all over again. "Do we talk about how you knew it was me at the door? Or how you know so much about vampires?"

The arm was a little longer than she needed, so she had to move the extra bone elsewhere in her body. Conveniently, there were plenty of places where she still had to shed and replace sun-damaged bone. Inconveniently, it took quite a lot of blood to do so, especially since the flesh was no longer warm.

Attuning the cold flesh to her body wasn't painful, exactly, but it felt like the worst pins and needles she'd ever had when she was alive. She grimaced as the sensation intensified. She'd already absorbed most of the corpse's organs, including the skin, and she was using the new, fresh flesh to slowly replace all the putrefied bits of her own body that continued to fall away.

Penny sighed and handed June the last two bags of blood. June sucked them down, one after another. They were absolutely vile, tasting, ridiculously, *disgustingly*, of vomit. She didn't really have functioning taste buds, so it must be from some kind of extremely unfortunate magical interpretation of what something 'should' taste like when it was, essentially, predigested.

Old, preserved, and separated blood was just *not* what she was meant to eat, even if it did technically suffice for the mechanical purposes of repairing her damaged body. The only thing that saved, or perhaps damned her, was that she lacked a gag reflex, so there was nothing to stop her from choking the stuff down.

When she was finished, she had enough fuel to get herself back to looking human. She put on Sofia's hair and face since it was easiest, but left her body mannequin basic, not bothering with biologically correct details.

The chunks of rotted flesh had sloughed off in heaps around her, but, mercifully, she'd started to freeze in the hours Penny had been gone, so the smell was no longer overwhelming.

Penny still hadn't answered her question. Instead, she'd retreated out of the freezer and gone to fetch a garbage bag and cleaning supplies.

With a huff, June started picking up the chunks of squishy flesh and dumping them in the bag. When she'd gotten everything that could be picked up, Penny handed her the cleaning supplies and went upstairs to leave the remains in the sun where it would rot away to nothing in seconds.

"You know, if you have a UV light, we could use it to clean up down here in seconds," June commented idly.

"Don't have one. I'll be back in a minute."

They didn't say anything else until the freezer was spotless and smelled only of the orange-scented cleaning solution. They got the rest of the basement floor and stairs— everything that hadn't been exposed enough for sunlight to do the job for them.

When it was done, June crossed her arms over her bare chest and waited.

Which was possibly slightly unfair, since June arguably had just as much to explain, but whatever.

"June, I..." Penny started, then faltered, looking pained. "It's not... I can't—"

June held up a hand and affected a sigh. "No, wait, stop." June really *didn't* have the right to push her, and she found herself trusting Penny completely, to a degree which might have startled her if she could only hold onto the desire to worry about it. Since she couldn't, she said, "The only thing that matters to me is that, for whatever reason, you not only recognized me, but you saved me. Can you at least confirm that you're a witch?"

Penny looked immensely relieved, her warm brown eyes finally meeting June's currently blood-red ones. "Yes, I'm a witch. It's not even a secret. I thought you knew." There was an uncomfortably long pause. "So what the hell happened to you?"

June wearily sat on a box and threw her hands up. "The fuck if I know. There was this...this *creature*. It was demonic, maybe, but it was wrong, like, tainted or something, and it was really fucking powerful. It tried to, I don't know, eat me, and so I ran. It didn't follow me into the sunlight, but I could feel it like, below the surface of the ground. I knew it would follow me into whatever dark place I could get to so I just... I ran here. I thought..." June realized she *hadn't* thought, really. It had just been her only idea. In hindsight it didn't make much sense.

Penny's face had gone grey, and she was frantically looking up something on her phone. She turned it around and showed June a picture of a screen shot of...of the fucking *thing*, on a subway, swallowing some poor girl. Some poor girl that June *recognized*, slightly, though she couldn't quite recall where from.

"Is this what attacked you?" Penny asked quietly, already seeing the answer on June's face.

"Oh shit," June whispered, not knowing what it meant, but instinctively certain it was *very* bad. "Who, um, that's her. What happened?"

"She murdered fifty people. Or rather, that black horror *possessed* her and murdered fifty people and then left her there. Do you recognize her?"

June almost did, but the girl's face was twisted with fear, and she couldn't quite. "Um, maybe?"

"The girlfriend."

"Oh *fuck*. Fuck." June's mind skittered from thought to thought, trying to make sense of what that meant. "But, *fuck*, how? He... It was two fucking days ago!" It had taken June twenty fucking years to pull herself together after she was released from the oblivion behind the seal durring the breaking, and another twenty to convince Lillian to let her become a vampire. Also, the Triad wouldn't let something like that fucking *nightmare* wreak havoc anywhere, let alone the mortal plane.

Penny looked just as upset as June was. "The Covens are meeting tonight to try to figure out what this thing is. I...we need to tell them everything."

June didn't even have a chance to process that last statement before another thought made her go cold. "What if it finds me? Fuck, how has it not already?"

Penny waved vaguely around them. "The wards on the building? Carla installed every ward known to mankind for me when I moved in. It must not be able to sense you through them. If it could have, it would have found you hours ago. Maybe. Shit." Penny dug her hands into her thick hair and pressed the heels of her hands into her temples. "The only way to know for sure is if you stepped outside, but without knowing what the thing is there's no way to keep you safe from it. Not unless..." Penny looked thoughtful.

June was not particularly enamored with the idea of never leaving this building again, but she was willing to consider it. "Unless?" June said for lack of anything useful to add.

Penny went over to a safe in the back corner of the basement. June waited while she opened it and fished around for a few minutes before pulling out an amulet. She tossed it over to June, who caught it reflexively.

She nearly dropped it. As soon as her skin made contact with the amulet, her whole body started tingling. She felt a flush of warmth and her senses immediately dulled. The room appeared to grow much dimmer, and a wave of weakness settled into her muscles. She itched like crazy as her flesh shifted, forced into a perfect replica of a living body, including a *heartbeat.* She felt the amulet pulse lightly in time with it.

June stared at the amulet in complete awe. She'd heard of such things, but the amount of magic and blood it took to make one was astonishing.

They were also *very* illegal. Like, *Treaty* illegal.

"Did you make this? How long will it last?" she asked, breathlessly.

June wondered if maybe she should reflect on just how excited she was to have something so incredibly dangerous.

Maybe later.

Right now, she was *breathless*, because she was *breathing*. She didn't need to think about it to do it, but she couldn't help paying attention to it now.

She hadn't needed to breathe in *decades.*

"Six months of continuous use, and yes, Dorothy and I made it," Penny said, unable to hide her smugness.

June didn't know who the fuck Dorothy was, or Carla for that matter, but that wasn't the point. June looked up at Penny, awestruck. "I can't pay you for this. Not with money, not without pulling some kind of heist. Gods, how did you even *make* it? I'd offer you any service you wanted in exchange, but I'd do that already. How can I..."

Penny smiled cryptically. "Don't worry about it. But let's see if the thing can find you outside the wards with that on. I don't think it will, but the sooner we find out the better."

June felt her heart rate increase in response to her sudden spike of fear. It was really weird. "Okay. Oh man, this is wild," she said, feeling her head rush slightly as she stood up too fast. Her body felt delicate and *loud*. All the normal living organs were in place and functioning. She'd been a little short on mass when it happened, so she was now built like a ballet dancer— not exactly skeletal, but with very little in the way of curves. Intellectually, she knew she was probably not going to fall over in a stiff wind, but compared to her normal vampiric strength she certainly felt like she might.

The fact that she had to breathe slightly harder after running up the stairs didn't help. Again, she probably wasn't unfit by normal human standards, but she *felt* like she was. Also not being able to *flicker* made her feel vulnerable.

It was *amazing*. Like standing on the edge of a cliff and looking down.

As soon as the sun, which was shining through the window, hit her skin, she instinctively flinched. When nothing happened, and her heart continued to beat in time with the amulet, now hanging around her neck, she marveled instead. She held up her hand to the light and admired the way the sun shone through her fingernails, like her hand was glowing with power.

Penny went around the back of the bar and rummaged around for a second before tossing her a t-shirt and jeans. "That's all I have for extra clothing. It's going to be way too big though."

"I have some things back at home. If we're going to see if this corrosive ooze-monster can find me, I could walk over and back." June put on the definitely-too-big clothes and the two of them walked outside.

The first moments of full sunlight were almost overwhelming. Even through her dulled senses, it was so *bright*. She felt lightheaded as her body reacted to her deeply ingrained fear of the direct sun, and she gratefully took the sunglasses Penny offered her.

"Let's take my bike. It will take too long for you to walk."

June spent the entire ride oscillating between fear and exhilaration. It wasn't June's first time on a motorcycle, but it was her first time as a living human. When she'd been actually alive, the only ways to get around had been walking, running, and maybe a canoe. The experience was *significantly* different when she was breathless, windswept, and inches from disaster.

Gods, it was broad daylight! If they crashed, she couldn't even take the amulet off.

When they pulled up in front of her apartment, June almost collapsed getting off the bike. Her legs were weak, and she felt oddly tingly after the constant vibration and wind.

"I'll wait here and keep the bike ready. If you see the thing, we'll be out of here in seconds."

The fear returned in force as she approached the condo. The door was still closed, and there was no visible damage, like nothing had happened. June hesitated at the threshold of the last bit of direct sunlight and focused on searching for that sense of doom that had preceded the thing's attack.

She felt nothing, so she slowly opened the door.

Her apartment was exactly as she'd left it— keys sitting on the plate by the door, guitars and amps and other instruments blessedly undamaged, though her couch was definitely toast.

There was no lingering smell of corruption or ruin. Just broken furniture and nothing.

June changed quickly, shoved some extra clothing into a bag and grabbed her phone, wallet, and keys. Even though the thing didn't appear to be coming for her, she wasn't going to tempt fate by hanging around somewhere it knew and could get to, even in the daytime.

When she walked out, Penny was talking to a snake. The small black and gold creature had looped itself around her arm. Both Penny and the snake looked over to her, and Penny looked like she was ready to speed off if June said the word.

"Done already?" Penny asked, surprised. June held up her small bag and nodded. She locked the door behind her before turning around.

The snake bobbed its head once and said, "Pleasure to finally meet you. I am Lor, familiar to Penelope."

"Uh, hi. I'm June, Vampire." A thought occurred to June, "Oh, wait, you should call me Sofia, that's the identity this face uses." June turned to Penny. "If I take the amulet off, can I pick a different face? Nevermind, not worth the risk. Sofia's face is fine."

The two of them nodded, but Penny added, "You can take it off for a bit if you want behind the wards back at the bar. Without physical contact, it will turn off and you'll revert back to your normal vampiric self." Penny gestured at her bike. "Come on. You can stay in the basement at the bar for now. That way you'll still be safe if you take it off. Probably better that you do—if you leave it on too long you'll need to eat and sleep, which I recommend avoiding. One of the side effects of the amulet is horrible nightmares."

June nodded, but hesitated, still unsure. She kept having the feeling that there was *something* she was missing, some obvious thing about Penny and Lor. It wasn't bad, and she still had that instinctive and unwavering trust of Penny, but it bothered her that she couldn't understand *why*. It was as if every time she tried to have the thought it slipped away, like water through fingers.

Penny saw her frustration and winced sympathetically, but she didn't say anything.

June grumbled nonsensically under her breath and climbed on the bike.

"I will take my leave. See you later, June," Lor said and puffed away in a flash of green fire.

When they got back to the bar, there was a police car waiting outside. June tensed up, still not quite used to the way her body reacted to fear so *strongly*. She felt like a wild animal, all fast heartbeats and short quick breaths, and the sensation made her dizzy. It was starting to get overwhelming, and she swallowed hard, forcing herself to calm down. She couldn't fleshcraft away any of the annoying biological responses, so instead she just focused on keeping her breathing even.

Penny must have felt her tension at the sight of two people stepping out of the car. She put a hand on June's shoulder and murmured, "It's fine, I'll handle this. I recognize the plate. Shit, we need a story about why you're staying here."

"Bad breakup, I don't want to be home alone for the next few days," June said, thinking quickly. "My eyes are all watery from the freaking wind anyway, and I'm excited to try out mortal crying." As soon as she said it, she realized there was a tightness in her throat, a response to her stress and frustration. She could probably use it as a trigger. "Honestly, I think I might need to cry anyway. It's been a stressful day," she finished, a little hoarsely.

Penny gave June's shoulder a slight squeeze. "Good news is, no one will suspect anything with you all out in the daylight like this. Change of plans. I'm going to tell the GPI and the Covens about a vampire who showed up dead on my doorstep this morning. It was only able to get a few words out about the black thing coming after it before it dissolved completely. Lor will tell the real details directly to the Triad down in the Underworld. No one here will go looking for you."

June nodded, feeling her tension ease slightly. It was a good story.

Penny went over and unlocked the door, and June followed behind her with her bag slung over her shoulder. June was still wiping her eyes, trying to get them to stop watering. She kept wanting to just turn off her tear ducts, but every time she tried she felt the thump of her heart beat and she couldn't *do* it.

The frustration made her eyes burn and water even more. She made a big production of trying to suck it up, rubbing her eyes and then pressing the heels of her hands to her face and taking a deep breath. That actually did work, and so she turned to give the investigator and Penny a watery smile.

When she did, she got her first look at the investigator, and her stupid living heart did a little flip. The woman was *gorgeous*, with dark red hair coiling in thick curls pulled back from her face in a messy bun. She had a muscular, healthy frame with luscious curves. Her eyes were a startling blue framed by long, thick lashes. No makeup, and they were slightly red-rimmed with exhaustion, but that didn't detract from their intensity—they looked huge and also kind of badass when paired with the firm set to her jaw and sharp clarity of her expression.

June was very unprepared for the way her body responded, flushing hot and cold at the same time before settling at a warm hum in the pit of her stomach. It was ridiculous, and it shredded her control. June found herself blushing and stammering in a breathy whisper, "Uh, hi."

Penny turned to look at her and obviously suppressed a groan. "Detective Scott, this is my friend Sofia. She's staying here for a few days."

Detective Scott locked gazes with June, at first looking surprised, and then confused. "Nice to meet you, Sofia." She continued to hold

June's gaze, silent for just a hair too long, and then, "If you don't mind, I need to speak with Ms. Reed about a case."

June's breathing was shallow, and the blood in her stupid human body wasn't anywhere near where it was supposed to be, but she managed to gesture her assent with a casual shrug.

The Detective's face was still professionally neutral, but she swallowed before she nodded and turned to Penny. "Is there somewhere private we can talk? I, well, what do you know about the incident in the subway?"

Penny smiled enigmatically and led the detective into her office. June went over to a couch in one of the moody little lounge areas and let herself fall into it.

Being human was physically exhausting, and *emotionally*, ugh, even worse. She let her head fall back against the magically clean cushions and tried desperately to *not* crush on a freaking *detective* just because she was smoking hot.

It wasn't a winning battle.

June was still brooding when Detective Scott stepped back into the main room, a small frown on her face.

"Done already?" June asked. Her voice was rougher than normal, and a little too high-pitched. It made her sound vulnerable, which, fine, she *was* and she was supposed to pretend to be also, but that didn't mean she liked it.

Detective Scott shrugged. "Ms. Reed asked me to step out while she called a few people."

June sat up. The detective had a good poker face, but June had been reading subtle body language as a means of survival for years. Detective Scott was pissed.

"Witches are a cagy bunch, huh?" June said, thinking of her own frustrating mysteries. Was there something in her vampiric contract that she wasn't allowed to remember? How the hell could she ever verify that?

Detective Scott smiled, seemingly in spite of herself, and leaned against the edge of the bar. It highlighted the gorgeous swell of her hip. "Yeah. So, how did you end up staying here?"

June told herself the detective was just curious. This woman was an investigator, and investigators were always nosy, even when they weren't on a case. "My ex showed up at my house this morning. I, uh, didn't want to be home alone." She tried to sound both nonchalant and defensive, just the right mix to fit her story. Normally it would have been easy, but her stupid body kept *doing* and *feeling* and it made it much harder to perform with her usually perfect skill.

Detective Scott's expression softened, and it transformed her face. June felt herself flush again, and she swore she could actually hear her heart beating faster.

"That sucks. Have you known Penny long?"

June shook her head. "Uh, no, not really, but my ex was, um, a witch, so I came here. Thoughts and Prayers has a reputation as a safe place."

June had no idea if that was true. It could be.

Detective Scott nodded. "That makes sense." She hesitated, then, "You know, there's some resources—"

The door to Penny's office opened, and Detective Scott cut off. "Sorry, I'll be right back out."

June slouched back and worried her lip with her teeth.

Why shouldn't she ask out the hot detective? It would only make her cover stronger, right? Well, unless something went wrong, or June let something slip, or a terrible, horrible monster tried to eat her in the middle of dinner or whatever.

But what other option did she have? Sit here in Penny's basement, worrying herself mad?

June got up and dug around behind the bar for something to write with. There wasn't any parchment paper, of course, but a napkin would do. Penny had really nice ones, too, embossed with the bar's logo, super-absorbent while also being tough enough to really use for cleaning. Not the best writing material, but good enough for the marker June found that Penny probably kept around for spellwork.

As soon as the door to the office opened again, June was ready. The detective's gaze went right to June as she walked over, smiling intensely. Penny, who was standing behind the detective, frowned when she caught sight of June, looking positively defeated, and maybe a little mad.

She didn't say anything, though.

"Call me if you want to go out. Toss it if you don't." June handed her the napkin and held her gaze for a charged moment.

Detective Scott blinked at her, startled, and accepted the napkin. She opened her mouth to speak when her phone let out a shrill chime.

"Sorry, I, um, I need to go. Nice meeting you." Detective Scott slipped the napkin into her pocket and left with the phone pressed to her ear.

THE MEADOW

When Aiden turned around, both the boat and Sam were gone. A powerful ache, and a flutter of panic, drove his eyes closed. Resolutely, he took in a deep breath of air scented with uncountable wildflowers all combined in harmony, letting it fill him up with soft tranquility. He tipped his head back to let the gentle sunlight fall on his face.

He was being ridiculous. One kiss, no matter how magical, did not justify this level of attachment. He'd known Sam for less than a *day*. There was absolutely no logical reason for him to feel so cast adrift over a little temporary separation.

The problem was that Sam was literally his only friend in this strange afterlife he'd found himself in. It would be all too easy for Aiden to drown himself in Sam, and that was a *terrible* way to start a relationship.

If a relationship was even what Sam wanted.

He must, right? Why else would he have kissed Aiden back so thoroughly? Unless Sam was just—

Something brushed against Aiden's nose and he jumped, his whole body tingling with the absence of a thumping heart.

A butterfly, which must have briefly landed on his nose, flew around his head once and then fluttered off. Aiden huffed and shook himself lightly.

The butterfly was right—nothing good would come of standing here and worrying himself silly. He took in another deep breath and marveled at the way it made him feel both peaceful and energized, like he should both take a nap and romp around chasing butterflies he had no intention of catching.

Aiden started walking in no particular direction, brushing his hands lightly against soft petals. The flowers grew chaotically, some down by his feet and some towering over his head like over-sized sunflowers. Unlike a normal meadow, there was very little in the way of grass, with only soft moss covering the ground between the forest of flowers.

Aiden paused to take off his shoes and socks before tying the laces together and hanging the shoes around his neck—it felt wrong to step on the moss in shoes. He half wished he could also take his clothes off too, but he didn't want to be caught without them.

He...wasn't ready to be quite that bold. Not on purpose, anyway.

The more he walked, the more that sense of peace pressed itself on him, crowding out the ever-present knot of fear that was not, apparently, a fixed part of his soul.

His anxiety was not *gone*, exactly, but it felt more hollow, like an echo. Like something that might heal, permanently, with time.

He stopped again, surrounded by flowers, and when he held out his hand a bizarre, crystal winged not-quite butterfly alighted on his upturned palm. It sat for a moment, tasting his hand with its curly straw-like butterfly mouth, wings beating a slow, tranquil rhythm.

The cool moss beneath his feet, the warm sun, and the silky petals falling mysteriously from the sky like impossible snow felt so *real*. Everything was dream-like in content, but it *wasn't* a dream. If anything, it felt more real than life.

Real, and safe.

Could he have ever felt this way alive? If he'd had a place that welcomed him and made him feel safe, if he could have afforded to go to real therapy, or immigrated to a real witch city? If he hadn't...

If.

The crystal butterfly on his palm took off, and Aiden watched it dance its way through the cascade of petals.

Now was the perfect time to let go of *ifs* that would never *be*.

He started walking again, slowly at first, but eventually relief and joy filled him until he couldn't hold back any longer. He ran, and soon he was leaping about, trying to catch the petals out of the air. He laughed as they slipped through his fingers and landed on his face, blowing away before amusement could turn into frustration.

An indeterminate amount of time passed before he noticed something strange in the distance. He stopped and squinted at what looked like a small copse of trees, dark shadows at the edge of the meadow that were far more exciting than foreboding. Instinctively, he turned towards them.

It was just becoming obvious that the copse of trees was not at all small when he heard a voice call out to him.

"You! It's *you*! Hello you!"

Aiden stopped and looked around. Why was the voice so familiar?

An enormous rabbit poked its head up out of a thicket of daisies just to the side. It had reddish brown fur, and a blue ribbon tied around its neck.

A blue ribbon Aiden *recognized*.

"Hello nice boy! You are here! Do you have something tasty for me?" The bunny's voice was audible to Aiden, and yet he knew the bunny was not making any actual sounds. The bunny hopped over to Aiden and snuggled against him, the top of his fluffy back coming just to Aiden's waist.

Hand shaking, Aiden stroked one soft ear in absolute astonishment.

"Bernadett?" he whispered.

"Yes! That is what you call me! You remember me! I am glad. I remember you. You are friend. Do you have tasty treat?"

"I...don't. I'm sorry."

Aiden had given her a treat almost every single day, from the first day of third grade until Bernadett died almost four years later. The sweet, energetic bunny had been the closest thing he'd ever had to a pet. She'd belonged to his third grade teacher, Ms. Charmerd, who lived down the street from Aiden.

Ms. Charmerd had, perhaps, been the only adult who never treated Aiden like there was something wrong with him. She'd been very old and retired the year after she taught Aiden. She never turned him away when he snuck over to visit Bernadett against his parents' wishes, even letting him come to the small burial she held for Bernadett in her backyard.

"I forgive you," Bernadett said, unconcerned. "Maybe next time? Oh! Come, you should meet the other friends!"

Bernadett hopped off at an impressive speed, and Aiden took off after her, somehow keeping up. She led him over to the grove, which he now saw were willows larger and more magnificent than any possible on earth.

Vertigo made him hesitate. Were Bernadett and the trees really huge, or was Aiden actually small? Did it matter?

No, it didn't.

Aiden moved aside the curtain of bright green leaves and peered in. He found himself looking up and up at a huge cathedral-like space filled with glowing motes of light. The ground was covered with bright green grass, cropped low. More willows, smaller and covered in blossoms, stood like sentinels at the far side, marking a border between the grove and what was obviously a much thicker and darker forest.

Just in front of the darker forest was a crystal clear pond lined with large flat stones to form a natural basin. It called to him and—

"Boy! See all the friends!"

The grove was not empty. A large gathering of animal-people looked up as Bernadett bounded in among them, announcing that she had found a friend she wanted them all to meet. The majority of them appeared to be mostly normal animals like Bernadett, strangely sized fluffy or horned mammals. Each one shoved a nose into his palm or brushed a fluffy tail against his face as they greeted him before returning to their romping play or sleepy lounging.

There were also more fantastical beings. A delicate rainbow colored creature with wings and scales and huge, iridescent eyes paused to wave as it curled its way through the branches of a blooming apple tree, drinking nectar from the blossoms. A pair of unicorns with fragile crystal horns, lion tails, and cloven hooves whickered at him from where they stood in a shaft of glittering sunlight cropping at the bright green grass. A winged horse the color of a dusky sky, deep blue except for the brilliant sunset at the very tips of the wing feathers, blinked at him sleepily from where it lay in a thick patch of multi-colored moss.

Aiden waved and nudged his way through the crowd, but his attention kept drifting away from the fantastical creatures and back to the pool of water.

Help, something whispered in the back of Aiden's mind.

Hypnotically, he took a step towards it.

"Boy?"

"Hush," a different voice said. "Look, see? Your friend is doing something. I want to see. He smells good. Magical."

The words meant nothing to Aiden, drifting towards the pool as if lost in a dream. There was *something*. A song, so familiar, totally forgotten, pulling him forward. He knelt on the smooth stones and reached into the pond.

A ghostly hand rose from the depths to grasp his hand.

Aiden gasped and arched back. Blazing colors filled his vision. The song in the back of his mind burst into full clarity, a symphony of meaning and memory just out of his reach. It swirled through and around him before flowing down his arm and into the hand holding onto him like a lifeline.

I've got you, Aiden thought firmly, inexplicably.

Aiden pulled, and a staggeringly lovely human face appeared in the depths, framed by hair the color of honey. It curled, magically dry as it broke the surface, almost but not quite hiding the tips of pointed ears. The face was masculine, the skin the color of bronze. When the eyes opened, huge and violet, they fixed on Aiden. A brilliant smile broke like the dawn, and Aiden found himself smiling back.

"You fixed him!" Bernadett cried and barreled into Aiden's side. Aiden fell back and nearly lost his grip, but the lovely person held strong and used Aiden's momentum to pull himself out of the water the rest of the way. He landed on top of Aiden with a soft, otherworldly grunt.

"Stupid! You could have ruined it!"

The voice from before belonged to a reindeer with huge velvety horns. The reindeer shoved Bernadett with their soft nose.

Bernadett thumped. "Nothing is ruined. Look, he is fine! He is better!"

He was also very naked.

Aiden froze, not sure what to do. "Um," he said breathlessly.

The beautiful, ageless man rolled off Aiden with a soft chuckle. He reached up and put his hand on the irate reindeer's nose. "It's alright, sweet girl."

His voice echoed strangely, as if it came from both near and far at the same time.

The deer snorted. "Fine. But do not call me *girl*. I lived several very *long* lives before the Seal locked me in oblivion. Also, I am not sweet."

He laughed. "Alright, as you wish. Bold protector, then?"

The reindeer snorted again, but this one sounded pleased. "Yes." She folded her legs under her and nudged the latest beautiful man who was also naked until he sat with his back leaned against her. She checked him over like a mother looking over a child for injuries. Finding nothing, she lowered her head to the grass and closed her eyes.

"Grumpy deer," Bernadett said, and flopped down against Aiden. "Nice boy, may I sleep here?"

"Um, yeah, of course," Aiden said.

Bernadett wriggled closer, forcing him into a sitting position so she could lean against his back before seemingly dropping off to sleep.

"Do they, um, all do that?" Aiden wondered out loud.

"Mother their friends and then pass out?" The beautiful elf-man laughed. "Maybe it's this place." His laughter faded into something more like wonder. "You look so different, you *feel* different, but it's you, isn't it?"

Aiden swallowed. Like the soul on the river, Aiden felt like he *knew* this person, but he couldn't *remember*. "I don't know," he said, and he leaned into Bernadett. "I'm Aiden."

"I knew you by a different name." He tilted his head to the side, his violet eyes fathomless. They seemed to shine with some kind of inner light. Aiden felt himself caught up, different from the way Sam's gaze held him. This was like an ocean tide, drawing him in, under.

"You...oh." The tide ebbed, and sorrow spilled across his gorgeous face. "Oh, sweet boy." He reached out a hand towards Aiden, but dropped it when Aiden stiffened. "I—sorry. Sorry. I am Kikeru."

Mourning the loss of something he couldn't remember, Aiden shook his head. "No, it's, I—" Aiden rolled to his knees, careful not to disturb Bernadett, and took Kikeru's hand. "There's something wrong with—" he broke off, unable to finish, then said instead, "It's not you."

Kikeru shook his head and squeezed Aiden's hand. "There's nothing wrong with you." His eyes shone again, and the tide drew Aiden back down. Kikeru's voice took on an even more otherworldly quality. "You're going to trigger a lot of change, more than you already have, but that doesn't make it your fault. None of it is your fault." The shine in his eyes grew until they glowed. "You're amazing."

Kikeru closed his eyes, and the strange light vanished.

Aiden sagged back onto his heels, released. He studied Kikeru, his beautiful face, his hopeful expression, filled with love and admiration Aiden did not, *could not* deserve.

An overwhelming sense of loss and longing made his eyes burn. "I'm not the person you remember."

"Aiden," he said, as if trying it out. "That's how it always is when you see an old friend for the first time after a long absence. You are still you, just...grown."

Aiden felt the truth in those words, but— "I don't remember you! How could I—" Hot tears blurred his vision, and he blinked them away. "I don't know what this all means."

Kikeru drew Aiden's hand up to his lips and pressed a kiss to his fingers. "I know. It's okay."

They sat in silence for a long time, holding hands without speaking, listening to the soft sounds of sleeping animal-people. Eventually, Aiden's sense of peace returned, but it was tenuous, balanced on a knife's edge.

"What did I do?" Aiden asked finally. "To you, I mean?"

Kikeru studied him, and a small smile curved his lips. "You found me and pulled me back together."

Aiden felt other questions try to force their way onto his tongue, but he clamped his teeth shut until they receded. Aiden had no idea how or why, but Kikeru clearly *knew* things, and he wasn't ready for the answers Kikeru surely wouldn't hesitate to give. "I don't know what I'm doing. It feels like I'm, I don't know, being rushed into something, but I don't know *what*, or *why*!"

Kikeru nodded, as if he understood. "Yes. That—" he cut off and studied Aiden for a long few seconds, expression softly inscrutable. "You don't remember me, but I remember you. When you're ready, I'll do what I can to help you." His expression grew distant, but they did not pull Aiden in this time. "It is hard to see clearly here. I need...a library? But it is not safe yet. They need...deniability?" Kikeru shook his head, and then brushed his curls out of his eyes with his free hand. "I will stay here until you need me. It's safer that way." His mouth twitched into a mischievous grin. "No one knows I'm here but you."

The reindeer at Kikeru's back snorted. "I am not no one."

Bernadett, without moving, said, "Me neither! And the others too! They are friends, not *no one*!"

The deer lifted her head to glare at Bernadett. "They don't know anything. Neither do you."

Bernadett jumped to her feet and thumped. "Do too! I know you've been protecting this pond since forever and *my* nice boy saved your friend who was in it! I am very smart!"

Kikeru laughed. "You are indeed. But would you do me a favor? Don't tell anyone my name? It is not a true name, but it would be enough." He nodded towards the other creature-people and leaned towards Bernadette conspiratorially. "We are far enough away from the others they could not have heard, but you know. Please tell no one, your nice boy's future may depend on it."

Bernadett leaned in almost nose to nose with Kikeru, ears standing straight up in attention. "Yes! I cannot go with my boy when he leaves, so I will stay here with you. Then your secret will be safe and I can make sure she—" Bernadett indicated the reindeer with a twitch of her nose. "—isn't mean to you or my boy."

The reindeer snorted. "I am not *mean*."

Aiden rubbed his hands on his thighs, restless. The Meadow's peace still hummed inside him, but softer, like it was going to sleep.

Or it couldn't compete with the weight of Aiden's rising anxiety.

Kikeru looked at Aiden sharply before nodding and standing up.

"Time for you to go, I think." He held out a hand to Aiden, who accepted and let himself be pulled to his feet. He felt a little floaty, and part of him recognized it as a symptom of being overwhelmed. "I'm sorry I do not have a true name to share with you yet, but I will remain here, I promise. I...need some time too."

Aiden nodded reflexively, and Kikeru turned to the reindeer. "Your name...Bora? It was so chaotic before, and I...is Bora still alright?"

The deer climbed to her feet in a way that made Aiden think of rolled eyes. "Yes, it is fine. Better than *deer* or *sweet girl.*" She shook her head in obvious disgust.

Kikeru smiled fondly. "Thank you. Bora, would you please show Aiden the...*deer paths* I think they are called? He will be able to use them."

Bora walked over to wuff at Aiden's shoes, still hanging around his neck. "What will you give me for this secret, strange human?"

Kikeru frowned. "Bora—"

"Will you bring us treats when you come back?" Bernadett asked, bouncing in between them.

Bora tilted her head to the side. "Yes, treats. Bring me a treat when you next come here. That is fair."

"O-okay," Aiden said. That felt like something he could probably handle, and it was actually a relief to have a task he understood.

The smallest weight settled onto him—did they just make a pact?—and Bora dropped to her knees and gestured at her back. "Come, ride. I will show you how to use the deer trails."

Aiden hesitated. He looked at Bernadett, who brushed against him with a murmured, "Treats!", and then at Kikeru, who smiled encouragingly and gestured for him to go.

He swung himself onto Bora's back, and she rose to her feet before leaping into the dark woods behind the pond.

Aiden had never ridden anything before in his life—well, except other humans—but his soul seemed to know how to do it. Instinctively he started moving with the motion of Bora's gait, effortlessly keeping his balance as Bora, despite her impressive rack of horns, flowed through the dense brush.

At first Aiden couldn't see the path she followed, but then Aiden felt himself *synch*. Suddenly, he could see the way ahead of them, and he thought he knew where they were going.

They stopped at an elm tree that *radiated* at Aiden. It felt like home.

Aiden slid off her back and put his shoes back on. Bora patiently waited for him to stand back up.

"Do you understand?" she asked, letting him pet her nose. She must have seen something on his face, because she added, "About the deer paths. Understanding Kikeru will come later. Maybe. Probably not, actually. His kind are annoying like that."

Aiden smiled ruefully. "I understand. Um. Thank you."

She gave him a quick, almost begrudging lick on his hand. "Do not be so afraid, strange one. You are strong, and you smell *good*."

Before Aiden could think of what to say to that, she bounded away and vanished.

When Aiden turned back to the tree, a woman stood there. A shaft of sunlight that was not there before shone on the place where she stood. Her hair was so full of flowers Aiden couldn't tell if it was gold, or green, or earthy brown. It cascaded around her flawless naked body, her skin golden and shining in the sun. Her face was radiant with youth and her eyes smoldered with the promise of heat and sex.

Aiden blinked, startled, and the woman's eyes went wide.

"Oh. Oh, it's you!" she said, voice full of wonder. "You *survived!*"

GREATER PROVIDENCE RI, SEPTEMBER 9TH 47 YAR

YES, STILL THE 9TH. IT'S BEEN A DAY.

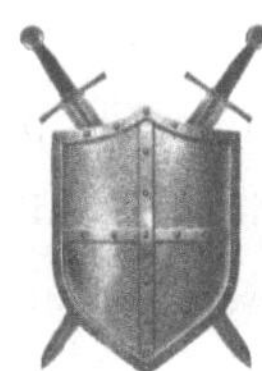

Emily stared at the napkin.

She shouldn't run a background check. She should toss it in the trash, or call it. There was a terrible monster on the loose and her partner had gone on leave and disappeared because a vampire murdered his rapist son. She had *things to do* and she absolutely *should not* use the phone number to run a highly questionable background check.

Also, who wrote numbers on napkins? It was so archaic, like from a pre-Rapture drama. Emily *wasn't* charmed by the weirdly romantic gesture. Nope. She was just really curious, because Sofia wrote her numbers weird too, like she was a calligrapher.

She'd been with Penelope Reed, which was suspicious, maybe?

Emily closed her eyes, ashamed for even pretending she could convince herself of something so ridiculous.

Her skin began to tingle where the seal rested against her breast bone, like tiny little pins and needles, not painful, exactly, but not comfortable either. She got the oddest impression it was judging her.

Emily shouldn't be doing this. She continued to tell herself that as she pulled up Sofia's full name. Sofia Jackson, age 47.

47? *Damn.* She looked *good* for 47. Like, would have carded her twice good.

A witch maybe? Or access to witch youth potions?

Compulsively, she continued to pull up details. Registered Nurse, working at the Providence Children's Hospital, no arrest record. Born in Georgia but seemingly cut ties with everyone there and moved here three years ago.

Emily's hand twitched over the mouse. She should stop.

She pulled up as much information as she could from Georgia, but unfortunately, or maybe fortunately for the sake of her integrity, she didn't have much access down there. God-fearing country had as much surveillance as witch country, but the Church of Unity kept a tight hold on the information, making even the FBI jump through a ridiculous amount of hoops for anything other than basic information.

It was the reason some of her extended family refused to move into witch territory. Why they trusted the Church more than the government was beyond Emily. At least the government let you vote on privacy laws. Sort of.

Maybe Emily shouldn't be throwing stones here. Her seal prickled in agreement, because it was rude and judgey, apparently.

She found the names of Sofia's parents, a sister, and a niece and a nephew. The kids had been in middle school and high school when their aunt had broken contact with them. There was no explanation for the split. No matter how hard she looked, without a warrant or more information, she was stuck.

That was it then. Emily should toss the napkin in the trash.

But...

It *had* been romantic for Sofia to give her number to Emily like that, especially after confessing how vulnerable she was. Maybe she just wanted a safe rebound date, which Emily didn't mind offering. She kind of liked the idea, actually.

She'd never dated a woman before, but she'd never been asked out by one before either.

Her stomach fluttered.

Emily called the number. She practically owed it to Sofia at this point. Because of the slight stalking. Emily should apologize.

"You have reached the Federal Bureau of Investigations, how may I direct your call?" Sofia said.

"Ha ha, very funny. This is Emily. Um, Detective Scott."

"It is? Oh, wow. So, that's a yes then?" Emily could hear the smile in her voice.

"Yeah. But first, I need to apologize."

"Oh? For what?"

"It's classified. But I *am* sorry." Weirdly, as soon as she apologized, her seal stopped prickling at her. What the hell *was* this thing?

Sofia laughed, and Emily's stomach fluttered again. "When do you wanna go out? Friday? *Sooner*?"

"Sooner, if tomorrow works for you. I work the weekends, so my Friday is Wednesday. But I need to warn you, I'm probably going to be on call for the foreseeable future."

"Tomorrow works for me, " Sofia said, which Emily knew. She'd seen her work schedule. "Meet me at Thoughts and Prayers at...?"

"Six-thirty?"

"Great. What kind of food do you like?"

"The kind you eat."

"*Me* too! We have *so* much in common. See you tomorrow!"

"See you." Emily hung up.

Emily dropped her head into her hand, feeling like she had just made both the best and worst decision of her life.

Except the damn witch-therapist who'd cleared her for duty had told her to try to find normalcy where she could. Dating was normal.

It was practically a job requirement for her to go on this date.

She finished logging her report on Ms. Reed's officially sanitized *Coven-approved* statement before the seal could start buzzing her again. She also tagged the dead vampire Reed reported as a potential suspect in her other case.

Was there a connection between the two events? First Olivia was targeted, and then the damn seal led her right to where Sean met his ultimate end at the hands of a vampire. A vampire that was now, apparently, dead, assuming it was the same one.

God, could there have been two vampires? Was the *creature* some kind of vampiric ghost?

Damnit, that didn't make sense. *Nothing* made any goddamn sense.

Emily pulled out the seal, or amulet, whatever it was. She wasn't sure if it *was* a seal, but something about the way it weighed on her made Emily want to call it that.

What did it know, and why did the Angel give it to her *now*?

She snapped a picture of the seal and spent the next hour fruitlessly searching for information. None of the images she could find resembled her seal enough to be useful. Worse, when she compared the picture she had taken to the seal, they were obviously different. It didn't make any sense. It was like her phone couldn't see the seal in its entirety.

Emily tried again, and then she tried taking a video. Every picture she took was wrong, missing symbols that Emily could *clearly* see. When she tried to draw the missing symbols by hand with a stylus, her damn tablet kept glitching. She even went and got a piece of charcoal from the magic store room so she could try and draw the symbol on a piece of shipping cardboard she scavenged, but as soon as she made the first stroke her hand went *numb*.

She was seriously considering interrupting Will's endless meetings with Coven leaders to ask for help when she received a high priority call from dispatch.

"Scott here, what's up?"

"How soon can you get to the hospital? There's a situation with the Weaver girl."

Emily was out of her chair and sliding her tablet into her bag before she finished answering. "I'll be there in fifteen. Is the situation under control?"

"In a manner of speaking. Officer Prescott was injured pretty badly, but he was in the right place to get treated. Anywhere else and he probably would have died, but he's stable and should make a full recovery. Well. Not quite a full recovery."

"What the hell happened?"

"I'll send you the security footage. We have Weaver in cuffs now, but she's... you'll see."

As soon as she put the address into her car she pulled up the footage on her tablet.

It was bad.

The video started with an image of Olivia in her hospital room. She'd been pretty heavily sedated when they brought her in, but clearly that was starting to wear off. A nurse finished checking on Olivia, taking her pulse and temperature, before walking out.

Prescott was stationed at the door to her room. There was no sound on the recording, but it was obvious that Olivia was talking to Prescott. For some reason, Prescott closed the door and walked over to Olivia. His back was to the camera, and he stood blocking the view of Olivia's face.

What wasn't blocked was her shoulder, which Olivia slowly freed from her hospital gown. She then obviously and, fuck, *seductively*, crawled across the bed towards Prescott, who was just as clearly undoing the front of his pants.

Emily started swearing at the screen as she watched the next few seconds. She had never before in her life been so angry at someone she knew. Prescott hadn't shown any signs of being such an irresponsible dick, and it made Emily feel stupid. Worse, it made no fucking sense. He *knew* the fucking cameras were there!

She would make absolutely fucking sure he lost his job for this.

Her anger was suddenly short circuited when Prescott jerked back, screaming. Olivia's face came into view and it was covered in blood. Her mouth was obviously very full, and she was *chewing*. Emily was so shocked and disgusted that she almost missed the way the whites of Olivia's eyes were shot with black.

Olivia swallowed, and Emily felt her stomach roll. Olivia licked her lips, smiled, and leaped onto Prescott, who had fallen to the floor, still obviously screaming, but not fighting back for some reason.

What happened next to Prescott was not visible on camera, but eventually people burst into the room and hauled Olivia off of Prescott. She had another chunk of flesh in her mouth, and it flew out as she screamed and fought. One of the nurses managed to give her a sedative. For a few moments longer she bit and scratched at everyone around her, until she suddenly went limp, her eyes rolling into the back of her head as she passed out.

Emily sat there, fighting her revulsion for the rest of the ride over. She left a message for Will, not wanting to wait for him, asking for someone who specialized in warding to come down to the hospital. He texted back confirmation and said he'd come as soon as he could. After, Emily grabbed a screenshot of Olivia's eyes and added it to the growing file of extremely fucked-up shit she had seen that day.

One of her deputies met her at the door and led her to the secure room where Olivia had been moved.

As soon as she started to get close, the seal pulsed against her skin, and then it started to hum and tingle, as if a low voltage was running from it into her. It didn't hurt, exactly, but it wasn't comfortable either. It wasn't quite the same as what it had done around *every* witch and familiar she came across, including Will and Sam. It was a lot more annoying, for one thing.

She didn't like it.

Olivia was secured in a room with an observation window. It looked like a surgery room, hastily cleared out. There were several cameras recording multiple angles, and Emily looked through the one-way glass at Olivia. She was alone and handcuffed to the bed.

Disturbingly, her eyes followed the movement of people in the observation room, and Emily suspected, in the halls and the floor above. An intercom carried the sound of Olivia humming tunelessly to herself. Her face had been somewhat cleaned off, but there was still a little blood at the corners of her mouth and nose. Her gown was also new.

The whites of her eyes were still streaked with black.

The deputy in charge was waiting for her next to the window. He looked terrible, like he was barely holding it together. Relief eased the lines on his face when he realized he was no longer the highest ranked person on site.

"She woke up a few minutes ago. We haven't been able to get anyone willing to check on her since...earlier. A divine healer treated Olivia when she arrived this morning, but she said she didn't detect anything unusual then. Now, though, the woman refuses to even come in *here*, let alone enter the room with the girl. Says she feels nauseated when she gets close. Do you... Are you going to go in and question her?"

Emily was going to, but she wanted to wait until the witches arrived to set up stronger wards. According to Penelope Reed, there was a strong possibility wards would affect whatever the *thing* was. Whether or not that would matter here wasn't at all clear, but it was better to try.

Emily went over the footage for the girl's entire stay and asked everyone who had been in contact with her, especially the EMTs that had taken her from the scene. There was no sign that the *thing* had reappeared to possess her again.

That didn't rule out it leaving something behind, though.

By the time she'd spoken to the last witness, a pair of witches had arrived to put up wards. Her stupid seal pulsed the moment they walked into the room. The witches didn't seem to notice, deep in a technical discussion about ward magic, but their familiars, a pair of owls, immediately turned to stare at Emily.

<<What *is* that?>> the first owl, a white snowy owl, asked in a stage whisper.

The other one, a barn owl, stage whispered back, <<Baby hunter. Not necessarily a threat now, the poor soul might still escape, but keep an eye on it.>>

Emily felt a chill run down her spine. That did not sound good. It was also rude.

Her seal pulsed at her the whole time they worked their magic— a low throbbing sensation that sat on top of the electric buzzing. Worse, she could *feel* the magic, a slight tingling sensation all over her body, an almost nails-on-a-chalkboard effect when combined with the seal's constant humming and pulsing.

If she wasn't careful, she was going to start raving like an anarch about all magic being bullshit.

Emily ducked into an empty room to try to take the seal off. In one swift motion, she whipped it over her head and placed it on a table.

As soon as she broke skin contact with the amulet, her head felt like it was trying to rip itself open, and her chest tightened, causing her to struggle for breath. Emily gritted her teeth, hoping it would pass, but it didn't. She made it maybe three seconds before she was clutching the amulet to her chest, sweating and panting. The pain stopped the moment she picked the thing back up.

Emily put the chain back over her head and stuffed it back under her shirt.

The experience did not help her mood one bit.

The humming from Olivia dulled to almost nothing as the witches added ward after ward. After the fourth ward flashed, set, the humming dropped low enough Emily almost convinced herself it was gone.

Olivia, whose eyes had continued to follow people through the walls, suddenly grunted. Her eyes started wandering, searching, and frustration creased her brow.

Emily walked over to the witches, who had just started drawing symbols for a fifth ward. "That last one definitely had an effect. I think she's stopped tracking people through the walls."

They looked encouraged by that, and erupted into chatter about the technical magical implications. They started laying down even more wards, faster now, to the point where the threshold of the door was completely covered in chalk and charcoal.

The witch's magic was still making her skin tingle, but when they finished the last ward the humming from inside the room was truly gone.

At least that was something. Emily still had no idea if she wanted to tell anyone about the seal and how it seemed to sense whatever was infecting or possessing Olivia. The owls hadn't said anything else, to her or anyone else, but they did keep giving her the stink eye.

The witches finally reported that they could no longer sense the wrongness, and that to the best of their knowledge, whatever was going on was contained.

Emily was struck by a chilling thought, and she asked the witches to take a look at every person who had been in contact with Olivia to see if they could detect the tainted demonic energy. They agreed, and went off to start checking people on Emily's list. They started with Prescott, who was isolated and cuffed, though still sedated.

As soon as the witches entered his room, they stopped dead. The two owls made a weird bird hissing noise.

<<He smells wrong, slightly demonic, but corrupted, like the girl. It is more muted, but definitely present,>> the barn owl said, still hissing.

Emily felt her stomach drop. Her seal hadn't reacted to Prescott at all.

Once the witches confirmed they did, in fact, sense corruption, Emily called for the divine healer. She also found nothing, could sense nothing, just as she had when Olivia arrived at the hospital. Emily had no clue what that meant, but the healer recommended calling a freaking *exorcist*.

Witches didn't much care for exorcists, and with good reason. The negotiations involved in getting a permit for one to visit Coven territory were extensive, but if the witches couldn't find a way to stop this thing, they might not have a choice.

Emily very strongly wanted to lock down the entire hospital, but she didn't have the authority. Instead, she ordered that everyone who had been in contact with the girl be inspected by the witches. She also notified the hospital management. They would need to take precautions, and she did her best to impress on them just how bad it would be if the media got wind of the situation. Fortunately, they seemed to understand the gravity of the situation, and were very cooperative.

When the witches finished checking everyone on hand, only two other people were showing signs of corruption. A nurse and another deputy. Both had been bitten by Olivia when they pulled her off Prescott.

The two of them were immediately put in warded isolation. Both complied without a fuss, and both were obviously, and reasonably, fucking terrified.

No one could say for sure if the infection would grow to the extent it had in Olivia, though the fact that only people who had been actually bitten were showing signs of corruption was something like good news.

Emily called the captain.

"Detective Scott, you have an update?"

"The girl from the massacre is apparently infected with some kind of corruption, and it might be contagious."

Silence.

"I've got three people besides Olivia, including two deputies, infected with this magical corruption. Only Olivia has shown any symptoms beyond giving witches the heebie jeebies. Have you heard anything about what happened with Prescott?"

"Not in detail, explain." Emily felt sick as she relayed everything she knew.

"Stay on site. You're still in charge of this case for now, but I need to contact the FBI and the North American Coven. I'll also need to contact the National Guard so they can go on standby in case of an infectious outbreak. Keep things contained if you can, but we need to prepare for the worst. How quiet can you keep this?"

"Right now only a handful of people know the infection, corruption, whatever it is, has spread beyond Olivia. I might be able to keep it quiet for a few days."

"Do it. We'll have to make an announcement before too long, but we need time to get more details. People are already freaked out enough as it is."

"Sir, the *thing* is still out there." Emily was very, very cold.

"I know. Call if you get any more information. I have everyone on high alert looking for this thing."

Emily hung up, and took a moment to center herself. Unconsciously her hand went to the seal, and it radiated comforting warmth into her.

"Oh, shut the fuck up," she told it, but couldn't stop herself from feeling comforted anyway.

Emily returned to the observation room and debated the wisdom of trying to speak with Olivia. The seal was still radiating warmth, as if encouraging her. They needed answers, and she had a gut feeling that she might be the only person who could go in there without risking something worse than death.

She put on an N95 mask and gloves, held her taser in her hand as a precaution, and went into the room.

As soon as she walked through the wards, Olivia's eyes locked on her. Immediately, the girl's face crumpled.

"What is happening to me? Why am I locked up?" she asked, her voice trembling. Tears started to leak from the corners of her black, corrupted eyes.

Emily hesitated. She probably should have asked for a therapist to be on call during this conversation, but it was too late now. The seal throbbed against her skin, humming just as strongly as before the wards went up. Still, Emily had been lied to quite a lot in her line of work, and she couldn't detect anything fake about Olivia's distress.

It was still suspicious as fuck.

She decided to proceed cautiously. "Can you tell me what you remember? What happened to you today?"

Olivia continued to stare at Emily, whimpering, tears still rolling down her cheeks. Emily was content to wait it out, though she made an effort to school her face into a sympathetic expression. It wasn't that hard. The poor girl definitely didn't deserve this, especially given what she had probably been going through with her now-dead boyfriend.

A boyfriend who was killed by a vampire two days ago. And a vampire had turned up dead this morning.

Emily was pulled away from the reminder of *that* unpleasant connection as she felt a slight pressure build in the room. It grew and grew, and Olivia was staring intently at Emily, her eyes leaking tears that suddenly tinted red, then turned to blood. The pressure popped and the seal thumped against her chest almost painfully.

Olivia's eyes went even more black and suddenly she arched back and roared.

</<*Fuck you, you fat bitch. How many donuts have you eaten today?*>/> she said, and in spite of herself, Emily flinched.

Laughing, Olivia jerked her arms with unnatural strength. The leather cuffs holding her wrists to the bed snapped. Much faster than she should have been able to move, she leaped at Emily, her hands curled into claws.

Emily reacted barely in time, grabbing a nearby chair and pushing it into Olivia to block her attack. Olivia snarled and tossed the chair aside, and it slammed into the one way mirror, causing it to crack.

Olivia leaped at Emily again. Emily tried the taser, but Olivia just laughed harder and ripped it out of Emily's hand.

Emily blinked, and Olivia was on her, hands wrapped around her throat.

The seal pulsed, and Emily saw a flash of brilliant golden light. Olivia screamed and fell back, her hands red and raw, as if they'd been burned.

Emily didn't think—she just ran back through the door to the room, trying to put distance between them.

As soon as the thing that used to be Olivia got to the threshold, still trying to get to Emily, she slammed against an invisible barrier. The ward was holding.

Emily stopped and spun around, ripping the mask off and panting. The seal was quiet again, though it pulsed slightly when the two witches came running around the corner. They stopped next to her in front of the open door.

They all watched in silence as Olivia threw herself against the barrier until her face and hands were bloody from blunt trauma. Her screams echoed down the hallway, but Emily sent a quick order to keep everyone else away.

Eventually the girl passed out. She crumpled to the floor, bleeding steadily from a head wound. Her breathing was very shallow.

The witches and Emily looked at each other. Their eyes met, and one of the witches gestured at Olivia's bloody form.

"If I had to guess, you are probably the only one that can go in there without risking getting infected."

<<I told you we needed to keep an eye on her,>> the barn owl said.

"Hush, Artemis. Now is not the time."

Emily ignored them. "I need to try to help her. Can you fetch a nurse for me? I want to try to stabilize her. Someone will need to talk me through it."

The first witch nodded, and the second ran off to find a nurse.

Emily stepped over the threshold cautiously. Immediately the seal began to pulse and hum, even stronger than before. Carefully, Emily checked Olivia's pulse. It was too slow. Emily still had her gloves on, and the girl's skin did not burn on contact. She carefully moved her so she was flat on her back. After some rummaging, she found a roll of bandages in a nearby drawer and wound them gently around Olivia's head.

There was a deep dent in Olivia's skull.

When the nurse arrived, she asked Emily to check a few more things, hooking up a heart monitor to the poor girl's chest. Eventually, the girl's heartbeat stopped, and Emily and the nurse exchanged a deeply sad nod.

There was no point in giving her CPR.

The nurse left, but Emily stayed to wait for the humming in her seal to subside. Except it didn't. It continued to grow. She stripped off her gloves and pulled the seal out from under her shirt to hold in her hand.

It gave a single violent pulse as the body on the floor twitched.

Emily couldn't stop herself from letting out a terrified yelp. The corpse hauled itself to its feet, blocking Emily's path to the door. Its eyes rolled, black except for a single bright red rim where the iris should have been. It screamed at her, a terrible, inhuman sound, and launched itself at her.

Emily held up the seal in an instinctive gesture.

There was a bright flash, and the...the fucking *zombie* threw itself across the room, huddling in a corner. Emily wasted no time leaving the room as soon as her path was clear. The moment she passed the threshold, the humming in the seal stopped vibrating again.

After a few more minutes of tense silence, the same witch spoke.

"Detective, I think maybe you should come speak with our Coven elders."

Emily's heart started to thump painfully, and she swallowed. "I've been ordered to stay on site. I think I shouldn't leave this, ah, *this,* unattended."

The witch nodded. "I understand. Would you be willing to speak with them here, in a private conference room? I think it is in all of our best interests to discuss the *implications* of what just happened."

The other witch, who was clearly much younger, said, "Will speaks highly of you."

<<Sam and Will are ridiculous, but we have no reason to doubt their judgment. Are you willing to negotiate?>>

"I..." Emily swallowed again. "Yes. Is—never mind, we can discuss it when your elders arrive."

"Thank you." She pulled out her phone and made a call, but didn't walk away.

Emily eavesdropped. She was obvious about it, which made it okay. The witch told whoever she had called what she had just witnessed. There was a pause.

"No, the individual in question has been extremely cordial and works with William Davis regularly."

Another pause.

"It seems very recent. Sam might even know exactly when, but he's...Sam." Pause. "Yes, I believe he's gone back to report, so the Triad likely already knows."

A very long pause. Emily forcibly unclenched her jaw.

"Understood. Yes." The witch hung up and looked back at Emily. "Detective, they cannot meet with you tonight. You have been granted a provisional permit for at least the duration of this crisis, subject to review if things should...change. It's not a requirement, but we would like you to check in with a witch at least once a day in person, is that acceptable?"

Emily nodded, then forced herself to ask, "Can we speak in private? I'd like to ask you some, ah, private questions." She felt like an idiot, but the witch nodded.

They moved into an empty room and closed the door.

"So, you know what this thing is?" Emily asked, showing them the seal. It pulsed ominously when she held it out and she immediately dropped it. One of the owls hissed.

"We suspect it is a Divine Artifact. There are classified records from the Breaking that indicate such things were given out to people who would eventually gain the powers of Divine Paladins." She gave Emily a meaningful look, and said, flatly, "Also known as Witch Hunters. Or exorcists."

Emily swallowed stiffly and tried not to shiver. "I'm not an exorcist." Emily could hear the uncertainty in her tone. The stupid seal warmed, probably trying to comfort her. She swallowed again, and gestured at the seal. Artifact. *Thing*. "I can't take it off. It hurts to try."

"That's not surprising." The witch sounded sympathetic. "Divinity rarely lets go of what it sees as belonging to it without a fight. I assume you haven't had it for long?"

"Um, last night. Twenty hours ago."

The witch nodded. "Thank you. I..." She looked like she wanted to ask another question, but she stopped herself. "I'm afraid I don't know anything else for certain. It is likely that you could still be separated from the Artifact, but it...well." She looked uncomfortable, then her expression glazed over. After a moment, she said, "You do not seem to have the same presence as a true exorcist, so it's likely not fully bonded with your soul."

Emily must have looked as horrified as she felt at the implied *yet*. The witch sighed, and rubbed at her temples. Witches in general did not age like normal people, so it was usually difficult to tell how old they were. Emily suddenly had the impression this witch was *much* older than she looked.

"Frankly, we don't have much in the way of procedures for dealing with a case like this. New Paladins are *extremely* rare, to put it mildly. In your nascent state, you could have gone undetected for months. During the Breaking, someone like you would have been used as a spy."

Emily set her jaw. "I won't be doing anything underhanded. If I can't find a way to get rid of this thing, I'll apply for the proper permits or, or I'll leave." She *really* didn't want to leave. This city was *home*. She liked it here and she really didn't want to move out into God-fearing country. Much as she complained about witches, everyone she knew living in Divine territory was a piece of work.

"As I said, you have been granted a provisional permit. It's already been registered with your ID. If you still want the thing removed when this is over, we will try and help you. Some of the Yaga may have experience with such things, and we can try to contact them on your behalf." The witch looked a little guilty. "I would offer to help you now, if you wanted, but given the situation..."

Emily nodded. She understood.

The look of guilt did not ease from the witch's face. "You must understand, the longer you have the Artifact, the stronger its hold will be. There is a chance it will bond fully with your soul, and there may not be any way to free you from it at that point."

The seal continued to seep soothing warmth into Emily, and it made her feel both comforted and violated at the same time.

"I understand."

A PLACE(ISH, GEMMA'S KIND OF UPSET) BEYOND TIME AND SPACE

"*What the hell do you mean you don't know what it is*?" Gemma's voice caused chittering tremors in space-time.

The thrones were there, but no one was sitting. The emptiness between each deity was charged with their combined agitation.

Lucifer rubbed at the scar on his abdomen, uncomfortable. "Um Gemma, could you not use that word? It makes me—"

"*Lucifer*!" Gemma hissed.

"Right, sorry, not the time." He cleared his throat. "Anyway, the thing isn't pulling on demonic reservoirs as far as I can tell, but—"

"I can *see* that! It's pulling on *mine. Through* mortal *souls*! And it's *breaking* them." The tremors got more pronounced. Something eldritch started to stir.

Lillian stepped forward and put herself in Gemma's path, making a placating gesture, pleading. "We're not sure what else we can do.

Whatever it is, whatever it did to survive the Chaos left it *wrong*, somehow. If we could get to the soul, er, souls, now, I'm sure we could rip them apart—"

Lucifer cleared his throat.

Lillian whirled to glare at him. "Lucifer, these aren't normal souls, we don't even know if they're sane enough to *have* free will, so just shut the fuck up."

Lucifer raised his hands in surrender, wincing, and Lillian turned back to Gemma.

"Whatever this corruption is, any demon that tries to touch it directly runs the risk of being consumed. It's just too big for anything we can field on the mortal plane. We *think* we can ward against it, but we can't be sure of anything at this point." Lillian spread her arms in a helpless gesture.

Gemma glared at Lillian for a long moment. Eventually, her aura softened, just slightly, and she turned to Zee. "Why isn't there anything in the Library on this thing?"

Zee poked their head out from behind Lucifer. "I don't know! We're a library, not a crystal ball!" Zee paused, eyes landing on Micheal. "Or, well, we're not a crystal ball right *now* because there aren't any Oracles left." They nodded pointedly towards Micheal, who pretended not to notice.

Zee flicked their gaze back to Gemma. "My best guess, though, is that this is a genuine *new thing*, and even an Oracle would have had trouble predicting it." Their expression changed, grew more somber, and they added, gently, "You know how the Chaos leaves its mark on raw souls, and this soul was both powerful and very, very angry before it entered the Chaos."

Gemma's face was a mask, but something dark flickered behind her eyes. Black smoke leaked between her teeth. "You think this is *my* fault? Chaos affects souls, yes, but not like this. What aren't you telling me?"

Zee's expression didn't so much as twitch. "I don't *know*. It's not in the Records."

Lucifer and Lillian exchanged a glance, faces schooled to blankness.

Micheal narrowed his eyes at them. "This *thing* is not Gemma's fault, it's yours, Lucifer. If you hadn't been keeping those souls in the Pit, if you'd just destroyed them like we—"

Lillian twisted and *warped*, appearing inches from Micheal's face. "*Enough*, Micheal. Why don't you instead explain to us why there's a *nascent Paladin* inside one of our cities?"

Zee nodded and stuck out their tongue. "Yeah, *Micheal*."

Micheal remained placidly calm. "We discussed this. The vampire issue was getting out of hand, and we agreed—"

"We didn't agree to shit, Micheal!" Lucifer said, getting in Micheal's face. "Did you even know about this thing when you made the Paladin, or are you just using this emergency to cover up your illegal—"

"It's a good thing she was there! Who knows how bad your mess would have gotten otherwise? If you were wise, you'd let us send in a whole team of Paladins. We could—"

Lucifer scoffed and shoved Micheal. "Oh, you'd like that, wouldn't you? Let your Paladins have free reign, and when they just happen to accidentally target the wrong soul—"

Micheal shoved Lucifer back, his fire blazing. "Your refusal to see reason is what created this mess! So what if a few less dangerous deviants get caught in the crossfire? *All* deviant souls are dangerous, and to protect the many, we must—"

Gemma stomped her foot, and a loud crack shuddered through space-time. Her voice thundered when she said, "I DO NOT WANT TO HEAR ANOTHER SECOND OF YOUR BICKERING. WORK *TOGETHER* TO FIX THIS." She exhaled primordial steam and turned to face Micheal, who took an involuntary step back. "That means you too, Micheal. You're off the hook for now, but I will remember what you did." She turned back to the Triad. "Find a way to fix this *before* it works its way into any fae spaces."

Lucifer held up his hands. "We're working as fast as we can, but—" He glared at Micheal. "—we can't hold the truce together if Micheal's going to continue flagrantly violate the Treaty."

Gemma growled, deep and low, causing the walls of reality to blur. Something scratched at the edges, chittering. Zee ducked back behind Lucifer, and Micheal looked nervous. "Micheal will behave going forward, so you've got nothing to worry about. *Right*, Micheal?"

Micheal nodded. "Of course. We would like to point out that we submitted a formal request for this Paladin, which was left pending. It was not *strictly* a viola—"

"MICHEAL *SHUT UP*," Gemma roared, and he did.

Gemma fixed her gaze on the Triad. "We'll balance the scales later. Make sure your people understand that so long as whatever Paladins are brought in do not violate the truce, they are to be allowed necessary access."

She swung her head around to glare at Micheal again and exhaled slowly. Sparks flew out and landed on Micheal's flawless face, leaving behind tiny spots of miasmic glitter. He didn't quite flinch, but his eyes darted around, following the skittering shadows. "Send in your help, but choose your agents well. *Do not* violate the treaty again."

Micheal nodded, looking worried. "That. Ah. We will find someone we can trust."

Gemma flicked her tongue out, tasting the air. "Good." She opened her mouth and let her teeth gleam ominously. "You will work *together*. This thing could destroy us all, and *I will not* let your petty squabbles be the reason it does. *Understood*?"

Micheal and the Triad nodded as one. "Understood."

GREATER PROVIDENCE RI, SEPTEMBER 10TH 47 YAR

June was going stir crazy. She was used to having the long stretches of the daylight hours to while away, but that was when she was naturally inclined to stillness and meditation whenever the sun was up.

She'd tried leaving the amulet on, hoping it would make her less bored, but it hadn't. The living body kept having urges, like thirst, or tiredness, or arousal, or having to pass water because she stupidly had a drink to quench her thirst. Using a modern toilet was much better than what she'd used before, but it was still an absolutely disgusting process.

At least the wine had been excellent. Penny, unfortunately, hadn't let her try to get drunk— *apparently* it might interfere with the amulet, or something.

Once the novelty of having a heartbeat wore off, it became massively distracting, and, worse, she had to breathe *all the time.* She couldn't even stop for thirty seconds without her body freaking out like it was about to die.

Living was somehow *more* of an inconvenience than she remembered. The time she'd spent in oblivion had passed in a blink, but even considering how long it took her to pull herself together after the seal broke, she'd spent significantly more time as a demon than as a living person.

Living was very stressful.

She decided to go for a walk as soon as the sun rose, because she'd spent the night cooped up inside Thoughts and Prayers, *not drunk*, watching the local regulars talk about their shoes. Or whatever.

June should have brought her guitar and given the place some live music. Ugh.

Maybe the sunshine would be a good distraction. The novelty alone should provide some kind of entertainment value.

It did not.

June stepped out into the bright morning light and winced. It took her pupils *eons* to stop aching like they were on fire, and even then it still kind of hurt. The sun was *bright.* She was, probably, safest from the abomination in direct sunlight, but she couldn't help but imagine that her skin was itching from the overabundance of UV exposure. It *wasn't* itching, but the knowledge that the only thing standing between her and a repeat of yesterday morning was a tiny piece of magically infused crystal and wood wasn't enough to let her feel comfortable.

The worst part was that, unlike the more civilized starlight, or the softly brilliant moonlight, or the streetlights that kept the city in a constant, warm glow, the sun *pressed* on her. It hung there in the sky, raging at her like an overly aggressive fanatic, smothering her with its relentless brilliance.

Even when still alive, she'd spent her happiest hours at night, looking at the stars with her aunt, the only member of her family who even tried to accept June as her true self.

Now, the heat of the angry ball of fire on her skin made her feel like she was dying all over again, heated wood surrounding her, choking her, roasting her alive. Just like then, she couldn't move away from it because it was *everywhere*.

June paused under the shade of a few overly-bright green trees, breathing deeply, forcing the memories back into the past where they belonged.

The unwavering brightness remained, unrelenting even from within shade.

It was maddening.

No.

The sun wouldn't stop her. She wasn't a slave to her past. It wasn't actually burning her, nor was it rotting her.

June took off down the street, bound and determined. This was an opportunity to get over a trigger she hadn't even known she had. She could learn about some fun, modern activities that people only did when the sun was out, and find something to like about the day.

She used her phone to see what people did only during the day.

Go the park. Go to the beach. Garden. Look at scenic views.

Every list she found was wrong. Absolutely all of those things June already did, at night, when everything was softer, and cooler, and less loud.

She tried anyway. She detoured through a nearby park and focused on smelling the trees and flowers. Unfortunately, the smell of people was overwhelming, no matter where on the paths she went. She tried to listen to the birds singing instead. That, at least, was noticeably different with the sun up, but, unfortunately, it was difficult to hear over all the goddamn *people.*

It would seem daylight activities were essentially the same as nighttime ones, except during the day people were packed so densely and chaotically that you couldn't go two steps without practically tripping on one.

And the fucking *children*. It was like boring Halloween, with the chaotic little scavengers screeching and whining and laughing at extremely unfunny jokes all over the place. Why were there so damn *many*? Weren't birthrates supposed to be dropping or something?

The park cleared out after the first hour or so, presumably because they'd all gone to school, but by then the sun was becoming positively apoplectic as it climbed higher in the sky. Worse, the tiny amounts of shade were reduced to fetid pools of barely useful dimness.

A few scattered clouds drifted across the sky in a parody of helpfulness, but, unlike the moody, silvery wraiths shrouded in moonbows and halos, they were just these, these completely useless shaggy white cotton balls. They drifted aimlessly across in the obnoxiously blue, opaque sky that completely obscured the rest of the universe.

No wonder living humans were so small-minded. They went most of their existence surrounded by human-generated chaos without a single reminder that the universe was vast and infinite and went far *far* beyond their insignificantly tiny rock world.

At least she no longer felt like she was dying. She was too irritated. All that waxing poetic about the sun, an endless number of books and movies stressing how she, as a vampire doomed to eternal night, should be *longing* and *bitter* because she could never see the sunlight without suffering an agonizing death, and it turned out the sun was boring as fuck and daytime was filled with an overabundance of self-absorbed assholes.

People were much more fun at night. At least then the assholes had the excuse of being drunk or stoned, and the screeching children went to bed.

June finally gave up and retreated back to the cold, dark bliss of Thoughts and Prayers. She found Penny there, busily getting the bar ready for the evening. She slinked over and silently started helping, stacking glasses and morosely thinking about how much easier it would be to do this if she could move with vampiric strength and dexterity.

"So, any new developments while I was out?" she asked eventually, desperate to break the silence fertilizing her melancholia.

Penny put down the bottle of scotch she was inspecting. "Yes, actually. Carla called. She was over at the hospital this morning with that poor girl, Sean's girlfriend. She's dead."

June dropped the glass she was holding and it smashed before her stupid, slow human reflexes could so much as twitch. Swearing, she went to pick the pieces up and ended up slicing her hand on one of the shards.

Red blood welled up on her palm and dripped to the floor.

"Shit, June, run down the basement and take the amulet off so that can heal. I'll come down and tell you what happened after I've got this cleaned up."

"Thanks," June said, frustrated, embarrassed, and a little shocked by how quickly her blood seemed to be fleeing her body. Instinctively she put her hand to her mouth, and almost gagged at the flavor.

She resisted the urge to spit and yanked the amulet off as soon as the door shut behind her. Instantly, the foul flavor vanished, and the blood was quickly absorbed back into her body. She sagged in relief until, driven by guilt at the mess she'd left for Penny, she looked at the inventory list on the white board and started hauling boxes out from the back.

Penny knocked before opening the door, and June made sure she was well out of the way of any errant sunlight when she came through.

What Penny told her made her glad she hadn't put the amulet back on yet.

As horrible as Olivia's death had been, the implications of it were worse. Corrupted demonic energy that could spread from person to person like a disease? June had never heard of such a thing, and judging by the way it tried to eat her, demons were almost certainly not immune. If it actually managed to eat her, she'd probably end up part of the horrible thing.

"The good news is, we've confirmed magic wards meant to enforce Neutral Territory are effective deterrents. We're looking into why that might be, maybe something about the way all magic, including fae, divine, and demonic, with aggressive intent is short-circuited..." Penny shook her head. "Anyway, demons can smell the corruption even before it...blooms, or metastasizes, whatever happens to drive people to kill. I don't know if you'll still be able to sense it when the amulet's on, but we can probably figure out a way for you to check people at night. Do you think—"

"Woah, hold on," June interrupted, frowning. "What do you mean me? I'm dead, remember?"

Penny made a dismissive gesture. "With the amulet on we can pass you off as a witch to the humans. As for the Covens, they deliberately don't keep track of how many vampires are in a given area. No one will look closely at you. We're spread pretty thin, so I doubt it will even be an issue, especially if you only take the amulet off in controlled environments like—"

June shook her head. *Controlled environment?* "No way. You want me to, what, hunt for people who've been infected? *No way*! That thing can *eat me*, and unlike you, I don't have any spells I can use to protect myself!"

Now it was Penny's turn to frown. "June, this is all hands on deck, world-in-danger levels of fucked up. We'll set you up with some spell bombs you can use to trigger—"

June stood up. "Penny, no. I'm not a familiar, I'm a *vampire*. I became one to stay out of all this magical political shit. I'm supposed to be *off grid*! I don't even have Library access!"

Penny stood up as well. "June, look, I get that you had a close call, but we can take—"

"No! *You* look, you saved my life and gave me shelter and this amulet and I am *so* grateful, but are you really going to use that to guilt-compel me to fight this *thing* for you? Or worse, take it away if I don't? Do I get any say?" June rubbed her hands on her face, feeling the walls of the basement pressing down on her. "That is not my job! For all we know the damn thing is sitting outside your wards all night, biding its time until it can try and *eat me*!"

Penny put up her hands. "Okay! Okay, you don't have to go out and hunt it! But could you at least watch the bar for me tonight so Lor and I can go instead? You can safely leave the amulet off while you're here, so you can scan the crowds that come in, make sure those who are infected really can't get past one of our wards."

"I...sure. After my date," June said, deflating begrudgingly. "But you need to—"

"*Date*?" Penny said. Then she slapped her forehead. "Shit, maybe I should have led with that—the detective who was here, the one you asked out *like a crazy person*? Apparently she's an exorcist, a proto-Paladin. You have to cancel your date."

June felt a complicated flutter of emotions, thrill and fear and...shit. Was that why she'd reacted so strongly to the detective? Because some suicidal part of her recognized a hidden predator and wanted to *hunt*?

But, no, she'd had the amulet on. It had to be real. And now that everyone *knew*? There was no way the little tap dance her heart was doing could be because Detective Emily was a secret exorcist.

Shit. June should want to go out with her less, not more. Except... "How did you find that out? You didn't notice before."

Penny pinched the bridge of her nose. "Lor went back to the Underworld to report before we got back here, remember? So no, I couldn't tell. Anyway, she's apparently the only person immune to corruption. The Divine Artifact she's bound to repels them, or something, which means we're probably going to have to call in an actual Divine Paladin, probably that dick who lives out by Fall River."

June chewed on her lip. "So, what you're saying is that near Detective Emily is the safest place in the whole city?"

Penny threw up her hands. "No! June, she's an *exorcist*! Clearly, she can't tell what you are under the amulet or she would have said something, but we don't know if that will last! Are you crazy?"

June was suddenly so angry her fangs started to bud, and she fought the urge to hiss. "So you're saying that even though she's done nothing wrong, nothing but *help*, I can't date her because she's, what, on the *other side*?"

"What! June, that's—No, you know what? You're right. You don't owe me anything. Go on your suicide date. If you end up blasted to bits by a fucking stealth-Paladin, that's on you." Penny tossed the amulet to June, who caught it. "Keep this on and *hidden*. If you, by some miracle, come to your senses and decide to help us instead of playing with Divine fire, I'd like you in one piece."

June resisted the urge to throw the amulet back at Penny and instead put it back on. Unfortunately, the stupid thing made her even more angry as her goddamn hormones or endorphins or whatever the fuck biology started messing with her head. "Fine! I will!" June grabbed her stuff and stormed up the stairs.

"Where are you going?"

"Back to my apartment! I'll call you if the thing comes after me with the amulet on once the sun goes down. That would be *helpful to know*, right?"

Penny followed June up the stairs. "June—"

"Save it. I didn't become a vampire because I wanted to, to, act like a fucking *responsible adult* or whatever. I'll talk to you later!"

June slammed the door behind her.

It took her three blocks in the blazing afternoon sun to finally calm down enough for her brain to start working again.

Shit. She'd handled that kind of badly.

But what the hell? Witches were supposed to be better than those religious fucks, but no. Apparently the kind of magic you used branded you, or some shit, and now she was Juliet and Emily was Romeo and June really didn't want to fucking die in the end like last time.

Well, fuck them all. She was going on her date, and she wasn't going to die, either.

June sent a text to Emily asking if they were still on. She half expected her to cancel because Emily, unlike June, probably wasn't a raging asshole who ignored evil monsters menacing the city so she could yell at her friend and storm out like a child. She was pleasantly surprised when Emily texted back that things were stable enough that she could take a few hours as long as they didn't go too far from the hospital.

This meant that June would have to meet Emily there, which was great because she didn't have to admit she wasn't going near Thoughts and Prayers. It also meant Emily wouldn't ask why she didn't want to see Penny, go all investigator on her, and figure out June wasn't really Sofia, or human, or a very good friend.

Damn Penny and her stupid, maybe slightly justified, biases.

And when had she started caring so much about Penny? Before Penny saved her life, she'd been just some acquaintance, or so she'd thought, but it didn't feel that way now. Maybe it never had. Penny had gone overboard to keep her safe. Was it just that Penny was scared of the terrible monster and wanted *all hands on deck*?

Maybe. And maybe after June had her date, she'd think about a way to help. Her *own* way, not collared like a trained dog so she could sniff people for contamination.

Assuming she survived the night.

The abomination hadn't found her while she was out in the daytime, but maybe that was because it wasn't *active* in the daytime.

June paused in the shade of a particularly dense tree and thought about Emily's curls. The way she moved, with uncompromised confidence and effortless authority while still being deliciously feminine. The way she obviously *genuinely* cared about other people, even strangers she'd only just met and witches she *had* to know were lying to her.

June closed her eyes.

It was worth the risk.

Purpose renewed, June started frantically researching how people dated when they weren't hunting for sexual predators. A movie was out since Emily was on call, but a lot of wooing seemed to involve music, which June could do.

She had a brilliant thought and checked the distance between the hospital and a place she knew that had a really well-organized open mic night. Upon discovering it was close enough, she called to sign up for a few slots and to let them know she was coming with a date. Rory, as always, was delighted to have her, and they talked about instruments and who else was coming for several minutes before she hung up and moved on to food.

Hopefully food wouldn't suck as much as everything else about living had so far.

The internet seemed to think that the best options for date food were French, Japanese, or Italian. There were quite a lot of opinions about which was best of those three, but images of two cartoon dogs kissing over spaghetti and meatballs were everywhere. There was even a whole *song* about spaghetti and meatballs.

Not to mention, the pictures were making her stupid mouth water.

Food had to be better now, right?

When June found a top-rated Italian restaurant halfway between the hospital and the bar where the open mic night would be, it felt like fate. She called and made a reservation for two.

By the time she got to her apartment, it was nearly time to go. She called for a rideshare and went into her apartment to change into clothing more suited for a date and also grab an acoustic guitar for later.

When she got to the hospital, Emily was waiting for her. She looked like she had put some effort into looking nice, with a freshly printed set of leggings and a loose, off-the-shoulder wrap top. She still had her yellow investigator coat on, probably because of the ongoing emergency, but she'd done something with her hair that made the curls a bit tighter and a lot bouncier. She wasn't wearing any makeup, but she didn't need to—her eyes popped anyway, just like they did yesterday. She looked great, but she was so visibly tired that June kind of wanted to give her a hug and wrap her in blankets.

She lost the impulse when Emily saw her and immediately perked up.

"So, vixen, where are we going?"

June had never been called that by a woman before, and she *loved* it. She beamed at Emily and gestured in the direction of the restaurant.

"Food, then a surprise. Unless you don't like surprises?"

"I hate them. But don't tell me, I want to guess," Emily said, eyeing the guitar case in June's hand. "I assume that has something to do with it?"

June winked, but said nothing as they walked down the street. It took Emily five minutes to guess their destination. June enjoyed watching her as she tried to walk and investigate on her phone at the same time. She got an adorable little line between her brows, and she kept having to blow her curls out of her eyes. Unlike when she was working, her hair was down, the curls framed her sweet face and made her look like a porcelain doll.

Humans all had such flawless skin, in this modern age, and perfect teeth. Their cheeks were plump and flush with health, and they mostly smelled like soap and flowers and spices. They seemed to age slower now, too, and June wasn't sure if that was all the magic in the air or just because they led softer lives. As a result, June couldn't really tell how old Emily was. Probably older than she looked to June, since she was a detective.

Emily looked pleased when they stopped outside the restaurant June had picked. They were seated immediately, and June had a moment of frustration when she realized she hadn't done any research on wine.

Fortunately, Emily had it covered, and she picked something red for them. Once the waiter left, she turned her full attention onto June.

"So, Sofia, how comfortable are you with being interrogated? I've been told I have a hard time turning my investigator off."

Right, June was *Sofia*. Shit, Rory knew her as June, and she had no way of hypnotizing anyone with the amulet on.

She'd have to come up with a plan.

"I can take it, though I don't promise I'll answer every question. I like being mysterious," June said, giving Emily a wicked grin.

Emily gave her one back, and her eyes dilated slightly with excitement. "Oh, good."

Thus began the duel.

June had been pumped for information before, humans were always curious, but Emily was on a whole other level. By the time the food arrived, June was only mostly certain she hadn't given anything important away.

June had ordered spaghetti and meatballs, obviously, while being quietly devastated that she couldn't order everything else on the menu as well. She was *hungry*. Emily, sharp eyed, had 'innocently' suggested they share main dishes and ordered a couple appetizers along with some other lemon-and-chicken dish.

June's heart fluttered. It was really weird and uncalled-for, honestly.

The food came, and June tried to hold it together. The smell was overwhelming, and her mouth watered alarmingly. It was everything she could do not to shovel the food into her face like a starving beast. She took a deep breath and focused on not drooling all over the table.

How did humans do this every day? Multiple times a day! When she was still alive, eating was usually just another chore to stave off death for another day, not this constant harvest festival of wonder.

June watched Emily use one of the utensils, a fork, to split the first appetizer in half. It was a ball of fried rice stuffed with cheese. She moved one half to a small plate and offered it to June.

June carefully picked up her own fork and used it to bring the other half to her mouth.

Pleasure, tingling, intense, incredible, washed out from her mouth, along her jaw, and through her entire body. With an obscene groan, she carefully chewed and swallowed and tried not to cry.

Her intense reaction was probably suspicious, but there was no helping it. She had not been prepared.

Food *did not* used to taste this good, even during a harvest festival.

The other appetizer Emily ordered was some kind of toasted bread with tomatoes and a broad-leafed herb. June did tear up a little as she took her first bite. There were so many *textures*. And *flavor*! Salt and sweet and warm, rich oil with a hint of bright bitterness, and peppercorns that popped against her taste buds like tiny fireworks.

It was intoxicating. Before she knew it, the appetizer courses were gone and Emily was watching June with a highly amused expression.

"Like this place, do you?"

June could only nod, still a bit dazzled.

She lost her head completely when the pasta arrived. Spaghetti, it turned out, was an *adventure*.

During the appetizer course, she'd been able to mostly ignore the utensils after that first bite. June wasn't entirely sure why there was a dull knife and a spoon, since she hadn't ordered any soup and the food

was tender enough that there was no need to cut it. The fork worked fine on the rice ball, like a tiny little hay fork. It was kind of cute, really.

The pasta, though, was another story. June watched as Emily picked up her fork and spoon and deftly used them to split the two dishes. She graciously gave June the larger portions for both, and June was touched.

June was also still salivating like a rabid wolf.

She picked up her own fork and did her best to try to look like she knew what she was doing. Other people were using their forks to swirl the pasta in their spoons or on their plate, and June successfully imitated them for her first bite.

Oh, Divine Fucking Hell.

The flavor of the sauce was *overwhelming*, bright and spicy and sour and rich with an intense depth of flavor that somehow put the first dishes to shame. The flavor of the red sauce was so much *more*. Even the cranberries the Narragansett had cultivated couldn't compare.

Then she chewed. The texture of the noodles was absolutely fascinating, with a bit of bite while still impossibly smooth and soft, but also, somehow, wriggly!

It was too good to eat patiently, properly. The damn noodles kept trying to jump off her fork.

She...

Well.

June lost her head.

When she got control of herself again, she looked over at Emily. She was sipping her wine, an even more amused expression on her face, clearly entertained by watching June barely hold it together.

June's gaze flicked around the room, not embarrassed, but strategically assessing the social damage she'd done.

Emily's amusement was not the common response. June could see that some of the other people at the restaurant were *not* happy with her table manners. Possibly even nauseated. Eyes skittered away from their table, napkins were flicked, and well-dressed snobs sniffed and wrinkled their noses.

They could fuck off. It wasn't like she had food on her face or anything. Just her hands. Besides, it had been fine to eat the appetizer bread with her hands. This wasn't *that* different.

Emily, eyes dancing, said, "So, how's the spaghetti?"

June made a sound *not* suitable for public, a little helplessly, and managed a slightly hoarse, "Pretty good." She had to force herself not to explain further, which was ridiculous—normally it wouldn't even be a temptation to drop hints that might reveal her nature to people who didn't already know and approve.

June blamed the wine, which, while not mind-blowing like the spaghetti, was just as excellent as the wine Penny kept at the bar. Better, probably.

It was also a lot stronger and clearly impacting her judgment.

Ohhh! She could blame the *wine*. If it worked on herself, it might work on Emily, too.

June looked up at Emily, intending to say just that, and said instead, "Those eyes of yours are unfair."

June was rewarded for her irrational pivot with a blush.

June wasn't so sloshed she couldn't see the opportunity to flip the script on the detective. She licked her fingers clean with slow deliberation while maintaining eye contact. "So, how many hearts have you broken with that face of yours?"

Emily's blush deepened, but she sounded calm when she answered, "Not as many as you seem to think. Most of the guys I've dated had a problem with my assertiveness. It probably doesn't help that most of the people I spend time with are either public safety workers or people being investigated for crimes. Oh, and lawyers too, but they're not really much better."

"Guys?" June asked, letting her mouth curve into a sly grin.

June sensed victory when Emily looked down at her plate to expertly twirl some pasta. "Yeah, guys."

"But you said yes to me, huh?" June was *extremely* pleased with herself, but she decided to go easy on the poor detective. She let her expression soften and asked gently, "How are you liking it so far? Am I to your taste? It's okay if you only like me for my fabulous mystique."

Emily looked up, startled. Their gazes locked again, and June heard Emily's breath catch. As she stared at June, June felt her smile grow until she was beaming.

Emily blinked, smiled, and flushed even redder. "I *do* like your fabulous mystique."

When they finished dinner, June checked the time and realized that, tragically, they did not have time for dessert. When Emily suggested she was too full for it anyway, June forced herself to pretend she was also not interested. Emily looked at her suspiciously, as if she wanted to call June's bluff, and June was again struck by just how little Emily missed.

June was in so much trouble, and she felt her own eyes dilate slightly at the thought.

When the check came, they mutually agreed to split it. They both scanned the code when the waiter showed them the bill. When the tablet flashed in confirmation, they both stood to go. June offered Emily her arm with a flourish. She had the guitar slung over her back, and Emily had to dodge it when June bowed. It set them both off laughing.

Emily took her arm anyway.

It was a short walk to the bar, and when they got there the bouncer waved them through without asking for a cover, since June was playing.

Rory, of course, called her over as soon as she walked in. "June! Perfect timing. Can you go next? One of those ridiculous Spanish songs, right?"

"Hi Rory, nice to see you. This is Emily, isn't she lovely?" June said, and Rory aimed his considerable enthusiasm at Emily.

"She is! A pleasure. Are you going to perform too? You can borrow any of the equipment you like, and there's a list of songs if you want to sing with the band."

Emily looked startled, then smiled delightedly before June could rebuke Rory for being pushy. "Sure, as long as nobody minds if I'm a little rusty."

"Not at all! The book is over there by the stage, let me know if anything catches your eye."

Rory left, and Emily turned to June with a raised eyebrow. "June?" Emily asked, her expression sharp and predatory.

June was ready. "Stage name. I don't want any of my night time hedonism to get back to my boss at the hospital."

Emily softened instantly, and June knew she'd successfully dodged that bullet.

"Ah, that makes sense. Do you ever play for the kids?"

June didn't, and she felt kind of bad about it, now. She opened her case and started rapidly checking the tuning on her guitar. "I should, shouldn't I? I work night shifts and they like to keep things quiet so they can sleep, but I'll have to see if I can play for them before bed."

The pair who'd been doing a decent cover of a Rolling Stones song finished, and Rory called June up to the stage. Emily waved her off and went to sit at an empty high top near the front.

June's fingers were slightly slower than normal, and it took all of her attention to play to her normal standards. She probably should have spent some time making sure her body had all the right muscle memory to play properly *before* jumping on stage, but that was hindsight for you—

Judgey.

She ended up playing two songs, because the audience called for an encore. June went to join Emily, but apparently Emily was next. She gave June a wink and hopped onto the stage when Rory called for her.

The band swung into 'All That Jazz'. Emily sang the opening notes.

June forgot how to breathe.

Emily was *good.* Emily was doing *choreography.* Emily was an upstanding investigator, a *Paladin,* and she was playing the murdering seductress to a fucking T.

As soon as the band realized Emily knew what she was doing, they adjusted, and Emily worked the small stage. Her voice was rich, like chocolate, and she almost didn't need the mic with the way she filled the space. June's mouth went dry when Emily dropped to the floor, and it became deliciously obvious how flexible she was. Emily's clothing allowed a lot more movement than June would have guessed, and the way it clung to her curves was almost more than June could take. Some of the band members started filling in the chorus vocal line, and, with a room full of musicians, soon Emily had everyone else singing as well, working the crowd like she'd been born to it.

It was stunning. Emily was *bold*, and she clearly had the skills to follow through. It was incredible, and incredibly sexy.

June was in *so much* trouble.

The room absolutely exploded when she finished. Emily gave a cheeky wink, and hopped back off the stage as if she hadn't just dance-fucked the entire room.

She was only slightly flushed when she finally pushed her way over to June, but her eyes were sparkling.

"That was great. I needed that," she said, and sat next to June.

June was still too stunned to say anything. Fortunately, Rory picked that moment to come over and gush. "My god, woman, you can *sing*. Can I convince you to do anything else?"

Emily smiled graciously. "Nah, not tonight. I don't think I can follow that up with anything that will make quite as much of a splash, and besides, your jazz list is seriously lacking."

"What!" Rory exclaimed, outraged, "What do you mean *lacking*? What songs do you want me to add? I'll get them ready by next week if you promise to come back."

They bickered about songs for several minutes, and June used the time to recover.

"L.O.V.E. is *extremely* underrated. It should be on every Jazz list. Actually, Nat King Cole should *be* every jazz list," Emily was saying, and Rory spluttered delightedly.

When Rory finally got called away, June was composed enough to speak again. "Well, *that* was *amazing*. I thought you didn't do surprises?"

Emily laughed. "I don't like *being* surprised, but I *love* surprising other people. Also, you're pretty freaking amazing yourself. How do you make your fingers move so fast?"

"Drugs," June said, deadpan, and Emily swatted at her. "But seriously, it's just hours and hours of practice. I spend most of my free time playing." June leaned in and whispered, conspiratorially, "It means I have *very* dexterous fingers." She waggled her eyebrows and gave Emily a suggestive smile.

Emily blushed again.

June felt like she might start glowing.

They stayed and watched a few more performances before Emily sighed and stood to go.

"I should get back. We still have an ongoing crisis on our hands. But thank you. This was really great."

June stood too. "Want me to walk back with you?" she asked, more eagerly than she'd meant to.

"Sure," Emily said, and smiled.

It wasn't a particularly long walk, and June managed to keep Emily talking about herself. June had the suspicion that Emily was letting it happen, and she hoped that was a good sign. Emily talked about how her music teachers had wanted her to go into theater, but her parents had wanted her to go to law school. In deference to her parents, she'd agreed to at least get her undergrad degree, and she found she genuinely *liked* law. While she was there, she realized that she didn't want to spend most of her time behind a desk, and that led her to becoming an investigator.

"Honestly, I don't think anyone was surprised. I was always an especially nosy person, and when most of your social circle is made of theater kids, that's *saying* something."

They stopped at the corner where they'd met up. June's rideshare pulled up just as they were arriving.

June met Emily's gaze and was shocked at how vulnerable she suddenly felt. They were standing very close, and her heart was thumping painfully in her chest, making her feel light headed.

"Thanks for calling me," she said, and she knew her heart was in her eyes.

Emily didn't look any less flustered than June felt. "Sure thing. We, ah, should do this again, maybe. I'll call you?"

June knew she shouldn't. Emily was a *Paladin*, and yeah, Penny definitely had a point about that, but she couldn't not. "Yeah."

There was a long moment, and then June whispered, "So, can I kiss you goodnight?"

Emily hesitated for a second then nodded firmly. June moved carefully, giving her plenty of time to change her mind. She put her hand gently on the back of Emily's neck and let their noses touch for just a second before pressing a soft, gentle kiss to Emily's lips.

Emily shivered briefly, and June pulled away before the kiss could become more, or less.

"Call me," June said and climbed into the waiting car.

She collapsed into the seat, and her head dropped back against the seat as the car pulled away.

June was in so much trouble.

NEXUS

"I...what?" Aiden asked, more confused than ever. Why did everyone here seem to *know* him?

The ethereal woman smelled like sun-thawed soil. She walked over, her steps light and graceful, and cupped Aiden's face with her hands. "You're Aiden, yes? The soul I, well, I was assigned to be your therapist, but..." She was searching him for something, maybe recognition.

She didn't find it, not really, but Aiden could feel himself wanting to remember, like all the other times. Aiden said, "We knew each other once."

The woman nodded and stepped back. "We did." A slight frown crossed her face. "I'll need to look into who recommended *I* come to you. The odds of this being an accident... they're terrible, you understand? There are so many souls who need help, and there are hundreds of us who…" She seemed to notice the way Aiden's shoulders were tensing. "Never mind. It's not important right now."

Aiden nodded, then stopped and shook his head. "I don't think I do understand. Um, I don't remember you. I'm sorry. I know I should?" He clasped his hands together and pressed them into his stomach.

The woman hummed soothingly and gestured for Aiden to follow her. "Yes, sweet. Blessed eternity, of course you don't understand. Let's see if I can help with that."

"Um." Aiden thought back, trying to remember if anyone had told him her name. "You're Esther, right? Sam said you'd find me."

Esther nodded, almost absently. "Yes, but he wasn't the one who recommended me to you. I assumed it was Zee, but now I'm not so sure." She made a thoughtful sound. "I suppose it still could be, but if so…"

Esther shook her head as if to clear it and took out a delicate pen that could have passed for a wand. She used it to draw a door on the elm tree.

Aiden expected it to open into some kind of office. Instead, Esther took them to a playground.

It was the same one that had called out to Aiden during his tour of Nexus. He stopped to admire the deep magenta of the grass, as bright and full of life as regular green grass, but also weird, and different. It rippled with blue when the wind moved over it. When he looked closer he could see that the veins of the grass were actually a deep cyan color, contrasting vibrantly with the purple blade and creating that illusion of blue. He ran his hand over it, and it took his breath away.

He would have admired it longer, but Esther had stopped walking, obviously waiting for him. She didn't look upset, only patient and perhaps still a little awed. Aiden blushed and hurried to catch up to her.

The grass was not the only strange thing about the park. The trees were an absolute riot of color, with every leaf different. It seemed to Aiden like there should have been repeating colors, and yet every one he looked at was a distinctly different shade.

"Are there more colors on the trees than there are colors?" he asked, too nervous to press her to explain what she'd meant about Zee or about their shared past.

What *was* he? Did he really want to know?

"Possibly," Esther said serenely. "The colors that you see on the trees here are a reflection of the colors you can imagine. Do you see a lot of colors?"

Aiden swallowed. "Um. Yeah."

Esther smiled at him, but didn't say anything else.

The two of them walked over to the playground. Without a word, Esther started climbing the jungle gym. Somehow, the bars always seemed to be at an optimal distance for Esther to climb, even though by all rights she should have been too big for it. When she reached the top, she hung upside down and her hair fell almost all the way to the ground.

Aiden wanted to climb too, but he didn't quite dare.

"What are you so afraid of, baby bunny?" she asked, smiling upside down at him.

"I... A lot," he said honestly.

"I see. Are you afraid of heights?" she asked.

"No."

"That's good," she said and waited.

Aiden sighed and then ducked his head to hide a self-conscious smile. It was always like this, a moment of irrational fear, and then calm determination, the certainty that he could do this, as irrational as the fear that preceded it.

Was that because he was old? Or because...

It didn't matter. It simply was.

Maybe...maybe he should let someone explain things.

He started to climb. He was slow at first, and the jungle gym adjusted itself, making it easy for him. As he got higher, he also became bolder, and he started leaping from bar to bar, which was always at the exact distance that would make him feel most comfortable.

Eventually he was swarming all over the thing, laughing, and Esther joined him, racing and playing games of leapfrog and tag.

Just as Aiden was starting to get truly bold, Esther dropped to the ground and looked up at Aiden, waiting.

Aiden froze.

"Why are you afraid, baby bunny?" she asked, suddenly serious again.

"Is this the therapy?" Aiden asked, cautiously. He felt better now, calmer. He could ask what he wanted to know.

"Yes and no. It's me, asking after my once little brother."

Her what? "When?"

"Oh, sweet, so long ago. Just before the Seal went up, when we didn't tell stories of gods, only of people who did great feats of magic."

Aiden felt the words land on him like stones. "So. So it's all true then? I'm... old, older than I remember, and all these people I've forgotten were from my past?"

Esther's eyes twinkled. "Yes. But do you know what it *means*? You *survived*."

"Um. No? I'm dead. Right?"

Esther laughed. "I mean your soul. Your soul survived intact after being put through...oh, sweet boy, we don't even know. More than

I can imagine. You're the first soul caught in a reincarnation loop to come here."

"The *first*?"

Esther nodded gravely. "And only, that anyone can tell. Perhaps more will surface. We don't have records of what happened to the lost ones. We don't know what lives you lived, or how living potentially *hundreds* of lives might have changed you." Esther reached up a hand to cup his face again. "You're old, *so* old, but you're also *new*."

Aiden swallowed, letting the information settle. "I still don't know what that means. I don't remember any life but the one I just had, or...well. Every time I meet someone from before, I get this feeling..." He drifted off, unable to find the words.

"Mmm, you're sensing the Library. Each time you connect with someone and they remember you, the Library gives you access to their memories of you."

"Oh," Aiden said. "No one told me." He hesitated, then added, "And I didn't ask." He'd been *not asking* a lot. Too much.

Resolved, Aiden *reached* and—*yes*. There they were. Aiden shivered, and then, almost compulsively, he admitted, "I'm afraid to look at them. What if they aren't..." Right? Good? They'd be both good and bad, like all his memories. "Are they really part of me even though I can't remember?"

Esther tilted her head to the side. Her expression was warm, soft. Understanding. "When a tree grows in the forest, the seasons it lives through become a part of its trunk, there forever, even though the tree does not have the biology for true memory. Souls are like that too. Normally, when they come here, those memories are waiting. For you, it will be different, but not *so* different." She smiled enigmatically, obviously pleased with her own analogy.

And, oh, *that* was a memory. It surged through him like white fire, undeniable. It smelled of wood smoke, of roasting meat, of hot clay and boiling roots. She'd smiled at him like that before.

Aiden closed his eyes and held the memory to his chest like a teddy bear. "I'm afraid of disappointing you all."

"Why?"

"Because, because I always do? I die, or leave, or am gay. Am a whore. And it's not something I can control, you know? I just *am* myself, and I *like* myself. It hurts, disappointing people I care about. I've been punished for being myself my whole life, and it doesn't matter if I don't deserve it, because I'd rather that than—than having to start all over again." Aiden felt tears well through his closed eyelids and drip through his lashes. He opened his eyes and they dropped down towards Esther, cool, glittering gems, and landed in her hair. Where they landed, iridescent flowers bloomed. "I'm not what they, *you*, remember. What you expect. I can't remember, but I did know you, before, in a dream of another me. I *know* it's true."

Aiden wanted to curl in on himself, but he couldn't, not without falling, and he wasn't going to fall. "But that *me* died, right? Died in a way no one else usually does. Over and over. And now I'm different. Too much my current self to remember, to even *pretend,* to be the person you remember me as. I'm failing to be what people want me to be all over again." He was babbling, and his chest ached, but he couldn't stop. Couldn't even manage to want to.

He needed *someone* to understand, even if that someone wasn't him.

Esther's eyes also filled with tears. "Oh, love. I'm sorry. Come here."

Aiden hesitated, then dropped down. Esther wrapped her arms around him. "You're quite the resilient little soul, you know."

He choked on a soggy laugh. He knew that. He'd been told that before. *What a remarkably resilient boy you are*, and *Damn kid, I never would have guessed what you've been through*. He'd been told a hundred different ways by a hundred different kinds of people that he was strange and strong and it was so frustrating because he still *hurt*, so much, so often.

"I'm tired," he whispered into Esther's soft hair. "But I can't rest. Not even here."

"Why do you say that?" she demanded very gently, petting his hair. "You know you're safe here, right?"

"I… Yes. I know I'm safe here. But it feels like something is pushing me, driving me forward? It's not just the memories. Things keep happening, I keep meeting people who knew me, and weird things keep happening with them, and there was this person lost in a pond, and I just, it feels like this whole place *wants* something from me, but I can't quite figure out *why*!"

"I see," Esther said. There was something stern and oddly protective in her voice. "Let's set that aside for now. Before you can face the future, you need to make peace with your past. Now, can you think about what you just said to me? About your fears?"

Aiden nodded and considered. He said, "I like being punished sometimes, because I understand it. It makes me feel safer. Does that make me, I don't know, broken?"

Esther squeezed him tighter. "Definitely not. The paths we take to happiness are as wild and weird as the lives we live. You've lived a lot of lives, bunny, so you're going to have a lot of paths to happiness, and *all* of them are *good* as long as everyone is on board with walking them. Understand?"

Aiden felt so *warm*. The words sank into his soul like drops of honey, and his tears redoubled. "Yes."

Esther gently released Aiden and looked at him for a good while, searching his face. "One more important question. Are you sorry? For the way you led your life? The most recent one, at least?"

"No." He said it immediately and with some anguish. He wasn't sorry. He'd tried his best.

But, shouldn't he be?

Shouldn't he be sorry he'd failed to live his life longer?

He regretted the things he didn't get a chance to try, but...but...

"No," he said again, more quietly. "But I think I'm glad I died." He cringed guiltily.

"Ahh," Esther said, a sympathetic sigh, and pulled him back into her arms. "And you think that is wrong."

"Yeah. I do. It *is*. And I shouldn't be rewarded for feeling that way. I should have gone to Hell. This should be Hell."

There was an ominous rumbling that shook the ground. Aiden froze and looked around, his chest fluttering with panic.

"Lucifer!" Esther said, angrily, letting Aiden go. "Honestly, this is a *therapy* session! What the *Hell* is wrong with you?"

The rumbling repeated, and then cut off abruptly when Esther stomped her foot. "Stop scaring him!"

Aiden looked between the ground and Esther, eyes wide.

Esther reached out and squeezed Aiden's arm. "Don't worry about that. Lucifer gets touchy about the word 'Hell'."

The rumble started up again, and Esther stomped again. "He has *bigger things to worry about*!" she said, low and angry. The rumbling cut off in a way that felt oddly begrudging. She cupped Aiden's face again. "You okay, sweet?"

"Um, yeah." He swallowed. "We can, uh. Just not say that word." Aiden was never going to say the word 'Hell' out loud *ever* again.

Esther rolled her eyes and patted his cheek. "You say whatever words you like, sweet. Lucifer, I am *quite* certain, owes you." She glared at the ground again, and then shook herself. "Where were we? Right." Esther smiled wryly. "You're right, it's bad that you're glad you died, but not because it's your *fault*. It doesn't mean you deserve to be punished."

Aiden pressed his face into Esther's shoulder. "I know I don't *deserve* it. But, but lots of people think I do. I *know* they do, because they told me so when they hit me, or sent me away, or—" Aiden cut off on a sob, remembering all the times he'd accepted punishment because there wasn't any other choice. When his father broke his arm for running off the football field, or his mother locked him in a closet for three days after she caught him with her makeup. He knew it wasn't his fault *now*, but it hadn't stopped the pain then, and it didn't stop him from *feeling* like he'd done something wrong to deserve it. "It *matters* that they feel that way. It shouldn't, but it does because I cared about them! I still do! Maybe I shouldn't care, maybe I should hate them instead, but I don't want to stop caring!" The memory of that last, cold night seeped into his chest, and he shuddered. "But I wasn't strong enough to endure that way, I guess."

Esther resumed petting his hair. "I somehow doubt that was the problem." She held him, her soul radiating warmth and comfort, and eventually it chased away the cold again. She said, "So, let me get this straight. You're afraid of being punished for things you did in life, *any* of them, even the ones you don't remember, even things you had no control over and don't think were wrong, but others *did* think were wrong. You also think you deserve to be punished because you think you were bad *at* life, at least this last time."

Was that what he was saying? "That's silly."

Esther took his hand, leading him away from the jungle gym. "Perhaps, little one, but that's alright. Feelings are often silly. They don't think. That's what *we're* for."

He followed behind Esther, digesting that.

"I don't know how to not be afraid," he said finally. "I... Fear has always been there, even if I know what to do with it and understand how to manage it, mostly. I think I've *always* been afraid. It makes sense, right? When could I have lived without fear? I know enough about history. I like men. I like *scary* men, dangerous ones, or ones it is dangerous to like. I think maybe I always have, in all the—all the other lives. Like it's part of the center of my, my soul-trunk, or something. Even if I'm old, like, so old there's no way to count the lifetimes, when would I have been safe? Has life ever been *safe*? Especially for someone different, like me?"

Esther squeezed his hand. "I don't know, sweet."

She didn't say he was safe now, either, because while he was safe *here*, that didn't mean he was safe *now*.

And he'd done it to himself this time, too. He'd immediately turned himself into a demon. After being warned, if vaguely, that it would make him a target, put him in danger, he'd practically *jumped* at it, without thinking it through, just because he'd liked Sam and wanted to...to...

"I do it to myself," he said. "Put myself in these positions. Am I bad? To do that?"

Esther didn't answer right away, leading him over to the slide. They climbed up the fake rock wall together in silence, and as Aiden stepped out onto a wobbly bridge, she asked, "Do you think you are?"

Aiden hesitated, then walked across the wobbly bridge with sure steps. "I *want* to think I'm brave. Strong. Beautiful. But only if it's true. Only if I've earned it."

Esther followed him quickly across the bridge, somehow managing to be graceful.

"What would need to happen for you to feel like you deserved it?"

Esther climbed up the final, short ladder to the slide and turned to wait for Aiden. Carefully, he followed her. She motioned for him to go first, and he did.

The slide was much longer and much steeper than it should have been. As he slid down, it was perfectly frictionless, and when he reached out the tube grew in size so that he could never quite touch the tunnel above him. Suddenly the slide dipped down, impossibly vertical. For a moment he was suspended in the air like Alice as she went down the rabbit hole. It lasted a suspiciously long time, and he looked at the walls of the slide with narrowed eyes, not entirely sure if it was reasonable for gravity to just *stop* working. Aiden got the weird impression that the slide was laughing at him, and suddenly gravity was back and the slide immediately twisted into a loop.

When he landed, he called up the slide to Esther, "This slide is kinda cheeky."

He heard her laugh the whole way down. A cascade of flowers preceded her arrival, and she landed perfectly, not a single hair out of place.

"The slide's not the only cheeky one here," she said, grinning at him.

Aiden stuck out his tongue at her and ran for the swings.

Esther followed him at a more sedate pace and took the spot beside him. The two of them swung in silence, sometimes in sync, and sometimes perfectly out of phase. Happily, the swings still made the *sound*, the comforting squeak of rarely oiled hinges. The chains, though, didn't pinch at Aiden's hands, which was nice.

Esther didn't repeat her question, but it rang in his head, over and over again.

He didn't know the answer. He should, though, if he ever expected to get what he wanted.

"This isn't what I expected from therapy," he said instead of answering.

"Oh? Did you go to a lot of therapy when you were alive? Most recently, anyway."

"No. Not really. Not the kind with psychologists, anyway. Just the school counselor, and she wasn't a therapist, just a nun who mostly agreed with my parents about everything. Oh, well, and Father Luke, but he *definitely* doesn't count." Luke had been his first, and his worst, lover. "I watched a lot of videos made by psychologists, though. They weren't actually therapy, but they helped, you know? Maybe they reminded me of stuff I already knew, or maybe they were just good enough for what I needed. Anyway, aren't you supposed to like, sit and stare at me and wait for me to crack open and spill all my secrets to you?"

"Is that what you want?"

"Maybe?"

Esther stopped swinging and stared at Aiden, her eyes warm and full of rainbows.

Aiden cracked.

"I don't know what I can do to deserve to feel that way. I shouldn't have to do anything, right? I'm just being an idi—" Aiden couldn't finish. Not because he didn't want to finish, but because he couldn't. The word had cut off in his mouth, the sound simply stopping, on its own.

He frowned. "Why does that keep happening?"

Esther smiled. "Souls cannot lie, Aiden. Even Demons. Especially Demons. Not with words, when they speak, and not with the faces they show."

"Oh. *Oh.*" That explained some things. "Oh."

They sat in silence for a while. Esther kept staring at him, but it was softer now, her eyes lifted in a smile.

Aiden said, "I haven't looked at my reflection yet. I don't want to see my face and hate it, like I did...before. It wasn't right. It didn't feel like mine. I thought I might be trans for a while, but that wasn't it. Then I thought maybe I was just manifesting my self-loathing, but that wasn't it either. I didn't hate myself, I hated my *face*. And other people didn't, which... Well, they usually thought I was just being shallow. Vain. I thought maybe they had a point, but it didn't feel like vanity. It felt *wrong*."

Esther nodded. "It happens that way, sometimes, with reincarnation. Or, at least it does now. Before the Seal, there weren't really many mirrors, and people didn't worry so much about how they looked, only how healthy they felt. There weren't enough humans living in one place for people to get picky over aesthetics."

"Oh," Aiden said again. He pushed himself off and started swinging again, and Esther joined him.

The sky above them was getting closer to sunset, but instead of a regular sunset where the colors only bloomed on the horizon, the entire sky filled with color. Aiden knew with absolute certainty the sky couldn't do that, because the colors were caused by the angle of the sun or something. It made him deeply, ridiculously happy that even though it wasn't supposed to be that way, the sky did it anyway, probably because it was beautiful and this was a place where people could be beautiful, even if it didn't make any sense.

"I belong here. In this place. I fit." He could feel it.

"You do," Esther agreed, smiling at him.

He still felt that tightness in his chest. Fear, and the echoes of old pain, some remembered, and maybe some not.

He trusted that fear. Fear meant he wasn't being reckless.

And, oh. That was it, wasn't it?

Aiden stopped swinging. "Pain makes me feel safe, and I'm afraid I'll break myself because I won't stop before it's...before it's too late. Like I...like I did. When I died. I think it wasn't the first time, either. I think I died young a lot." His eyes burned. "How can I deserve to feel strong when I hurt myself so much?"

Esther stopped swinging as well and went to stand in front of him. She opened her arms, and Aiden threw himself into them again. He muffled his sobs in her soft hair, and he felt a few new flowers appear and bloom next to his cheeks, as if they were drinking in his tears and using them to grow. The thought that they might actually be doing that made him smile, and then cry harder.

"It's okay, baby. There's people here who will help you, no matter what, okay? You're going to be okay," she said, and he heard the unconditional love in her voice. It broke him, a little, that a virtual stranger could just *love* like that. With no strings, and from a place of such *strength*.

It was everything he wanted to be. And he could see it, too, not quite a memory, but an understanding.

He could do that. *Had* done it, with his parents, Father Luke, some of his ex-boyfriends. He'd offered them unconditional love, even though they hadn't given it in return.

It had hurt him, the lack of reciprocity, but he could handle that. Because he *was* strong.

Aiden stood there with her for a long time even after he stopped crying. When he pulled away there was a massive cascade of iridescent flowers that fell out of her hair. They glowed faintly in the liminal darkness.

Esther reached down to pluck one up, holding it in her hand. "Oh, sweet one. Look at these. Aren't they lovely?"

Aiden nodded. They were. "Didn't you make them?"

The moon was beginning to rise again, and even though last night the moon had been full, tonight it rose as a thick, smiling crescent. Aiden smiled up at it, and he noticed that the rainbow trees were glowing in the deepening twilight, like the flowers.

"No, sweet. *You* did." She held one to her nose to smell.

Aiden froze. "Are they weird? Special?"

"I don't know," Esther said slowly. She started gathering up the rest. "I'll keep them safe, just in case. Okay?"

"Okay," he said. Then, "I think I'd like to find a mirror."

"I know the perfect one."

She took his hand and led him to a small thicket of trees. Aiden could feel the edge of the deer paths, and Esther gestured for Aiden to take the lead.

He stopped. "I don't know where I am supposed to go."

Esther smiled at him. "Go where you want to."

Aiden frowned at her. "I want to go where you think I should go."

Esther's expression grew slightly wicked. "And if I tell you I want you to go where *you* want to go?"

Aiden thumped his foot on the ground and frowned harder.

Esther laughed, and relented, "Alright, alright. Just start walking. I'll correct you if you turn off the path."

Aiden looked at her seriously. "Why?" He was asking about more than the literal path.

Esther smiled, deep and full. "Wouldn't you do the same for me? If our positions were reversed?"

"Yes," he said, instantly.

"Why?"

Aiden frowned seriously. "Because seeing people stumble around in the dark and hurt themselves is *terrible*. But it's also important to let people find their own paths. So, so the best thing you can do for someone is let them know where they are, and offer help, and hope they'll take it when they're ready."

Esther smiled and booped Aiden on the nose. "Just so."

Aiden frowned, this time not at all seriously, and Esther laughed.

They didn't have to go far before they came to a waterfall. The cliff seemed to be hundreds of meters tall, and Aiden couldn't even see the top of it. The mist at the bottom glittered with fragmented rainbows, and the stones were all crystal and full of starlight.

"Is this your home?" he asked Esther, unsure where they were.

"No, sweet. It's called the Falls of Reflection." Esther nodded at the waterfall. "There is a mirror through there. It's not special in any concrete way. Only because of where it is."

"Won't I get wet?" He bounced on the balls of his feet, his body electric with nerves.

"Not if you don't want to. Do you want me to come in with you?"

Aiden was torn. He thought about it and answered, "A little, but I think I should go alone anyway."

Esther nodded and gave his shoulder a tiny squeeze. Aiden took a breath, starting to get used to the way he didn't need to, and then let it out and ran towards the falls.

He forced himself not to hesitate, but he still flinched as he ran into the water. The water split for him and he passed through without so much as a drop landing on him, and he staggered to a halt.

The cave beyond the falls was magnificent. The ceiling soared high above him and glittered with the same starlight as the stones outside, only much brighter. He looked down at his hands. They were familiar, solid and his, but also not, lacking any callous or scar. The lighting was exactly right to show every detail without being harsh.

He took another deep breath and held it. He could probably hold it forever, standing in this magical cathedral, frozen in time. He'd never have to face what he would see in the mirror. He'd never have to find out who he might be when he had the freedom to be himself, when he couldn't lie to himself about it and his reflection would show only the truth.

The face of his soul.

He hoped it wasn't some horrible mashup of a thousand lives. That would be terrible, to see hints of a thousand people he couldn't remember being.

Or worse, what if he just had no face? He'd been so many different people and all of them were gone so now he was no one, like that poor soul from the river that he couldn't remember but he hoped with his whole heart was okay.

What if he looked like an ancient mummy? Not that old bodies weren't still beautiful, but Aiden didn't like being seen as old. He didn't want people to expect him to be wise. Not when he wasn't sure that he was.

Aiden let out the breath and turned to face the mirror.

He stood in complete shock for several minutes. His knees felt weak, and he absently let them collapse, still staring at the unexpectedly lovely creature in his reflection.

His face was...perhaps it *was* a mix of a thousand faces, but it wasn't a hideous homunculus. It was familiar, and soft, and friendly, young and also ageless, like a nymph. An ancient, boyish sprite. His skin was flawless, almost luminous, and his eyes were huge, only partially because they were wide with shock. They were filled with the same sort of rainbows that Esther's had.

Aiden wasn't entirely sure what they meant, the rainbows, but he felt, instinctively, that he would need to work very hard to be properly worthy of them.

There was more. He wasn't entirely human. He had rabbit ears, long, white ears, with bright pink tips. He could feel them there, now. He had felt them all along, actually, only he hadn't let himself recognize it. In his shock, they stood straight up, making him look silly and adorable.

He did not have time to dwell on his ears, though, because he also had *antlers*. They came out from artfully shaggy silver hair, right at the base of his bunny ears. They were covered in soft lavender velvet, and he counted seven points. He reached up a shaking hand and touched them. His whole body shivered, and an unexpected wave of arousal washed through him.

He dropped his hand, and his cheeks practically glowed, a cartoon of a blush. His bunny ears, seemingly of their own accord, turned and pressed back against the back of his head and neck.

"Oh," he whispered, overwhelmed. He stared for a long time, trying to make sense of what he was seeing and not quite managing it. "Well. That explains why everyone keeps calling me *bunny*." He suspected the bunny ears were expressive, likely telegraphing his emotions more than even his face, which would at least partially explain why everyone seemed to see right through him all the time.

The rest was probably just part of being a soul. A poker face, which he *could* do if the need arose, was a kind lie, after all.

"Dang it! I missed it! I was really hoping I could see your face when you first noticed them. Have you found the tail yet?" Sam's unmistakable voice asked from somewhere behind him.

Aiden jumped several feet in the air and spun around.

Sam stood at the entrance to the cave, Esther just behind him. She looked about as close to annoyed as he had seen her and she lightly cuffed Sam on the back of the head.

"Ah, whoops. Sorry. I guess not," Sam said, not exactly chagrined.

Aiden twisted to look at his butt and was less surprised than he felt he ought to be when he discovered a small fluffy tail poking out from a slit in his jeans. A slit he must have put there without *realizing*.

Just how much had he been ignoring over the past few days?

A word popped into his head, the voice of his mom, or, no. It *was* his mom, but not the one he remembered. It was some *other* mom, a mom from a dream, or maybe from a different life, saying *hurry up, scuttlebutt*. He'd known the word when he was alive, even looked it up once, trying to explain to his friends that he wasn't making it up. It was the name of the kind of tails deer and bunnies have.

And now him, apparently.

He waggled it back and forth, and studied it intently. Interestingly, when attached to an otherwise human body, there was almost no way to tell the difference between a deer tail and a rabbit tail. It looked more like a deer tail just then, curled up with adrenalin, or whatever passed for adrenalin in a soul-body, but Aiden was willing to bet when he sat down it poked out more like a fluffy bunny cotton puff.

He waggled it again, and Sam made a strangled sound. "Tell him to stop, please. I can't. It's too much."

"How long have you been stalking us, cat?" Esther asked, gently chiding.

"Hey! Aiden told me to find him in Nexus! When I saw he was with you, I hung back. I was being *patient*," Sam said. He didn't seem even the slightest bit sorry.

"Hmmm. So, is there something you needed to say to him, Sam? Something that couldn't wait?" Esther asked, arching a delicate brow.

Aiden turned to look just in time to see Sam's face fall. His posture turned beseeching and he looked positively devastated. It was very uncharacteristic to how he usually acted, and Aiden was suddenly very scared.

"Aiden, I'm so sorry. I never explained to you what it meant to sign up with the Library."

Esther turned to Sam, genuinely shocked. "You didn't? Sam!"

Sam let out an anguished yowl. "I know!" He hunched his shoulders and took a few steps closer to Aiden and stopped. "Lucifer told me to take him there, so I thought he, well I didn't think. I didn't even question it!"

Aiden grew very, *very* cold.

"Lucifer told you to take him to the Library on his second day? Why?"

Aiden made a small sound of protest in the back of his throat, but they were too far away to hear him.

"Something to do with the emergency on earth. Look, I don't know why, the point is that I did and I fucked it all up!" He turned back to Aiden, and there were *tears* in his eyes. "Aiden, when you signed up at the Library, you *changed*. You're no longer just a mortal soul. You have a <[name]> now, and that means you're a Demon. I should have made sure you understood what that meant."

"I, um," Aiden said, the words *emergency on earth* still echoing in his thoughts. "What does that mean? What's the difference between a mortal soul and a Demon?"

Sam opened his mouth to answer, looking even more upset, somehow, so Aiden said, "Wait, I can do it." He <[accessed]> the Library, not bothering with a screen in his haste, and then he knew.

Being a Demon meant that he would never join Divinity, unless he let himself get torn to shreds first so that his identity was scattered. It meant his soul could host a shard or Mantle, and all the akashic knowledge stored in the Library. It meant he could do any number of important jobs, including entering the mortal plane as one of several different kinds of demonic manifestations, one of which was being a familiar like Sam.

It was all stuff the scary owl person had kind of implied to him before, so none of the information felt new. He hadn't used a screen to access the knowledge, so it was still a little vague, like something half remembered. He figured if he wanted to know more, or in more detail, he would need to use a screen to organize his thoughts better.

"Oh," he said. "Okay. It's fine."

Sam's ears flattened into his hair, almost disappearing. "But it's *not* okay! You're now going to be hunted by any angel or divine creature you come across!"

Aiden tensed up again. "Are there divine creatures down here?" What if they tortured him to try to get Sam's <[name]>? He would *never* give it up, but, how long would they—

"What? No, of course not. I meant if you ever wanted to reincarnate. Demonic souls are still allowed to reincarnate, but when you do you keep the knowledge of your <[name]> and you can access some magic without needing a familiar bond. It *sounds* fun, but without the benefit of an active Library connection it can be *super* dangerous, and if an exorcist or an Angel finds you, they'll try to rip you apart! You might not even know why!"

Once Aiden sorted through the meaning of the torrent of words, he relaxed. "Oh. That's okay then." The idea of reincarnation was *viscerally* unappealing. He was *done* being different people.

Which...huh. He'd thought that before too, back at the Library. It made sense now.

Sam pulled Aiden away from that train of thought with another yowl. His tail started twitching back and forth in agitation. "You don't understand! I think part of me did it on purpose, because I wanted to catch you and I didn't ask you and—"

"Sam, it's okay," he said, a bit of frustration, and fear, leaking into his voice. He walked over and took Sam's hand. "The Librarian explained it all, remember? Besides, I, um, wanted you to catch me," Aiden smiled shakily. "Please, I forgive you, okay? I get to do that."

That stopped Sam, finally, but he still looked upset. Aiden fought to stop himself from shrinking away.

"Aiden, I shouldn't have *tried* to catch you until I was sure you knew what you were getting into!"

"Sam, it's *okay*, really." Aiden's eyes burned with frustration, but he resolutely kept them dry. "You gave me your <[name]> even though I didn't know what it meant or how important it was, so I think that makes us even. I would have said yes anyway. I had this feeling when we were there... I think I *needed* to become a Demon."

"Pfff, that's obvious," Sam said immediately, and then brightened, "Oh! All that weird magic stuff!" He frowned. "But what does that have to do with the monster? Have you—"

Aiden released Sam's hand and stepped back. "No."

Sam looked like he'd been punched. "Fuck, you're right. What am I doing, dragging you into this? I'm going to tell Lucifer he needs to leave you alone. *I'll* leave you alone. Whatever this thing is, we'll handle it some other way, and you'll be safe. Detective Paladin—"

Sam kept talking, but all Aiden heard was static. "You're with a Paladin?" Horror crawled up his throat, and he started shaking. *I'll leave you alone.*

"Yeah, she's cool though. I think. Anyway, it's not something you have to worry about. I won't let them send you in to fight."

Aiden shook his head, feeling himself start to come apart at the seams. "I can't fight."

Sam looked startled. "Oh, wow. Like, *can't*? I mean you said it, so it must be true. All the more reason for me to tell Lucifer—" Sam cut off, and his expression turned stricken. "Oh no. Not *now*." He reached for Aiden, then stopped and dropped his hand. "I have to go."

Aiden pushed his way through the ice and asked, "To fight the monster? With the Paladin?"

"Yeah. Aiden, I'm sorry. So, *so* sorry. Can we talk later? Please? I'll leave you alone after, if that's what you want."

Aiden nodded. "Come to my room," he whispered, feeling like a ghost. He wanted to reach out to Sam, tell him he had nothing to be sorry for, *beg* him not to go, but he was too slow.

Sam evaporated into green fire and was gone.

Aiden fell back to his knees and curled into a ball, trying to hold himself together.

Esther's arms joined his, and, slowly, Aiden stopped shaking.

"He gave you his <[name]>?" Esther asked, softly.

Aiden nodded. "But now he wants to leave me. If he even lives that long."

Esther made a low, soothing sound. "That's not what he said."

Aiden held still. "He said *I'll leave you alone.*"

"If *you* want. Aiden, he gave you his *<[name]>*."

Aiden unclenched. "I don't know what that means."

Esther let him go and waited until Aiden knelt on the ground, whole and stable again. "It can mean different things for different people. For Sam, I'd guess it was because he chose you."

Aiden whimpered. "But what does that *mean*?"

Esther took his hand and squeezed it. "Ask him. And tell him you don't want him to leave."

"I want to give him my <[name]> too. I can't fight, but maybe I can...do something else."

"I'm sure you can. Demonic powers aren't my area of expertise, but I bet Sam will help you if you ask. I bet he'd love to help."

Aiden sniffled. There wasn't any physical *reason* to sniffle, but he kind of wished there was. Then he told Esther his <[name]>.

It took a while.

When he finished, Esther was wiping tears from her eyes and smiling. She whispered, "Thank you for your trust, love."

Aiden nodded. "Was that okay? You... I needed—"

Esther leaned over and whispered a <[name]> in his ear. Aiden felt it settle inside him near the other ones, Sam's and his own.

"But, why?" he asked. "That wasn't why I told you mine."

"I know. But you're special, and I want you to have someone you can call anytime. I'll find you anywhere, if you need me." Her smile sparked like sunlight on dew covered flowers. "And I'm pretty sure my name is safer with you than even with me."

"I'll keep it safe," he vowed. The words crackled between them, but, oddly, no sense of weight descended on him.

"Yes. I don't think you could do anything else." Esther stood and offered Aiden a hand.

He took it and used it to pull himself to his feet.

When they reached a deer path that led back to Nexus, Aiden turned and gave Esther a hug.

"Um. Thank you," he said, managing only to whisper it.

"You're very welcome, baby bunny. Would you like to have regular weekly sessions? We can meet in the park to start, and move on from there if you ever need to go anywhere else."

Aiden looked up at her, painfully hopeful. "Weekly?"

She smiled down at him and stroked his ears, the tips of which were resting against the back of his neck. "Of course. We can do it more often if you need to, but I think weekly will be more than enough."

"Um, yeah. Weekly sounds good. I like sunset time."

Esther's smile brightened, and it shone like spring sunshine. "Of course you do, sweet one." She studied him. "Do you want me to stay with you longer?"

Aiden wanted to say yes, but he knew that wasn't what he needed. "No. I... I need to be on my own for a little. So I can tell Sam that even though I would be okay without him, I don't want to be."

She gave him another quick hug. "Alright. Don't hesitate to call me."

Aiden lifted his chin. "You too. If there's um. Something you can think of that I can do."

Esther's smile turned enigmatic. "Oh, I'll think of something. I'm sure if I keep an eye on your Library entry, something will pop up."

Aiden nodded firmly. "Yeah."

Then he turned and went back to Nexus. Alone.

GREATER PROVIDENCE RI, SEPTEMBER 11TH 47 YAR

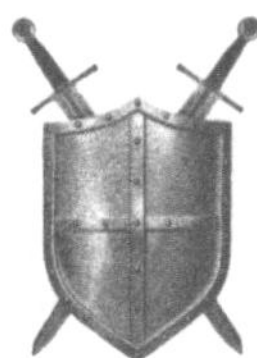

Emily slept at the hospital for the third night in a row. There were no new developments, good or bad, but everyone agreed that keeping Emily nearby was prudent. It was clear that nothing more could be done for the possessed until the FBI exorcist arrived. The Covens had fast tracked his permit, but unlike Emily, whose case was unique and unprecedented, this permit had to go through the proper channels and be approved by City Hall as well. The final approval was expected sometime later in the day.

The three people who had been corrupted at the hospital were still there, and though none of them had gotten worse, none of them had gotten better, either. The going hypothesis was that the final transformation might be triggered by cannibalism since that was what seemed to trigger Olivia, but it wasn't something they could test. Until they found the source of the corruption, or the trigger for the transformation was somehow healed or removed, the three victims were being kept in complete isolation.

Emily had set herself up with a satellite office, but she was getting restless. Her priority case was stagnant and the rest of her assignments were still being handled by the captain. She helped as much as she could by keeping up with the paperwork and digging through footage where required, but it was not the same as going to interview people herself. The captain was *fine*, obviously, but they'd been elevated to captain for a reason—they were much better at administrating than the actual ground work.

Emily shuddered to think of all the green deputies the captain was sending out so they could get *experience*. They needed experience, of course, but not on *her* cases.

A little before lunch, she couldn't sit still any longer and she went to take a walk around the building. As soon as she let herself think about anything besides work, her phone felt like it was burning a hole in her pocket.

She really wanted to call Sofia again, but she was terrified of what would happen if she did.

Never in her life had a date gone so smoothly, and her stomach still did flips when she thought about how it felt to be kissed by a girl. By *Sofia*. It was soft and sweet, and it felt so *warm* to remember it. She'd been kissed before, but they always asked for something from her after. Sometimes she wanted to give it, sometimes she didn't, but the demand was always there, pushing her, putting pressure on her to perform, or yield, or just to give *more*. She'd never had a problem saying no, but it wasn't the same as not *needing* to.

It felt dangerous, this tremulous feeling she had, like if she kept going she might really get hurt if it didn't work out. There were also her parents to consider. She didn't *think* they would have a problem if she dated a woman, but what if they did? It had never come up before. They still whined at her every holiday about when she was going to settle down and make babies. They didn't seem to care whether or not she wanted kids, nor did they seem interested in pressuring her brother, who at this point was much more likely to have kids than she was. At least he was married.

Emily reached the cafeteria and pushed the thoughts of Sofia's hot and spicy personality and so, *so* soft lips from her mind. That was more than enough self-indulgence for now—she'd have plenty of time to consider what to do about the little vixen when the crisis was over.

She had just gotten back to her desk with her food when an emergency call lit up her phone.

"This is Detective Scott."

"We have an ongoing emergency at Roger Williams University. There's... The kids there are... They're..." The dispatcher swallowed audibly, and gave an exact location on the campus, at one of the student dormitories. "We need you and as many witches as you can bring with you to get there as quickly as possible. The Covens are being notified directly, but there's no *time*. The national guard has been called, but they may not be able to—" The dispatcher swallowed again. "You're cleared to request as many portals as you need."

Emily took off at a dead run down the hall. "Make sure everyone on scene knows about the contamination risk, don't let anyone leave if it can be helped, and get pictures for facial recognition if it can't."

"Understood, Detective." A pause, and a whisper, "*Hurry*."

Emily dodged nurses and cleaning bots while she dialed Will. The witches were the same ones from Monday. They had eventually introduced themselves as Carla, the elder, and Kal, her apprentice. Emily skidded to a stop in front of them just as Will picked up, and she put him on speaker.

"We have a situation at Roger Williams University. I need every witch who is willing and able to portal there and help contain a possible outbreak situation. Carla, can you or Kal portal us there?"

"They can't, not if they're going to be any use warding," Will said, "but Sam and I can portal to you at the hospital and bring all six of us. Does that work?"

Carla looked briefly at Kal, who nodded sharply, and Artemis, the barn owl said, <<Yes, that works for us.>> Carla repeated the owl's words for the phone.

"Okay, I'll be there in less than two minutes. I'm aiming for the hospital's emergency pad, make sure it's clear for me."

Ninety seconds later, Emily and the witches were waiting next to the portal room. It was a simple steel-walled room with a large double wide entrance. There were sigils painted everywhere, and Kal and Carla rapidly touched a sequence of them, causing each one to take on an ethereal glow. Every time they did, her seal pulsed at her, humming more and more with each sigil they lit up.

There was a huge copper circle in the middle of the room, and it suddenly erupted in heatless fire. When it did, Emily's seal went crazy, and she clenched her jaw, bracing against the burning. The snowy owl looked at her and let out a sympathetic hoot.

Will rose through the floor, his eyes blazing. The figure of a man made entirely out of the same unnatural fire stood next to him, but it shrank and resolved into a cat just as the flames abruptly vanished. Will was already moving, drawing symbols in the air with his magic dagger. Emily followed the witches, who crossed into the circle as soon as the flames vanished.

None of them spoke, letting Will focus on his task. When the circle again erupted in flames, Emily gasped as her head split with agony. Her knees buckled and she sank to the floor, her vision going white. She did not scream, she did not have the breath to scream, but she also *refused* black out. The seal pulsed, and it tried to reach out, as if to interrupt the magic about to spin them through space-time.

You will not, Emily thought, violently, and gritted her teeth. She forced herself back to her feet, shoving her anger and determination against the seal, preventing it from interfering.

The seal did not let up, but Emily was equally implacable. Eventually, her vision cleared, and the stalemate between her and the seal stabilized. The witches were looking at her warily, and she gestured at the circle. “It’s fine. We need to go!”

Will looked dubious, but did as she asked and pressed his hand to a glowing sigil in the center of the circle. Emily felt the world lurch, and there was a powerful feeling of vertigo. It *hurt*. She kept all her focus on the seal, keeping it in check—the pain remained steady. It wasn’t incapacitating, but it made her so *angry*.

If she hadn’t focused her anger on the seal, would she have lashed out at the witches around her?

She continued to focus her anger on the seal.

When the sense of vertigo vanished, so did the fire, and the pain, and the anger. Emily couldn’t help falling to her knees again, her whole body shaking. Blood rushed in her ears, and her vision was blurred with the remnants of furious tears.

Will reached out a hand, but pulled it back when Emily shook her head. “No, just, give me a second,” she said, her voice rough, but calm.

With another massive effort, she stood. She braced herself, lowering her center of gravity into horse stance while her head swam, but after a few deep breaths, the dizziness receded.

The seal was not quiet, though it was no longer painful. It vibrated with that same itchy electric-hum from when she was in the room with Olivia, except even *stronger*.

When the rushing in her ears quieted, Emily finally noticed the screams.

Carla and Kal were already moving, their own knives out and glowing as they ran in opposite directions around the small cluster of buildings. As they ran, brilliant purple and green light streamed behind them. The two owls flew above them, calling out information Emily had neither the time nor education to understand.

"Emily, you should move to the side," Will said, touching her arm lightly. "I'm going to set up a temporary landing zone here and hold this circle so more of us can come through. You need to talk to the humans." His eyes were still glowing, and, strangely, so were Sam's.

Emily shook herself and nodded. She squeezed Will's shoulder once before striding off to look for the emergency responders.

They had set up a perimeter, which Emily realized was what Carla and Kal were using as a guide for whatever magic they were doing. As soon as Emily started looking, she spotted a man in tactical gear walking towards her.

"Please tell me you're Detective Scott and this is the cavalry," he said by way of greeting. He had the sharp efficient calmness of someone in the Guard, and there was a gun in his hand, pointed at the ground. His eyes met hers briefly before he continued to scan for threats.

"Yes, and I hope so. Can I get the code for the coms?"

He gave them to her, and she entered them into her phone and spent several minutes listening to them and asking the man questions. The information was pretty scattered, but at least two individuals inside the dorms were tearing people to shreds. Someone had pulled the fire alarm, and the first Crisis Security Responders to get to the scene had gone in and tried to taser the two attackers.

It hadn't worked. They'd been ripped apart in seconds.

So far no one injured had come out of the building. A few kids had managed to get out, but the infected individuals were currently tearing people apart in the stairways, and most people were still trapped inside.

Campus security had set up the initial perimeter and started clearing the area. The captain, who was coordinating civilian forces from the GPI main office, was well aware of the potential transmission of the condition. On their command, the kids who'd escaped the carnage were being sequestered in separate, empty classrooms while they waited for Emily and the witches.

As for what was still happening inside the dorms, all they could do was wait after the first two responders died. The National Guard had been on standby—one of their Fortress Carriers was anchored above Narragansett Bay just west of Bristol—but they had only arrived on scene a few minutes before Emily.

"I'm Sergeant Grey Callihan, by the way," the man said, after Emily was roughly caught up.

There was a sudden flash of brilliant witch-light, and a dome of magic sprang up around the dorm buildings. Emily's seal pulse once, so hard it felt like she'd been punched, and then it went quiet.

Sergeant Callihan glanced at her, concerned.

Emily rubbed absently at her chest and nodded towards the dome. "To the best of my knowledge, everything actively hostile is now contained within that dome. There are more witches arriving. Have someone direct them to start checking people for signs of corruption. I suggest beginning with the kids who escaped the dorms, but honestly, we need to check as many people as we can. Lock down the campus, if possible."

Sergeant Callihan winced, but nodded. "What about inside? We aren't just going to let whatever is happening in there happen, are we?" His expression said he was afraid they had to do exactly that.

Emily shook her head, grim, but determined. "No. I'm going in to see if I can stop them. I have immunity to whatever they are, I think. There's someone else coming, a Divine Paladin. His name is Hunter Graham. He's still waiting on his damn visa. We can't wait for City Hall to get its shit together and let him through the Providence Wards, but if I don't stop them, he should be able to."

Sergeant Callihan gave her a level look. "You're not going in there alone."

Emily set her jaw. "I'm not going to ask anyone to go with me. It's not *safe* for them to. *I* at least have a chance, and god forbid this...whatever, corrupted magic, gets into someone with actual military training and weapons." She paused long enough for Callihan to get her meaning. He blanched and nodded. "Just... If I'm successful and anyone makes it out, have the witches scan everyone who comes through the ward they set up. Most will be able to get through, even if they've been infected. Wards seem to only physically stop people who are already showing symptoms, like black sclera or veining."

He studied her, and then pulled out a gun, a .45 sig. "Do you know how to use this?"

She nodded. "Yeah. My uncle lives in Divine territory, and he likes target shooting. He taught me." She'd protested it at first. She was an investigator, not security or Guard, and she wouldn't be carrying anything more dangerous than a magically calibrated taser, but her mom had practically forced her to go.

Once she'd gotten past her irritation, she'd been surprised at how much she enjoyed it. She still went shooting at a club in Rehoboth with her uncle sometimes.

Calihan handed it over along with an extra clip. She ejected the clip and checked for a bullet in the chamber before reloading the gun and clicking the safety on. She knew from experience it was the easiest way to prove she knew what she was doing.

Calihan nodded and took her over to one of the Guard techs so they could wire her up with several body cameras, front and back, and a pair of military earpieces, all of which she quickly paired to her phone. She switched her live comm channel over to a private call with just the Sergeant.

He tried to get her into some body armor too, but she refused. She wasn't trained for it, and it would only slow her down.

Besides, she wanted to have easy access to the seal.

"You keep us constantly updated, you got that? Help people escape if you can, but if it looks like those things can get through whatever defenses you have, you get the fuck out, understand?"

Emilly scowled at him, but nodded. "Understood. Wish me luck."

"Good luck. *Fuck* you're brave," he said, and Emily ran through the ward without another word.

As soon as she stepped through, her seal started reacting again. She let her instincts pull her around to the back of the building, and, after finding the door locked, hesitated for only a second before trying to kick her way in. The seal pulsed lightly with each strike, and she could feel it giving her strength.

Three kicks and she blew through the door like it was made of cardboard.

At least the stupid thing was good for something besides electrocuting her and telling her to murder people.

The door opened into an emergency stairwell. There was blood everywhere, with scattered chunks of torn flesh. The fire alarm was still blaring, but her earpieces filtered it down to something bearable.

"Shit, Detective. Did you just kick your way through a solid security door?" Sergeant Callihan asked, his voice coming through her ear pieces by way of the coms.

"Yup."

She started going up the stairwell, following the sounds of screams. Screams were good. Screams meant not everyone was dead.

She ignored the way her shoes stuck to the floor, the way the air tasted like a copper sewer pipe. She sorely missed the mask Will had spelled for her.

When this was over, if she wasn't reduced to bloody chunks by fucking zombies, she was signing *herself* up for a full *year* of therapy, no complaints.

"You have someone watching my back, right? Through the body cameras? I won't say no to someone acting as an extra pair of eyes for me."

"I'm watching your back, Detective," Sergeant Callihan told her, and Emily felt a little less like she was about to get herself killed.

She kept going, checking each floor as she went, listening to Sergeant Callihan's instructions on how to proceed. Emily started to get the inexplicable feeling that the seal's humming was actually trying to tell her something, and she cracked a small door in the wall between her mind and the seal to listen to it.

It stopped feeling like an aimless electrical charge and instead gained a distinct *direction*. Three pulls, two very strong—urgent and moving—and one much more faint and stationary.

She followed the stronger pulls, and there was a slight pulse when she reached the correct floor. She heard the sound of woods splintering, and more screams.

"I think the things are up ahead. One on this floor, one on the floor above me. I can sort of sense where they are. I'm going to try to stop the one on this floor."

"Be fucking *careful*, Detective."

Yeah, right, she thought, and ran directly towards the danger.

The first *thing* used to be male. It was feeding on a still-twitching body inside one of the rooms, but it looked up as Emily came to stand in the doorway.

Its eyes were completely black except for those awful red rings, and the tips of its fingers had the flesh flayed away from the bone, exposing blackened claws. There were inky veins running all over its body, and it was mostly naked, the tattered remains of clothing hanging on in a few unhelpful places.

It roared and threw itself at her. To her own amazement, rather than freezing or screaming, she leveled the gun and fired. The bullet hit the thing square in the chest. She emptied the entire clip, two more shots into the chest until it staggered back, and the last seven into its head.

She didn't miss a single shot. The seal was warm against her skin, calming her, giving her unnatural focus and precision.

The gun clicked once, empty, and she ejected the clip and put in the second one. She aimed but didn't fire.

The body on the floor was flailing around, clearly still, well, not *alive*, but animated. Its head was essentially mush, but the flesh was quivering, and the black veins were pulsing and drawing the flesh back towards the stump at the neck.

"Get out of there, Detective. Use the time it will take to pull itself back together to evacuate people," Sergeant Callihan said in her ear, his voice steady. Emily moved.

She started knocking on doors, calling for people to get to the stairs and outside. She could feel the other *things*, one moving around above her, and one still stationary below her. As she focused, letting more of the seal's influence past her defenses, she started to get a sense of where the other, living people were, their souls radiating at her with frenetic terror.

She cleared the entire hall. Only a few people needed to be pulled from their rooms and shoved down the hall by force. At Callihan's suggestion, she went back down to clear the rest of the levels below her. It didn't take long, because most people on the lower levels were already dead. Possibly, *hopefully*, most of them escaped earlier.

One girl limped out of the room where she could sense the stationary *thing*. Emily aimed her gun into the room behind the girl, but nothing jumped out—it must be locked in a bathroom or closet. Emily didn't take the time to ask questions, just instructed one of the other kids to help her get out.

"Sergeant Callihan, I think there's another one of the *things* in this room, but it's not moving. I think I should just leave it there. It seems weaker." As long as it stayed put, she had other priorities.

"It's your call, but for what it's worth I agree. Keep moving."

Once that was done, she ran back up to the top floor, the only place there were still-living people. The two monsters were below her now, but the one she hadn't shot was clearly finished with whatever occupied it before. It was now moving quickly towards the stairwell.

Emily gathered everyone alive in a common sitting area right next to the stairway. The kids were terrified. She scanned them quickly, looking for someone who might still have a few wits about them. One girl met her eyes, and one boy.

Emily pointed at the two of them. "You two are in charge. I need you to wait here while I try to distract the thing. I will shout 'Go Go Go!' when it's time for you to run, understand? You get everyone down those stairs as quickly and safely as you can. Don't leave anyone behind, and don't let anyone fall, got it?"

Both of them nodded, and impulsively Emily reached out and touched each of their cheeks, gently *pushing* strength and courage into them. They visibly steadied, and started lining people up, the girl taking point and the guy taking up the rear, a fire extinguisher brandished like a weapon.

She gave them an approving nod and ran back down the stairs. The thing crashed through the door below her, and Emily felt a pulse of strength from the seal.

Trust.

She jumped over the railing to land in front of the *thing*, the gun still in her hand. It screamed at her, obviously female, and she was just as fucked up as the other one had been. Emily shot it three times in the face and then leaned back against the railing and kicked the thing with both feet. It flew down the hallway where it lay, writhing.

The other *thing* she had shot was still lying on the ground below her, but her instincts were screaming at her that she only had seconds.

"Go! Go! Go!" she screamed. She waved the kids past her while she watched the monster twitch and crawl slowly towards them.

Emily followed behind the boy with the fire extinguisher, gun ready, covering their retreat. She *reached*, and the seal responded, burning slightly against her skin.

There was no one else alive in the building.

"Sergeant Callihan, the building is clear of living people and all the monsters are in here with me. Can you see if the witches can put up another ward around just this building?"

"We can, detective," Carla answered for herself. Apparently Callihan had tapped her into the channel. "You let us know if those things try to head our way."

"Will do."

It was a tense several minutes. She split the rest of her bullets between the two active monsters, running between to pulp their heads again while the witches worked.

She could *feel* the magic, like a burning itch, and the seal was even louder now. She told it to *shut up*. She needed to focus and the witch magic was *not* the threat here.

It burned her slightly, as if it was angry, but then the anger vanished and it eased off on its reaction to witch magic.

Thank fuck.

This time when the ward snapped into place, the seal only pulsed mildly. Emily gave the seal a grateful pat under her shirt, almost in spite of herself. It pulsed at her again in amicable acknowledgement, radiating calming warmth. She had the unsettling feeling that she'd just come to an agreement with the thing, and she was slightly terrified by what that might mean for her.

With the ward up, Emily wasted no more time in leaving. As soon as she passed through the inner ward, the seal went quiet. The strength the seal had been feeding her drained away.

She made it maybe three steps before her knees gave out. She crashed to the ground for the third time that day, and a wave of exhaustion hit her hard. Her whole body started to shake, and it was all she could do to keep from passing out.

She pushed furiously at the exhaustion, but it didn't work. Anger wasn't going to give her a second wind this time.

She focused instead on breathing, on not letting her arms collapse, vaguely aware of people arriving, surrounding her. Someone helped her into a sitting position and a bottle of water was held to her lips. She gulped it gratefully.

"No, Sergeant, there's no corruption on her, and I don't see any injuries," someone, probably Carla, said. "If I had to guess, she's just exhausted from whatever Divine magic she was using in there. A new witch in her position would have passed out using that much power."

Emily was *not* going to pass out. She might not be able to see, or stand, but she *would not pass out*. The seal seemed to approve of her determination, and she felt just enough of the warmth return to her that she finally stopped shaking.

She said, "Sergeant Callihan, can you patch me back into the main coms?"

"*Fuck*, woman. Take a break. That Paladin will be here in less than thirty minutes, and the witches are working to round up everyone with any sign of corruption." Emily opened her eyes to find him kneeling next to her. He was holding an empty water bottle. "I'll link you back in, but you are going to see one of the paramedics right now, and you are not doing anything else until they say you're clear."

Emily was too tired to argue, so she just nodded. This was far from over, and she needed to keep it together. Taking a break would be hard, but she knew enough about stress to know if she didn't take the time now to rest, recenter, and let other people do their jobs, she wouldn't last much longer.

For the moment, there was nothing more she could do.

She repeated that to herself like a mantra.

GREATER PROVIDENCE RI, SEPTEMBER 11TH 47 YAR

June surveyed her grocery and take-out harvest.

After getting back from her date with Emily, June had spent the next twelve hours researching modern food. She'd been overwhelmed by the sheer *amount* of information there was.

The only food she had eaten when she was alive that modern people still ate regularly was popped corn, though she'd never eaten it *drowned* in butter and salt. There were some few other familiar-sounding things, but the more she looked into them, the more it became clear they were not at all the same.

A huge number of what she'd known as medicines had been turned into candy. Marshmallow, licorice, peppermint, and even sassafras, sort of. Apothecaries had apparently started using sugar to make their medicine more palatable after, ugh, gross, *slavery* made sugar cheap. Gradually people stopped even bothering to put the medicine in and just ate the confections with some kind of flavoring approximating the medicine it was originally meant to be.

And that was *nothing* compared to what they'd done with wheat and corn.

In the years she'd been a vampire, she'd somehow managed to avoid noticing there were entire online communities of humans who discussed which restaurants and bars made the best version of particular types of foods. Furthermore, a significant portion of the entertainment industry as a whole was dedicated to food preparation. She'd known modern humans were obsessed with food, sure, but this was on a scale she never could have guessed. There were *thousands* of hours of videos and shows that revolved only around food, and even some restaurants that did weird science on foods just to create new food experiences.

It was madness, and June couldn't believe how much she'd been missing.

For this first experiment she had a good sampling of various kinds of foods, several for each modern meal type—breakfast, lunch, and dinner. Some she'd ordered from restaurants based on the reviews she found online, and some food she'd found at the grocery stores closest to her apartment. The neighborhood she lived in also had several very excellent cafes, so she'd gotten a variety of food from them as well.

She'd also purchased a small witch-oven that cooked with some combination of spells and sub-light frequency electromagnetic radiation. It could heat the food inside to optimal serving temperature in a matter of seconds. All she had to do was enter in the number displayed clearly on each of the take-out boxes.

June had also gathered a large heap of what was apparently considered 'junk' food, though not because it was actually bad food. All of it was shelf-stable and did not need to be heated. From what June could tell, their nutrient profiles were fine, certainly non-toxic, though there were definitely higher sodium and sugar amounts. Even more strange, none of the foods required any rinsing or preparation— they could be opened and immediately consumed.

Magical.

Many of the 'junk' foods were considered pre-Rapture relics, considered unhealthy only because they made you sick if you ate too many of them for too long, but, like candy, they maintained a popular presence in modern food culture.

She had candy, too. Not much—she knew what sweet was supposed to taste like, and most of the medicines they were descended from—but some of the more colorful and strangely textured candies caught her eye, especially the chocolates and creatively shaped gummies.

She started with a box covered with a cartoon man in a green hat full of tiny, dry confections. The store labeled it 'cereal'. It was, in fact, nothing of the sort, because it was mostly sugar and held only the vaguest resemblance to a cereal grain. The dry bread-shapes covered in powdered sugar were accompanied by suspiciously chalky and unnaturally colorful candies the box claimed were marshmallows.

Whatever the firm, colorful shapes were, it was *not* a curative tincture. They didn't even smell like marshmallow.

According to the instructions, she was supposed to eat the dry bread shapes with *milk*, like an instant, cold stew for the very ill. Straight-from-the-teet milk, without any sort of cooking or processing into cheese or butter! June checked online, just to be sure, and every source she could find confirmed that was how she was supposed to eat the stuff.

She'd had no small amount of trepidation over her first bite, but it was...

Magical.

The milk had been cold and thick, refreshing and creamy in flavor and without so much as a hint of sweaty animal. Combined with the crunchy cereal and half-rehydrated candy, it was a symphony of texture and intense flavor unlike anything she'd ever tasted before.

She carefully noted on her ranking chart that modern cereal was just below spaghetti on the 'perfection' scale.

Next she tried a salt-cured bacon and egg 'sandwich' purchased from a place that had good reviews. It, too, was magical. The bread was ostensibly a biscuit, but it was far too light and smooth, made of some kind of science-wheat that made it soft and tender and white as snow. The sausage and cheese were so flavorful they made her mouth ache with pleasure, and there weren't any vegetables at all. Unfortunately, the egg was more of an afterthought, and it was weirdly flavorless compared to the other foods.

She put that down as 'promising'. Impatiently, she skipped over the rest of the breakfast things to try the hamburger she'd gotten, which was basically the same thing but without the egg.

It was *perfection*. The meat was flavorful and soft, the cheese was warm and gooey, and the bright red tomato and crisp pickles were almost violently flavorful when combined with the strange pink sauce on the fluffy, cloud-like bread.

The fries that came with the burger were more disappointing. They were *fine*, and she ate them all before she could stop herself, but they weren't anything more than crispy fat-fried potatoes covered in salt. The 'ketchup' that came with them was much more interesting, shockingly sweet and tangy and barely reminiscent of the tomato proudly displayed on the little packet it came in.

Then she tried the pizza.

She had been mistaken before.

Pizza was the best.

Pizza should have been reserved for *gods*. It was too good for mortal palates.

The bread was chewy and soft and had just a hint of char. It overflowed with cheese and sauce and very thinly sliced bright red sausage. Even though she was getting close to being overly full, she regretted having only gotten one slice. She thought she could eat maybe ten slices if they were in front of her.

And there was still *so much more* food to try!

She lost her head again after the pizza. Her chart was abandoned in a frenzy of crunchy corn-and-cheese puffs, water fiery with carbonation sweetened to the point of insanity, and chewy, sour-sweet nonsense that made her whole body shiver with sensation.

It was a cornucopia of color and flavor and intense pleasure. She never wanted to stop eating.

Unfortunately, her mortal body disagreed.

She managed to make it into her bathroom before her stupid, *awful* body ejected nearly everything she'd just consumed.

It was nowhere near as wonderful the second time around.

When her body finished its betrayal, June collapsed on the plush shower mat and passed out, exhausted.

"What have you done this time, idiot child?" her father asked.

June ran.

She didn't stop, didn't think. She just ran.

Laughter, familiar and hideous, followed her as she ran through the forest. Huge, ancient elms towered overhead, but none of them were the right ones.

Where was the path?

She needed to find the path.

If she could just get to the path, she could find—

June stopped.

She didn't skid to a stop. There was no momentum. She just stopped.

"What the fuck is this?"

The world around her felt real, vivid, but it wasn't.

It was a fucking dream.

"I do not want to deal with this subconscious angst shit." *June said to her magically regurgitated memories.* "I left the underworld because I didn't want to deal with this shit. I kill bad guys, I heal kids, and I do my own fucking thing. I *do not* want to deal with my baggage, especially not with a shitty nightmare!"

The forest around her grew indistinct, and her brothers' sick laughter faded away.

<<That was fast,>> someone June did not know said behind her.

June whirled and saw a fucking angel *standing in a gold-washed meadow that had* not *been there a moment before.*

"Are you *doing this?" June demanded, using anger to cover her fear. "How?* Why?*"*

The angel laughed, the sound like burning bells. <<I am not, little abomination. You *are. I am here with a message.>>*

June backed up. "I don't need a message from the likes of you." If she was doing this, if this was her dream, maybe she could—

<<You need to stop being a coward. We're all in this mess because of you. The least you can do is help.>> The angel smiled, and June

wondered why it didn't burn her. <<Even we *are helping. If you do not help, her hand will be forced, and her soul will become ours forever.>>*

"Emily? No*! You leave her* alone*!" June screamed and launched herself at the angel.*

He vanished in a blinding flash, and June fell down and down and down.

</<Too late, you stupid fucking coward,>/> Sean said, his voice twisted, wrong. </<There's nothing you can do. You're alone, just like you wanted. No one needs your help. Why would they?>/> Black tentacles wrapped around her neck, forcing their way past her clenched teeth and down her throat. </<But I *still want you.>/>*

June woke up screaming.

She ripped the amulet from around her neck and threw it out of the bathroom and across the room.

"Fuck," she said, hoarsely.

Penny hadn't been kidding about horrible nightmares.

The moment the amulet was gone, her body started working double time to shed its magically induced mortality. The nausea and headache vanished, and her senses re-sharpened.

June let out the last breath she'd inhaled and did not bother breathing in another. She waited in tense silence. It was still daylight outside, but June was in the dark, without wards or amulets.

She waited for what felt like hours.

Nothing happened.

Eventually, when the smell in the room really started to bother her, she concluded the *thing* wasn't coming. Mindlessly, June shoved all the remaining food down the rarely used compost disposal and cleaned up the mess.

She wasn't giving up on food. Not forever.

Just for today. That was okay. Waiting a day didn't mean she was surrendering.

It was a strategic retreat.

Drained, though thankfully not yet in need of a hunt, June collapsed on the wreckage of her couch. She plugged her phone in—it must have died while she was passed out—and powered it on. As soon as it connected to the network, it started going off with nearly a dozen missed calls and messages from Penny.

Grimly, June read and listened to her messages. Then she went to a local news blog site. As she watched the various videos, read the warnings and the calls for anyone with symptoms to *report to the nearest clinic*, guilt twisted in her stomach, and her nausea returned.

June typed several messages to Penny, apologies, questions, excuses. She typed others to Emily, asking if she was okay, if she needed help, confessing everything.

June deleted them all and rolled over onto her stomach.

"Shit. What the fuck could I even do to help?"

GREATER PROVIDENCE RI, SEPTEMBER 11TH 47 YAR

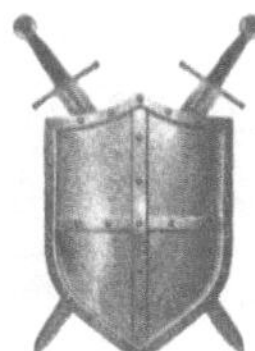

Emily was cleared by the paramedics just as the Paladin's helicopter landed. She had a sneaking suspicion Callihan had told them to wait until the Paladin arrived to give her the all clear. There wasn't anything *wrong* with her, she was just tired, but the paramedics had insisted she sit and eat a bunch of energy bars anyway.

The soldiers and campus security had cleared a space for the helicopter in one of the parking lots near the dorm rooms, and Emily made her way over as the rotors slowed enough for the Divine Paladin to jump out.

Emily hated him instantly. Irrationally, possibly, because the reason she hated him might have been slightly related to the way her seal seemed to fucking *love* him. It fluttered with warmth as soon as she laid eyes on his stupidly handsome face.

He was dressed in completely impractical white-and-gold tactical armor, with a gun on his hip and a freaking *sword* on his back. A Church of Unity symbol was emblazoned on his chest in red, surrounded by gold Latin lettering. His FBI badge was on his shoulder.

"It stinks of demonic magic here. How am I supposed to find this *corrupted* magic? It's *all* corrupted." Emily heard him from several hundred yards away, and he was waving grandly at all of the various ward circles.

Hatred confirmed and justified.

The Paladin walked over to Carla, who was checking on one of the wards around ground zero. Artemis flapped their wings and hissed a warning at the Paladin, which he completely ignored.

Emily picked up her pace, moving on an intercept course. She spotted Sergeant Callihan moving in as well.

"I need to speak with the witch in charge here," he demanded, loudly. Carla ignored him. "I want to know exactly how you can sense this supposed corruption on living people. Better yet, take me to where—"

Emily put herself between the Paladin and Carla and extended her hand.

"Hi, I'm Detective Emily Scott, and I'm acting as liaison between human law enforcement and the Providence Covens. All communication between you and Coven members needs to go through me. This is Sergeant Callihan, and he's in command of the Guard militia here."

Callihan nodded at the Paladin with a carefully neutral expression. "Agent Graham and I have met before."

The Paladin never even looked at Sergeant Callihan. His attention focused on Emily, appraising her with his astonishingly blue eyes. The stupid seal gave a small *thump* of pleasure, and she scowled as Hunter's expression lit up with a brilliant smile. "A pleasure to meet you, Emily," he said. His voice was like fucking chocolate. "Agent Hunter Graham. Please, call me Hunter."

She wanted to slap him, especially since he'd almost certainly left out her title on purpose, but since that wasn't an option, she nodded sharply and spun away. "Agent, Sergeant, I'll meet you at the command center. I need to speak to one of my magical consultants." Also known as Will, the *actual* liaison.

She was fairly certain she was doing Will a favor by running interference between him and Hunter, but she needed to ask him if that's what he wanted before she dug herself in any deeper.

And she wanted to get away from Agent Shiny Ass.

From somewhere behind her Sergeant Callihan said, "If you'll follow me, Agent, I have a command center set up over here. I'll brief you on the situation."

Sergeant Callihan was good people.

Emily found Will sitting next to the portal landing, mechanically eating energy bars and drinking water. She gave her seal a mental warning, and it resigned itself to only the slightest of mild pulses when she got close. Will's normally warm brown skin was looking rather ashy, and Sam was stretched out on the pavement, clearly asleep.

Emily didn't know demons slept. She supposed if one was going to, it would be a cat demon.

"Hey Emily. You look like how I feel," he said, scrubbing his face and offering her one of his energy bars.

She was still hungry, so she took it with a grateful smile. "Like a badass who saved like, twenty kids?"

Will's returning smile was startled from him, but it settled into his eyes and he noticeably brightened. "Yeah. Like that."

"Cool, so the Paladin is here, and he's an asshole. I told him I was the acting liaison because he waited all of four seconds to start throwing his shiny golden dick around. I'll fess up if you want, but I have a feeling we might get better results from him if I run interference."

Will adjusted his glasses and climbed wearily to his feet, scooping up Sam on his way. Sam made a small noise somewhere between a growl and a mew in protest. Will draped Sam around his shoulders, who seemed content to ride there as they walked.

"Does that mean I don't have to be in charge of team magic anymore?" he asked, sounding like he was almost too tired to banter.

"Ah, no, you're still in charge of team magic. I'm offering to be your asshole translator."

"Great, translate away. Where is he?"

"In the command center with Sergeant Callihan. If we walk slow, he might be briefed by the time we get there. How many infected people have you found?"

"We're up to six, including a girl who really wants to talk to you. I think we should go there first."

Emily nodded, and they walked over to the series of small classrooms the witches had warded to hold the people showing signs of corruption. A crisis responder watched the door, and she nodded deferentially to Emily. There was a hint of hero worship in the young woman's eyes, and Emily wanted to groan. Instead, she gave the officer's shoulder a squeeze and pulsed a bit of the warmth from her seal at her.

Now why the fuck had she done that?

Will indicated the room that had the girl Emily needed to talk to. Emily looked through the door's window and recognized her as the girl who'd been in the room with the monster that wasn't moving around. Her arm was in a sling, and her foot was propped up on a chair with some ice. There were bruises purpling an otherwise fairly pretty face, and Emily was surprised when she realized she knew the girl—she was a member of Sean DeNardis's social circle, and she'd interviewed her just...fuck. Only three days ago?

The girl, whose name escaped Emily at the moment, was playing a game on her phone. She looked relatively calm, but there were obvious tear tracks all over her face.

Emily opened the door and stepped through the ward, indicating that Will should wait outside. She left the door open though, so he could hear.

"Hello again. I'm glad you made it out okay."

The girl looked up at Emily with wide eyes. Recognition had her relaxing, and a sad, but also grateful, smile spread across her face.

"Thank you for saving me, Detective Scott. I'm glad you made it out, too."

Emily sat down in a chair next to the girl. Her seal was silent, so the girl was probably safe enough for now.

"I heard you wanted to talk to me. I don't have much time, but I can spare a few minutes."

The girl swallowed and a tear rolled down her cheek, but then she set her jaw and nodded. "I...I think..." She took a deep breath, and said, "The two monsters, I think they're two of my friends. Or, they *were*. Richie, Jen, and my boyfriend, Cal, have—had—been acting really weird the last couple of days. I let it go, thinking it was just because they were upset about Sean, you know? But I ended up confronting Cal about it, right before, um, before it started. He was being really pushy and abusive, you know? He's never been like that before, but I didn't want to put up with it. He, uh, he punched me, and when

I went to leave he grabbed me and threw me against the wall. When my head cleared, I looked up at him, and his eyes had gone all weird and black, and he was standing over me, *crying*. He kept saying he was sorry.

"I asked him what the hell was wrong with him, but I don't know how coherent I sounded, because my arm felt like, or, I guess it *was* ripped out if its socket, dislocated, and I was crying too. I was so angry, and afraid. He...threw me too hard, like, he's not really that strong, and it didn't, *doesn't* make any—"

She stopped, and her breath hitched. She held it for a second and then let it out slowly. After one more deep breath she continued. "I think I said something about his eyes, because he went into the bathroom and let out this...this sound. It wasn't fully human. He locked the door to the bathroom and told me to run, but when I went to leave I saw what was happening in the stairwell and I went back into the room and shut the door. I just waited there. I guess I was in shock, or something, because I just stood there, listening at the door, until I heard the gunshots, and then you were there.

"He cried the whole time, these wracking sobs, right up until the sound of the gun. Then he got quieter, though he was still whimpering. He... Did you find him?"

Emily's stomach hurt, and she fought to keep her face as neutral as possible. What the fuck was she supposed to say? She'd left him there, because he...because it had felt like...

Her seal gave a pulse, and Emily felt a flash of anger at it. It pulsed again, and tried to radiate that stupid warmth at her. Emily didn't want its fake comfort, so she pushed at it as she reached out and took the girl's good hand. "I'll let you know what happened to him as soon as I can, okay?" she said, meeting the girl's eyes and shoving the seal's stupid warmth at someone who deserved it.

The girl's body suddenly relaxed, and she smiled and nodded. "Okay."

Emily left, and Will shut the door behind her.

"You heard?" she asked. Will nodded and searched her face. In consideration of whatever he found there, he stayed quiet. They walked in silence until they got to the command center.

"It's not your fault," he said very quietly, just as she was opening the door, when it was too late for her to try to do something to deny it.

Sneaky bastard.

Hunter looked up from the footage he was watching on a tablet as they walked in, and his delighted expression when he saw Emily made her want to turn around and leave.

"You did very well, Detective. You're barely imbued, but it's clear you have access to enough Divine power to hold your own. I'm impressed."

"Thanks."

"Can you describe to me what you were feeling, how your Relic was reacting?"

Emily did her best to describe it, making sure to highlight that it was a distinctly different sensation than what witch magic felt like. Hunter looked slightly dubious, but he had the sense not to challenge her on it.

"I'm going to go in there. There is something I can do, a kind of cleansing. You won't be able to do it unless you fully embrace your Relic. We call it Divine Light. It burns away any demonic energy, leaving demonic souls powerless. I'm hopeful that it will work on whatever these things are."

<<And what if it doesn't?>> Sam asked unexpectedly, still draped on Will's shoulders. Emily had almost forgotten he was there. <<It's

not like normal magic. It's...off. We don't think it's pulling from underworld power sources. We think it might actually be pulling power directly from the souls it's infecting, somehow.>>

"Sam is concerned that it might not be that simple," Will said, for Sergeant Callihan's benefit. Hunter stared at Sam, his jaw clenched, and did not respond.

Emily jumped in when the silence went on too long. "Also, I have recently learned that there is reason to believe that one of them may be less... less turned than the other two. I believe an infected boy locked himself in a bathroom on purpose, and he didn't move from there the whole time. I think we should focus on dealing with the other two first and see if we can still reason with the boy. If he is still there."

Sergeant Callihan, who had been watching the exchange with sharp eyes, said, "I agree with Detective Scott. Agent Graham, do you need backup?"

Hunter's focus was still on Sam. Sam was staring back, steady and unblinking. Emily tensed, ready to jump in between them if she needed to.

<<I'm Sam, by the way.>>

Hunter broke the glaring contest, finally, and looked over to Sergeant Callihan. Sam, deliberately casual, licked at one of his paws.

"I think it's best if I go in alone, but have everyone on standby just outside the wards. If things don't work the way I hope they do, I may need to call for help."

No one disagreed, so Hunter was geared up with body cameras and an earpiece. Sergeant Callihan also gave Emily another gun and clip, this time with a holster she could put on her belt. She made sure her cameras were still on in case she needed to run in for some reason.

Other than the witches and officers still working on screening people for corruption, everyone gathered around the dorm building. Nothing seemed to be moving, and the wards were several layers thicker than when she'd left an hour ago.

Carla came over to Emily and held out two small crystals hung on leather cords to Emily. "You and the Paladin will need these to pass through the wards now. It won't physically stop you if you somehow lose them, but it will hurt like hell if you try to pass through without them," she placed them in Emily's hand, and added, "We will need them back."

Emily nodded, but before she could pull away, Carla caught Emily's wrist.

"Make sure the Paladin does not walk away from here with that amulet. I'm trusting you."

A test, then, and a warning. "Understood. I'll make sure you get them both back."

Emily handed the crystal to Hunter, who grimaced when it touched his skin. Emily wanted to roll her eyes. The witch magic in them did buzz slightly against her skin, but it didn't feel bad, or wrong, just present. She suspected what Hunter felt wasn't any different and he was just projecting his prejudice.

Unless what he felt *was* different. Fuck. She knew so little about the damn thing. Emily reminded herself that making that assumption was likely just *her* prejudice. She didn't think so, but she needed to at least offer him the benefit of the doubt. Or, she *should*, because it was the right thing to do.

While they waited for the equipment to go through a final check, Sam spoke up, loudly enough that Hunter could definitely hear.

<<So, for the record, just so we're clear, I asked this guy 'but what if you're wrong' and his response was to pretend I don't exist.>>

Will's face didn't change expression, but he did respond, quietly enough that only Emily could hear. "That's correct, Sam."

<<We know he can hear me, right?>> Sam was not quiet. <<Like, we're *sure* he can hear me? Detective Cute and Cut, you can still hear me, right?>>

Emily looked at Sam flatly. "*Cute* and *cut*? What is *that* supposed to mean?"

<<There, see, she can hear me, which means he *must* be able to hear me.>>

Hunter was pointedly ignoring them. Some of the soldiers, who could only hear the human side of the conversation, were giving them weird looks.

Will said, "Sam, maybe now is not a good time for this."

<<It is. Trust me. I was a soldier, I died in a trench. I'm an *expert* on joking to lighten the mood.>>

Emily turned to stare at Sam. "You what? You died in a trench? Like, in the World Wars?" Emily's brain caught up with her mouth. "Wait, was that rude to ask? Don't answer that."

Sam twitched his ears in her direction, but he kept his attention on Hunter, his cat eyes dilated, his tail ticking lazily back and forth.

"Sam, I'm not sure that's how being an expert works," Will said, still quietly, but Hunter was standing close enough that he must be able to hear. "Are you sure you're not just trying to needle the Paladin?"

The Paladin in question took off through the ward without ever once looking at them.

<<I don't like your question, Will, so I'm going to pretend you didn't ask it. Now zip it, we have to pay attention. I'm going to be validated any second now. I can practically taste it.>>

Will adjusted his glasses with a heavy sigh before they all turned their attention to the feed from Hunter's body cameras.

Hunter moved up the stairwell confidently, evidently knowing where he was going. He came upon both of the active monsters on the third floor landing. They were locked together, ripping chunks out of each other. It didn't *quite* look like they were trying for murder, though. They were moving like they were...

"Oh my god," someone whispered. The camera went suddenly static, and even through the wards Emily felt her seal hum with warm recognition of whatever Hunter was doing. When the camera cleared, the two monsters were still there, but the blackness had been burned away. Both had stopped moving. The bodies began to bleed steadily from half-healed wounds, and then an awful keening sound came from the twisted bodies.

"*Dominus Patris*," Hunter whispered, and Emily grew cold at the sound of his voice. "Something is *very* wrong. The souls are... I cannot explain it. I cannot see the souls, but I can feel their anguish, their *madness*. The souls are still lingering within the bodies, but the bodies are... They should be dead. I do not sense any more demonic magic, but they're still—"

"Sam and I are coming up," Will said, and he and Sam took off running through the barrier. Emily gestured for Sergeant Callihan and the others to wait, and then she followed behind Will and Sam, pulling her gun out and pointing it at the ground as she ran up the stairs.

Sam grew in size as they ran, eventually reaching the size of a panther.

That was a neat trick.

They reached Hunter quickly. He had his sword out, and he was watching the horrors writhing and keening on the floor with an unreadable expression. Emily could understand why. The moment she'd passed through the ward, her seal had begun feeding her information. It still pointed towards the boy in the closet, identifying the blatant wrongness, but what it sensed from the now corruptionless people in the stairway was somehow worse than before. They weren't corrupted anymore. They *anguished.*

<<I see the souls. Oh, *fuck,*>> Sam said. He stopped next to Hunter, who tensed but made no other move.

"Sam, please describe what you're seeing," Will asked, stopped just behind Emily, his dull knife ready in his hand.

<<I don't really know how. It's like they've been gutted, or maybe desiccated? They should be falling apart, scattering. The bodies should be dying. But it's like they *can't.* I don't know what they are. These things, they shouldn't *exist.*>> Sam sounded traumatized, and Will relayed his description over the comms for the benefit of those who could not hear him.

"Tear the souls apart, Demon," Hunter said, without hesitation, his jaw clenched.

Sam swiped at the body, but his huge paw passed right through, leaving no damage. <<It's no good, I can't get to it inside the body. Will?>> He looked at Will, who nodded.

Emily stepped back when Sam suddenly leapt at Will. The two of them *fused,* and Will rapidly transformed in a swirl of fire into a half-cat, half-human creature. His glasses were still perched on his nose, and Emily fixated on them. It looked ridiculous.

Emily's seal buzzed at her, reacting to the surge of demonic energy, but she was getting better at telling it to fuck off, forcing it to treat the witches as neutral rather than *enemy.* It did hurt a little, like a very short lived but still painful headache.

Will/Sam tore the bodies apart. All she saw was gory destruction, but they must have done something to the soul as well, because she felt it the moment the wrongness faded.

Hunter apparently did as well, because he lowered and then sheathed his sword.

There was another swirl of fire, and Sam fell out of Will, who staggered. Emily caught him before he toppled down the stairs, and Sam, who was still huge, steadied Will's other side. Will was shaking, leaning heavily on both of them, but otherwise he didn't seem hurt.

They stood looking at the now still and silent mess for several seconds.

Emily could still feel the stationary zombie. It hadn't moved. They should go to it, deal with it. But Emily was tired, and overwhelmed, and she needed answers. *Right now.*

"Okay, I need a minute here," she said, sliding the safety back on the gun and putting it in the holster. "First, Sam, Will, I need to know what the hell you just did. Is it normal for witches to fuse with their familiars like that? Also, Sam, why the hell did your paw pass through the body? Are you incorporeal? If so, how the *hell* are you supporting Will right now? And how are you huge?"

Emily knew that now was not really the time for these questions, but a larger part of her didn't care.

"Um," Will said, his voice rough. "So, it's no secret that familiars are only corporal to their bonded witch and other familiars, but most of them try not to advertise it too much, since it makes people uncomfortable. Before you ask, the messenger bag is spelled specially for Sam because he's a spoiled brat."

<<I resemble that remark!>> Sam said, his exaggerated indignation somewhat ruined by how tired he sounded.

"Okay, great. I can't believe I've known you for years and I somehow missed that, but okay, whatever. What about the were-cat thing you just did?"

<<It's technically something all witches can all do, but we usually don't. It's, ah, not comfortable for either of us. It feels like being mildly electrocuted while you do it. It's not *necessarily* dangerous, physically, but do it too long and we could both go a little nuts. We're talking *hours* too long, like, all in a row, so it's not something to worry about right now.>>

Will had stopped shaking, and he took most of his weight off Emily. He gave her a worried look, which was ridiculous, because *he* was the one who could barely stand. Hunter was looking at them both, his expression inscrutable but also a little judgey. Emily wanted to tell him to shut his face, which was when she realized she needed to rein herself back in.

Emily took a deep breath. "Alright, let me see if I followed what has happened here. Hunter, you used that Divine magical blast to burn away any traces of demonic magic. What would *normally* happen when you do that?"

Hunter glanced briefly at Sam and said, "Normally, Divine Light would strip the demonic soul of its magical connection to Hell. This leaves it powerless and often unconscious. Then, unless we have a trap set up to imprison the soul, it falls back into Hell, unable to stay on the mortal plane."

<<Where many souls then immediately fall apart. They're usually not allowed to use that power anywhere inside Witch territory,>> Sam added. <<Even when the soul survives intact, getting hit with one of those blasts will knock a demon out for weeks, and damage or shatter a witch's familiar bond. He has a special permit to use his blast on the corrupted humans.>>

"Okay," Emily said, "So you did the blast, and the demonic magic is gone, but the soul is still there. Let's talk about the bodies. The bodies should have been dead, but they weren't. Or they were, and the soul just stayed there anyway? How does that work?"

<<Yeah, it *doesn't* work. That's not supposed to be a thing,>> Sam said.

"Clearly, it *is* a thing, since it just happened, right?"

<<Right. Technically, it's possible for demonic magic to re-animate dead flesh, that's kind of how vampires work, but the Paladin's blast stripped that away. I'm not sure what was going on, other than it was horrible.>> Sam sounded legitimately shook.

Emily was too, which was why she plowed ahead. "So, the next thing that happened is Hunter told you, Sam, to tear it apart. I assume this means demons can tear souls apart?"

<<Actually, any soul can tear another soul apart. You all can't because your souls are still fused with your mortal flesh.>>

"Okay, but only souls with demonic magic can stay on the mortal plane without flesh, right? Except for this thing, sort of. But it's gone now because Sam fused with Will and they tore it up."

<<"Right,">> they all said, Hunter included.

"Okay, gone where? What happens to torn up souls?"

<<The same thing that happens to intact souls. The fragments lack an identity, but they still have... Call it an echo of being someone. It's enough that the soul pieces can show a preference to either join Divinity, enter the Underworld, or reincarnate,>> Sam said.

"And we know these soul bits are doing that?" Emily asked, and there was an awkward silence.

<<I'll get back to you on that.>>

"Great, you do that."

Will cleared his throat. "I have a theory. I hate it. You're all going to hate it."

Emily glared. “If your theory involves the words ‘Zombie,’ or ‘Apocalypse’, I don’t want to hear it.”

Will said nothing for several seconds. “I wasn’t going to say ‘Apocalypse’ because I think we’ve just proven we’ve got a way to fight them, as long as we cooperate.”

“Okay, that’s...actually really good news. I don’t hate your theory.”

“<<I do.>>” Sam and Hunter both said. They glared at each other before Hunter continued, “but I don’t see any alternative. I think you might be right, witch.”

The way he said it pissed Emily off, and she got right in his face. “His name is Will, or William, or Witch Davis. Address him properly, Agent Graham. We’re working *together*, which means you need to stop acting like Will and Sam are the enemy.”

Their eyes locked for a long moment. Emily refused to back down, daring him to contradict her.

His eyes were very, very blue, and Emily did not like noticing. The seal warmed against her skin, giving another one of those little thumps, and she felt an answering flutter in her chest.

Fucking *no*. She did her best to squash that feeling. At the same time, Hunter’s expression changed to one of resignation, and he nodded and gave her an almost tender smile. “Point taken, Detective.”

Emily did not like the way he said *Detective*. Or rather, she didn’t like that she *did* like it.

“You all know you still have your comms on, right?” Sergeant Callihan drawled in their ears.

Right. Crisis ongoing.

Will said, “Okay, so now that’s settled, don’t we still have one more of the zo—*things,* to deal with?”

Hunter and Emily both turned to look in the direction of the boy who had locked himself in a bathroom. Hunter sighed. “I’ll take point.

Witch Davis, are you and your familiar at all protected against Divine Light?"

Will shook his head. "It's impossible to ward against a direct, focused attack, but we'll be fine as long as nothing is aimed directly at us."

"Great." Emily said. "Will, Sam, hang back. We're going in first, and once Hu—Agent Graham does his thing, you two can follow, got it?"

They nodded, and Emily tried to ignore the way Hunter looked at her with a pleased half smile. Shit. How many times had she used his first name?

She didn't have time to worry about it. Emily pulled out her gun again and walked just behind Hunter. The hallway floor was sticky with blood, but she was almost used to the horrible smell by now.

Hunter stopped in front of the dorm room where the last zombie was holed up. He pulled out a key card. Someone had apparently thought to give him a master key.

He pushed the door open, his hand glowing with golden light. Her seal warmed in reaction, and this time Emily didn't have the energy to fight the feeling.

As soon as they stepped inside the small room, they could hear crying. There was also a soft, rhythmic thumping sound.

"Cal? Are you in there?" Emily called out. The sounds of crying and the thumping both stopped. Emily tensed, and neither she nor Hunter moved. "Cal, we're here to try to help you," she said, as soothingly as she could. She prayed she wasn't lying.

"I'm here," came a voice through the door. It was raw, but human sounding. "I don't know what's wrong with me. I want to—</<*I want to hurt people.*>/> *No*! I don't—" he cut off, and there was a keening sound.

Emily glanced at Hunter, and he looked as anguished as she felt. “Cal, will you open the door for us?” Hunter said, his voice soft, gentle. “I’d like to try something that might help. Do you think you can do that?”

There was a long moment, and then a choked, “Yes. Please, help me.”

As soon as the door opened, Hunter flared into brilliant golden light. Emily flinched instinctively, but it did not actually hurt her eyes. She could still see fine.

The boy looked terrible, his eyes fully black, bloody tear-streaks running down his face. His skin was veined in black, though less than the two who were fully gone.

The Light gathered in Hunter’s hands, and he held them out to the boy in benediction. The boy screamed, and the light burned away the blackness. He fell back and hit his head on the seat of the toilet, convulsing and screaming, though his voice was almost too hoarse for sound.

The light faded and Hunter rushed forward. He dropped to his knees next to the boy and cradled his head, trying to keep him from hurting himself as he continued to writhe. Hunter began to say a prayer quietly under his breath. Silver light flowed from his hands into the boy’s head and it ran down his body. The convulsions subsided, and the screaming stopped.

Hunter stopped praying and the light receded. The boy lay very still, his breathing much too shallow.

Emily could feel through her seal that the boy was dying. It was like a guttering candle. There was no longer a sense of wrongness, but the soul was still damaged enough that her seal reacted to it. She put her gun away and crouched down.

"His body is healed, but he is still dying," Hunter said. He sounded heartbroken.

"Let's move him to the bed."

Sam and Will appeared in the doorway as Hunter gently laid the boy on one of the two beds in the room. Sam approached the boy slowly and gave him a sniff. <<His soul is damaged, drained. Not as badly as the others. If I can get him to the Triad quickly, they might be able to help him stay whole. If I don't, I think his soul will fall apart as soon as he dies. Or it might get stuck in the body, like the others. I...don't know.>>

Hunter, who looked absolutely exhausted, stared at Sam for a long moment, his expression unreadable. The boy's breathing grew shallower, and there was a slight, wet rattle. Sam gave Hunter a single slow blink, and Hunter nodded.

"Take him. Let the boy have his choice."

Sam's body became indistinct, and gentle flames licked to life as he shifted from panther to man. The flames were not bright, but it still hurt Emily's eyes to look at them. She did anyway. Hunter's body tensed, and his expression was pained as Sam moved closer.

Sam reached a hand into the boy's body. <<Will you come with me?>> he asked, his voice very kind. There was no answer that Emily could hear, but as Sam pulled back, a pale shadow-hand appeared, grasping Sam's glowing one. Sam pulled the boy's soul free, and Emily could see it outlined in Sam's fiery glow. Sam gathered the boy into a hug, and they both fell away in a flash of green light.

The body stopped breathing, and they sat there in silence.

Emily was very surprised when after only a few minutes there was another flash of flame and Sam, back in his normal cat body, reappeared. He looked more indistinct than normal, and when he spoke, he sounded far away.

<<It worked. The boy’s soul will need a few days to recover before he can make his choice, but Lucifer thinks he will choose to join Divinity. I expect that makes you happy, Agent Graham.>>

Hunter shook his head wearily and sat down on the other bed. He dropped his head into his hands. “None of this makes me happy, Demon.” Emily fought the urge to put a hand on Hunter’s shoulder and lost. She pushed warmth into him from her seal almost without meaning to. Some of Hunter’s tension left him, and he gave her a grateful half-smile.

Will crouched down next to Sam and rubbed his ears. Sam attempted to purr, but even that sounded tired. “Good work, buddy. Go have a rest and talk with that new friend of yours, I know you’re still upset. I’ll call you if I need you, I promise, but I think we’re done for now.”

Sam rubbed his face against Will’s hand. <<You should rest too, Will. You haven’t pulled that much magic in one day since your trials.>> Sam turned to blink slowly at Emily. <<You too, Detective. I know your day is far from over, but a power nap never hurt anyone.>>

Before Emily could answer, Sam disappeared in another puff of heatless flame.

Sergeant Callihan’s voice came over the comms then, as if he’d heard Sam, even though he couldn’t possibly have. “You all need to take a break and check in with the paramedics. When you’re done, meet me at the command center and we can discuss how to proceed from here.”

NEXUS

Aiden woke with a warm, furry body sleeping on his face.

"Sam!" Aiden said, overjoyed. It came out muffled. There was no reaction from the cat on his face.

Aiden picked Sam off his face and sat up. Sam still did not wake up, and his body was limp. Aiden felt his whole being go tight and cold.

"Sam?" he asked, giving him a gentle shake. The body felt warm to Aiden, but Sam did not respond. He did not breathe.

But that was okay. He didn't need to breathe any more than Aiden did. Aiden told himself that, several times, but he felt his eyes burn with tears. Could demons die? Aiden didn't know.

"Sam, if this is a joke, it's not funny," he whispered, and there was still no response from Sam.

Panicked, Aiden reached inside himself and *called*, using Sam's <[name]>.

This, finally, got a response from Sam. His head snapped up, and he blinked blearily at Aiden.

"What? Aiden, are you okay?" Sam asked, his voice suffused with exhaustion.

Aiden's relief was a force of nature, and he burst into tears with the strength of it.

"Aw, bunny, shhh. What's wrong?" Sam's head lowered back to the bed wearily.

"You— you weren't waking up!" Aiden said, still crying. He tried to calm himself, but all that did was give him hiccups.

"I'm sorry, Aiden. I know we need to talk, but I'm so *tired*. I just...I need to sleep..." Sam's voice drifted off, and he went limp again.

Aiden sat there sniffling and hiccupping and petting Sam for several minutes. He still felt slight flutters of panic, so it took him several moments of deep breaths before his thoughts stopped spinning.

Why? He needed to understand why. Sam wasn't going to be able to tell him, and he floundered for a moment before he remembered the Library interface. Aiden *reached* and <[accessed]>.

He drew a box in front of him, like he'd seen Sam do. A holographic screen popped into existence, hovering in front of Aiden at exactly the right distance to be comfortable. He typed [why would a demon be too tired to wake up?]

The screen started listing things. It was a very long list, and it did nothing to help him calm down. In particular, the descriptions for 'curse' and 'soul damage' made Aiden go all cold and tight again.

Impulsively, desperately, he typed, [Why is *Sam* so tired *right now*?]. Aiden wasn't entirely sure how he put the emphasis in, but it was there.

This time, there was only one answer on the screen. It read <[Sam channeled a very large amount of magic for his witch in a very short period of time.]>

That was a much more specific answer than he was expecting.

Encouraged, he typed, [When will Sam wake up?]

<[Error—user does not have access to future knowledge.]>

Aiden made a small frustrated sound, and tried again. [How long will it take for Sam to wake up?]

<[Error— user does not have access to future knowledge.]>

Aiden read over his question, and, thinking carefully, tried, [About how long should it take for Sam to wake up from his most recent channeling of a lot of magic?]

This time the answer came back instantly. <[Data concerning typical recovery times for excessive magic use for Sam is limited. Best estimate, given past records and cross-referencing with other familiars of similar experience and strength, is one quarter day cycle, Nexus time, with a margin of error of up to one half cycle.]>

Aiden sat for a moment, letting himself process the information on the screen, finally calming down. Aiden tried, [How long has Sam been asleep?]

The answer the Library gave him was in Earth *years*. It took a moment for Aiden to figure out the Library had given him the total amount of time Sam had slept *ever*.

"Crap, they weren't kidding about needing to ask the right question," Aiden muttered to himself, and kept typing. He had to ask the same question several ways before he felt confident he understood what he had learned.

Once Aiden concluded that Sam had been asleep for possibly one-eighth Nexus cycle and would likely sleep for at least another quarter cycle more, he started asking other things. He looked up his own account and found his current status listed as <[Registered Demon, Suspected Integrated Mantle, type unknown, demonic skills unknown, strength untested, magic type unknown, soul age unknown—verified pre-Seal.]> There was also an uncomfortable amount of information there about his human life, as well as an alarmingly long list of 'past life fragments'.

They were organized into three main groups: one branching from Kikeru, one from Esther, and one from a soul called Amun. There were several dozen other groups marked as <[waiting for confirmation]> and Aiden closed the window, lacking fortitude to look further.

He would, though. He could do it.

Just, later.

Aiden glanced at Sam, who was still curled into a furry ball on top of the comforter. Determined, Aiden turned back to the interface. [How can I help Sam be safer?]

<[Error—user's file is incomplete. Question cannot be answered at this time.]>

Aiden strangled a frustrated scream and pressed his hands to his eyes. Eventually he calmed down enough to type, [What actions can I take to complete my file enough to answer the previous query?]

The interface screen filled up with so much information that Aiden couldn't even read it. Frantically, he deleted his last question.

Aiden took a deep breath, and let it out.

[Is there a simple action I can take right now that will help complete my file enough to help Sam?]

<[Yes.]>

Aiden started to type, paused, and then asked, [How many?]

<[42.]>

Aiden narrowed his eyes. There was something suspicious about that number, but he couldn't quite figure out what.

He typed, [Which actions do I currently have the skills, mental fortitude, and time to do before Sam wakes up?]

<[Create objects using the wardrobe, trade goods or services, try to randomly manifest powers by doing dangerous things, like jumping out of a window, or accidentally picking a fight with someone on the street, or—]>

"How the Hell do you *accidentally* pick a fight *on purpose*?" Aiden said, out loud.

The room shook, and Aiden clapped his hand over his mouth. "Sorry," he whispered, eyes wide.

The shaking stopped.

Aiden decided he would use the magic closet to make items and then go out and sell them. That was simple, and something he already knew how to do, sort of. He swiped a hand through the screen and slid out of bed.

The massive pile of shirts on the floor, still there from the day before, stopped him short. With a sigh, he drew himself another interface so he could ask where he might trade them and anything else he decided to make. The Library gave him a massive list of options, and it was easy enough to rank them by both proximity and style.

He also asked how he could carry large amounts of things and had a moment of vertigo that led to the sudden awareness that he had his own...pocket dimension...thing...where he could keep pretty much anything he could pick up in his hands.

There was a small warning about magical overuse if he tried to store too many things at once. Aiden searched for his limit, but only got another intensely frustrating error message.

That was fine. As long as he was careful, filling up his pocket dimension with clothing was probably a good way to add information to his file.

Aiden nodded to himself, took a deep breath and focused. He reached out a hand, placed it into the pile of shirts, and grabbed hold.

There was a loud pop. Aiden's eyes flew open.

The entire massive pile of shirts was gone.

Panicked, Aiden <[accessed]> and asked how much magic he had left.

<[Error—magic limit unknown.]>

Frantically, Aiden typed, [Am I close to running out?]

<[...No.]>

Aiden relaxed, then frowned. [How do I know when I get low?]

<[Symptoms of low magic include extreme fatigue, headache, and hunger.]>

[But I've never felt that!]

<[Error—not a question. Also, duh.]>

Offended, Aiden typed, [Who is typing out these answers?]

<[Depends]> was the answer, followed by a very, very long list of names, including his own.

Aiden swiped a hand through the interface and turned back to the wardrobe.

After a moment's consideration, he focused with as much delicacy as he could possibly manage on what he wanted to make—a green silk scarf. He pulled open the wardrobe door and barely felt a twinge of disorientation as the magic left him.

A single scarf was there, just as he'd imagined it. The color was the exact shade of Sam's eyes.

He smiled and set it next to Sam for him to find when he woke up.

Aiden threw himself into his task, delightedly pulling all different kinds of clothing from the closet. He was able to make different weights and knits of fabric in whatever colors he wanted, and he marveled at the way it changed the way the clothing looked.

It was *amazing*. Once, years ago, he'd tried printing out some of his designs with his old, cheap clothing fabricator, but everything he made was always off, the recycled fiber fabric never holding to the shapes he wanted. He knew the shapes he wanted were possible—some of his clients wore really nice clothes—but he could never afford the fabric to make them, not while he was saving up to move to witch territory.

Aiden winced, remembering how close he'd been to making it. Another year and he would have been able to afford the immigration. He could have gone to school and gotten an art degree. He could have done character design for video games, or maybe even gotten into real fashion. If he hadn't been so dependent on drugs to deal with his anxiety and after-work drops, he could have—

Aiden pushed the thought away. It was too late to worry about it now.

He moved over to the writing desk and drew a screen on it so he could start sketching out full outfit sets, including accessories. He even found a set of pencils and paints in the writing desk drawers, exactly what he needed.

Which was probably because, like the things he made with the wardrobe, Aiden had created them himself.

There was something deeply soothing about doing something familiar, and Aiden found himself relaxing into a confidence he hadn't felt in a long while.

When he was satisfied he had enough things to trade, he made a few more small baubles to use as gifts, and then decided to make something for himself to wear for the day.

Something with pockets. Pockets always made him feel more prepared, even if they were only filled with acorns or random nice-looking rocks.

He designed himself a knee-length flared coat with huge, oversized pockets. It was made of a heavy, iridescent, silk-like material. He also created a pair of low-slung white pants and a skin tight shirt with a picture of a rainbow cake and the words 'Where is the lie?' printed in holographic lettering.

When Aiden opened the wardrobe on that last set of clothing, satisfaction settled deep into his core. He got dressed, feeling like he'd finally *done* something.

Even if it was just making a bunch of silly clothes.

It took him several minutes to psych himself up before he could bring himself to look at his reflection again. When he finally did, it took several more minutes for him to be comfortable with the very new and unavoidable experience of liking what he saw very much.

The clothing was perfectly tailored, and the colors and style lines managed to accent every single feature without being gaudy. He almost fearfully let himself admire the way his eyes were a bit too large, shining with sparkling, shifting rainbows, supernaturally bright.

He looked, unquestionably, good. Not just attractive, or like a sex object, but *good*. Like how he'd always wanted to look, like how he wanted to *feel*. There was a softly radiant sweetness to his face, a lustful brightness to his expression, and more strength in his body than he thought he had any right to while still looking somewhat delicate.

So many years hating his reflection. So many years spent wanting to be good, trying to be good in the only ways he knew how, but being told he was bad.

But here, in this place without lies, he looked *good*.

He held his own gaze for as long as he could, feeling shattered, but in a clean way that promised healing.

When he finally let himself turn away, he went back over to the bed to sit with Sam for a little longer before he left. He didn't want to leave Sam—there was so much unsaid between them—but he was determined not to leave the job half done.

He used the writing desk to make some really nice paper and wrote Sam a message explaining where he was going and that he would be back soon and left the room.

Hugo was waiting for him outside the door. Aiden gave him his best and most earnest smile and pulled from his pocket the small gift he had made for him.

Hugo stared at the amethyst and silver brooch for several moments, long enough that Aiden started to feel like he might have made a mistake. He was about to apologize when Hugo slowly held out his hand.

"It's a gift," Aiden said nervously. "To thank you for keeping me safe. I don't want anything in return, except maybe friendship, but you don't need to do that if you don't want to."

Hugo looked at him in a way that clearly said, 'Don't be ridiculous,' and fastened it to his lapel.

Aiden bounced in the elevator, clutching the garnet and gold pin he had for Septimus.

By the time Hugo opened the doors for him, he'd almost completely lost his nerve. The only reason he managed to hold out the pin to Septimus when he got to the front desk was the nod of encouragement Hugo had given him.

Unable to meet Septimus in the eye, he looked down at his shiny hightops and said, "It's a gift. No strings. As thanks. For letting me stay."

Septimus coiled his fingers around Aiden's wrist, and Aiden looked up, startled and tingling with nerves.

"You're very welcome, ssssweeet one. Thank you for choossssing to ssstay with usss. Thank you for thisss." Septimus took the pin with his other hand, keeping his gentle hold on Aiden's wrist.

Aiden was caught, hypnotized by Septimus's eyes. They were fascinating, beautiful, golden and unblinking. Aiden felt himself swallow and blush, unable to stop staring. Septimus rocked his head, hypnotically, and Aiden almost smiled, almost surrendered. He *wanted* to, quite badly.

But when he thought of Sam up in his room, an echo of his last boyfriend's voice said in the back of his mind '*you filthy slut'*.

Aiden flinched and looked away, and Septimus released his wrist instantly. He flicked his tongue out and said, "You do not owe usss anything, love, and no harm will ever come to you here. No one will ever take from you sssomething you do not wish to give, and more importantly, what you are willing to offer will never be used againsssst you. Do you underssstand?"

Trembling slightly, Aiden nodded. But still... "What about things I want? Want to give and receive, but that I am afraid of. That I'm afraid to *want*?"

Septimus placed a slender finger under Aiden's chin and lifted his face, gently. This time when he met Septimus's eyes, he was not caught, but there was still something deeply soothing about the analgesic gaze.

"You are accepted here, sssweet, no matter what. Now go. We will be here when you come back. When you are ready, I will show you why people visssit thisss hotel." Septimus released Aiden and gave him a weirdly un-snake-like wink. "You will fit in beautifully, ssssweeet. You are, I think, jussssst what we need."

Aiden felt fluttery, but in a way that warmed him and soothed away his shame. “Okay,” he whispered, and then he turned and raced out into the city.

This time, Aiden knew the eyes that followed him were looking at him, and not Sam. He didn’t feel threatened by them, but he found himself jumping from light pole to light pole, only meeting a person’s gaze for the briefest moment before he disappeared. It made him feel free.

A few of their faces stuck in his mind, and he found himself hoping he had stuck in their minds as well. If they met again, later, he wanted to see if any of them would be fast enough to catch him.

The sky was dusky, the moon setting and the sun rising. The air smelled bright, suffused with the sweet scent of dawn. As he zigzagged down the street, the light noticeably changed, transitioning from night to day. Food smells filled the air, coffee and cake and something spicy. Aiden found himself outside the cafe Sam had taken him to, but he remembered the scary barista and he decided he should keep moving, following a slight pull that felt like where he wanted to go.

He stopped suddenly in front of a huge glass window display. It looked like a fancy department store, the sort only very wealthy people shopped at. This one displayed clothing that refused to be categorized. There were cloaks made of smoke, and outfits that looked like they might give someone a fancy powerup in a video game. Aiden was frozen in place with longing, wanting to see them up close, touch them, understand how they were made.

He was suddenly, irrationally ashamed of his stupid amateur clothing. He took a step back, ready to give up and return to the Hotel and hide under his covers, promises and plans abandoned.

He might have done just that if a unicorn hadn’t stepped out onto the street and trotted over to him.

"*Where* did you get that coat?" the unicorn asked. The voice seemed female, but Aiden was hesitant to assume, and even more hesitant to check.

He said, "Um."

The unicorn wuffed at him, nosing at the coat with a soft pink nose. The unicorn was shockingly tall—Aiden could have tucked himself under their chin without crouching if they stood straight.

"I do not recognize this designer. That is impossible, I know *every* designer. Who made it?" they asked. Their horn was golden and spiraled, and their tail was long and prehensile, with a fluffy golden tuft at the end, like a lion. They were an impossibly pure white except for golden feathers above each cloven hoof and a shining golden mane. "It was not Zee, though the shape is admiring of their style. This is not their magic, though. Not another Librarian either."

Aiden said, "Um."

The unicorn continued to nose at him, muttering and discarding names Aiden didn't recognize. Aiden stood frozen as they moved to his hair. Aiden's instincts told him the unicorn meant him no harm, but he still didn't understand what was happening.

The unicorn's breath was warm and light and smelled of flowers and sunshine. They suddenly pulled back, and studied him, their eyes full of rosy sunrises. "*You*. It must have been. This material is unique, like it was made by some new kind of magic. It's subtle, hidden, perhaps most would not notice, but *I*, of course, could never be fooled." The unicorn huffed. "Who *are* you? *What* are you? Do not say 'Um' again."

"U—I'm Aiden," he said, ears pressed flat to his head, tail quivering behind him. He reached back to try to stop it.

"Hmmm. Why do you look like you are going to run away?"

"U—" He stopped himself from saying um, but they obviously knew anyway.

They pranced lightly behind him and nudged him towards the open storefront, careful not to jab him with their horn. "Come on newbie, show me what you brought. *Imagine* being afraid of a *unicorn.*"

"You could stab me," Aiden said, but he meekly walked forward into the store while he said it. Inside, it smelled like fancy.

"Why would I do that? Are you sick? Wounded? You don't smell injured. You smell *unique*. Show me what you have."

"I thought unicorns were supposed to be, like, elusive. You're pushy."

The unicorn laughed, and a bunch of butterflies popped into existence. They fluttered around the store. One of them landed on Aiden's nose, and he sneezed.

"You're cute. *Show* me."

Aiden *reached* into his little pocket dimension and took out the outfit sets he'd crafted. They appeared on the floor between them, and the unicorn snorted, tiny golden sparks flying out.

"Not on the *floor*. On the display!" They nodded to the corner of the store, where a persistently indistinct figure stood in a circle of spotlights. Aiden started to reach down to pick things up, but the unicorn nosed him out of the way and tapped the clothing with their horn. They all flew over to the display, and the indistinct figure split and formed into shadowy models, each one wearing one of the outfits Aiden had crafted.

Aiden felt himself flush deeply with embarrassment. He wasn't sure how he'd ended up *here*. He'd thought he might find some kind of underworld flea market to trade his clothes at, not a specialty designer store! Was the city playing a trick on him? Had he done something wrong?

The unicorn studied each piece as they laid them out, and Aiden started shaking with the need to run.

"The structure is a bit amateurish, but it actually adds to their appeal, I think. You've designed much but made little, right? Or you had limited access to unusual materials, perhaps?"

Aiden nodded mutely.

The unicorn made a slight noise of approval. "I thought so. Most of the newbies these days relied too heavily on those fastfab clothing printers in life. Makes them ignorant of the way quality fabrics are supposed to behave."

Aiden opened his mouth to protest—he'd *wanted* to use better materials, he'd just never been able to *afford* them—but she continued speaking without pause. "May I add some tailoring? I'd like to take them and sell them here, but depending on who wants them they will need to change shape. Humanoids, mostly, but you never know, it might work for some of the more ephemeral cryptids too."

"You like them?" Aiden asked, disbelieving. He couldn't quite understand how she could want them displayed near the rest of the clothing in the store.

The unicorn turned to look at him. Their expressive, aurora eyes went suddenly somber.

"Oh, honey, I'm sorry. I should have noticed. Yes, I like them quite a lot. They're extraordinary, truly."

Aiden frowned furiously, but without any malice. Why did everyone have to see how insecure he was so *easily*? His reaction seemed to shock another laugh out of the unicorn, and more butterflies appeared.

"That must get inconvenient," Aiden said, holding out his hand so one could land there.

"Mmmm. I have no idea where they come from, or where they go. Maybe it's the same hundred or so butterflies, or maybe they're illusions. Let me know if they ever explain themselves to you."

Another one of the butterflies landed on his ear, which was standing up now. "Why would they tell me?"

The unicorn just rolled their eyes at him. "So, will you let me take the clothing," they asked instead of answering, "and add the tailoring magic? I'll teach you how to do it yourself, if you want, as long as you promise to give me the first pick of anything you make to sell for at least one earth year."

Aiden was thoroughly overwhelmed. He still hadn't quite wrapped his head around the unicorn's use of *extraordinary*. He felt like he had to at least try and negotiate even though he wasn't sure there would be anyone else who wanted the clothes he made. He was surprised that this crazy unicorn wanted them.

Haggling over the price of his services, even when he didn't quite understand why someone wanted them, was familiar territory for him, though. "Six months, and okay, as long as you tell anyone who asks they were made by me," he said, only slightly tentatively.

"Done." Obviously delighted, the unicorn pranced over to him and touched their horn to his antlers. There was a flash of golden light, and Aiden shivered at the contact with his antlers. He could feel the weight of the agreement settle on him like it had with the other promises he had made.

Aiden blinked at the unicorn. He had expected more negotiating, and now he was even more confused. Had he undersold himself? Aiden had no idea how that could be, but there was no other explanation. He resolved to be more careful in the future.

Unconcerned with Aiden's obvious befuddlement, the unicorn continued, "Now, if you wouldn't mind, I'd like to do some tests on their durability. I'll take possession of all of these sets, of course, this lot won't be sold on consignment since I'll be modifying them. During later exchanges we can negotiate consignment or not, depending on how well these sell. What is your asking price?"

Aiden said, "Um," again, and tried not to wince. He decided he should maybe talk to Esther about practicing better ways to handle confusion at their next session. Before the unicorn could snort at him again, he blurted, "I don't know what they're worth."

He flushed and hid his face behind his ears. What had he been thinking? He'd thought, maybe, that if he found a flea market, he could shop around and get an idea of the market before trying to sell. This—he was completely unprepared for this. And now he'd given that away.

The unicorn didn't say anything for an uncomfortably long time. Eventually, his face still noticeably warm to the touch, he let go of his ears and peeked out.

"There you are," the unicorn said gently. "You *are* new, huh?"

Aiden nodded miserably.

"How long?"

"Um," Aiden said, and winced. "I mean, two days? Nexus time?"

The unicorn blinked. "Two days? *Two days?*" They tossed their head. "You mean, since you became a Demon, yes? Not since you *arrived*?"

Aiden shuffled nervously. "Um. Only one day a Demon."

The unicorn blinked again. "How long ago did you die? If you don't mind me asking?"

"Um. I'm not sure? The last date I remember was September 7, 47. Um, YAR."

"Oh, *sweet,*" the unicorn said, in a tone Aiden didn't really understand. A low, soft, soothing sound radiated from their horn. "Did you come here, to my shop, on purpose?"

Aiden bit his lip, and then shook his head in the negative. "Sorry."

The unicorn snorted, but more softly than before. "Sorry? You regret being here?"

"No!" Aiden said, quickly, letting go of his ears completely. "I'm, um. Sorry for not coming on purpose? And wasting your time?" Aiden winced again, because while it was the truth, it sounded absurd when he said it.

The unicorn laughed so hard and long that they had to open the door and let some of the butterflies out.

"Alright, sweet, I shall be blunt, and I will refrain from playing any mercantile games with you from now on. You can trust me." The words landed like an offering of fealty between them. "I will owe you in favor-debt what these are worth to me right now, which is probably about what I can sell them for because you don't have any brand recognition yet. The lucky bastards who get here first are going to be *so* pleased with themselves later." They nosed at one of the outfits. "This fabric is incredibly unique and, if I'm not mistaken, *highly* magical."

"It is?" Aiden studied his coat cuff. "This too?"

The unicorn nodded seriously. "That most of all. It's beautiful, and it's also, I suspect, a rather miraculous kind of armor." She studied Aiden long enough that he swallowed audibly, twice. "Did you do that on purpose? Or did you make the material instinctively?"

Aiden considered before answering, even though he didn't really need to. "Instinct."

The unicorn nodded again and let out a slow huff of air. "Alright then. I have already agreed to teach you tailoring magic with a deal that was, I admit, *extremely* to my advantage. I apologize. I shouldn't have sealed that deal without making sure you were fully prepared to engage in Demonic-level commerce. I can only say, in my defense, that I was excited."

Aiden nodded and chewed on his lower lip. "That's okay. I forg—"

The unicorn snorted violently. "Hush! I am not finished!" The unicorn took a deep, steadying breath. "I will offer a second deal now. Allow me to train you, and to help you discover what I am quite certain is a dangerously new and powerful kind of magic. Specifically, I can offer to help you understand the crafting of magical clothing and accessories, which is what you have created here, and help you turn what is currently unpolished instinct into something you can use with intention."

Aiden hesitated, then asked with a flash of insight, "Is this why Nexus brought me here?"

The unicorn tossed their head and tail in a way that gave Aiden an impression of immense pleasure. "Almost certainly."

"Oh. Okay. Good." He swallowed again. "So, um. What do you get out of the deal?"

The unicorn stared at him like Aiden was slow. Aiden *hated* being looked at like that, and he scowled and said, without thinking, "Oh, come on, I'm supposed to believe the privilege of teaching me is enough?"

Horror washed through him, and he backed away. "I'm sorry, I didn't—"

"That is *exactly* what you are meant to believe, because it is the *truth*."

Aiden flinched back at the force in the unicorn's tone.

"Your magic is *unique*, and I am starting to think you don't have the slightest understanding of what that means."

Aiden felt tears well up in his eyes, and he tried to scrub them away before they fell, ashamed at his overreaction. He backed away farther, accidentally knocking into the cloak made of shadows.

Deliciously soft tendrils wrapped around his arms and neck, cool and silky. A wave of dizziness washed through him. He felt lighter, like he was floating. He tugged tentatively at the tendrils, and they coiled tighter.

Aiden froze and stopped breathing, eyes wide and still blurred with tears.

"Damn it," the unicorn swore, then they swore again, softer. "I'm sorry, sweet. Don't move."

The unicorn *shone* at the cloak, their horn radiating magic like warm, thick sunshine. The shadowy tendrils slid away, releasing Aiden, and the unicorn used their tail to gently guide Aiden forward and away from the cloak.

"I'm sorry," the unicorn said again. "Perhaps you should find yourself a better teacher than me."

"No!" Aiden said, surprised by the strength of his own reaction. "No, I don't... I just—" Aiden cut off, and took a breath. He didn't want to lose an opportunity because he was still so easily triggered. He'd get better, he *would*. He could do this.

His voice was steady when he said, "I would be honored to learn what you have to teach me."

The unicorn held Aiden's gaze for a moment, and then gently pressed their nose to his forehead. It was warm and soft, like living velvet. "Alright, sweet. Give me a few days to study these items, and then come back. I'll leave it up to you whether you experiment some more on your own, but be careful—your intentions will almost certainly manifest themselves in the items you create in some way, and without more control, the effects might be, ah, unpredictable."

Cold fear settled into Aiden's chest. "I made some other things, gifts. Are they dangerous?"

The unicorn started to snort, then stopped themself and let out a slower huff of air. "No. No, at least, not to the people you gave them to. But they might be larger gifts than you intended, and you'll want to be careful who you give out gifts to, if they're anything like these items. Not everyone would use gifts like these wisely."

"Oh," Aiden said. He trusted everyone he'd given gifts to, and Sam and Esther both told him it was okay to trust his instincts. "Okay."

"*Oh, okay*, he says. Like it is nothing." The unicorn tossed their head, and then nosed Aiden out the door. "Go, on your way, and come back in a few days. You feel the signature of this place now?"

"Yes?"

"Is that a question?"

"Um."

The unicorn laughed, and half a dozen butterflies followed Aiden out the door. They stayed with him as he walked down the street, a smile tugging at his lips.

GREATER PROVIDENCE RI, SEPTEMBER 11TH 47 YAR

YES STILL.

Hunter refused to leave the dorm building until after he went around praying over the torn bodies of the dead kids for the better part of an hour. Forensic officers would be working to document the scene for at least another day, so no one tried to hurry him. He'd seemed less tired after he'd come out of the building.

But less was very relative.

Will and Emily took showers at a nearby gym while Hunter prayed, and then changed into clothes that didn't reek of blood and death. Will left to take a short nap in an empty classroom while Hunter took his own shower. Emily waited for him— she needed to get the crystal amulet back from him so she could return it to Carla.

He cleaned his ridiculous armor as well. There wasn't a ton of blood, it wasn't like they'd been rolling in it, but there was enough. She was surprised how easily it all came out. It made Emily wonder if there was some kind of magic involved. When he finished, he was back to the pristine white and gold warrior priest that he'd arrived as.

His face was still etched with sadness and exhaustion, though, and he didn't seem nearly as much of an ass as when he first arrived. If it weren't for the seal, she might actually like him. She might have even prayed along with him.

She couldn't pray, though. The stupid thing might take that as an invitation.

He handed her the crystal without protest. Emily didn't know what to say. Her irrational, or, to be fair, *defensive* hatred warred with empathy and a grudging respect.

Emily tucked the crystal into her pocket and muttered about meeting him at the command center.

He just nodded at her tiredly.

A witch Emily hadn't had time to meet earlier was with Carla. She looked like she could be anywhere between fourteen and forty, ageless in a way that was less, or more, than human. Her eyes were darkened with dramatic makeup, and her hair was long and silver. She dressed in long, lacy robes that were covered in stars and moons, all of which glowed faintly with unnatural light. Her familiars—she apparently had two—were a pair of ravens, one white that sat on her shoulder and one black that sat perched on a carved staff. She even wore a wide-brimmed hat with a long point that sagged artfully to the side, a personal sigil made of seven stars surrounding a crescent moon dangling from the end.

She screamed witch as loudly and with as much cliché as humanly possible. It might have been ridiculous if she didn't carry herself like a queen. Emily still would have thought she was ridiculous, but her seal pulsed at her in alarm even after she shoved at it as hard as she could.

Emily handed the crystals to Carla.

"Thank you, Detective. This is Selena, one of our elders. She would like to speak with you as soon as there is time."

The obviously powerful witch shook Emily's hand, despite how uncomfortable it made them both. She studied Emily for several minutes before saying, "You are a puzzle. I think I see why they want you, but I cannot imagine why they took the risk."

She drifted off without another word.

Carla sighed. "Selena is the Providence Coven leader, as well as a prominent member of the Northeastern High Coven."

"Is she always like that?" Emily asked, keeping her voice low.

"She's usually worse," Carla said back, conspiratorially. "She's toning it down for the emergency. You better get going, Selena will join you all in the command center. Someone will need to *act as liaison* and run interference between her and the Paladin." Carla said pointedly, winking to take the sting out of her words.

Emily winced, then saluted Carla with a sheepish smile and followed after Selena.

Ten minutes into the meeting, Emily wasn't sure interference was even possible.

"We don't have a choice. If we don't try, for all we know they will all turn," Hunter said, for the third time.

"We cannot do it without knowing whether or not it will kill them," Selena said, also for the third time. Selena and Hunter had been glaring at each other from across the table since the meeting began, arguing about whether or not they should use Hunter's Divine Light power on the infected people. Emily didn't want to side with Hunter, but she had to admit he did have a point—they couldn't just keep holding people indefinitely, and the people back at the hospital had been there for days with no signs of improvement

"We should ask them. Explain the risks, let them make their own choice," Emily said as reasonably as she could, interjecting before Hunter and Selena could go another round of 'greater good' vs 'unethical risk'.

Both Hunter and Selena turned to look at her when she spoke, but Emily saw in their faces that even though they both knew that was the right way to do it, neither of them would concede yet.

They ignored her and went right back to their verbal jousting, neither one listening to the other. After another *hour* of it, Emily decided she was too tired to deal with the bullshit, and she stood up. "I'll be right back. Feel free to keep going."

Both Will and Sergeant Callihan looked downright *betrayed* as she left. She felt slightly bad about abandoning them, but not bad enough to stay.

She went to where they were holding the corrupted students before she could change her mind. The security officer at the door waved her through without so much as a single question, and Emily went straight to the room where the dead boy's girlfriend was. Her name was Helen—Emily had finally looked it up in her GPI files.

Emily knocked and waited for the soft, "Yes?" before she opened the door.

The girl read Emily's expression and immediately burst into tears. Emily reached out to hold the girl, and her seal buzzed *very* slightly at her when she made skin contact.

"He's dead," the girl said into Emily's shoulder, and Emily made a soft sound of confirmation. "Did he—" she choked, then continued wetly, "Did he kill anyone?"

"No," Emily said gently. "He was still locked in the bathroom when we found him. We... We tried to cleanse him, but he was too far gone. There was damage to his soul, and he died. But his soul is still intact and he moved on as himself, unlike—" Emily cut off, kicking herself. This girl was friends with the other two as well.

Helen's breath caught in response to Emily's stupid slip, and she pulled back, looking terrified. "Unlike what?"

It was too late to turn back now. "Unlike the other two. Their souls were ruined."

"Oh my god. Oh my god. Is that going to happen to me? Wait. You said *cleanse*. Can you fix it?" Helen looked at Emily, barely breathing except for the occasional slow, hitching exhalation and sharp, gasped inhalation.

Emily fought the seal's attempt to push warmth into the girl on the off chance it affected her decision. "We have a way to cleanse the corruption, but we don't know if you will survive it. We think you have a good chance, because your infection is less advanced, but we don't know. It's your choice, no one will—"

"Do it." Helen's expression turned fierce.

"I cannot stress enough how dangerous it is."

"I don't care. I don't want my soul *ruined*. I can see in your face that what happened to Riche and Jen is much worse than death."

Emily nodded, unable to deny her feelings on the matter, and stood. "I'll be back soon."

She would have said the same if she was in the girl's position. Maybe that was why Emily had come here—she recognized the girl as a kindred spirit and wanted to give her the choice.

Hunter and Selena were still going at it when she slipped back into the room. She caught Sergeant Callihan's attention and nodded for him to step out into the hall with her.

"I have a volunteer. For whenever those two stop their pissing contest."

"Fuck, woman, you should have just said so!" He turned back into the room and said, "Enough, there's a volunteer."

Selena looked at Emily, her eyes narrowed. "I will speak to this volunteer first. It is important that no coercion was used."

Emily bristled instinctively, and she was happy to see Will stand up and start to defend her, but then she thought better of it and put a hand on his shoulder. Selena was right to check— Emily was compromised. Her seal very well might have done something. She couldn't know for certain.

Emily said, "Her name is Helen. Her boyfriend is the one who locked himself in the bathroom." Selena met Emily's eyes briefly, and then nodded in acknowledgement of Emily's understanding before leaving the room.

Hunter was watching Emily with an inscrutable expression, maybe slightly worried, and Emily wasn't sure if she should be insulted or concerned that she really had influenced the girl after all.

Will and Sergeant Callihan went to check on the screening checkpoints. It was an impossible task, and one Emily dreaded the results of. They still didn't know anything about how the corruption spread, or how long the poor kids had been infected.

It could have been days.

It took Selena at least half an hour to check the girl over. She even brought in a witch that apparently specialized in mind magic to make sure the girl was choosing to do this freely.

Emily wasn't sure what she would do if there were traces of mind control, if the seal was fucking with people besides her.

Emily and Hunter waited in tense silence outside the room while the witches did their examination. When the specialist came out, he and Selena walked down the hall to speak, but Emily still heard the man say to Selena, "Honestly, in her shoes I would be just as insistent."

Right? Emily wanted to call over, but she didn't. She was too relieved. Selena nodded and walked back over to Emily and Hunter. It was only then that Emily realized she'd been standing next to him. As if in *solidarity.*

Fucking seal. It was too late to move away now.

"She's clean. We will ward the room so that the Divine Light does not penetrate beyond the walls. It should take roughly fifteen minutes. You can burn the corruption out of her as soon as we finish." She looked at Emily in a way that was definitely not an apology, but it gave Emily the impression she'd passed another test. "You both might want to wait outside. It may get uncomfortable for you while we build the seal up."

Emily did not need to be told twice. Even outside, the damn thing was letting her know the witches were working. Hunter followed behind her, and the silence stretched between them as they stood on the campus sidewalk.

Sunlight slanted through trees still summer-green where it managed to wink through the tall campus buildings. Most were pre-Rapture in this part of the campus, but they had all obviously been repaired and reinforced with modern hempcrete to match the witchy aesthetic of the rest of the college. The air had the soft golden quality of an early fall afternoon, smelling like earth and incense and the faintest hint of ozone from all the magic in the air.

Emily was almost resentful that the day was so beautiful, considering what had happened here. What was happening.

The seal tried to warm her, responding to her need and Hunter's proximity. She forced it back. She would feel her own damn emotions.

Hunter broke the silence, interrupting her stubborn quest to wallow in her *very reasonable* melancholia. "I have the feeling that you don't like me much, Detective."

Emily almost winced. "It's been a stressful few days."

He quirked another one of those sad half-smiles at her. Emily once again failed to ignore how attractive he was, in that chiseled golden-boy way of his. "I can imagine. You know, there are fewer than seven thousand Divine Paladins in the whole world, and all of them were either imbued before the Rapture or were born with the power. Your Artifact, the way it's partially bonded, is *very* rare."

"I'm not a Divine Paladin. I'm not an exorcist."

"You could be. You might need to be. I cannot help but feel that you were chosen for a reason."

Emily's jaw ached as she clenched it so hard her teeth felt like they might crack. Eventually she said, "I wish I knew why. I'm not even all that religious."

Hunter looked genuinely surprised. "You're not? You must at least believe in the goodness of the Divine Will, in finding eternal peace within its judgment."

"I..." she drifted off. She *did* believe in the idea dedicating herself to a greater good, and Unity had always sounded so *nice*, but... "I don't like the way the Church of Unity treats witches."

Hunter studied her, looking earnestly contemplative. "Fascinating." He continued, "You wouldn't be the only member of the Church of Unity to think we need to work to bridge the gap between witches and the good people of the Church. It's difficult to save people who won't even speak to you."

"See, that's part of your problem. You assume they want to be *saved*. You can't force people to accept help."

Hunter's smile changed to something more wry. "You can, actually. *We* can. But clearly you don't believe we should."

"You're right. I don't."

He was back to that pensive expression. "And yet here you are, in possession of a Paladin's Relic." He said it like it was a question not for her, but for himself.

She was saved from further questions by Selena, who waved them over. "I will walk you through the wards. Are you both going in, or just Agent Graham?"

"Both," they said together, and Emily wanted to hit something, especially when Hunter smiled warmly at her.

Helen looked mulish when they opened the door, but she sagged in relief when she saw Emily. Selena grabbed both of her and Hunter's wrists, and Emily felt an aggressive tingling as she was pulled through the ward by the shockingly strong little witch.

"*Do not* aim your Light directly at the walls, floor, or ceiling. It will be considered a breach of Treaty if you do." Selena walked back out without waiting for a reply, closing the door behind her.

Hunter knelt down in front of the girl, who was still sitting with her broken leg propped up. She was obviously both scared and determined.

Emily said, "This is Agent Graham. He is the one who will cleanse you. Are you ready?" Helen nodded, and Hunter placed both hands on her head. He began to pray.

It was not like when he blasted the boy back at the dorm. This was slower, and the Light fell from Hunter's hands to rain over the girl. Emily had to admit, in spite of herself, the Light was objectively beautiful.

The girl's breath hitched, and she let out a small, pained sound before relaxing with a sigh. Her face became blissful, and then her head rolled back and she passed out.

Emily caught her, and her seal *sang* when the Light touched her. She was swept up in it, and for a moment she thought she could feel the girl's soul. She wrapped herself protectively around the soul, bracing it up while it shook and then settled.

It took Emily a few moments to come back to herself after the Light faded, and when she did she found the girl cradled in her arms, breathing evenly. Hunter was breathing raggedly, still kneeling.

"It's done!" Emily called, and the door opened.

Selena stepped through the wards, and the white raven familiar said, "The corruption is gone. The girl's soul is intact."

Selena gave them both a genuine smile. "Well, good. I'll ask the rest if they are willing. Are you two able to keep going?"

Hunter rose tiredly to his feet. "Yes. We will continue. We must." He glanced at Emily. "We must do it together, I think, for these results to repeat themselves."

Emily clenched her jaw at his presumption, but nodded her agreement.

They went back outside while the witches adjusted the wards. Hunter took her hand, his face suffused with tired joy. "You held her together. I felt it. You are meant for this work."

Emily shook her head while her seal pulsed in agreement. "Let's not get ahead of ourselves. We have a long afternoon ahead of us still."

It *was* a long afternoon. Emily cradled each soul as Hunter used his Divine Light, and each time she was swept up in the beauty of the feeling. Afterwards, she felt sick at how easily she surrendered to it, but not enough that she hesitated to help the next person.

Even if it let the seal dig into her own soul a little deeper.

When they finished with the people who had been found on campus, they left to head back to the hospital. Emily was *exhausted*, but she couldn't bear the thought of waiting to cleanse the three people waiting there, and Hunter, who looked about ready to fall over, agreed without hesitation. They didn't know if waiting would cost them.

Emily had to help Hunter walk over to her car—he wouldn't let anyone else touch him—and he fell asleep as soon as he fastened his seat belt.

The car ride itself was the only concession to their exhaustion. Aside from the fact that Hunter patently refused to use a portal, the time it took to cross the city would give them some time to recuperate. Will was staying behind at the university while Selena portaled over to the hospital with Carla and her apprentice Kal.

When the car pulled up in front of the hotel, Emily woke from her half doze and waited a moment, hoping Hunter would wake up on his own as well. His face had relaxed from what she now felt certain was a carefully crafted political mask into something softer, more human. She wondered for a moment what he was like when he wasn't essentially alone in enemy territory, and then cut off that line of thinking sharply.

"Hunter, we're here," she said, realizing only after she said it that she'd used his first name again. Damn it. "Agent Graham," she said, louder. When he didn't wake, Emily hesitated a moment before she gently shook Hunter's shoulder. As soon as she made physical contact her seal flared with warmth, just like every other time. Hunter's eyes fluttered open, and for a moment they met hers in a completely unguarded expression. She felt more of those unwanted chest flutters, until he ruined it with a knowing smile.

She made a noise of disgust and got out of the car, shutting the door with more force than necessary. She took a moment to collect herself, feeling her exhaustion fraying her composure. Hunter waited for her without saying anything, and they walked in charged silence to where the infected people were still sitting behind wards.

They started with the least corrupted people and worked from there. To Emily's relief, the corruption burned away even easier from the nurse and officer who'd been bitten while subduing Olivia.

It was more touch and go with Officer Prescott. Emily was barely able to hold his soul together while Hunter burned the corruption away. When Selena came in with her familiars to examine him, she read Emily's expression and looked worried.

<<There is more damage to this one than the others. He may pull through, but it will take time,>> the white raven said, and the black one flew over to rest above his bed. Prescott had passed out during the cleansing like the others, but his breathing was much more shallow.

"Hugin will stay and watch over him," Selena said. "Are you ready to deal with the other?"

Right. Emily had been avoiding thinking about the thing that...about Olivia.

Another witch was waiting outside the room. She looked wild, her long dark hair pulled into a messy braid with leaves and small twigs sticking out of it. Her clothing was leather and fur like she was a barbarian cosplayer. Her familiar was, alarmingly, an absolutely *massive* wolf. They smelled strongly of forest and wolf—hardly a whiff of human body odor. Emily wondered how much of their appearance was affected.

As soon as Emily and Hunter rounded the corner, the witch fixed them with a predatory glare. The wolf growled ominously.

"Chill, Alyssa. I told you they were coming," Selena said, not rolling her eyes but sounding like she wanted to, at least a little.

<<They smell,>> the wolf complained. Hunter snorted in derision, but did not say what he was obviously thinking.

"Try anything, exorcist, and I'll remind you why Divinity agreed to the Truce," Alyssa said, darkly. Hunter looked at the sky beseechingly.

Emily decided to ignore them unless the posturing escalated. She turned to look at what was inside the room. Olivia, *it*, had completely destroyed every piece of furniture and equipment over the course of the last three days. The floor was littered with debris and dried chemical spills. The poor creature had built itself a bizarre nest in the corner, and it alternated between a keening sound and raving screams.

"How are we doing this?" she asked quietly. All eyes turned to look at what was left of Olivia.

"Alyssa is here because she specializes in fusing with her familiar. She also has some grandfathered pre-Rapture protection from Divine Light. Once you burn the corruption away, Alyssa and Scarlett will deal with what is left."

Selena walked away, and they waited in tense silence until she was far enough to not be at risk. Hunter's hands began to glow, and he ignored the way the wolf, Scarlett, growled at him.

Emily felt the Light build until, at the last moment, Hunter stepped through the ward and blasted the creature.

Emily really saw what happened this time. The thing screamed and writhed, convulsing on the ground until it went still. The light cut out more suddenly than before, and Hunter swayed on his feet, obviously shivering. Emily stepped up just in time to catch him as his knees gave out, and she helped him sit outside the wards on the far side of the hallway. The brief moment she was behind the wards was enough for her to be certain that the soul was corruption-free and *shredded*. The *sounds* coming from the now corruptionless flesh would haunt her nightmares.

Alyssa and Scarlett merged, and Emily did not watch as they tore apart the last remains of the poor girl.

It was over.

For now.

Hunter shivered for several minutes, but as soon as it stopped he started trying to climb back to his feet. Emily offered her hand to him without thinking.

"Thank you, Emily," he said, and she tried to pull her hand back, feeling suddenly scorched by their clasped hands. He held onto it, and she tensed, looking him in the face, feeling the seal pulse with soothing warmth. The half smile crept onto his face. "I go now to the Sanctuary to rest. Let me know when the thing that started this is found." He cupped her hand in both of his, and went on, his voice soft. "You could come with me. There's much I can tell you about your Artifact that the witches will keep from you."

Emily pulled her hand back. It was much harder than it should have been for her to put that distance between them. Hunter, disappointed, let her go, and she stepped away. "I think I'll go home, thanks. Send your direct line information to the PPD and I will contact you as soon as we have a lead."

"You will be welcomed joyously when you change your mind." He left, moving slowly but confidently.

Once he was out of earshot, Alyssa, who had split from her wolf and was leaning against the door frame, said, "What a creep."

Emily nodded even as her seal continued to spread manipulative warmth through her. "I'll let forensics know the scene is theirs. Are you going to be around in case the thing shows itself again?"

Alyssa looked Emily up and down, measuring. "Yeah, I'll be close." It sounded like a threat.

Emily went home. She probably would have gone back to the office instead, except she was ordered by the captain to take the next day off unless they found something.

She still planned on filing her report before she even thought about resting.

But before she started on it, she called Sofia.

As soon as Sofia answered, Emily said. "Want to have lunch with me tomorrow? I'll be on call, but they're not letting me go into work unless I rest first, and I'd rather rest with you."

"*Hell* yes! Where?" Sofia said instantly, her happiness, and an unsubtle amount of relief, obvious.

"I'll text you an address. See you."

"See you!"

The seal pulsed at her, as if in disappointment.

The seal could go fuck itself.

GREATER PROVIDENCE RI, SEPTEMBER 12TH 47 YAR

June couldn't understand why Emily had called for another date, but she wasn't going to complain.

The GPI captain released an initial report around mid-morning covering the events that took place at Roger Williams. June watched it live, sick to her stomach.

The captain was careful to only confirm what everyone basically already knew through various social media leaks—there was a magical corruption that was infecting people in the city. There was no mention of the word *zombie*, or even the much more popular term being used on social media: Reavers. Instead, they stressed that it was possible to prevent *deterioration* and recover fully as long as authorities were contacted during the early signs.

The captain outlined the two known ways to get infected—being possessed by the black essence or being in direct physical contact with a person who had been infected. There was a pause and they showed a short clip of the *thing*, which made June shudder. Part of her was surprised the *thing* actually showed up on camera.

A magical disease specialist came on to describe in detail all the symptoms people should watch out for, which included a list of every abusive behavior known to man. Anyone who saw blackness around the irises or black tinted veins was supposed to call 911 immediately.

June turned the report off when a politician came on to lay it on thick about how they had a joint task force of local witches, emergency services, the National Guard, and a pair of trustworthy exorcists.

She picked up the amulet, still on the floor where she tossed it last night, and put it back on.

Mortality settled on her again. There were no lingering side effects from yesterday, just the normal dulling of her senses and the constant thrum of a heartbeat, the endless gasping for breath.

She stubbornly spent the rest of the morning researching ice cream with the vague idea that after lunch she and Emily could go for a walk and eat ice cream together, because popular media seemed to indicate ice cream made everything better.

The problem was, June had never had ice cream, which meant she didn't know what her favorite flavor was. Apparently 'favorite ice cream' was an important thing to know about yourself in the modern world. Worse, finding out could be very complicated, since not all ice creams were created equal, and it also came in bars, sandwiches, and cakes.

By the time Emily texted her the address for lunch, June had decided vanilla was the best place to start. How an exotic South American flower came to be considered *common*, June had no idea, especially since the other popular flavors were chocolate or strawberry. Chocolate maybe she could understand, and cookie dough sounded interesting, but strawberry?

Perhaps modern strawberries were also magically enhanced, like all the other food she'd encountered. A quick search indicated that was almost certainly the case, but she didn't have time to go down that rabbit hole if she wanted to meet Emily on time.

And she *really* wanted to meet Emily on time.

June decided to walk since the restaurant was fairly close to her apartment. Did that mean Emily lived nearby? Was that a good or bad thing?

She checked the place out on her phone as she jogged from tree to tree, trying to avoid the brilliant sunshine. It was Ethiopian, apparently, and June spent the time it took to get there researching Ethiopia and its food.

A cacophony of birds screeched at her from every tree. They perched along benches and the tops of statues, some colorful, some grey and white and inoffensive except for the way they looked at her hungrily. Were there always so many damn birds?

June missed listening to the owls.

Emily was waiting for her when she arrived, looking like she had finally gotten some decent sleep, even if there was still an understandable strain around her eyes. She was dressed casually again, her curly hair tumbling around her face. In the sunlight, her hair looked rich and glowed with warm colors, like a darkening sunset.

June wished she could see her with her vampire eyes with moonlight scattering soft rainbows over her face. June's dull human senses made her feel like she was missing something.

"I'm not late, am I?" June asked, checking the time on her phone. It was still several minutes to their agreed meeting time.

"No, but I always like to arrive early," Emily said, giving her a warm smile.

"Uh-oh. And to think, I really liked you. I'm a 'best effort' sort of gal. Clocks are prisons of the patriarchy, or something." June frowned, dramatically serious. "We may be destined for failure." She tried to say it somberly, but couldn't quite prevent the wicked smile that broke her false sobriety.

"Destiny can go fuck itself," Emily said, almost too emphatically. June laughed, and Emily went on quickly, "And as long as you're not deliberately making me wait, I think we can work it out."

"No, no no, never deliberately. Wait, are people late on purpose?"

"You would be surprised," Emily said, and June got the impression she was speaking from experience.

"Ugh, rude. And, like, not in the fun way." June kept up a pretense of jovial flippancy, but inside she was seething. Deliberate lateness was a manipulation tactic. She'd had several great hunts start off that way.

Maybe June should look into some of Emily's past boyfriends.

Except no. Emily was an investigator. And a Paladin, of a sort.

She probably wouldn't like it if June did that.

The restaurant was pretty full, but Emily had apparently made a reservation in anticipation. The smell of the place almost had June drooling, but she managed to hold it together.

June was pleased to see people eating without a bunch of unnecessary utensils. It felt homey.

Oh, shit. Had Emily picked this place on purpose? So June could use her hands?

Her mortal heart fluttered.

Much to June's delight, they ordered a sampler of all the different things on the menu. It looked like some kind of painting, a rainbow of food laid out on a thin, spongy trencher. It was mostly stewed, which was normal to June, but it was spiced in ways that June hadn't even imagined was possible. She especially liked the foods that were so spicy they actually hurt her mouth. The combination of pain and flavor and then the afterglow from so much sensation at once had June groaning in pleasure from start to finish.

She also successfully managed to pace herself. Something about Emily's presence encouraged her to exert self-control.

Emily wasn't quite as interrogative this time, but she gave it a half-hearted effort. June decided to throw her a bone, and talked at length about the various bands she was in. She didn't hang out with any of the other musicians socially, but between practice and gigs they were the closest thing she had to a friend group.

June wondered if she should cancel the rehearsals she had coming later in the week. If the thing came after her, she didn't want any of her bandmates becoming collateral damage.

Maybe if Emily came along? Would she even want to?

And, fuck, she definitely had to call out sick from the hospital.

She'd make it up to the kids, bring her guitar and play for them, once everything went back to normal.

If everything went back to normal.

"So, you're a member of two metal bands, one of which only releases music online, a jazz band, and a Led Zeppelin cover band? And the cover band is the one that has the most gigs?"

"Yup. It's called Toxic Blimp, because Ruby, the lead singer, has a terrible sense of humor."

Emily laughed, indicating that she, too, had a terrible sense of humor.

"I have a rehearsal with them tomorrow night. Do you maybe want to come?"

Emily looked overjoyed for a moment, then her face fell. "Maybe. It depends on how things are going."

A chill ran down June's spine. "Yeah. Of course. Sorry."

June launched into a story about the time Ruby dared the drummer to take lead vocals while she played drums for a rehearsal, and how it ended with June frantically trying to play every instrument at once.

She left out the part where she'd had to wipe everyone's memory of just how fast she'd been moving.

When they finished eating, Emily asked if she had anywhere to be. June did not, obviously, and she used the opportunity to suggest they go for a walk and seek out ice cream after. They paid, and Emily led them towards North Burial Ground.

The cemetery, which was more of a park these days, was old, almost old enough for June to worry about recognizing some of the names on the oldest gravestones. Not quite, though, since most of the people June might have recognized would have been buried in small family plots, if anyone bothered to bury them at all. She didn't think anyone had buried her, and they certainly wouldn't have done it in such a grand place, with a monument that lasted for ages.

No, her mortal bones were long gone, and good fucking riddance.

They turned on to one of the lovely gravel paths, both quiet under the weight of a place from long before the Breaking and the Rapture. The sounds of the city faded as they walked, and the air was filled with the scent of wildflowers and cut grass.

"So, what made you call me? I mean, with everything going on, I wouldn't have thought you would have time for me," June asked finally.

Emily sighed and looked up at the branches of a tree they were passing under, a sugar maple blushed with the first hints of fall color. Emily looked like a goddess standing beneath it with her wild hair and green eyes. "I needed a break. To do something else, you know? And I guess...I guess I didn't want to do what I was told."

June was a little confused and alarmed. "Someone told you not to date me?"

Emily looked at June, startled, and rubbed at her chest. "No! No, what I mean is, I wouldn't have thought you were my type. I already told you I've never dated a woman, but the truth is that I've never even dated someone who was a stranger to me, who hadn't been asking to go out for a while. It's always been classmates and coworkers, and honestly, I've regretted it every time. In more than one case, it soured our friendship when dating me wasn't what they expected."

June had trouble imagining that, of being close to someone for years and only then being intimate with them. "So, you weren't attracted to them?"

Emily smiled wryly. "Not as much as they were attracted to me. No, wait, that sounds conceited. I should say, not as attracted to them as they thought I *should* be. As if, because they didn't think I was returning their affections with enough... desperation, maybe, I wasn't holding up my end of the deal."

June could hear the loneliness in Emily's words. "Huh. I wasn't aware that relationships were supposed to be emotionally transactional like that. Sounds like they should have worried less about what you *should* have felt and more about what you *did* feel."

Emily's eyes went huge in her lovely face, and then she looked away, hiding behind her curls. "Right?" she said, obviously trying to sound flippant, but it came out rough.

June reached out a single finger and gently turned Emily's head back so their eyes met. "Right," she said, trying to let Emily know with the way she said it that Emily hadn't done anything wrong.

When they started walking again, Emily let her hand brush against June's, and June entwined their fingers together. They walked in silence for a while, and June felt a little light-headed.

It was probably the sun. She glared at it, which proved to be a mistake, because it was much too bright. It won, and June winced.

"You okay?" Emily asked, always observant.

"Oh, yeah, I'm fine. The sun and I just disagree on what an appropriate level of brightness is."

Emily steered them towards a path with denser trees. Most of them appeared to have been planted post-Rapture, and they had the telltale shine of fairy wood. Emily walked right in, which impressed the hell out of June, since humans usually avoided anything fae-touched.

"So, the spooky trees don't bother you?" June asked, feeling a weight lift off her as she passed under the thick boughs. Most humans believed the stories of fae who kidnapped people who wandered under fairy trees. They were false, mostly, unless you were foolish enough to wander around outside the city wards. Anything fae-touched inside the city would be Neutral Territory, perfectly safe unless you were really against being teased, or maybe magically stoned.

"Why should they? These are from the Rapture. They're a memorial, just like all those headstones, and they're *living* memorials, which makes them better, I think," Emily said, without a hint of tension. "Do they bother you?"

June gave her a wicked grin, "Not at all. I love spooky. But, I have to ask, you didn't bring me here to kidnap me, right? Because then I might have to call for help. I hear there's this one badass investigator who wouldn't rest till I was found."

Emily's eyes sparkled. "I better be careful then."

June tugged lightly on Emily's hand, pulling her closer. Emily moved in without resisting. "We don't need to be careful. If you don't want to be." It was a terrible line, really, but June committed to it, letting her gaze fix on Emily's lips.

Emily laughed. "That's probably one of the worst lines I've heard, but you know..." Her hand curled around June's neck. "I think I'm in the mood for terrible lines."

June smiled wickedly and backed Emily up against a tree. She searched Emily's eyes, making absolutely sure she was okay with this.

Emily nodded. "Please", she whispered, her cheeks flushed.

June kissed her gently, letting Emily feel the softness of their joined lips. She licked Emily's lips once, her tongue darting out and then back, before she moved to trail a line of kisses down Emily's neck. When she reached the pulsing vein, June reflexively sucked hard, pulling the flesh into her mouth, but not biting. Emily gasped and bucked, and June slid her fingers inside her waistband and then paused, asking permission with a gentle tug.

"Oh my god, don't stop," Emily said, panting and breathless. She slid her hands up the back of June's shirt, running her nails lightly along June's spine.

June shivered, and worked her hand deeper. She moved her kisses back to Emily's mouth. Emily opened hungrily, sucking on June's bottom lip with an appetite that matched June's with interest. There was some fumbling as Emily adjusted and unbuttoned her pants to give June better access, and then Emily was shivering and scratching at June's back. Emily fought June for control of the kiss even as her body yielded to June's stroking fingers.

June made a sound deep in her throat, a groan of pleasure mixed with a growl of challenge as they struggled. She took revenge after Emily got hold of her tongue by pushing her fingers inside Emily and pressing in exactly the right spot.

That was it for Emily. She came apart.

June escaped Emily's mouth when she gasped, and used her free hand to start unbuttoning Emily's shirt, kissing as she went.

Halfway down, June's hand brushed against the pendant resting against Emily's chest.

There was a *very* painful flash of light, and June found herself on the ground, panting. Emily, still flushed, looked down at her absolutely shocked.

"What the—are you a—" she tried to say, but the words seemed stuck.

June's amulet was almost scorching, still hidden under her shirt, but the heat was fading fast. Was the heartbeat pounding in her ears slower than it should be?

"Uh," June said. "Ow."

Emily's shock did not lessen, but she visibly pulled herself together. "What was *that*? Are you not human? Why didn't I sense anything earlier?"

"Uh," June said. Her heartbeat was *definitely* too slow.

Emily's shock was starting to transition to anger. "What *are you?*" There was another pulse of light, and June jerked away, suddenly afraid.

She opened her mouth to lie, but found she couldn't. The light that radiated from Emily pulled the truth from her mouth. "I'm a vampire."

Emily shook her head. "No. You can't be. The sun." The Divine Light continued to pull on June, but June couldn't say anything else. Her tongue felt thick, and she started choking on the need to *confess* but the absolute inability to say anything more. For the first time in a very long time, June felt like she was suffocating.

"Stop," she croaked, gasping.

Emily did not stop. "*What are you?* Tell me!"

Desperately, tears running down her face, she said what she could. "I'm a vampire. I'm in hiding because the *thing* is after me, that's why I can go out in the sun. It can't get to me in the sun. I—" She cut off again, choking, truly *unable* to say more.

What was *wrong* with her? "Please, I can't—" she managed, sobbing while she gasped for air that she somehow couldn't get past her tongue. Blackness started filling her vision.

The light vanished, and Emily's expression went from angry to horrified. She sank down to the ground, staring at June.

"What the hell?" she whispered, staring. "God, I'm so sorry. I don't know what just happened."

June barely heard her. She stared back, her chest heaving, finally able to breathe again. Her heartbeat was still too slow, and everything was a little too bright. After a moment, she wiped at her face and said, "I don't know what happened either. I guess I shouldn't have touched that thing on your chest."

"It really hates you."

The silence stretched for a long time. June's skin started itching, ever so slightly. Eventually, June said, "Um. Should I...run away?"

Emily wiped at her face. "God, maybe. I think I have the thing under control now, but don't come any closer." Emily's brows creased in a frown. "Were you going to eat me?"

June's eyes went wide. "No! I wouldn't! I only eat, like, rapists and sexual predators, not beautiful hero-ladies."

Emily, rather than being reassured, looked stricken. "Are you the one that killed Sean DeNardis?" she asked, as if she couldn't quite stop herself.

Uh-oh.

June nodded and looked down at her feet. Her breathing was shallower now, like she didn't need as much air, and she felt light-headed. "I need to. Um, I need to hunt them. Rapists. It's my Geas." June wasn't sure if she still *had* to answer, or if she was doing it just in case the holy Artifact tried to choke her again. Probably the latter.

"Your Geas," Emily said, flatly. "What is a Geas?"

"It's a thing vampires have. Whoever makes us places a Geas on us, it's part of the, ah, contract. A Treaty thing. It specifies what our prey is supposed to be. Once we fulfill it, if it's something that can be fulfilled, we get to hang out on earth as long as we want." June started slowly climbing to her feet. Was that the faintest scent of rot? "Mine won't end until there are no more rapists."

Emily stood as well, straightening out her clothing. "Because your Geas is to kill rapists."

June nodded. "Yeah. I wasn't like, forced. I chose to answer the call of *this* Geas." June wasn't entirely sure why she needed Emily to know that. It might have been easier to play the victim.

"God, you're like a perfect torture for my conscience," she murmured, clearly to herself. To June she said, "You know I was assigned to your case? Right now, you're supposed to be dead."

"I almost was." June smiled weakly, her body feeling slightly shaky with a combination of mortal adrenaline and, fuck, a trace of UV destabilization. "If it helps, I also use my blood to cure kids with cancer. That's why I took Sofia's identity after I killed her. She was, um. Hurting kids."

Emily stared at her, and then looked at the sky beseechingly. "*No*, that *doesn't* help. God damnit, you *lied* to me! I—wait. Took Sofia's identity. So, what's your *real* name?"

"That's a more complicated question than you would think. I have a Demon name, a soul name, but no way I'm telling you that—I'm not *completely* suicidal. And your divine thingy can't make me say it either—it's part of the Treaty. As for my birth name, the one I had when I was human, that person is dead, and so is that name. I go by June now, to my friends." June paused. "You should call me June."

"Right. June. Not Sofia." Emily thought for a long moment. "Can you change your appearance?" Emily still wasn't looking at her, but her posture wasn't as tense.

June felt a smile slide onto her face. "Yup! Makes hunting rapists easier—I change to look like their *type*, you know? But not this face—this is the identity I use to heal the kids. If you blow my cover, I'll still be able to get away, but I won't be able to help them anymore."

Emily groaned again. "You're really fucking evil. My own personal Hell. I should hate you."

June looked at Emily hopefully. "Should?"

Emily ignored the question.

There was another moment of heavy silence.

"So...should I run?" June asked again. Her chest squeezed.

"Probably," Emily replied, but she just put her hands in her pockets and started walking. Her movements were stiff, like she was in pain. "Stay away from the Church of Unity Sanctuary, okay? Hunter would murder you in a heartbeat."

June warily, *hopefully*, fell in beside her. "Who's Hunter?"

"The exorcist. Calls himself a Divine Paladin." Emily let June walk with her, but she maintained her distance, her posture closed.

"Oh shit, really? Those guys are the heavy hitters. They hunt vampires especially. Did you know?"

Emily said, half sarcastically, half fatalistically, "No, I hadn't heard." She glanced at June. "This thing is turning me into one, you know. A *Paladin*." Emily practically spat the word. "You should probably run."

The silence stretched awkwardly. June should *definitely* run. She should ditch this identity, warn Penny, and leave the city. She should run and never think about Emily again.

June didn't run. Instead she asked, "Do you want it to?"

"No." Emily said and winced.

June's heart ached. "Does it hurt? The Relic?"

Emily let out a strained breath. "Not as much as at the beginning. But it *knows* about you now. It wants me to turn you in, or kill you. "

"Oh," June said sadly.

They walked for a few more minutes before Emily asked, "Why aren't you running?"

June shrugged. "I don't want to."

"That's really stupid," Emily said.

"Is it?" June asked, walking ahead and turning around so she could search Emily's face.

Emily didn't say anything and kept walking, eyes fixated on the graves near the side of the path.

June's skin was really starting to itch now, in the direct sun. Her heart was still beating, and her lungs still demanded air, but something in the amulet was broken.

June pulled out her phone to call for a ride. She needed to get out of the sun.

After June slipped her phone back into her pocket, Emily sighed. "So, what's your relationship to the witch, Penelope?"

June fidgeted with her sleeve. "I don't know? I can't really...I can't even *think* about it, let alone talk about it. We're friends, I guess."

Emily swore again. "I'm supposed to *work* with them. Is Will involved? William Davis?"

"Uh, no. I don't know anyone by that name. Is he a witch?"

Emily nodded, but she seemed to relax a little.

A *very* little.

"So, why Sean? It's him, right? The thing? Why did he come back as this monster?"

Was it Sean? Oh. Shit. *Oh shit.*

June swallowed. "I dunno. Vampires are sort of off-grid. No going to the Underworld, no Library access. It's supposed to be a way to escape."

"This has never happened to you before, right? A victim coming back after you?"

June stopped walking, stopped breathing, feeling like she'd been punched. "No! Do you think this is my fault?"

"No! Of course not!" Emily swore under her breath. "It's just this *stupid* seal keeps acting like the two of you are connected. It's probably stupid. It *is* stupid."

June's mind went a little fuzzy, and she was forced to start breathing again. "I've killed dozens of Seans and they've never done this before."

"*Dozens*?" Emily tensed all the way up. "June—" she cut off, swallowed, and then said, "How can you be sure they deserve it? That they weren't just, just making a mistake?"

June laughed, bitterness making it feel jagged in her throat. "Oh, it's easy, really. Once I spot someone I suspect, I get them alone, give them power over me, and then say no. They'll show their true colors, every time. People like that, they're not making mistakes. It's not a fluke. It's a sickness, a cancer rooted so deep in their soul that even death doesn't cure them. All you can do is send them somewhere the only people they can hurt are like them." June should shut up. "It's called the Pit, though not everyone there is irredeemable. The best part? They all go there willingly, every time the Triad asks. It excites them, knowing they can hurt as many people as they want, knowing they'll either win, or be destroyed. " June paused, then amended. "Or, well. None of them actually believe they'll be destroyed."

"Shit," Emily said, looking sick. "Shit."

It wasn't an agreement, but it wasn't a disagreement, either. That was fair. It was more than fair, considering Emily was a *Paladin*.

Eventually, Emily asked, "How did he escape then? Become this monster?"

June looked away. "I don't know."

After another long silence, Emily asked, "What's wrong with your skin?"

June looked at her arm. It was decidedly grey. "I think my amulet got damaged. I should go."

"Will you be okay?"

June felt a weight lift off her. Not everything, not by a long shot, but enough. She grinned. "You care?"

Emily scowled. "Shut up. This whole situation sucks."

June's smile bloomed into something more heartfelt. "I still like you too, even though you tried to choke me to death with that weird light."

Emily growled in response, but June thought it seemed forced, like she was fighting a smile.

June's stupid human heart fluttered like a butterfly about to take flight. "I won't lie to you anymore. I promise, any question I *can* answer I'll answer truthfully from now on." Shit, June *meant* it too. What the hell was wrong with her? "My oath as a Demon," she declared. The magic of the oath snapped between them.

Emily jumped. "Was that some kind of Demon magic?"

June smiled at her, sweetly, sadly, her heart in her throat. "Yeah. I...look, I know I've been lying, but you get why, right?" Emily nodded, short and sharp. "Well, now I can't, ever again. You can ask, and I'll tell you all my secrets. My fate is in your hands."

It was a stupid thing to do. *So* stupid.

But June had to do it, *needed* Emily to have that power over her.

They walked in silence the rest of the way back to the entrance. The ride June called was waiting at the curb. June, impulsively, gave Emily a peck on the cheek, consequences be damned, before dashing away. Emily froze, but no weird light or angry shouts followed, and June was in the car and on her way before Emily had time to react. When June looked back, Emily was staring after the car, her hand over her cheek, looking very conflicted.

June let her head fall back against the seat and swore. She was an idiot.

A reckless idiot who was *done* being a coward.

Penny picked up on the first ring. "Are you alright?"

June was an ass. "Yeah. Shit, I'm sorry for going dark. Look, I want to help. Tell me you have a way for me to help." June shifted in her seat, and she caught a whiff of herself. "And, um, also, the amulet isn't working right. I think maybe it got, um, accidentally broken? But that's not why I want to help."

There was a heavy sigh. "Where are you, can you go out into the sun at all?"

"Uh, yeah. I'm rotting, but very slowly. I'm in a cab. Can I come there? And do you have a cleaning charm handy?" The car's cleaning charms were almost certainly not up to the task of June's current funk.

"Yeah, come here." June put the phone on speaker so she could tell the car to reroute to Thoughts and Prayers. Penny continued, "Look, there is a way for you to help, but it's pretty dangerous. Are you familiar with a Justice Summoning?"

June winced. "Uh, yeah. But don't you need to be in the Underworld for that to work?"

"We have a special modified version. It will call only to people on the mortal plane. My Coven will cast it, and you can wear the amulet—no one will know what you are, so your cover won't be blown, but, well. You'll need to be there, face him."

June didn't tell Penny her cover was already blown. She maybe should have. "No worries. Being bait for abusive monsters is kind of my thing."

Penny snorted. "Yeah. Listen—" she inhaled deeply. "*Thank you.*"

June felt her stomach twist. "I should have offered sooner."

"No, you shouldn't have. There was nothing you could have done, and you were right when you said this wasn't your fault, so thank you for helping. We really need it."

"Maybe those kids wouldn't have died if I'd offered to help right away."

"No, June. We only got the modified spell finished today. We were going to try casting it on Sean using the bones we recovered from the river. Assuming it took, the spell would have summoned all his living victims as well, so it's good you called."

Yeah it was. "Would you have called me?"

There was a long silence. "You weren't answering. I went by your apartment about an hour ago. I thought maybe you left."

June closed her eyes. “Sorry.”

“It’s fine. You’ll be here soon?”

“Yeah.”

NEXUS

REMEMBER WHEN I SAID TIME IS SQUISHY IN THE UNDERWORLD? KEEP REMEMBERING.

When Aiden got back to the Hotel, he found Sam waiting for him in the lobby.

He flung himself at Sam, who opened his arms with a mildly surprised look on his face. As he clutched at Sam, Aiden was embarrassed to find that he was shaking.

He'd known, intellectually, that Sam was fine, that he would wake up, but it hadn't felt real until he saw Sam standing there. It was ridiculous, and Aiden felt like an idiot, especially since Septimus was at the desk, trying to be discreet.

"Aiden, are you okay?" Sam asked, patting Aiden's ears. Aiden realized Sam was back to being naked, and Aiden felt awkward about his own clothing, even though he really liked them.

Aiden huffed and mumbled, "Yeah, I'm sorry," into Sam's shoulder. His *naked* shoulder.

"For?" Sam asked, sounding baffled.

"For being an—" Aiden cut off, unable to say *idiot*. The other words that flickered into his head, *stupid*, *dumb*, *irrational*, all of them stopped before he could voice them. Not being able to lie apparently included about himself, which...well. That was probably a good thing. "Um. For acting like *this*." He waved his hands vaguely.

"For acting like you are happy to see me? Or acting like you are worried about something? Neither of those things are something you need to apologize for, bunny." Sam still seemed bemused, but he didn't stop petting Aiden.

Aiden pulled back and took a deep breath, holding it in until he felt himself grow steadier, and then letting it out with a puff. "Okay, yeah. But I *am* sorry. I'm being really clingy and insecure, and I shouldn't put that on you."

Sam's fluffy ears flicked. "I see. Well, you're forgiven, then." He grinned, showing his fangs. Then his expression grew more serious. "But *I'm* the one who should be apologizing." He fingered the scarf, which was tied around his neck in an oversized bow. "Thank you for this, it—" he cut off and looked away for a moment before looking back. "Do you realize what you've made here? It's...Aiden, it's some kind of artifact, magic like nothing I've ever seen before. I don't deserve this, not after I—"

Aiden pressed a hand to Sam's lips to stop him, and then quickly pulled his hand away. "I told you before—I accept your apology. *I* get to decide when you're forgiven, and you don't get to tell me how to feel," he said shyly.

Sam took Aiden's hand gently and pressed it back to his lips. Aiden let himself fall into Sam's wonderful, amazingly *open* green eyes. Sam smiled against his hand, like he could feel the way Aiden was falling, and nodded solemnly before giving Aiden's hand back.

Aiden shivered with butterflies from ears to tail. "Thank you."

Sam shifted Aiden so he was pressed comfortably into his side. "May I still apologize when I do something wrong?"

Aiden curled into Sam. "You *better*. And you can argue with me about whether or not I need to apologize too, as long as you forgive me also. Just...maybe don't argue with me about whether or not I get to accept your apologies. I have a...a hang-up about forgiveness, and it means a lot to me when I can be generous with it."

Sam's eyes practically glowed. "Bunny, I think maybe we should have a discussion on what a 'hang-up' is supposed to be."

Septimus made a hissing noise that somehow imitated a throat being cleared. "*I* don't mind at all if you want to keep going down here in the lobby, but you might prefer to go back to your room?"

Aiden flushed. Part of him kind of liked the idea of putting on a show, but would Sam?

"Do you want me to go back with you?" Sam asked.

"*Yes*," Aiden said emphatically. "We, um, have a lot of stuff to talk about."

Sam gave Aiden a squeeze. "Sure do."

They were quiet on the elevator ride up to the room. Hugo was still wearing the pendant. Aiden watched Sam admire it, and he clenched up.

Would Sam be mad Aiden had given gifts to other people? Would it be better or worse to admit he didn't know how valuable they were at the time?

Aiden dashed into the room too quickly with the doors opened. Hugo made a rocky sound, and Sam nodded. "Yeah, I will."

As soon as the door closed behind Sam, Aiden steeled himself. "Before you say anything else, I need to tell you something. Something important. It's okay if it makes you change your mind about me."

Sam stepped away from the door and took Aiden's chin lightly in his claws. "Nothing you can say will change my mind about you, bunny. We're *souls*. I can feel the truth of you."

Aiden closed his eyes and said in a rush, "Yeah, but I'm a whore. I *like* being a whore. So if that means you don't want to hang around with me anymore, I understand, I do, just don't—"

Sam pressed his fingers to Aiden's lips. "I'm going to kiss you now. Is that alright?"

Eyes wide, Aiden nodded.

Sam kissed him. It started soft, but Aiden was impatient. He fell into Sam, wrapping his arms around Sam's lean shoulders. Sam let out a pleased little growl, and Aiden parted his lips, inviting Sam to deepen the kiss.

He did, and Aiden's head swam with the taste of it. Aiden hopped up and wrapped his legs around Sam's waist. Sam smiled into the kiss and laughed, stumbling a little before making it over to the couch.

When they finally separated, Aiden covered his face with his hands. "I mean it. I...I love deeply, you understand, but I also love easily. And even when I don't, um, feel that way about someone, I really like sex, and I'm good at it too. I—" Aiden broke off, unable to go on. He braced himself for rejection.

"That's fine, bunny. Monogamy isn't very common around here."

Aiden dropped his hands, not quite sure he heard that correctly. "What?"

Sam booped Aiden on the nose. "You heard me. Monogamy isn't common. We're not alive, bunny. What kind of psycho thinks it's reasonable to tie yourself exclusively to one person *forever*. That's not partnership, that's consumption." Sam pursed his lips. "Which, yeah, that happens down here too. Some people really feel like two halves of the same soul. But then you're not two soul's anymore, you're one soul." Sam smiled. "Honestly, it's kind of good to know for sure you won't ask that of me."

Aiden was so happy he felt like sparks might burst out of his middle. "I would never ask you to do that. And anyone you want to have sex with is cool, with or without me. Like, maybe that lion guy?"

Sam looked momentarily confused, then he laughed. "You mean Jacques? Nah, he's like that with everyone. He's been asking me for years. He'll probably ask you next time you see him."

"He will? And you really don't mind?" Aiden felt his chest flutter.

Sam rubbed a thumb along Aidens cheek and he started to purr. "Yes, really. Souls can't lie, remember?"

"Oh, yeah." Aiden chewed on his lip. "So, you wouldn't mind if I maybe did some sex work?"

Sam blinked once, slowly. "Nope. I think it's a good idea, if you like it."

Aiden buried his face in Sam's chest and breathed in. Sam smelled wonderful, like home. "Do you want to have sex? Like right now?"

Sam froze, then his arms went around Aiden. "Yeah. Am I paying you, or is this a gift?"

A gift. Gods, no one had ever phrased it like that with him before. "A gift," he whispered.

Sam trailed a finger up the back of Aiden's spine, and Aiden shivered. "So," he said. "I also have a minor confession to make. Before we start."

"Mmm?"

"So. I'm a. That is to say. I've never, um."

Aiden sat up, shocked. "No way."

Sam looked off to the side and rubbed at one of his fluffy cat ears. "It's no big deal. I told you, I died pretty young."

"But, all those people you knew! You were naked *all day* yesterday! You're so *confident*!" Aiden couldn't wrap his head around it.

Sam shrugged, still looking away. "I never met anyone I liked as much as you before."

Aiden had been hired by plenty of virgins, so he stopped embarrassing Sam and slid to the floor to kneel at Sam's feet. "I can show you what to do, if you want. Or I can do it to you. Or both." Aiden started to tremble slightly in anticipation.

Sam smiled and caressed one of Aiden's antlers. A wave of arousal unlike anything he'd ever felt before surged through Aiden, and he gasped.

"How about you start with taking off those pretty clothes, and we can work from there? I bet you'd rather I just play with you until I figure things out, right?"

Aiden shivered and whispered, "Yes."

Hours later, they'd discovered a few things. Sam was a very fast learner, soul cum was not sticky and it tasted oddly fizzy, lube was not necessary for souls, and Aiden's antlers were very, *very* sensitive.

Aiden snuggled up to Sam in the middle of the bed when they both finally felt satisfied. A thought occurred to Aiden.

"Sam."

"Mmm?" Sam was purring contentedly.

"*Sam.*"

"What?"

"I'm a horn-y bunny."

Sam smothered Aiden with a pillow. Since Aiden still didn't need to breathe, the only thing this accomplished was to prove that Aiden, at least, was in fact *not* too spent to continue.

"Are you kidding me, kid? That is just ridiculous."

Aiden bucked slightly, taking it as praise. When he tried to reply the pillow muffled his voice, which struck Aiden as very odd. He didn't need to *breathe*, but the pillow still stifled his words?

In the state he was in, all that did was make him even more aroused.

Sam lifted the pillow off Aiden's face and Aiden whimpered, disappointed. Sam climbed out of the bed. He was still wearing the scarf Aiden made him, and it rested on his back, still tied in a bow, like a pair of great gauzy wings. Aiden felt warm all the way through.

The warmth vanished when he saw Sam's face. "I need to go. I'll come back as soon as I can, I'm sorry." He was staring off into the distance, but he re-focused on Aiden and gave him a deep, longing kiss before vanishing in a flash of green fire.

Aiden wrapped himself in one of the silky sheets and curled into a tight ball.

It didn't feel like all that much time passed before he reappeared in another flash.

"You're back! Is everything okay?"

Sam scratched at his hair, and started pacing, clearly frustrated. "No, there's just nothing more for me to do, so Will, my witch, sent me back. He might summon me again any second."

Aiden shifted into a sitting position, still wrapped in the sheet. "Sam, you said—" he cut off, and asked instead, "How bad is this thing you're fighting?"

Sam stopped and turned to face Aiden. There were shadows in his eyes. "It's the worst thing I've ever seen." He swallowed. "I told you, I don't care what the Triad wants, there's no way I'm letting them drag you into this."

Aiden hunched in on himself. "But what if they're right? What if I'm needed, and if I don't help something horrible happens to you?"

Sam opened his mouth to speak, but nothing came out. He frowned. "If something happened to me, it wouldn't be your fault."

Aiden straightened his spine. "But you can't promise nothing bad will happen. And you can't say something about my magic wouldn't help stop that from happening."

Sam winced. "I can't."

Aiden looked down at his hands. "I want to learn about my magic."

The bed dipped when Sam sat down. How did that even work? There wasn't gravity.

"But?" Sam asked, softly.

Aiden shook his head. "No 'but'. I'm scared, yeah, which I guess is pretty obvious, and I feel really rushed, but I still want to try." Sam scooted closer to Aiden until he was just out of reach. Aiden leaned into him with a sigh. "Will you help me? I'd like your help."

Sam petted Aiden's ears. "I'm not the best help you could get."

Aiden looked up and met Sam's green, green eyes. "Yeah, but you're the help I want."

Sam smiled. "Alright then. What have you tried so far?" He fingered the scarf, still tied around his neck. "You made this. Do you know what you did?"

Aiden hid his face in the sheets. "No. I made of bunch of stuff and I sold most of it to this pushy unicorn—"

"The *Unicorn Fashionista*?" Sam asked, nearly incredulous. "That's amazing! She's *famous*!"

Aiden mumbled something deliberately incoherent and fiddled with his hands. "She's going to give me some lessons." Then he looked up. "Wait, how do you know which unicorn I meant? There's lots of unicorns down here, I'm pretty sure."

Sam kissed Aiden's nose, which Aiden immediately wrinkled and rubbed. "When you speak, you project more than just words most of the time. You send along impressions, scents, even pictures. It's not uncommon for new souls to do that, and some people never stop, liking the way it smooths things over." Sam rubbed his ears self-consciously. "I've never been big on it myself. Not receiving. Projecting. I like that *you* do it."

"Oh," Aiden said. Another reason why he was so transparent. He was glad to find he didn't mind.

"So have you tried anything else?"

Aiden shook his head. "The Library gave me a list of things to try, but some of them were ridiculous. It told me to *accidentally* start a fight! How do you purposefully *accidentally* start a fight?"

Sam's mouth twitched. "I can think of a few ways. So, that's the recommendation that stuck out to you the most?"

Aiden opened his mouth, then closed it. "It was, I guess. And trading goods and services, which I already did."

Sam tilted his head to the side. "What did you trade?"

Aiden gestured at the wardrobe. "All the clothes I made. To the Unicorn Fashionista? That's her name?" Aiden had forgotten to ask for a name.

"More of a title. So, no services then? I thought you said you liked sex work?"

"I do. I just..." Aiden couldn't bring himself to finish.

He hadn't wanted to do it and risk Sam being disappointed. Or worse.

Sam's brow furrowed with concern. "Bunny, I already told you, I don't care if you have sex with other people." Sam considered Aiden for a moment, and then gently grasped both his shoulders and looked him in the eye. "Look, you know what? Let's go find some clients for you. Someone *not me*, okay? I'll even tag along for emotional support until I get called back to the mortal plane, if you want, so don't you dare think this is a rejection."

Aiden trembled and whispered, "Okay."

Sam studied Aiden. "You're okay with me ordering you around some? You'll tell me if I push too hard? I can be pushy and I don't—"

"Would it make you feel better if I had a safe word?" Aiden asked, quickly, before Sam could spiral. "We probably should have done that right up front anyway, but I trust you, I guess."

"A what?" Sam got a vague look on his face, like maybe he was trying to access the Library, but it wasn't being helpful.

"A safe word. It's a word we both know that isn't likely to come up during rough play. If I ever feel overwhelmed or unsafe or unwilling, I use the safe word and you know that I need you to stop. That way you can be pushy, or chase me and catch me, and, um, do whatever you want to me, and you'll know that you have my consent. We can also do colors if you prefer, green for *keep going*, orange for *slow down*, whichever you find easier to use. Any time you worry I might be getting overwhelmed, you can just ask."

Sam looked slightly stunned. "That's brilliant! Let's do both. What's the safe word?"

"Carrot sticks," Aiden said immediately.

Sam burst out laughing. Aiden frowned at him.

"Bunny, you're a—you're a—and you want—" Sam was laughing so hard he couldn't get the words out.

"I hate carrot sticks," Aiden said grumpily. "It's a perfect safe word."

Sam laughed harder. "You do? But you—"

Aiden thumped his foot into the bed, and Sam collapsed completely. It took him ages to stop laughing. Aiden waited, arms crossed, an overly dramatic frown on his face.

Sam finally pulled himself together enough to ask, "Okay, well, you're okay going out to find some clients? You don't need any carrot sticks or whatever?"

Aiden made a face. He *hated* carrot sticks. "Bleh, no. *Yes.* I'll find someone not you." Sam looked at him expectantly, and Aiden clarified, "To have sex with."

"Good. Don't be cheap about it either. You're worth fancy favors."

Aiden blushed and slid off the bed to get dressed.

When they were both ready—Aiden fully dressed, Sam contently nude—Aiden tugged lightly on Sam's arm.

"Before we go, I want you to have this," Aiden said, and told Sam his <[name]>.

As before, it took a bit of time.

"That's uh, quite a long one," Sam said weakly when it was done. "How, um, how many times have you reincarnated? Wait, don't answer that, it's rude to ask."

Aiden looked at his feet. "I don't know anyway. It's...probably a lot."

Sam tugged on one of his ears, and Aiden looked up, startled. "Well, there's probably going to be a lot of people who know you, then. Don't feel like you need to stress about it. Unless they only recently pulled themselves together, most people will be happy to wait for you. Eternity tends to breed patience, especially in a place like this where time doesn't necessarily play by the rules."

Aiden threw himself at Sam, burying his face in his chest. "Thanks," he mumbled. For what, Aiden wasn't entirely sure. Maybe for taking it in stride. Maybe for everything.

"No problem, kid."

"I'm not a kid," Aiden mumbled, but Sam probably felt the way his mouth curved in a smile.

When Aiden finally pulled back, Sam had a piece of chalk in his hand. "So, you know what this is for?"

Aiden nodded, eyeing the chalk suspiciously. "Drawing doors."

"Right." Sam drew a circle on the floor. "But you can also use it to make a rabbit hole."

Aiden huffed in irritation.

"No! That's really what they're called!" Sam grinned. "A rabbit hole is what you use when you don't know where you need to go. It's a little like the Styx that way, but instead of it being driven by the mutual needs of many people, a rabbit hole is just for you."

Aiden nodded. "Like the movie."

Sam snorted. "Like the book. All you younger people are so obsessed with movies. Are they really that great?"

Aiden nodded solemnly. "Yes. Maybe we should stay here and watch movies instead."

Sam paused. "Is that what you really want? To stay here?"

Aiden bit his lip and looked down. "No. But I do really want to watch movies with you."

Sam wrapped his tail around Aiden and resumed drawing the circle. "I'm looking forward to it." He finished the circle and jumped in, pulling Aiden in with him. "Now, focus on what you want, and point where we need to go."

Aiden closed his eyes and focused on what he wanted. He felt a very slight tug, and he liked the feel of it, so he turned his whole self in that direction and sniffed.

There was a sudden lurch, and Aiden reflexively grabbed Sam's hand. His eyes flew open, and he found himself falling through a field of glowing orbs that danced and sang with small, high-pitched whispers.

A wisp of dark golden light appeared and swirled around Aiden's head, laughing. It danced and beckoned him to follow. Aiden briefly looked at Sam, who nodded, and Aiden flew after it with the ease of a dream.

Eventually the world faded back into existence, and Aiden found himself on a deer path. He started running, pulling Sam along behind him. The wisp stayed just ahead no matter how fast he moved, until Aiden, with Sam close behind, arrived at what looked like a medieval tavern, plopped right in the middle of the dark woods.

The light wisp seemed to bow, and then it puffed out of existence.

"Seem like what you wanted?" Sam asked, nodding at the building. It was dark and subtle, with strangely colored lights glowing in the thick, blurry windows.

It looked a little bit magical, and a little bit seedy. Aiden nodded, slightly electric with anticipation, and took a step forward. He stopped when a fluttering sense of wariness came over him. "It feels dangerous in there."

Sam's tail curled around Aiden's waist, a gesture which Aiden *finally* realized was protective rather than possessive. He warmed at the realization. "We can go somewhere else if you want. There's plenty of other places, and we can draw another rabbit hole easily enough."

Aiden smiled gratefully, but shook his head. "No. I want to go in. I just...wanted to check in." Wanted to make sure *Sam* didn't want to change *his* mind.

Sam watched Aiden, searching his expression. "Okay. I'm going to make you take the lead here. If you get spooked say so, okay? I'll be right with you."

Aiden still hesitated. Part of Aiden had figured Sam would stay in control, pick the client, that sort of thing. He was familiar with that dynamic. But he could feel in Sam's words that wasn't his intention. He really wanted Aiden to do this on his own, and was only here as backup. "It's just, I don't understand. You said you want me to find someone else, that you're really okay with it, but... No one's ever... You don't think I am horrible for wanting that?"

Sam cupped Aiden's cheek, careful to keep his claws clear. "Earlier, you told me you felt sorry for being too clingy. You said you wanted to learn more about your magic. This is me, helping you do that. Trade in sex is *normal* here." Sam flexed his hand, and his claws pricked Aiden's face lightly, deliciously, and Aiden shivered and closed his eyes. "This place, Aiden, the Underworld as a whole, is a refuge for the unconventional, for the heretic and the deviant. All the souls here, or, at least the ones that last, have rejected culturally imposed moral standards. So long as you are considerate of others, *anything* you want to do is not only fine, but *good*."

Sam kissed Aiden, gently, and pulled back before Aiden had time to react. "You wanting to have sex with other people doesn't mean you're bad and it won't change how I feel about you at all."

Aiden was still trembling, and he found himself holding Sam tightly. "How do you feel about me?" Aiden asked, barely a whisper.

Sam started purring. "I feel like I want to be with you as much as you'll have me around." He rested his chin on Aiden's head and leaned his forehead lightly against Aiden's antlers. That, coupled with the claws still pressing gently into his skin, made him feel electric.

"Look," Sam continued, "does it bother you that I have to leave all the time to go be someone's familiar? That I could have to leave any second, even in the middle of all this?"

"Yes, but not because I'm jealous." Aiden was very distracted, but he tried desperately to focus on the conversation.

Sam nodded sagely. "Then there you go. You can date me and still do what you want with other people, okay?"

Aiden felt suddenly very hot and cold at the same time, and he tilted his head back to look at Sam. "I can date you?"

Sam's face lit up like a sunburst. "Yes, *please*. But you still gotta go in there. You need it." He stepped back from Aiden and turned into a cat with a puff of green light. "I'm not dressed for this place," he said by way of explanation, blinking brilliant green eyes up at Aiden. Aiden bent down to pick him up and Sam let him.

Sam immediately started squirming, nosing at his coat. "Is this a huge pocket? Oh, Aiden, you sweet little bunny-bun, did you put a perfectly cat-sized pocket in your coat for *me*?"

Sam slithered his way into the oversized pocket and curled around in it a few times until he finally got settled. Aiden hadn't made the pockets huge specifically for Sam, but he didn't have the heart to correct him. Oddly enough, Sam didn't seem to weigh down the coat much. Aiden could feel him there, though, warmth radiating through the coat and into his leg. Loud purrs emanated from the pocket like a tiny motor.

Aiden took a deep breath and opened the door.

GREATER PROVIDENCE RI, SEPTEMBER 13TH 47 YAR

June had texted her late the night before. Emily didn't look at it until morning, after the witches called.

> *It's not just for you. It's because you make me want to do better. Not because you ask it of me, or expect it of me, either. You remind me that doing the right thing, even when it's dangerous, is worth doing.*

> *They don't know you know. I'll have the amulet back on, it's working again, and a different face, one you don't*

know. No one will know I'm not human but you. Not unless you want them to.

All the witches told Emily was that they had a spell that might work, and to meet them at the cemetery. June had explained the ritual they would try, and that it was experimental. She'd downplayed the danger she would be in, but it was obvious.

"God damn it Sof—June," Emily said, and closed her eyes. "My own personal Demon."

She wouldn't tell anyone who June was or her connection to Sean.

Especially not Hunter.

The seal pulsed at her angrily. Emily ignored it.

Emily got to make her own goddamn decisions.

She sent her car over to pick up Hunter from the Fall River Sanctuary. The National Guard could have sent a helicopter, but the witches made it clear there was no rush, so the car would be fast enough.

Emily walked over to the cemetery from her apartment. She scanned the streets, wondering if any of the people she passed were June, if she would recognize June without Sofia's face.

Did she want to? What would it mean if she did?

Will and Sam were waiting when she arrived. Sam was sulking loudly enough she could hear it before she even passed through the gates.

<<—tell he didn't want me to go,>> Sam was saying. He had on a strange green scarf Emily had never seen him wear before, tied around his neck in a large bow. <<There's this core of steel in him that's fathomless, and he can be so, so wise, but he's also so delicate at the same time. I'm sure he's fine without me, but I don't think I'm fine without him, which is just ridiculous! I've known him for like, no time

at all! Eternity couldn't be long enough! He is all light and rainbows and sweetness, but then he gets this *heat* in his eyes and—>>

"So you said," Will replied, patiently.

Sam cut off with a little mew of sorrow. <<I need more time with him. There's still so much unsaid! What if I get destroyed or eaten by the horrible demon zombie? I'll never get to really know him! You know this is new for me, and I'm, like, failing before I even get a chance to try!>>

"Sam, I don't think you're failing," Will said, but Emily could see the worry on his face.

"I won't let anything eat you," Emily said, startling herself. "And I won't let Hunter hurt you either."

Her seal vibrated at her neutrally. Not quite like the way it reacted when June made her oath, but not entirely dissimilar either. Emily wasn't sure what the hell that meant, but she took it as a good sign.

Sam stared at her with wide eyes. <<Shit, Detective. Thank you.>>

Before Emily could process the uncharacteristic sincerity in the cat-demon's voice, she saw Hunter approaching. "Incoming."

When Hunter reached them, he gave a curt nod to Will and then had eyes only for Emily. He completely ignored Sam's presence. "Em—Detective Scott, have you given any more thoughts to fully accepting your Relic? We would be better equipped to fight whatever this Hell-spawned monster is if you did." Sam squawked something about Hunter not being allowed to say *Hell*, but Hunter ignored him. "Given the danger, it would be irresponsible for us to not have every possible weapon at our disposal. We have enough time before sunset for me to teach you the basics."

Sam grumbled incoherently under his breath, though Emily might have caught the word *slavemaster*. Will patted his head, looking as annoyed as Sam. He watched Emily, waiting to see if she wanted help.

Emily's jaw clenched. "Can you just *explain* the basics to me? I would prefer not to bond any more with the thing unless there is no other choice."

Hunter's look of disappointment should not have made her feel small. That it did pissed Emily off even more.

Sam, his cat face glancing between Emily and Hunter, said, <<So, you're a vampire *hunter*.>>

Hunter, as if he knew what was coming, closed his eyes and let out a heavy sigh.

<<And your name is Hunter,>> Sam continued.

Hunter turned to walk towards the spell staging area. It was set up in a large, empty clearing surrounded by rune-carved stones in the center of the cemetery. It was the remnants of a circle some of the first witches used during the Breaking to stabilize the city.

Will and Emily walked behind Hunter, and Emily kind of wanted to pet Sam. Hunter did not acknowledge Sam, but there was a twitch in his cheek, like he was clenching and unclenching his jaw repeatedly.

<<Don't you think that's a little *much*?>> Sam said.

"Sam, he didn't choose his own name," Will said, but he didn't really sound like he was chiding. Hunter was *right there*.

<<Yeah, but someone did. And I want to give them a hug.>>

Will said, "Sam, he wasn't born an exorcist. They didn't know."

"I actually was. Born one," Hunter said unexpectedly.

Sam jumped onto Will's shoulder, who accepted it with equanimity. <<No. Fucking. Way. Where is your mom? I want to know this woman.>>

"She died," Hunter said, not bothering to turn his head to look back at them, sounding cold. "During the Rapture. Torn apart by a *vampire*. I never knew her."

<<What, really? What did your mom do to end up vampire prey?>>

"SAM!" Emily and Will both exclaimed. Will smacked Sam lightly on the nose. "Don't victim-blame."

<<Oh, you're right, I'm sorry, that was uncalled for.>> He licked a paw with incongruous urgency. <<More importantly, you're old as fuck. You were born before the Rapture, during the Breaking! So you're what, like, fifty?>>

"Sam, you know it's rude to talk about a magic users' age," Will said.

"Magic user!" Hunter whirled on Will, indignant, then looked away quickly. Apparently he was more upset about being put into the same category as witches than the insult to his mother.

Sam rubbed at his ear, tail twitching. <<I'm just saying that for a geriatric Divine bitch he's pretty fucking cut. I'd tap that, if I wouldn't like, catch fire from the Divine cum.>>

"SAM!" Both Will and Emily exclaimed.

Hunter stormed off.

Will looked a little guilty, but Sam only draped himself across Will's shoulders, lazily closing his eyes. Emily almost went after Hunter, but stopped herself. Instead, she turned to Sam with her hands on her hips.

"Was that necessary?" she demanded.

Sam blinked at her, then nodded sagely, <<Yeah, I think it was. He was pressuring you into binding your soul into slavery.>>

Emily felt a chill run down her spine. "What?"

<<Binding your soul. To Divinity. Like, for keepsies.>> Sam cocked his head to the side at her horrified expression. <<Shit, no one spelled it out, did they? Fucking angels. Asshole probably just handed it to you, right? With a beatific smile?>>

"Carla said they could separate it from me, maybe," Emily said faintly.

Sam went back to licking his paw, using it to clean his face. <<She knows more about that than I do. All I know is that thing you're wearing is a fucking slave collar, and if it fuses with you fully like that hunter wants, I wouldn't bet on you getting free from it intact.>> He stopped cleaning and looked at her for a long moment before giving her a slow blink. <<We'll try and help you, even if it bonds fully, but I want to make sure you understand—If you really want to be free of that thing, you should take it off now, no matter how much it hurts. You've done enough. We can do this without you.>>

Emily felt slapped. For a moment, she couldn't focus on anything other than *we can do this without you*. She found herself shaking her head, and she almost choked when the seal warmed at her, soothingly.

"I don't think I can do that. I can't just leave. Are you so certain I won't make a difference? That if I do leave and this thing escapes again, it won't be partially my fault?" she asked, quietly, but with intensity.

For some reason, Sam flinched. After a moment, Will said, "No," and he sounded very sad. "No, I don't think we could be certain you wouldn't have made a difference. But that *wouldn't* make it your fault. It's not your responsibility, not if you don't want it."

And there it was. *There* was the reason she couldn't just take it off. Because it *was* her responsibility. It was her *job*. She *chose* to be an Investigator, an honor-bound servant to the greater good, and there was nothing more important to her than that.

"Then I'm staying. I..." She swallowed, and then set her jaw. "I need to go talk to Hunter. I'm not going to *fuse* with the thing unless there's no other choice, but I'm going to be prepared in case I do."

Will nodded, resigned. He briefly grasped her shoulder. "Alright." He turned to Sam. "Listen, buddy, why don't you head back for now.

I'll call you when and if this spell works. You should tell your boyfriend how you feel, okay?"

<<He's not even technically my boyfriend, I already *told* you we haven't had a chance to—>>

Will rubbed Sam's nose and he cut off. "Go home. Emily, I'll be over with the rest of the tracking team. Most of them don't have as much experience as me, and I need to make sure they know some of the more obscure tracking spells. Even if the summoning doesn't work, it will surface again eventually. When it does, it won't get away from us again."

They split up, and Emily went to find Hunter. He was standing near a small private mausoleum just outside the witches' circle, looking up at the sky. When Hunter spotted her approaching, his look of relief surprised her. Was he scared?

"Hey. So. What are these basics I need to know?" she asked, doing her best to ignore the way the goddamn seal *swelled* with comforting warmth. When Hunter smiled, it *thumped* again, and Emily felt a little sick.

"So, you have reconsidered? You will embrace your Relic?" His face was full of hope.

"No," she said, and it physically hurt her to say it. She told herself it was because the seal stopped feeding her warmth, hitting her with pins and needles instead, and not because of the way Hunter's face fell again. She plowed on, "But I meant what I said. I want you to tell me what you can, in case I do need to do that."

He nodded and knelt on the grass, gesturing for her to join him, which she reluctantly did.

"When the time comes to accept the Relic, all you will need to do is *believe* in it. Believe in the Divine Will, believe it is your rightful God and that you are His chosen conduit. Believe that your purpose is to serve Divinity and then *yield* to that belief." He took a deep breath and let it out slowly. "Do you pray often?"

Uh, no, but she didn't really want to admit that. She'd had enough Judegy Hunter Face for one day. "When I need to," she said instead.

He nodded, accepting this. "Were you ever taught *how* to pray?"

Her mind flashed back to the Sunday school she'd attended in Fall River. Her parents had believed it was important that she get a moral education to balance with the 'witch-filled public schools'. "Yes, but it was a long time ago. When I was a kid."

"Tell me what you learned."

"It's a little like meditation. I quiet my mind and I focus on gratitude for everything that is going well and I ask for guidance on things that aren't. I... Up until very recently I never heard anything but my own mind. I would focus on what I needed, clear my thoughts, and usually something would float to the surface, the answer I was looking for."

Hunter smiled, and Emily's heart caught. He was really lovely when he smiled like that, and it wasn't fair. "That's good. Now that you have the Relic, though, it will respond more directly. If you go into that same state that you use when you pray, your Relic will hear your gratitude and reward you. It will hear your requests for guidance and show you the right path. It will hear a plea for help and give you power."

And if I do something it doesn't like, it will punish me, Emily added, silently to herself. The seal pulsed at her, as if to say <<*Yes. This is what Divinity is. Unity and obedience.*>>

She whispered, "Oneness, an extension of the whole." She only realized it was out loud when Hunter nodded, beaming at her. She wanted to flinch, but instead she clenched her jaw and kept her face neutral.

Hunter searched her face for a moment, then went on, "While the Relic is still separate from your soul, its power is limited. Throttled. On its own, the Relic is not a living thing. It cannot contain the full glory of the Divine. Once you have fully embraced the Relic, it will be part of you, and you will channel Divinity directly."

His smile turned wry. "I have a confession to make. I said earlier that I was born an exorcist, and that is true, but I was like you are now for most of my childhood. The Relic that was left for me by an angel on the day I was born was kept from me until I was twelve. I always felt it, calling me, and it hurt to be away from it, but the priests did not feel that I was capable of bearing the responsibility until I was older. After they gave it back, I did not bond until I was nearly seventeen."

He bowed his head for a moment, and then looked back at her, his expression more vulnerable than she'd ever seen. Part of Emily wondered if this was an act, a performance to manipulate her, and it terrified her because if it was, it was *working*. She couldn't see the lie in his expression, and she'd spent her career looking for the truth in other people's lies.

"I held off those five years because I was angry. I had spent a lot of time training with the other exorcists, even before they reunited me with my Relic. They were...scarred by the events leading up to the Rapture. Many of them had their faith broken and reforged by the return of Divinity, and all of them lost loved ones. It made them harsh, even though they were guided by the Divine Will."

He sighed and looked up at the sky, the sun falling on his face. "When I was young, all I knew was that a Divine Angel had given me the Relic, and the older exorcists were *keeping* it from me. I resented them for it, and I resisted the bond out of spite when they finally gave it back to me."

He closed his eyes. "It hurt. The whole time, it hurt. I believed the Relic was punishing me for letting them take it away from me. Because I had been separated from it for so long, I was used to the pain, so it wasn't difficult to keep resisting when it was in my hand again. I suppose I wanted to make the choice...mine, somehow."

He smiled, ruefully. "It wasn't logical. I was a teenager, and I'd been in pain for a long time. I lived for years in that state of limbo, not quite an exorcist, but still able to access some of the gifts. I spent those years miserable and afraid, with only my anger to hold on to."

Hunter opened his eyes and looked at Emily. The late afternoon sun, warm on her back, lit up Hunter's blue, blue eyes. He did not flinch at its brilliance. He took her hands, and she did not pull away.

"I was wrong, Emily. Eventually I set aside my anger for the greater good, and when I did, I regretted the years I'd spent resisting. I realized it was never the Relic punishing me, it was *myself*. Divinity is *forgiveness*. If you give yourself to it, if you let go of your imperfections and deviant thoughts, it will raise you higher than you could ever be alone."

They sat there for a long while, Hunter looking peaceful, Emily quietly at war. Part of her wanted to give in, to fall into the words Hunter was saying, but the larger part was having none of it. She believed in a greater good, she *did*, but the idea of sacrificing her free will to it was *wrong*. She wasn't sure what to make of Hunter's confession, but it terrified her.

That he believed what he said, she had no doubt, but for fuck sake, what he described was *horrible*. He'd never had a choice. He'd been *groomed*, and now he believed he was wrong for even wanting to *have* a choice.

The seal didn't care for that line of thinking. It buzzed at her, alternating between warmth and discomfort, making it hard for her to hold on to her sense of self. It was very similar to how she'd felt while she held the infected souls as Hunter cleansed them with his Divine Light.

Except this time there was no Divine Light, just Hunter, and her hands in his, the two of them kneeling in the grass, surrounded by monuments to the dead. She felt like she was drowning his eyes. He smelled like incense and sunlight, and it all nearly overwhelmed her.

But it didn't.

You can, actually. We can, Hunter had said about *mind control.*

She blinked, and took a deep breath. Rather than push back forcefully, she instinctively felt that would be a losing battle, she decided to try to placate the seal by accepting the warmth. She yielded to it without letting go of her sense of self, allowing it to flow into her and then *through* her. She imagined her resistance less like a dam holding back a flood and more like a storm drain, still strong and defined, but not allowing the flowing magic to build any pressure.

To her immense relief, her thoughts cleared enough that she felt like herself again.

"When you use your powers," she asked, carefully, "you say things, under your breath. Are there words I need to know?"

Hunter's brow furled. The spell he had been weaving—and it *had been* a spell, Divine magic was definitely still magic—didn't break, but it did slip, slowly draining away so that when it was gone it was as if it had never been.

"I was raised in a monastery. I was taught to recite pre-Rapture scripture while I prayed, and I find comfort in doing it still. It's not necessary, though. The intent is what matters, the purity of thought and clarity of heart."

Emily nodded. "Alright. Thank you for sharing with me. Is there anything more to the Paladin powers I need to know?"

Hunter still looked slightly perplexed, but he said, "It would be better if I could practice with you. You've seen me do it enough now, you must have a sense of what you will need to do, but the first time you use Divine Light, it will be...overwhelming. If it comes to an emergency, the witches may not like what happens when you imbue."

Emily pulled her hands back, and climbed to her feet. "I'm going to see Sergeant Callihan and see if he has any equipment for me. I'll be back shortly."

Hunter watched her go, and her seal thumped at her. Her heart thumped back.

Fuck.

Fuck. For a moment there she couldn't even remember why she was resisting. Like it was just a habit. Like she was a petulant child, saying no because she didn't understand.

But she *did* understand, and she *would* resist as long as she could, no matter what.

Callihan linked her into the comm system and gave her a set of ear pieces and another gun to borrow.

"You going to bring Hunter in?" Emily asked, gesturing at the electronics.

Callihan grunted. "Yup. When he comes by and asks."

Emily's mouth twitched. "Hopefully he'll remember to come over."

She took her time walking over to the witches, letting her head clear. She found Selena hovering near Penny and several other witches, who were arguing with each other about rune placement.

"Detective, thank you for being here. They are about to activate the spell. Please be ready."

Emily nearly stumbled when a thin, beautiful doll of a teenage girl standing next to Penny winked at her.

It was June. She *knew* it.

Suddenly the seal was burning again, and Emily almost smiled. The last of her muddled thoughts burned away. The seal did not like June, but Emily did, and so *it* did this.

No matter what Hunter believed, Divinity had no interest in forgiving June. It wanted her destroyed.

The Relic wasn't a *gift*, or whatever. It was a trap, a slave brand, trying to seal away her will.

And she *would not* give up her will.

Except.

Emily knew, deep down, that if she had to, she would embrace the seal and do what she needed to do. She would sacrifice herself to do what she thought was right.

Hear that, soul-seal? I'll let you in if I have to, but not one moment before.

Apparently, that thought was enough to shut the seal up. Sort of. It stopped hurting her, anyway.

"Detective Scott, you look troubled. Is something wrong?" Selena asked. Emily shook her head and pulled herself together.

"No, not yet anyway." Emily came to a decision. "You should know, if something happens and I need to fully bond with the Relic, there may be some chaos. H—Agent Graham implied that I may lose control at the moment of bonding. I wanted to give you permission to protect the witches from whatever I do, so long as it doesn't keep me from taking out the *thing*." She met Selena's eyes and held them. "I mean *anything*. Once the *thing* is destroyed, don't let me hurt anyone."

Selena studied her. Emily wasn't quite sure how to read the woman. The witch's ageless face wore a hard expression, but she might also have been a little impressed.

“Thank you for telling us, Detective. I hope that it does not come to that, but if it does, we are prepared.” She gestured at the circle. “The wards we are using here should contain the *thing* once it’s inside. They’re designed to be one-way, anything can go in, but nothing can come out until they are taken down. It will also diffuse any Divine magic radiation. If it was directly targeted by a blast of Divine Light, it would likely collapse, but we’d have enough time to take... steps.” She nodded at Alyssa, lurking off to the side. The terrifying woman winked, and Emily nodded at her.

Selena gestured at the spell circle again. “The *thing* should be summoned directly into the center of the circle. You will be able to hit it from outside with weapons or Divine Light, and no one but the witch inside will be in danger. She is prepared for the risk, and has been amplified with several magical advantages to give her a good chance at avoiding being hit.”

Emily looked at June, who quirked a tiny half-smile but didn’t turn away from Penny. Penny finished drawing a symbol on June’s forehead, squeezed her shoulder, and started walking around the edge of the circle. June walked into the circle.

“We’ll wait for her to reach the center, and then we will activate the spell,” Selena said.

The silence was tense. After a small eternity, June reached the center, a good thousand yards away.

Three witches stood equidistant around the circle, the farthest just barely in sight on the far side. As one, they raised their hands, and white light flashed.

A sound that resonated through her soul reverberated out from the circle, now a massive white dome. The Relic recognized it. It felt like *justice*.

The sound went on and on until it finally faded away. The circle edges continued to glow softly, indicating the magic was still active, but nothing else moved. Emily hardly dared breathe.

At least, for the first five minutes.

Selena sighed. "I was afraid of this. We will hold the spell for a full cycle of the sun, just in case."

Emily couldn't stop herself from asking, "Is there something about the *thing* keeping the spell from working?"

Selena shrugged. "There are a dozen reasons I can think of. We know the thing can move underground, and quickly, so the sunlight shouldn't be a barrier. The dome extends underneath to account for that. Perhaps the thing is inside someone and it is coming here on foot. Perhaps it is entirely resistant. We do not know."

Emily nodded her understanding. "I'll be here."

"Thank you, Detective."

Emily nodded again and turned to go. She should update Hunter on the situation, let him know it might be a while. Remind him to get linked into the coms.

Before she got far, a series of texts from June lit up her phone.

> *If I die, will you use your detective skills to figure out what my favorite ice cream would have been? I didn't get a chance to try them all. I think I might like vanilla best, I love the way those candles smell, but do you think cookie dough would be better? I don't want to be a vanilla person. It has bad connotations even though it doesn't make any sense. Did you know vanilla is from, like, an orchid? I didn't have vanilla when I was alive, before. It's very underrated. There's like, a million different kinds of vanilla.*

Emily paused. Hunter was fine, sitting by the mausoleum, deep in meditative prayer. He could wait a bit.

She sat on a nearby bench and texted back,

> *That's not really how detective skills work. I might be able to guess, but I'll need you to answer a few questions first.*

June replied with a smiling cat emoji.

NEXUS

Aiden was immediately blasted with pulsing dance music, a strange fusion of medieval instrumentation and modern techno bass. Firelight sconces in a riot of impossible colors decorated massive wooden pillars and beams, carved with scenes of cryptids doing all sorts of things. The air was thick with spice and incense, and the layout was strange, a jumble of tables and chairs and balconies that should have made the large room feel cluttered, but didn't.

Before he could second guess himself, Aiden plunged inside, Sam still tucked neatly in his pocket. He attracted attention as soon as the door shut behind him. Everyone inside was dressed well, but anachronistically, a blend of modern fabrics and historical formal wear.

"I am not dressed correctly either," he murmured at Sam. Aiden, in his bright coat, stood out like a lantern in the rainbow-dark.

Sam butted against Aiden's thigh from inside the pocket. "You're dressed amazingly. Standing out will only make you seem cooler."

Many of the people were dancing, generally in pairs or small groups, but plenty were sitting around heavily carved wooden high topped tables, drinking colorful, glowing liquids. A bouncer dressed in a black leather vest and fine silk shirt was standing just inside the door. He nodded at Aiden, and arched an eyebrow at Sam when he momentarily poked his cat-head out of Aiden's pocket, before waving them in.

Aiden walked farther inside, then froze, unsure where to go. There were booths in the back, shrouded in opaque shadow, except for a few that were better lit and obviously empty. There was a small stage, also empty at the moment. The music appeared to be coming from everywhere at once, with no obvious speakers. Aiden spotted a cute wolf boy in a corner with a set of *wooden* headphones on who might have been some kind of neo-medieval DJ.

From his pocket, and somehow over the sound of the music, Sam said, "Go say hello to the bartender. If you don't like them, we can leave, but if you do like them, they'll probably help you find what you came here for. Make sense?"

"Yeah," Aiden said and walked over to the bar. The person behind the highly polished black wood counter came over to Aiden immediately. They were dressed in a black waistcoat and gold fishnet shirt with a scarf styled to be reminiscent of a livery collar. Golden hoop earrings shone brightly against their dark skin, and black and gold hair curled and coiled like snake tails.

"Hi, I'm Kabi," the bartender said, giving Aiden a quick once-over. "I've never seen you here before. How can I help you? "

"Um. I'm Aiden, and yeah, I'm new. I was drawn here?" Aiden swallowed thickly. Kabi considered him for a long moment, and Aiden took a breath and met their eyes. Kabi smiled, a friendly curving of the lips with no hint of heat or snare.

Aiden analyzed his instincts, and decided that this person *felt* nice. Trustworthy. He smiled back.

"Okay then, Aiden. Do you want a drink, or were you planning to wait for someone to buy one for you?" They gave him a wink.

"I'll wait," he said. He bit his lip, then lifted his chin defiantly. Sam's warmth radiated reassuringly from inside his pocket.

Kabi laughed. "I doubt you'll wait long. If they don't choose the drink for you, what do you want?"

"Something sweet and colorful?" he asked, not sure what the options were.

Kabi reached over and patted Aiden's cheek. "Of course you do. Alright then." He glanced up and nodded behind Aiden. "Looks like you already have your first taker."

Aiden spun to see an attractive, mature looking man approaching. He wore a tight black doublet crested with white feathers, black breeches with gold buttons, and gold leather boots. His eyes and lips were gold and his hair was tied back in a neat cue, white as snow. There was a subtle sense of power to him, oddly similar to Sam, even though they otherwise felt nothing alike.

A flash of insight—he was a Demon like Sam.

Or, and, well. Himself too.

The Demon leaned against the bar and looked at Aiden. "Kabi! What do you have here?" He looked at Aiden with luminescent eyes. Aiden was instantly snared, and he shivered.

The Demon's mouth curved in a slow smile.

"Ask him yourself, James," Kabi said.

James's smile sharpened. "Well, then, what do *I* have here?"

"Aiden," Aiden said, so quietly that the music should have drowned it out.

The Demon leaned in, and Aiden blushed. "Well, Aiden, what are you here looking for? Because I think I found what I want."

"Oh," Aiden said, and for a moment he felt horribly self-conscious. Sam was still in his pocket, but he didn't say anything, or even move. Finally, Aiden huffed out a breath. He'd done this a hundred times when he was alive, and he said, almost automatically, "If you want to play with me, we need a contract to set terms."

James inclined his head. "Of course."

Aiden blinked, suddenly freed from the Demon's gaze. He panicked briefly when he realized he hadn't really thought about what kind of terms he would need. He instinctively <[accessed]> and searched for a standard contract that fit his needs. For once, the Library didn't give him any sass, possibly because he was already very familiar with contracts like this from when he was alive, and he quickly found what he wanted.

He opened a screen, and it formed between him and the Demon. Unlike the normal display, this screen formed itself into a glowing scroll. James took it in a golden-gloved hand.

His eyebrows went up. "You're okay with kidnapping?"

Aiden buried his face in his hands, but nodded.

"Hunter's balls, rabbit, aren't you a treasure? I'll owe you a fortune of favors inside a month. How open is your schedule? It says you have black-out times, and you'll use your safeword if I come during one of those."

"Um, it's pretty open right now, but can we maybe keep it to no more than four hours a week? I'm still getting settled." Aiden chewed on his bottom lip, feeling both excited and nervous.

James hooked a boot behind Aiden's knee, but didn't pull Aiden closer, yet. The contract still hovered between them. "I'd like more, but it will have to be enough. Let's schedule the first encounter. I'd offer to take you tonight, but—"

A clawed hand reached in between them from above and somehow snatched the contract, even though it was kind of a hologram. Aiden blinked stupidly at the empty space left behind.

"Oooooh! What is *this*?" Aiden looked up, following the sound of the voice. A puckish Demon with an abundance of fox tails hovered in the air above them, clutching the stolen contract. He was dressed in flowing white and red robes, and his scarlet hair, longer than he was tall, writhed around him, flames dancing between the locks. His eyes were swirling pools of fire, nestled in a startlingly pretty face. Those eyes caught Aiden instantly, and the pretty fox-man smiled.

Aiden shivered and licked his lips.

"Stay out of this, Yakeru. I found him first," James said, indignant, and reached up to snatch the contract back. It *doubled*, leaving each Demon holding a copy. Yakeru laughed and rose higher, sitting on an exposed beam near the ceiling. Were there six tails, or seven? Aiden couldn't quite tell.

"Yes, but *I've* found him second, and second is the best according to you Americans."

"Don't be ridiculous, we're not even speaking English. That idiotic rhyme doesn't apply," James turned back to Aiden. "I accept the contact with the terms as stated," he declared, and it vanished in a puff.

Yakeru, who still held Aiden's attention, grinned, revealing sharp fangs, "Me too, unless the little usagi says otherwise." Aiden didn't say otherwise. He couldn't. It would have been a lie.

The other contract also puffed away.

When it did, James let out a horrifying screech and exploded into a ball of light. The ball formed into an absolutely *gigantic* eagle that flung itself at Yakeru. Aiden suddenly found himself hidden behind the bar, unsure of how he had gotten there, curled into a tight ball and shivering. He was so startled he could barely think.

Kabi crouched down next to him and said, "Hush, sweet. This is normal—it's kind of their thing. Those two look for any excuse to fight, and the bar is well equipped to contain it, okay?"

Aiden nodded mutely. He was fine. Just, he hadn't expected things to escalate so *quickly*. It was disorienting. After a few seconds his mind unfroze enough for him to think again.

"Hey, Sam?" he whispered. "Did I just accidentally start a fight?" Aiden reached towards his pocket, but Sam wasn't there.

Cold shock shattered into abject horror when he heard the scream of a large cat.

Sam.

Aiden twisted into a crouch and peered over the counter. A huge black panther was arched in a defensive position in front of the bar.

The panther—*Sam*—screamed again, the primal, animal sound raking against Aiden's soul. It meant "*Cut it out.*"

Yakeru, now completely covered in fire, still hovered near the ceiling. He had a flaming staff in his hands now, and he was using it to block James's huge golden talons. Yakeru's eyes spun, and fireballs formed around him in a halo. They flew at James, who dodged out of the way with impressive feats of dexterity.

Everyone else in the bar had cleared away from where they were fighting, watching with mild interest from the sidelines, as if this was indeed a regular occurrence. The tables and chairs had been rearranged into a loose circle, marking the edge of the fighting area. Each flaming sphere splashed harmlessly against an invisible barrier at the edge of the furniture. One came at Sam, and he leapt out of the way, letting out an angry hiss. It splashed behind where he had been standing, hitting the bar off to Aiden's right.

Aiden flinched, but didn't look away.

Sam swiped at James, leaping upward and slashing at some feathers with one of his large paws. This finally caught the other Demon's attention, and James wheeled to face Sam.

"Stop it!" Sam growled. James's only response was to let out another piercing screech and rake his claws at Sam.

There was something wrong with the scream. It cut like it was filled with shards of glass.

"Idiot!" Kabi said quietly, obviously to themself. "He knows better than that."

Sam didn't move quite fast enough. His scarf, still tied around his neck, got in the way at the last second, and the claw only grazed the tip of his tail, catching only fur.

Sam yowled and twisted, bringing his fangs to bear. James backwinged and twisted, getting into position to come at Sam again.

Yakeru, taking advantage of the new distraction, flung another fireball at James. It hit him square in the back in an explosion of red and orange light, and James screamed so loud Aiden saw cracks form in the air at the edge of the invisible barrier.

A gong sounded somewhere in the room. <[Warning: Non-consensual fighting is forbidden in this realm. Pit portal will activate in five seconds.]>

Aiden felt something shift, and oil-slick magic seeped across the floor inside the barrier.

Yakeru laughed, and the sound was wrong, dark. *Corrupted.*

Kabi stood up. "Something's wrong."

"*You assholes*," Sam screamed and threw himself at Yakeru, knocking him out of the air. "Stop it *now*."

Yakeru landed in the oozing blackness on the floor, and his laughter cut off. The swirling fire in his eyes grew darker, red shot with black. "Fuck. Off. Cat."

<[Pit portal will activate in three seconds.]>

Black tentacles curled out of the corrupted magic on the floor. Sam noticed them first, and hissed, "What the *fuck*?"

Kabi followed Sam's gaze and growled at the tentacles. He flung his fireballs at them, one after another.

One after another, the tentacles ate the fireballs.

James screamed and raked at one of the tentacles, and then he screamed again, this time in agony as pieces of his claws were left behind, consumed.

<[Pit portal will activate in one second.]>

Aiden recognized the corruption. He'd met it before.

It was going to eat Sam.

Aiden jumped over the bar, landing in the center of the makeshift arena.

<[Pit portal activating—]>

"No!" Aiden screamed, his whole being crying out with him.

Every black tentacle swerved inward towards Aiden. Sam cried out, a denial, but Aiden didn't have time to hear it before the darkness swallowed him whole.

It condensed, reaching for him, hungry and desperate. It passed through and around Aiden, but could not touch him.

</<*Give me* more!>/>

"No," Aiden whispered. He stood his ground and *absorbed* the darkness trying to consume him.

The darkness *screamed*.

Aiden endured.

<[Pit portal activation canceled]>

All at once, the corruption vanished. The silence that followed was deafening. Aiden fell to his knees, shaking, *burning*, and he looked at his hands and realized they were glowing softly. He let out a small, helpless sob, and at the same time *pushed*. The burning sensation faded, and a cloud of iridescent sparks showered around Aiden like holographic snow.

After a minor eternity, the sparks stopped falling. They remained piled around him, glinting faintly.

"Stop fighting, please." Aiden said into the stretching silence, and he wrapped his arms around himself. "It's safe now, but please d-don't start again." From behind him, Sam's human arms reached around Aiden, holding him gently while he shook.

Aiden could feel every eye in the tavern staring at him. Despite that, after a few seconds his trembling subsided.

James climbed to his feet, also human again, and stared at Aiden with undisguised astonishment. Yakeru dropped to the floor next to him, his flames extinguished, looking both abashed and completely awed. The rest of the tavern's patrons started whispering amongst themselves in a quiet wave before silence returned.

"How did you *do* that?" Yakeru asked, all mischief gone.

"You shut down a *Pit* portal," James added, wincing as he carefully pulled off his ruined gloves.

"That wasn't a normal Pit portal," Sam said, irritated. "And what the hell were you two thinking, escalating into a Pit fight?"

Aiden braced for a grumpy rumble from Lucifer, but there was nothing.

James studied his broken nails. "I wasn't thinking. I have no idea what came over me."

Yakeru narrowed his eyes at James. "You've been off since you tried to visit the Pit a few days ago. I thought you said the place was a ghost town?"

James curled his hands into loose fists and winced. "It was, I think." He frowned. "I can't really remember. I just know that as soon as I tried to open the doorway, something went... wrong."

Sam squeezed Aiden tighter. "Did you report that to the Triad?"

James looked up at Sam, frowning. "No. I should have. It never even occurred to me." He shifted his gaze to Aiden. "I apologize, deeply. I don't know what that was, but it was my fault."

Before Aiden could answer, Sam said, "No, I don't think it was." He gave Aiden's shoulders a squeeze. "You should go report to the Triad. Both of you. I'll be along."

James and Yakeru both nodded and turned to go.

"Um. Wait," Aiden said.

They waited. Everyone waited.

"I don't, um. Know what happened. But I'm not... I also don't think it was your fault."

Both demons nodded solemnly. Yakeru said, "You are *something*, usagi-kun. We'll be in touch, yeah?"

Aiden nodded. "Yeah."

James bowed low. "It's been an honor to meet you. See you soon."

Aiden, unsure what to do when someone *bowed* at you, waved weakly.

Yakeru drew a door, and the two of them stepped through.

Aiden continued to sit on the floor leaning against Sam. The rest of the bar shifted around them, going back to normal. Kabi came out from behind the bar, their hair-snakes coiling sedately around their head, and pressed a sparkly blue and pink drink into his hand.

"I put it on James's tab. He owes it to you." Kabi looked at Sam. "You want one too?

"Yeah, sure. Do you have a jar for this stuff?" He gestured at the glittering substance on the floor. Kabi nodded, and ducked back behind the bar.

The music started back up, and Sam rested his head on Aiden's shoulder. "So, you've definitely learned more about your powers," he said mildly.

Aiden snorted into his drink. "Sort of."

Sam petted his ears. "I'll admit, that was more terrifying than I would have liked, and more than a little confusing, but you're not in this alone. What you did—" He gestured at the glitter. "I think it might have been huge."

Aiden set down his drink and scrubbed at his face. "What does it *mean* though? Does anyone even know? Or is it just another thing about me that's *new* and *special*?" He picked up his drink and cradled it, feeling the way it glowed cooly into his palms. "It's...a lot. Being *special*." He took a sip of his drink, and it danced on his tongue, the flavors like nothing he'd ever tasted before.

New, he thought. A smile tugged at the corner of his mouth in spite of himself.

Sam used a clawed hand to turn Aiden's head to the side. He rubbed his cheek against Aiden's, slow and soft. "I like that you're special," he said. "I like you."

Aiden blushed furiously, and closed his eyes to hold back a wave of tears. "You never met me before I came here, right? In some past life?"

Sam started purring, and tugged on one of Aiden's ears, which were pressed back against his neck. "Right. Is that okay?"

Aiden nodded and hugged him. "It's *really* okay."

Sam hugged him back. Then he stiffened. "Shit, Aiden, I—I have to go, right now. Will you be okay?"

Sam looked absolutely heartbroken. Aiden gave him a kiss. "Yeah. You be safe, okay?"

Sam vanished in a puff of green fire.

Aiden took a deep breath and didn't let the terrible sense of loss and fear seize hold of him.

Kabi came back around the bar with an impressive looking crystal jar and a small broom and dustpan. "He a familiar?"

Aiden nodded absently, his attention fixed on the crystal jar in Kabi's hands. "That looks special."

Kabi pushed the jar into Aiden's hands. "So are you. Don't worry about it, it's a gift."

Aiden took the jar carefully. Kabi went to start sweeping up the glitter dust, but Aiden put out a hand to stop them.

"It's my mess," he said. "Please. Let me."

Kabi smiled. "How could I refuse?"

Aiden carefully dumped every speck of the shiny dust into the jar. On closer inspection, it appeared to be made of tiny crystals, each one faceted and shining with rainbows. They didn't glow, or give off heat, but when they touched Aiden's fingers they *tingled*. He finished cleaning up quickly and sealed the jar.

Before he left, he threw himself at Kabi for a hug.

"Thank you," Aiden said.

"You're very welcome, sweet one. You know I didn't do much, right?" he said, clearly touched.

Aiden shook his head. "You helped."

Kabi let out a slightly helpless laugh. "Come back anytime. I'll see what I can do to make sure things don't get quite so...explosive."

Aiden nodded, gave Kabi one last squeeze, and left. He thought about going back and asking Kabi if he had any of that magic Demon chalk, but he thought better of it and took a deer path back to the hotel instead.

He continued to *not* let the knot of fear and longing in his chest overwhelm him.

"Be safe, Sam."

GREATER PROVIDENCE RI, SEPTEMBER 13TH 47 YAR

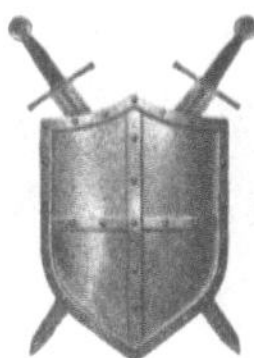

One moment, everything was quiet, the sky kissed with sunset, the stars appearing one by one.

The next moment a geyser of slick blackness boiled out of the ground, far, far too large for the witches' circle to contain. The world *lurched*.

Hunter was thrown back against the mausoleum. There was a sickening crack as his head made contact, and he slumped to the ground, unconscious. Silver light haloed his body immediately, but Emily didn't have time to find out if that was good or bad.

</<*That little shit. What the fuck did he do to me?*>/>

Emily's breath froze in her chest, seized by the sharp, horrible wave of recognition. The voice was wrong, corrupted, but that didn't matter.

Emily *knew* George DeNardis's voice.

The darkness slopped and dragged itself across the ground, converging inside the witch circle. Emily couldn't tell if it was her imagination, but the corrupted magic seemed somehow thinner, more ghostly, as if it was now weaker than when she'd first seen it in the subway.

Emily could see George standing inside the circle now, his body covered in grave dirt, but otherwise intact. The oily magic was rushing into his body, pouring down his throat, seeping into his pores.

The Relic informed Emily that the body was still alive, not yet fully Reaver, but whatever was left of George's soul—if there *was* anything left—was not in control.

</<*You,*>/> the thing said, </<*You got away from me before. Not this time. Maybe after I eat you, I'll be back to full strength.*>/>

Emily didn't know if June replied, but she was moving a moment later. The amulet flew through the air, landing outside the circle, and June began teleporting around, moving too quickly for Emily to follow.

The darkness, however, had no trouble at all.

Emily watched, horrified stupid, as June led the thing around the inside of the circle in a deadly game of tag. The darkness was definitely moving slower than Emily remembered, but it still wasn't slow, and it turned to follow June's flicking form with uncanny accuracy and supernatural speed.

"Detective, we need the Paladin to take the thing out," Selena said, suddenly beside her. "Soon."

Email turned to Hunter, still slumped on the ground. His face was a bloody mess, but the silver light was brighter than before now, and she could see his chest moving, obviously breathing.

She ran over and skidded to her knees, putting a hand on Hunter's forehead, unsure how to help. Her Relic responded, and silver light poured out of her hand, and the silver halo glowed the slightest bit brighter.

Something slammed into the witch-barrier right behind her, and Emily's head jerked up.

June was running along the inside of the magical dome on all fours, moving quickly.

"Shit shit shit!" June chanted, panting, obviously winded, until she cut off with a grunt as the thing grabbed one of her legs and flung her to the ground.

Emily could do nothing but continue to watch as June landed barely ten feet away, right at the edge of the dome. A human hand appeared out of the darkness, wrapped around June's ankle, and a terrible, bone-chilling laugh echoed from everywhere at once. Instead of pulling June towards it, the darkness crawled up June's leg in thick, pulsing veins, embedding into her skin, dissolving the flesh as it went.

June didn't scream, didn't make a sound. She just twisted and *ripped off her own leg* before scrambling back and away. She spotted Emily, and said, "Remember about the ice cream," before she vanished, flickering away again.

Her Relic informed her that Hunter would wake in another five minutes.

In much less than five minutes, June would be gone, eaten, and Sean would be who-the-Hell-knew how much stronger for it.

Emily closed her eyes against a sudden ache and threw herself through the witches' barrier, hoping it would be enough to keep her from hurting too many people. She whispered, her heart in her throat, "I accept."

The seal resting against her chest *burned*, a fire that seared down through her skin, through her bones, into her soul. It shattered, and a blaze of golden light burst out from inside her.

It washed out everything, including her sense of *self*. For a moment all she could see was light, and all she could feel was warmth. There was a long moment where all she felt was peace.

She was one with the Divine.

Then she felt it.

Demons.

Wrongness.

She had to *burn it all.*

She screamed, light still clouding her vision. But she could sense it still, the wrongness. It was *everywhere.*

The Divine Light rose within her until she was *bursting* with it. Her head swiveled, and some sense beyond sight identified two sources for the darkness—one, smaller, that felt strangely clean, even in its iniquity, when compared to the *other*. The other... The other was *sickening*, full of rage and twisted beyond comprehension, and it was *huge*. It was an *ocean* of putrid darkness.

She went for that one first. She ran, blindly, towards where she could feel the fetid corruption spewing like a burst sewage pipe. She moved like lightning, granted divine wings. Her hands were brilliant with Divine power.

The *thing* tried to escape her. It flinched away, screaming incoherent obscenities in a voice stripped of soul.

She moved faster, blasting light at it, pinning it in place. Her hands wrapped around its formerly human throat. Light rose inside her, an unstoppable geyser of radiant brilliance.

Together, she and the darkness *burned*.

It seemed to take ages, an eternity of blissful agony, because there was *so much*.

And then it was gone.

Emily blinked, a very distant sense of self struggling to assert itself. She felt empty, like a charred husk. Her hands were wrapped tightly around the neck of her partner, his familiar face replaced with a scorched mask.

Emily released her grip and collapsed to the ground with the body, a devastated sob escaping her throat. It was hoarse, her throat raw.

She was so *tired*.

She blacked out.

When she woke, it was because a Demon was touching her. She flinched, but the Relic was exhausted. It tried to surge with Light, but there was only a hollow sucking sensation. The Light was there, but she was too scorched to pull it in. It came, but only in a slow, agonizing trickle.

Emily blinked. Remembered. She felt the De—*no*.

No.

Emily felt *June*. June was kneeling next to her, patting her head, asking if she was okay.

The Relic, the *fucking* Relic was everywhere. Inside her, around her, choking her. It *raged*.

She started shaking with the need to *hunt*. The small amount of Light that had filled her tried to scorch June, but Emily was in control now. She pushed it back.

No.

"June," she whispered. "You need to get out of here. Get to the other side of the wards. I'm barely holding on." She pulled away from June and curled into a ball, trying to hold in the Light.

"Emily, are you—"

"*Run away from me, NOW!*" she screamed. June *flickered* and was gone.

It took her a moment to unclench her muscles. There was no more demonic presence, no more darkness, and the Light receded. She could breathe.

Emily touched her chest, where the weight of the seal was *gone.* There was nothing there now, no weight, because it was *in* her, now. There was no single source for the pulsing, the tingling, the warmth. The strength.

It was no longer a Relic. It was *her.*

And she felt a *wrongness.* Right next to her.

The corpse at her feet began making a rasping, gurgling sound. It suddenly *heaved.* Emily shrieked and jumped away, pulling Sergeant Callahan's gun on it but not firing. There was a sickening distortion, a discordant energy coming from the body, and it smelled like death.

She couldn't fire. God, the *sound* the body was making made her ache, but the face was too familiar.

Sergeant Callihan's voice came over the comms. She'd forgotten they were in. "What's going on there, Detective?"

Shit. "It was inside George DeNardis. His fucking son took over his body and now they're both probably in there, inside a *fucking* corpse. God, it's trying to *crawl.*" She sounded hysterical.

She might have been a little hysterical.

Will's voice said, "Emily, we need to send someone in to...take care of it. June says you burned away all the corrupted demonic energy, but that there is something still trapped in the body, like before. We need to free it. You sent June away because you felt out of control, right? Are you still out of control?"

Emily backed away from the body, towards where Hunter lay outside the circle. He hadn't moved, but she felt Divine warmth coming from him, so she knew he was still alive. "Yeah. No. Maybe." She took a deep breath. "I think I'm in control now, but be careful. I don't know what will happen when one of you walks through the wards."

There was a short moment of silence.

"Emily, Sam and I are going to step through, but we won't approach right away. Tell us if we need to run, okay?"

Emily nodded, even though no one could see it. "Yeah, okay. Do that."

Demon.

She could *feel* it.

She had to—

No.

It was Will. He was her *friend.*

She took a deep breath and held on to her sense of self through pure stubbornness.

She was *Emily.*

Emily forced down the rising Light, her breathing ragged. She *burned* with the need to hunt.

Emily thought, *No. They are my friends. I will not hurt them,* and willed her body and soul to accept it.

The seal punished her. Her vision whited out, and her whole body seized with electric agony.

She refused to cry out. She accepted the pain. If pain was what it took to keep her friends safe, she would bear it.

All of a sudden the pressure released, the Relic...conceding? The static awareness of demonic magic was still there, but it was once again only a mild discomfort, the familiar mild, low-voltage current. It was still uncomfortable, but it was also something she could easily handle.

She sagged, relieved.

"Emily?" Will asked, still far enough away that his voice only came over the comms. He sounded quiet, steady. Like a friend.

"Yeah, I'm okay. I've got it." And it was true.

"Okay, Sam and I are going to stay near you, and Alyssa is going to come in to deal with the body, alright?"

She swallowed, and let out another breath. "Yeah, that's fine. Hunter is still out cold, but I think he's okay. He's breathing normally, and I can kind of feel it, even through the wards."

"Understood. The paramedics are on standby for when the situation is fully contained." Sergeant Callihan said.

She felt Will come closer, but her control was fine. He appeared, a witch light floating by his shoulder. Sam was walking beside him, panther-sized, that same bright green scarf floating behind him like a pair of wings.

"I'm coming in now," Alyssa's voice said.

Demon.

She--

Stop. *Enough.* Fuck. Emily coughed, and shivered as the sense of electricity intensified. *Ally,* she firmly told herself, and the pain increased again. Again, she accepted it, stubbornly.

After an agonizing moment, the pain once again subsided.

This was her life now. Fuck.

She could feel them both moving around her, like how you can feel a fly that buzzes around a room. But they were *not* flies, they were *friends*. She could feel them like *magical energy sources*. Because they were *people*.

Something deep in her soul seemed to grumble, but then it settled and went quiet.

She looked up and found Will giving her a worried look.

She said, "I'm fine. I can feel you all as magical energy sources moving around. That's all."

"Cool." Alyssa's voice said, and there was a *pulse* of demonic power, more intense than ever before.

It only lasted a moment, but Emily staggered with the force of it. "This sucks. Magic is really *loud*," she said, wincing, and Will laughed.

<<**Honestly, I'm really impressed. You're holding it together amazingly well**,>> Sam said, and his voice hurt her ears.

Emily winced again. "Uh, yeah. Ow. *Real* well." Sam tilted his cat head at her in question, and Emily gestured at him with vague embarrassment. "Your voice hurts."

<<Sorry,>> he whispered. It hurt marginally less, and she nodded gratefully.

"You got it, though. You stopped it. The *thing*, whatever it was, is powerless now," Will said.

She nodded, and took a deep breath, standing firmer. She'd stopped it, and June was safe. Will was safe. Everyone was safe, now.

It had been worth it.

Still, she couldn't watch when Alyssa transformed into a huge wolf-like monster. Her head throbbed painfully with the surge in witch magic, and light flickered angrily at the corners of her vision whenever she glanced at the hulking form. She covered her ears to block out the sound of flesh tearing as Alyssa destroyed what was left of George and his son.

That was why she missed it when Hunter woke up.

<<Oh sh—>>

There was another surge of power, only it felt *wonderful*. Radiant light exploded around them, full of Divine purity.

It wasn't coming from her.

"No!" she yelled, realizing what was happening. She ran forward, putting her body between the beam of Divine Light and the witches.

Hunter growled, mad with Divinity, and threw himself into the circle. He moved past Emily in a blur she was almost too spent to follow.

Almost.

She tackled him to the ground, trying to disrupt his aim.

It didn't work. The Light shot out of Hunter just before she hit him, warm and fierce and horribly seductive. She wrenched her head up to look, and where Sam had been a moment before was a shower of strangely sparking rainbow glitter that quickly faded into nothing. Will was on his knees, gasping in pain.

Hunter tried to push her off, but she clung to him, pinning him to the cool grass. He struggled, obviously crazed, but he didn't try to hurt her to do it. Warmth bloomed between them, and his eyes blazed with Light, without a single hint of blue.

"Hunter, *stop.* They are *friends,*" she said through gritted teeth. She hoped, desperately, that Sam was okay. She remembered someone explaining that he wouldn't necessarily die or whatever from the blast, but Will was groaning in pain and...shit. Hunter was reaching for his *sword.*

Her body felt oddly numb, and her head was rushing. The numbness slowly turned paralytic and painful as they struggled. The Relic did *not* like her restraining Hunter.

She heard a monstrous roar somewhere behind her. Alyssa.

Hunter needed to stop, *now.* Desperately, she slapped him. She had enough time to see his eyes clear of Light, his expression shocked, before a wave of incredible pain cracked through her entire body and she blacked out.

This time when she woke, she was in Hunter's arms. Her body felt wrung out and weak, but the pain was gone. Hunter was kneeling on the ground, and silver light flowed from him into her. She was propped against him, and facing Will's back.

Will was standing between them and a wolfish monster.

The rushing in her ears cleared , and she heard Will say, "—accident. Sam survived and our bond isn't broken. *No lasting harm has been done. Stop it.*"

There was a deep growl. It wasn't a human sound.

Emily said hoarsely, "What the *fuck*, Hunter?"

"Exactly my thoughts," Alyssa hissed, her voice still less than human, but her posture gradually started to relax. She did not separate from her wolf, but she held up her hands in surrender to Will. "Fine. Whatever you want, Will. But legally, that bastard's Mantle belongs to you now, whether you claim it or not, and he knows it. I'm not leaving you alone with *either* of them."

"No, I mean what the *fuck*, Hunter. Why the hell did you blast Sam? And why did I *pass out* when I slapped you?" Emily said. She wanted to move, but she was wary of doing so while the silver light was still flowing.

Hunter sighed, his breath brushing lightly against the top of her head. "The Relic in your soul recognizes me as another part of Divinity. When you slapped me, what you felt was backlash for hurting yourself, basically. You were, however, right to do it. I was out of control. If you hadn't stopped me, I might have done worse. Your friend Will has shown an extraordinary amount of honor in defending me and not taking advantage. I am truly humbled."

"Yeah, he's good people," Emily said firmly. The silver light finally trickled to a stop, and she held her breath for a moment. The low buzzing was still there, but she felt no other pain.

Carefully, she pulled away from Hunter and climbed to her feet. "So that's it then? It's over?"

"Seems like it." Will said, moving towards her to give her a hug. He frowned when Alyssa moved to stop him, and he pushed past her. Alyssa growled at Emily when they embraced.

Emily almost wished Will had listened to Alyssa. It *hurt*. It hurt to touch him, and worse than the pain was the sorrow that nearly choked her.

She just wanted to hug her friend in peace.

"Sam's okay, right?" she asked, releasing him. The pain receded as soon as she let him go. There was some numbness where she had pressed against him, but that too faded.

That was fine. She was fine.

This was fine.

"Yeah, he...we got lucky. It was a direct hit, but something weird happened. The scarf he was wearing—" Will shook his head. "I don't really know. It doesn't matter. He survived, and should be okay soon. I'll text you when he can be summoned safely, okay?" He met her eyes without the slightest hesitation, but all that meant was she could see how, despite his words, his expression was worried.

"Okay, yeah, thanks," she said, and rubbed her arms unconsciously. Her skin felt tight. "So, are the wards good to come down now?"

Selena's voice said over the comms, "Yes, we'll bring them down now. Detective, we will need to speak soon, to discuss your new *condition*. That can wait till later, though."

"Great!" Sergeant Callihan's voice said. "All of you stay put and wait for the paramedics."

NEXUS

Aiden woke with a start, a hand on his shoulder. Sam? No, the hand didn't *feel* like Sam. Aiden opened his eyes, alarmed, to find Lucifer standing over him, his star-filled eyes troubled. His expression made Aiden go very cold.

"Sam's alright. There was a bit of an incident, but he's going to be fine. He's only sleeping," Lucifer said gently. Numbly, Aiden nodded. An extraordinarily beautiful woman stood behind him. She wore a fitted gown of darkness dotted with starlight, and it pooled at her feet. A delicate crown of black thorns and blood red roses sat on her head. Her hair was long and white in the crystalline, luminous way of snow in the moonlight. She looked at Aiden with very large, glowing eyes, brilliant and silver and full of ancient wisdom.

Lucifer gestured at her and said, "This is Lillian."

“Hello,” Aiden said, sitting up and pulling the comforter with him. Lillian smiled soothingly.

“Sam is in the Atrium right now, but we were hoping we could bring him here,” Lucifer said.

Aiden was still numb, and the question made no sense. “Here? Why here?”

Lucifer looked at Lillian for a moment, and then back at Aiden. “He...doesn’t have his own place. Up until recently, he was something of a stray.”

Lillian spoke, and her voice sounded like magnificent secrets. <<You two have bonded rather beautifully. We think he would prefer to wake here, and he’ll recover more quickly with you as well. If you’re not comfortable with that yet, we will take him somewhere else to recover.>>

“No!” Aiden said loudly, and he blushed and went on in a whisper, “He can come here.”

Lucifer nodded and smiled. “I thought so. I’ll go get him. Lil, no need to wait for me to start.” Lucifer walked out of the bedroom, and there was a flash of light.

Aiden looked at Lillian, nervous. “Start?”

Her smile warmed considerably. <<There is something you want to talk with me about, right? And something you’d like to show me?>>

Aiden blinked at her for a moment, and then some combination of memory and Library access cleared his thoughts. He *did* need to talk to her about a few things. He pulled the comforter tighter around himself. “Can I get dressed first?”

<<Of course. I’ll wait out here,>> she said, walking to the sitting room.

Aiden dashed out of bed as soon as she was out of the bedroom. He threw on some clothes, the first t-shirt and pants he touched, and his coat.

As soon as he was ready, he rushed out, not bothering to check himself in the mirror. Lillian was sitting on the sofa, a small screen open in front of her. She looked up and smiled at Aiden.

He froze in place, intimidated by the amount of power radiating from the woman. Then he squared his shoulders and *reached* for the jar of magic glitter, stored safely in his pocket dimension before he'd crawled wearily into bed. It appeared in his hands, and he walked over to sit across from Lillian.

She waited for him to speak. He had many questions, all of them very important, but instead he asked, "What happened to Sam?"

Lillian folded her hands neatly in her lap. <<Circumstances were such that he needed to work with an exorcist, a Paladin to be specific. I think you were aware of that? Sam was hit with Divine magic. He arrived in the Atrium, magically drained but otherwise fine, cocooned in a strange, bright green material.>> She gave Aiden a meaningful look. <<I have never seen anything quite like this material. Do you know anything about it?>>

Aiden did not breathe. "The scarf I made?"

Lillian nodded.

Aiden rolled the jar of dust between his hands. He pressed his hands into the intricate facets until they hurt. "I don't know what I did, not really. But he's okay?"

<<Yes. It's somewhat miraculous.>> Her expression shifted. <<And dangerous. It is outside the terms of the Treaty. Not a violation, not quite, but— Do you know about the Treaty?>>

Aiden nodded, then shook his head. "I heard it mentioned, but I haven't thought much about it, not enough to understand. Am I in trouble? Is Sam?"

Lillian looked thoughtful. <<No. But what that scarf did... We must proceed carefully. Divinity will not like it.>>

Aiden's first instinct was to hide or run. But he didn't *want* to run. For most of his life, or, at least the one he could remember, he hadn't had anyone willing to fight *for* him. People had wanted things from him, wanted him to be something he wasn't, but Sam didn't. Sam never asked for a single thing Aiden wasn't already offering, and he hadn't hesitated to help Aiden since the very beginning. He'd accepted Aiden as he was like no one else ever had. He was almost too good to be true.

Or...*was* he too good to be true?

A horrible thought came to him.

"Was Sam working for you three the whole time he was with me?" he asked before he could think better of it. As soon as the words left him, he regretted them. He was terrified of the answer.

Lillian's eyes were kind. <<No. When he brought you around Nexus and to the Library, yes, but everything else? No. Did you think we would have asked him to tell you his <[name]>?>>

"I don't know. I guess not. I just...was afraid. Am afraid. I think part of me knows what it's like, to have someone you can really trust, but I don't *remember* having that." He frowned, "Also, Esther told me her <[name]> too, so I wasn't sure—" He cut off, considered, and tried, carefully, "It wasn't just because they were watching out for me?" Aiden blushed. He'd had to phrase it as a question because part of him already knew the answer was *no*.

Lillian's eyebrows rose. <<She did? Well. I suppose I shouldn't be surprised. She does that when she finds someone she considers one

of her own.>> Lillian's smile grew distant and fond for a moment before she refocused on Aiden. <<It's never casual when someone gives you their <[name]>. Both Esther and Sam clearly trust you, an extraordinary amount. If I had to guess, they told you their <[names]> because they want to love you.>>

Aiden's blush grew hot enough he genuinely worried it might be glowing. He wanted to love them too. But he was confused. "You guess? You didn't know she gave me her name too? I thought you guys knew everything that happens down here."

Lillian laughed lightly. <<No, not at all. We know what people tell us, though. Sam has spoken about you a lot. I think he talks to everyone he knows about you.>> She frowned. <<Perhaps we should ask him to be more subtle, in light of current events.>>

The warmth that bloomed in Aiden's chest was possibly the best feeling he could remember having. Well. Top five. He'd had a lot of really good moments the past few days.

Aiden took a breath and made a decision.

"Can I be one, too? I mean, can I be a familiar, and help Sam? Help protect him?"

Lillian studied him for a long moment, and Aiden refused to squirm or shiver. He did continue to blush though, which was frustrating. He couldn't seem to stop it.

<<It's a possibility,>> she said carefully. <<There's...hmm m.>> She hesitated, then said, <<You're unusual, so there will be some special negotiations involved. You'll have to go through some training too, and pass a few trials. The shard situation...>> She shook her head and reached out to press a cool hand against his cheek for a moment. <<It's not a gentle job, you understand. There will be fighting involved.>>

Aiden understood what she was saying, and he nodded firmly, even though he was trembling. "I understand. I think I can help anyway, even though I can't, like, *fight*-fight. May I at least try?"

<<Yes,>> she said thoughtfully and leaned back. <<It may even be the best thing you can do. But it is not my decision alone. It's a commitment for the lifetime of the witch you bond with, and witches can live very long lives. There's a lot of trust involved, and we do not take the process lightly. But first, perhaps we might discuss that?>> She gestured at the jar in his hands.

Aiden looked down at the jar, surprised it was still there. "Oh yeah."

<<Indeed. May I see it? It's been a while since I've seen a new form of magic.>>

Aiden looked up at her sharply. "What?"

Lillian extended a hand, and Aiden passed the jar over, trying not to hesitate. She took the cover off and reached in, taking a small pinch out of the jar. She rolled it between her elegant fingers for a few seconds, and then *licked* it. Her eyes flashed with color for a second, and a startled laugh burst from her.

"*What?*" Aiden asked again, baffled and a little disgusted. She'd just licked something he'd scraped off a barroom floor.

<<Oh, you sweet thing! How extraordinary!>> Lillian said, still laughing. It was a lovely sound, like wings fluttering at night, but there was an edge to it, a hint of wickedness.

Normally, Aiden would have been quite charmed. At the moment, he was too annoyed, and he thumped his foot on the plush carpet. "What *is* it?"

Lillian sobered, but her eyes were still dancing. <<I'm sorry. It's just, what you have made here truly *is* a new kind of magic. I've never

tasted anything quite so delightful. I don't even know what to call it.>> She considered him. <<What have you been calling it?>>

"Um. Magic glitter," he said. His blush, which had finally cooled slightly, flamed back up with a vengeance. He wanted to roll his eyes at himself, but he was too embarrassed to even breathe.

At least he didn't have to.

Lillian laughed. <<Of course you have. Hmm. Let's call it Prism magic then. Sound right?>>

It did, actually. "Um. Uh huh," he said, not sure *why* or *how* he knew it was right. "Um. How did I do it, though, and what is it?"

Lillian raised an eyebrow, <<Shouldn't I be asking you that?>> Aiden tensed, and Lillian immediately reached out and took his hand. <<Shhh, I'm sorry. You just did it, right? There was a need, and so you did it?>>

Mutely, Aiden nodded.

<<That's how it works for us sometimes,>> she said, soothingly. <<It's okay if you can't explain it.>>

"Us?" Aiden asked, confused.

Lillian smiled. <<Us. Souls from before the time of the Seal. Powerful ones that resisted Divinity before the Seal was created. Souls like you.>>

"Me?" he said, voice cracking. Old was one thing, but *powerful*? Rebellious? That couldn't be...

Except Lillian couldn't lie.

Lillian nodded, and patted his hand. <<Yes. Most of us ended up in oblivion during the eons the Seal was in place. Esther is also an old soul. She told you, yes? There are a few others. We are not gods, because we came *before* gods. You could say that we are the souls that inspired the *idea* of gods.>>

"I'm *not* a god," Aiden said, horrified at the idea.

Lillian smiled again. <<Of course not, silly. That's what I am saying. During the time of the Seal, there was a lot of *pressure* on the ambient magic. Humans, both living and those trapped in oblivion, as well as other, non-human people, believed—still believe, very strongly—in the existence of gods. That belief shaped the trapped magic for eons, and so when it burst free during the Breaking, some of that magic manifested itself by fusing with the broken pieces of the Seal. We call those shards.>>

Lillian cupped one of her hands, and Aiden had to blink away tears as sudden light bloomed, then faded to show a...He might have called it a crystal, but it was obviously *alive*. It twinkled cheerfully at him, like a star made of ice.

<<When I get a hold of a shard, I can modify it so it can bond with a soul, allowing them to use and store magic. Normally, a soul only radiates magic, like a flame emitting heat. With a shard, they become more like a glowing coal or battery-powered light, able to hold more energy than what is within a single flame. Most shards are very small, like this one, because most beliefs are very personal.>>

With another blinding flash, the crystal vanished. <<But there are some beliefs, some ideas, that many people believe in. Those beliefs fused with larger pieces of the seal and they developed personalities. We call them Mantles. We control some of the Mantles, which are bonded to souls that resonate with the Mantle. You might call them gods. Some call them Demon Lords. Divinity claimed and absorbed other Mantles, some to embed in living human servants, some modified into entities you would know as Angels. Divinity has modified those Mantles in ways I find distasteful. We believe there are a few Mantles still missing on earth, as well as an unknown number of shards, some of which are controlled by the fae. Finding them is very important if we want to continue to resist Divinity.>>

Lillian waved her hand delicately. <<But that is not something you need to worry about yet. You will learn more during your training. What's important right now is that you've used magic in a way that should have required a Mantle.>>

"I don't have a shard," Aiden said, almost desperately, "and I certainly don't have a *Mantle*. Right?"

<<No, you don't. You are something else.>>

They sat there for a long moment. "I don't understand," he said, finally.

Lillian smiled, and it was beautiful and terrifying. <<Neither do I! Isn't it extraordinary?>>

Aiden felt slightly frozen. He wasn't sure what to think about all that. He pushed the problem away for later and asked, "What do I do with that?" He pointed to the jar.

Lillian shrugged. <<Whatever you like. It's yours.>>

Aiden frowned. "But what does it *do*?"

Lillian looked mischievous. <<You'll have to find out. That's one of your tasks.>>

Aiden thumped, and Lillian laughed again and handed the jar back to Aiden. He took it gently, as if it might explode. "So, can I still be a familiar? And help Sam? Even though I'm weird?"

Lillian smiled, and it was strangely smug. <<Yes, sweet. If you pass the trials, and Sam's witch finds you acceptable, and it is what you *really* want, I'll make sure it gets a pass.>>

Aiden nodded, firmly. "It is."

<<It's settled then. Once Sam has recovered, he can help you get started with your training. You'll need to meet his witch also. It's a bit of a process, and I'll send you a short list of tasks you need to complete. Sound good?>>

"I guess so." He wasn't entirely sure what he had gotten himself into, but he didn't think he was being tricked. Not really.

<<Can we come in now? Watching you tease the bunny is fun and all, but I'm tired of waiting,>> a voice said. It sounded like Zee.

<<You might as well. I think we're just about finished here. Ask him if you can try his magic glitter. It's *wild.*>>

A doorway appeared and Zee walked through. Aiden had forgotten how *beautiful* they were. He realized that he'd styled his own coat to be an almost chibi version of Zee's, and he flushed.

At least he hadn't worn a matching scarf.

<<Nice coat, bunny,>> Zee said with a wink. Aiden tried to hide his face in his hands, but he was still holding the jar. He thrust it out towards Zee and mumbled something about trying it. Zee accepted it delicately. <<Why *thank* you. Don't mind if I do.>>

Lucifer walked through the door next, and he was carrying Sam. It was the first time Aiden had ever seen Sam sleeping in his human form. He looked like a ghost, glowing very slightly, especially where the scarf Aiden had given him was wrapped around him like a full-body bandage. Aiden rushed over and hovered while Lucifer carried Sam over to the bed.

<<Shattered Divine, bunny, what *is* this?>> Zee exclaimed from the sitting area. <<Be careful who you give this to, we don't want any *riots*. Lucy, come over and try this.>>

Lucifer raised his eyebrow at Aiden, and Aiden gave Lucifer a distracted nod. Lucifer put Sam down on the bed so Aiden could fuss, and walked over to Zee.

Aiden ignored the Triad while they discussed his glitter—nothing they said was helpful, just more *wow, how odd, what could it be?* nonsense. Aided tried to arrange Sam's limp form so he would be comfortable. He adjusted the covers three times and then forced himself to stop.

Aiden looked down, admiring how lovely Sam was. He'd never had the chance before, since Sam slept as a cat normally and Aiden wasn't quite brave enough to study his face when he was awake. Sam wasn't *pretty*, not in the way Zee was, but he was gorgeous in a roguish way. He looked younger, asleep. Like he was actually the nineteen he'd died at.

It hurt to see him like this, even though it was beautiful. So much of who Sam was came out when he moved, or smiled, or teased Aiden. He was so *good*.

Aiden understood that what he felt was love, but it was a fragile thing, new and lacking the foundation that only grew with time and shared memories. He wanted that time.

"Do you think he'll wake up if I kiss him?" Aiden asked quietly, half hoping no one heard him.

The Triad went quiet, and Aiden looked up to see them looking at each other.

Zee said gently, <<That's a sweet thought, but... I mean, anything is possible, especially given your weird magic, but I wouldn't risk it until you ask. It's kinda rapey.>>

Aiden blanched and nodded. "Good point. I'll wait for him to wake up and ask him if I can try it next time. Maybe there won't even be a next time."

They looked at each other again, and Lucifer said, "You do realize he probably won't even get the reference, right? He died before Disney. Magical kisses that wake up sleeping loves weren't really a thing before that."

Aiden was shook. "*What?* That's...that can't—" A flash from the Library confirmed that it, in fact, *was*, and Aiden sat down. "That's more than I can process right now." Aiden flopped back and curled up next to Sam's sleeping form. "He better wake up soon. We have *so many* movies to watch."

Lillian gave him a kiss on the cheek, leaving his jar of glitter on the nightstand. <<He will, don't worry. Besides, we all know you're the princess in the relationship anyway.>>

Aiden huffed and thumped his foot on the bed. "*I'm* not the one falling into a magical sleep every other day."

Lillian and Zee laughed. Zee said, <<You blush at everything, you have talking animal friends, a fairy godmother, and you have *rainbow glitter magic*. You're definitely a princess, bunny.>>

Aiden tried to think of an argument, but instead found himself wondering. *Was* Esther his fairy godmother? But hadn't she been his sister? What did that make her now?

Aiden supposed *fairy godmother* was as good a description of their relationship as anything else.

The Triad walked out of the bedroom, and there was a flash of light. Aiden felt a pressure lift off him. The sense of their huge presences, which had been weighing on him from the moment he woke, receded, and he knew they were gone.

Aiden huffed again. "We can *both* be princesses. H-E-L-L is very progressive," he said to Sam's sleeping form. When the room rumbled softly, Aiden stuck his tongue out at it. He swore he could hear Zee laughing.

GREATER PROVIDENCE RI, SEPTEMBER 14TH 47 YAR

June didn't know what to do. It was early morning, still a few hours before sunrise. She was in the basement of Thoughts and Prayers. Penny was doing inventory while June fleshcrafted herself back together. She'd been given a fresh leg by the witch leader, Selena, right before they'd left the graveyard. June was starting to wonder where the hell they kept getting these bodies from, but she figured they wouldn't answer. Witches kept their secrets within their Covens.

She asked anyway. "Hey Penny, who's your corpse supplier?" Penny just rolled her eyes. June made a show of sniffing the leg. "Smells like mystery," she said, and Penny ignored her. June examined the disembodied limb, but she couldn't tell a thing about where it had come from. The skin was an unhelpful grey-tan color, unmarked. The foot might have been female, but it was extremely difficult to tell. Maybe it wasn't from within the city. Aside from the poor souls killed over the last few days—

"Woah, these aren't like, bodies from the—"

Penny looked up. "No! Fuck, June, of course not."

June waited for Penny to explain further, but she didn't.

Okay, so not those bodies. But the deaths still probably weren't natural—most people here had unrestricted access to both witch surgery and divine healers, as well as good therapy. Between all that, the death rate was very low. The only way people really died these days, aside from the occasional horrible monster or normal-type murder, were accidents related to magic scorching.

Hey, that was a theory. "Penny, are these corpses from idiots who died trying to channel magic without a familiar?" June sniffed again, trying to detect a hint of ozone. There was none, of course, just the smell of fresh meat.

Penny sighed. "June, what's wrong?" She was annoyingly perceptive to June's moods.

Emily, June thought, but instead she said, "Thanks for lending me the amulet." She took it out of her pocket and offered it to Penny.

Penny shook her head. "No, keep it. Come see me when you need it recharged. You deserve it."

Hell *yeah* she deserved it. Getting her human identities out in daylight would go a long way to preserving them, especially now that everyone sort of knew there'd been a vampire lurking around the city. Sofia was compromised, maybe, but she had plenty of other faces Emily didn't know about. She could spend some time using them in the daylight, making it even harder to tie them to her vampiric nature.

June was also determined to find out her favorite ice cream. And pizza topping. This time she wouldn't binge herself sick and ruin all that good food. She could have self-control.

But later. She had time now. All the time in the world.

June grinned and put the amulet back in her pocket, not letting it touch her skin. She barely refrained from giving Penny a hug. Penny didn't like hugs.

When she finished absorbing the leg, she fleshcrafted it to match the rest of her body and stood up to stretch. For the first time in days—though it felt more like weeks—she was herself, whole and in her preferred body. The monster was gone, and she could go back to her unlife.

Except, of course, for Emily.

June wanted to call her, but she hadn't dared. She'd sent a quick *Thank you for saving me* text on the ride back to the bar, and Emily had texted back *Don't. I need some time. It's harder than I expected, now. Don't push it. Please.*

She *should* ditch the phone, ditch the city, maybe. Emily had said she would keep her secret, at least by implication, but that was before. Now? What if that brand on her soul forced her to do something, or...just, what if *something*. She hadn't told anyone that Emily knew about her identity. Knew that she wasn't dead.

"You know," June said, "You still haven't explained why you helped me. We're friends, obviously, especially now, but..." She drifted off, and her brow furled. Why couldn't she keep hold of her train of thought?

"But nothing, June. Like you said, we're friends. And now you have the gratitude of the Northeastern High Coven, the Providence Coven, and my own Coven. I mean it, come back anytime you need that amulet recharged. It's the least we owe you."

June narrowed her eyes at Penny, still not satisfied. The amulet was still illegal, wasn't it? How was this all okay?

Then she sighed and decided to let it go. Penny clearly wasn't going to explain what was between them, so it wasn't like she had any choice in the matter.

"I'm thinking of hunting outside the city for a while," she said, packing up the few belongings she'd brought over. "I might go over to Taunton, or maybe Fall River." June hadn't really planned on it until she said it, but she just didn't feel right hunting in Greater Providence anymore.

Emily might find out about it.

Maybe if June wasn't hunting in Emily's territory, things would be easier for her. June could stay in Providence, maybe let her bandmates become real friends, especially since she could go out in the daylight now. She would keep working at the hospital, and maybe things would be... easier, that way.

Penny nodded. "That's not a terrible idea. Be careful out there, though. Fall River might not have its own resident exorcist, but it's still full of Church of Unity sympathizers and Taunton is practically a war zone, no matter what the media says. Alyssa lives near there, so I'll let her know you'll be hunting in the area. She'll keep an eye out for you." Penny considered June for a moment. "I assume you're going to keep your identities here intact? If you're going to be hunting that far afield, you should get yourself your own car, or at least a bike."

June stuck out her tongue, "Ew, no. I can move faster than a car. It will be fine. Between the amulet and my speed, I'll be fine." She'd need to invest in a special pouch for the amulet—she had no intention of going anywhere without it.

June picked up her bag and slung her guitar over her shoulder. Since she couldn't hug Penny goodbye, she instead said, with more sincerity than she usually spoke with, "Thanks for saving me."

Penny gave her a weirdly maternal look. "Any time. Thanks for helping to save the city. Take care. I'll see you around."

"Yeah," June said, and left.

Before she stepped outside, she checked the ICWW website to see what the witches had scheduled for the weather in Providence for the rest of the night. She was happy to see that it would be warm and clear. It usually was, but you never knew.

She ducked her head for a moment, crafting her face back into Sofia's, and started for her condo. There was no moon, but the stars over the city were magnificent, brilliant in the way that only a witch-managed night could be.

When she checked her phone regularly every fifteen minutes, no one was around to judge her for it.

A PLACE BEYOND TIME AND SPACE

Micheal shifted uncomfortably. “Are you certain it’s still there?”

Gemma growled at him, and he shrank back. “Did I *fucking* stutter? *Yes*. I can still feel the corrupted magic.”

Lillian spread her hands in a placating gesture. “We destroyed the escaped *thing*. I’m certain.”

Gemma waved her hand dismissively. “I’m not saying you didn’t. I’m saying the *corruption* is still there.”

Zee frowned and pulled up a screen. “Where?”

Gemma roared, and space-time shuddered. “I don’t KNOW! I can feel it there, crawling like insects under my skin, but it’s *hiding*. Inside the mortals, probably, but I cannot find which *ones*. I don’t even know if it’s only the human ones!”

Lucifer stepped in front of Zee and Lillian, arms spread out protectively. “We’ll keep looking. We’ll find it.”

Gemma growled again.

Lillian said carefully, “We might have to consider what we will do if we cannot contain it.”

There was a crack, and everyone cringed. "I WILL *NOT* LOSE MY HOME TO THIS SHIT!"

Zee leaned around Lucifer and said frantically, "We won't let that happen! No one is suggesting we abandon Earth, ever! We have a way to fight the corruption. We just need to keep ahead of it. Which means *Micheal* has to play nice, for real this time. No more friendly fire."

Micheal sneered, but did not meet anyone's eyes. "It was not on purpose. I—*we* cannot just turn off our instinctive defenses."

Lillian spread her hands, a sly smile on her face. "Then we need to give the demons a way to protect themselves." She caught Lucifer's eye, and there was a small spark of rainbows in their depths.

Lucifer said, with false nonchalance, "We may already have a way. Th—"

Micheal slashed at the air. "*No.* The treaty forbids it. I cannot allow you to have a way to counter Divine Light. What is the point of even *having* a treaty if you can just—"

Gemma got up in Micheal's face. "The treaty can fucking well change, Micheal! You broke it first, multiple times, so you will accept whatever reparations I deem appropriate, and this is one of them!"

There was a moment of stunned silence.

Micheal cleared his throat. "*One* demon. Defensive only, absolutely no inclination to attack. If you can find someone like that, I'll make sure the treaty holds with Divinity."

Gemma narrowed her eyes. "That's oddly specif—"

Lucifer, Zee, and Lillian said, all at once. "Done."

End

www.ingramcontent.com/pod-product-compliance
Lightning Source LLC
Chambersburg PA
CBHW020307030826
48979CB00029B/2289/J